Gallows Wake

Helen Hollick

Taw River Press

Published in 2022 by Taw River Press
https://www.tawriverpress.co.uk/

British Library Cataloguing in Publication Data
A CIP catalogue record for this book is available from the British Library.

978-1-7399371-4-0 Gallows Wake (paperback)
978-1-7399371-5-7 Gallows Wake (eBook)

Formatted by Avalon Graphics
www.avalongraphics.org
Published in 2022 by Taw River Press
https://www.tawriverpress.co.uk/

THE SEA WITCH VOYAGES

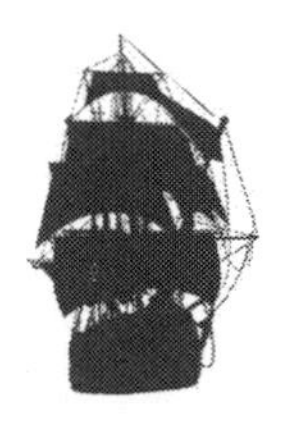

Sea Witch: The first voyage
Pirate Code: The second voyage
Bring It Close: The third voyage
Ripples In The Sand: The fourth voyage
On The Account: The fifth voyage

To Follow
Jamaica Gold: The seventh voyage

When The Mermaid Sings

A short read prequel to the Sea Witch Voyages
How Jesamiah became a pirate
Coffee Pot Book Club Book of the Year 2022
BRONZE AWARD WINNER

When the only choice is to run, where do you run to?
When the only sound is the song of the sea, do you listen?
Or do you drown in the embrace of a mermaid?

Throughout childhood, Jesamiah Mereno has suffered the bullying of his elder half-brother. Then, not quite fifteen years old, and on the day they bury their father, Jesamiah hits back. In consequence, he flees his home, changes his name to Jesamiah Acorne, and joins the crew of his father's seafaring friend, Captain Malachias Taylor, aboard the privateer, *Mermaid*.

He makes enemies, sees the ghost of his father, wonders who is the Cornish girl he hears in his mind – and tries to avoid the beguiling lure of a sensuous mermaid...

An early coming-of-age tale of the young Jesamiah Acorne, set in the years before he becomes a pirate and Captain of the *Sea Witch*.

https://viewbook.at/WhenMermaidSings

PRAISE FOR HELEN HOLLICK'S SEA WITCH VOYAGES

"A stylish blend of mystery, betrayal, intrigue, smuggling, murder, love, sex, Barbary pirates, and mysticism – all neatly wrapped in a spirited sea tale." *Quarterdeck*

"A story populated with fictional characters that bring the eighteenth century to life – A pirate adventure you won't forget." Cindy Vallar *Pirates & Privateers*

"Superb. They are not just rollicking good reads, these books, but the meticulous research put in by the author shows." *Amazon review*

"Goodness me, Helen Hollick can tell a ripping yarn! My wife handed me her Kindle... she didn't get it back for several days!" *Amazon review*

"Another compulsive read. The fifth journey of Captain Jesamiah Acorne picks up right after the cliffhanger of book #4. I loved the introduction of Maha'dun, the Night Walker. Such a colourful and rich character." *Amazon Review*

"I would stop any book I'm reading to continue this saga." *Goodreads*

"Filled with adventure, suspense and a little supernatural, *On The Account* is an epic voyage slicing through rough seas on *Sea Witch*... Treachery, treason and murder abound aplenty, and of course, there is love amongst the debris." Pauline Barclay *Chill With A Book Awards*

ACKNOWLEDGMENTS

My thanks to Cathy Helms, for her wonderful cover design and professional formatting, and to Annie Whitehead for her editing – the ship, *Lady Of Mercia* is named for her novel of Anglo-Saxon England, *To Be A Queen*.

At the risk of this sounding like an over-enthusiastic Oscar acceptance speech... for her experienced eye, my thanks to author Caz Greenham who writes highly entertaining children's books about Eric Seagull. To authors Marian L Thorpe and Robyn Pearce for casting their equally as experienced eyes over the final proof. (Any missed bloopers are my own additions!) And to Connie for being an early version reader. Thank you Nicky for the Spanish translations. To my neighbour, Captain Charles, for his 'Navy things' advice, and to village residents, Heather and Tim, for their support, enthusiasm and supply of cake and sparkling wine shared of an afternoon beneath 'The Go Outside', my patio gazebo.

I have never been aboard any sailing vessel larger than a small Mirror dinghy, so a very special thank you to nautical expert, and good friend, author James L Nelson for checking my 'sailing bits', and for not laughing too loudly at my errors – any that remain, are my landlubber's fault, not his.

And thank you to ***you***, the reader (hopefully, one among many!) My sincere apologies for the long delay in getting *Gallows Wake* written and launched. Various issues caused various problems, not least of which was a change of publisher and some subsequent difficulties, and then 'that' pandemic thing which kept many of us locked down or isolated for, well, you know how long.

During that time I wanted to do something different, so turned to crime... in the fictional sense, that is! I wrote the first two titles of my new cosy mystery Jan Christopher series set in the 1970s. They are available from Amazon or bookstores.

There will be more Jan Christopher mysteries, and Jesamiah will be sailing off on another adventure in Voyage Seven, *Jamaica Gold,* very soon.

Helen
September 2022
https://helenhollick.net/

In memory of the real Richard Tearle,
who passed away in April 2021.

A much missed, very dear friend
who thoroughly enjoyed 'his' escapades with a pirate.

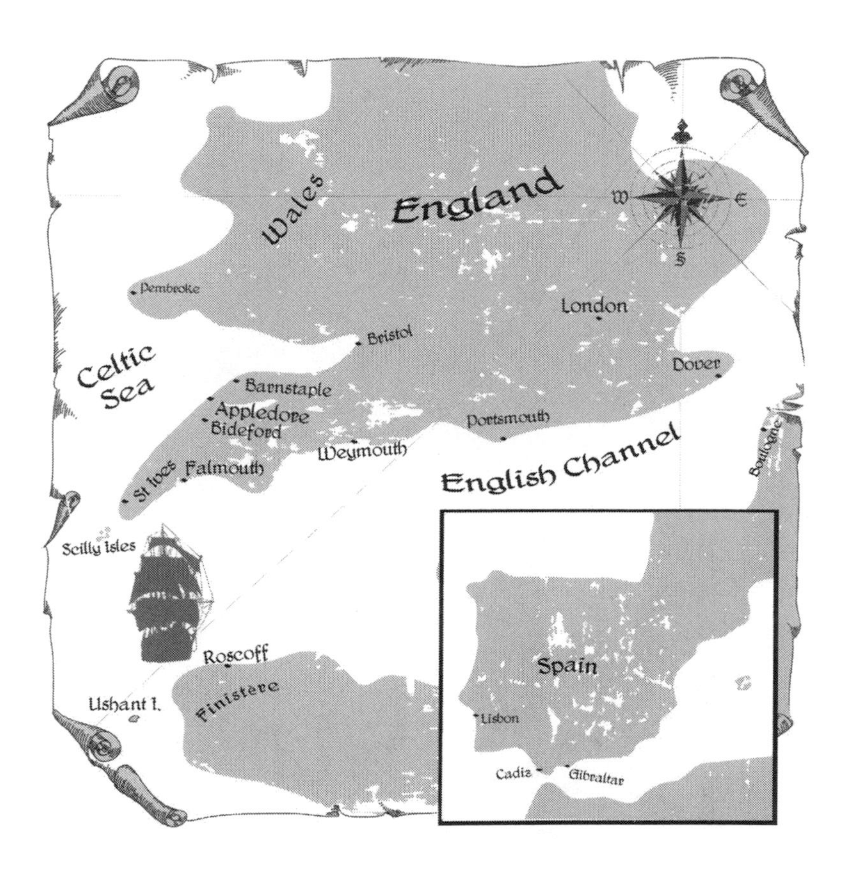
Wales
England
W
E
S
Pembroke
London
Bristol
Celtic Sea
Dover
Barnstaple
Appledore
Bideford
Portsmouth
Weymouth
English Channel
Boulogne
St Ives
Falmouth
Scilly Isles
Roscoff
Finistère
Ushant I.
Spain
Lisbon
Cadiz
Gibraltar

Plan of the sails and masts of a square-rigged ship

Sails

1	Flying Jib	8	Main Topgallant Royal
2	Jib	9	Main Topgallant
3	Fore Staysail	10	Main Topsail
4	Fore Topgallant Royal	11	Mainsail or Main Course
5	Fore Topgallant Sail (pronounced *t'gan's'l*)	12	Mizzen Topsail
6	Fore Topsail (pronounced *tops'l*)	13	Mizzen Sail
7	Foresail or Fore Course		

Masts

A	Bowsprit/Jib-boom	F	Main Topmast
B	Foremast	G	Main Topgallant Mast
C	Fore Topmast	H	Mizzenmast
D	Fore Topgallant Mast	I	Mizzen Topmast
E	Main Mast	J	Ensign and Ensign Staff

WEIGH ANCHOR

CORNWALL
NOVEMBER 1715

The mob was angry, their anger fuelled by the rain which had been cascading from the sky seemingly forever. It had persisted through the spring, making the land difficult to plough, then washing the new-sown seed away. When the skies cleared in the early summer the sun had shone, relentless, for eight weeks, scorching the ground into hardened ruts. What little that had struggled to grow withered and died. Then, as drought had finished parching the land, the autumn rain returned and did not stop. By the onset of winter, the rivers were swollen, bursting their banks and the mud along the lanes was ankle deep.

The crops were ruined. There had been nothing to harvest. No hay to cut for the beasts, although many of them were also dead or dying. Lambs, calves and piglets had aborted; sheep, cows and pigs slaughtered because they too had starved, or their sodden hooves were rotting away. The coming winter would be bleak, as it had been the previous winter; aye, and the one afore that. Nor had the pilchards come. The grey, sullen, sea was as empty as the fields and the bellies of the people and the beasts.

The blame was put on the woman who had been seen rescuing hares from the traps set for them. Hares were the devil's creatures. The woman should know better, for she was wife to the Reverend

Garrick – the 'white-choker, fore-and-after man'. Fishermen and farmers were wary of priests. All went to church on a Sunday, for it was expected of them, but no West Country man would utter the word 'church' for fear of drawing God's attention and subsequent wrath and retribution. *Chapel, Steeple, Meeting House, Tower*, but never *Church*.

The woman was not one of them; she was mistrusted. A Devon maid, not a daughter of Kernow. When the rain did not cease, when famine stalked the land alongside the Reaper, suspicion of witchcraft fell in her direction. And when a knife was driven into the Reverend's heart, the woman was seized, without mercy or compassion, by the angry mob.

For all that the man himself was disliked – and many another would have rejoiced in slitting his throat had opportunity arisen – the sin of murder could not go unpunished. For murder was the Devil's work, and all knew the woman to be the Devil's maid.

As the rain poured and the cold, cruel, wind blew above the cliff top, she was dragged to the gallows tree and hanged.

Even though it was not she who was the witch.

CHAPTER ONE

AUGUST 1719 - GIBRALTAR

"Rot? How could there be rot? Master John Benson, back at Appledore several months ago, checked and repaired everything needing checking and repairing." Captain Jesamiah Acorne stood, legs spread, arms folded, chin tucked to his chest, his leather three-corner hat pulled well forward over his eyes against the glare of Gibraltar's late afternoon summer sun. He was seething with frustrated anger and failing to keep his annoyance under control.

"Benson? I do not know him. Good chap, is he? And where is Appledore when it's at home? Never heard of it." The master shipwright, an English Kentish gentleman by his accent, pulled the stub of a worn graphite pencil from behind his ear and scribbled a few more calculations on the wedge of crumpled paper he held in his hand. Frowned myopically at what he'd written, then said: "It will take us several weeks to find and fit a new mainmast."

Jesamiah swallowed down a bellow of outrage.

"You can have rot and not know it, Cap'n," Chippy Harrison said, looking as grim-faced as Jesamiah.

"You're my ship's carpenter. You should have known about it," came the unjustified response.

The answering retort was as tart. "I told you about it as soon as I did know. 'Tis not easy to spot when rot's starting to take hold at the mast partners or the hounds supporting the crosstrees. There were no sign of anything back in Devon. Benson, as good as he is, would not have found it. Nor would I. As I recall, I advised you to look further, but you were in a hurry to sail."

"All right, I get the gist," Jesamiah answered, muttered churlishly, "You still should have seen it." He knew, as well as anyone, that discovering rot, especially where it was well hidden, was nigh on impossible even to an experienced eye. Plus, he had indeed said no to further investigation; Chippy was right, so the blame, in the end, was his own. However, knowing facts did not help ease the frustration or annoyance.

Chippy Harrison, ignoring his captain's disgruntled expression, continued defending his reputation as a ship's carpenter, his arms waving about to emphasise his points. "We could not have seen every little detail. If we'd taken everything apart, we'd still be wallowing in Appledore harbour."

Jesamiah took a mental deep breath. Maybe that would have been a good thing? Had they not sailed for Spain his best friend and second in command, Claude de la Rue, would still be alive, and the god-awful things which had happened might not have happened. On the other hand, worse things could have occurred. If there *was* anything worse than losing a friend and having your wife kidnapped. He closed his eyes a moment, remembering but wanting to forget. It had been back in the spring, and his wife, Tiola, was now well and safe, but good people, women and children included, had died there in that house in Spain. Horribly. Aye well, he wished he were still in Appledore or anywhere else, come to that, but he wasn't, he was here in Gibraltar with a rotten mast which needed replacing, so it was no good chasing the what-ifs around in pointless circles.

Until a few days ago, he had been happily cruising between the islands of the Canarias, a Spanish-held region and archipelago situated in the Atlantic Ocean, sixty or so miles from the western coast of Morocco. The eight main islands had proved lucrative for trade, Tenerife, Fuerteventura, Gran Canaria, Lanzarote and La Palma being the best places to sell his original cargo of fine furniture and wine. In ancient days, the chain of islands had been known as

The Fortunate Isles. Jesamiah had mentally changed it to Fortune Islands, for with the profit from the furniture and wine, he had acquired a hold full of gold in the guise of tubs of expensive Cochineal dye and bales of ready-dyed crimson wool, all of which he had sold halfway across the Atlantic in the Azores, for another handsome profit and an alternative stock of goods to sell back in the Canarias. But good fortune deserted him when the damage to the mast had been discovered. Reluctantly he had headed for Gibraltar, the nearest port where he could expect suitable repairs. He had hoped for a speedy replacement mast and somewhere different to sell what was left of his cargo. The latter had gone well, the former was looking distinctly unproductive.

The shipwright sniffed loudly and, tucking the pencil stub back behind his ear, announced, "From our first quick look, it has not too badly taken hold, but bad enough. We will know more when we strip her down. We will need to strike the t'gallants and topmasts and all the yards, rigging and such, then pull the mast and put a new one in." He sniffed again and squinted at his rough notes and calculations. "A lot of work. Could easily eat up four, five, maybe six weeks if we have trouble getting a replacement mast."

"Six *weeks*!" Jesamiah spluttered. "I can't wait around here for six weeks! Ain't you got a suitable mast in that bloody great warehouse of yours over there?"

"I might have. I will not know until I look."

"Well go and look, then!"

The shipwright, refusing to match Jesamiah's foul temper – the situation was nothing new to him – scratched at the stubbled whiskers on his chin. "I cannot be doing that, Captain, not until the morrow. A few hours ago, I might have had a chance for a quick rummage, but," he withdrew a gentleman's gold watch from his waistcoat pocket, squinted at it, "I am about to lock up for the night. My wife will have my guts for her stocking garters if I arrive home late for supper."

Jesamiah swallowed a few choice words about wives and what they could do with their garters, stockings and suppers. Said instead, "A few hours ago I was clearing my hold ready for your inspection." Added, "What's it going to cost?"

The shipwright looked again, more solemnly, at the scribblings on the top sheet of his notes. Made a few adjustments. "This is only a rough tally. I will get a more accurate estimate to you tomorrow morning." He made another adjustment and showed the result to Jesamiah, who whistled incredulously.

"'Struth! And they call honest seamen pirates! For that much," he said, thrusting his face closer to the shipwright's, "I expect the work to be done in no more than three weeks."

"I'll do my best, Captain, but we have several frigates in harbour; any Royal Navy vessels requiring my attention will take precedence."

The thought, *sod the bloody Navy,* ran through Jesamiah's mind, but judiciously he only said, "Help him look for a mast first thing tomorrow, Chippy." He nodded a curt dismissal to both his ship's carpenter and the Gibraltar shipwright, turned on his heel, thrust his hands deep into the pockets of his old buckram coat and strode away, not trusting himself to glance along the wharf towards where his beloved *Sea Witch* was moored. The mainmast had developed rot, despite his ship being a relatively new build of only a few years. It seemed obvious that the penny-pinching numbskulls who had built her had cut corners and used old materials where they thought they could get away with it. Oh, Jesamiah would dearly love to get his hands on the original builder's invoice – the man who had commissioned her had been robbed! His scowl warped into a grin. That would have been the Dutchman, van Overstratten, his wife's first husband. Pity he was dead; it would have been amusing to have gloated.

Jesamiah walked on, his grin returned to a grimace. The entire mainmast would need replacing with a new one; no ifs or buts about it. He could have tried to make it back to the Azores, but he wasn't certain about the quality of the Portuguese shipyards. Gibraltar had been the best option, the nearest reachable, safe, British harbour. Not that he was entirely certain that the place, with its excess of Royal Navy officers, common sailors and the proximity to his various enemies across the border in Spain, was a safe harbour. The Canarias was one thing, under Spanish control, aye, but with such a mixture of populations from Europe and the Colonies – discounting the hundreds of poor African buggers, enslaved against their will to work the land, dye the wool, serve the rich – that Spain itself hardly mattered. Mainland Spain was different, and Gibraltar was a bit too close for comfort. But needs must. Unfortunately.

The embryonic English colony was a tiny promontory of land of less than a few square miles, most of it uphill, a good bit of it nothing but rock as barren as a desert. The ancient Greeks regarded the towering outcrop – the Pillar of Hercules – as one half of the gateway guarding the entrance to the Mediterranean. Its counterpart, the high peak of the Moroccan Rif Mountains, Jebel Musa, was twelve miles distant on the far side of the Straits. The British Royal Navy held the same view as had the Greeks regarding the strategic importance of this narrow, seven nautical-mile stretch of sea lane giving access to and from the Atlantic.

The Spanish had lost The Rock to the Dutch in 1704 during one of the interminable wars. The Dutch had then signed it over to the British in 1713 as a bargaining point for the Treaty of Utrecht when Anne, officially the last of the Stuarts, had reigned as queen. Any rights or wrongs of how and why Gibraltar was now owned by the government of Great Britain – who were determined to hang on to it – were dismissed by the British, and contested by everyone else. Hence the heavy presence of the Navy and their frigates. Jesamiah did not particularly care who claimed the damned place. Who ceded what, when and why to whom rarely held sway for long; until the next war started and a bargaining point was required, or one side gained victory over another.

For himself, he was uneasy anywhere near the Navy but being too close to the Spanish was more unsettling. Too many Spaniards, for varying reasons, wanted him dead by equally varying obnoxious methods, and the British Navy tended to have as much of an unpleasant desire to hang pirates, even ex-pirates like Jesamiah who had signed their names in King George of Hanover's Book of Amnesty. Avoiding a squall with either of them was going to be difficult. The next few weeks were not going to be particularly pleasant.

He scowled as a group of Navy tars, worse the wear for drink, pushed past him, one catching his shoulder with quite a force.

Accidental or on purpose? He let the matter go. He was in the mood for a fight, but was not so stupid as to brawl when it was five against one. He walked on, hunch-shouldered, up the hill.

"You want some company, sailor?" A woman slipped her arm through Jesamiah's and matched her stride to his. "You look like you've lost a gold guinea and found a clipped farthing," she added, smiling coquettishly up at him.

"Not even a farthing, darlin'. Sorry, I ain't good company this evening."

The woman persisted by giving his arm a squeeze. "I'm sure I could brighten you up. I know where there is a very comfortable bed with a goose-feather mattress, fresh, fairly clean, linen and a good lock on the door."

"No. Ta all the same."

The woman stopped, folded her arms beneath her breasts. "Well, if you are not interested in making love to me, your wife, Captain Acorne, the least you could do is tell me why you are in such a foul grump of a mood."

Jesamiah walked on a few paces, stopped, turned around and walked back to his wife. He put his fingers beneath her chin and tilted her face upward slightly, bent, kissed her lips. "I'll make passionate love to you tonight, Mistress Tiola Acorne, but for now I need a good, strong drink or two. Or three. And a dark corner where I can sit and brood about the prospect of being anchored in this bloody place for more weeks than I care to think about."

Tiola kissed him back, then cocked her head to one side. "The rot is bad then?"

"The rot is bad. We need a new mast and the idiot who lords it over the shipyard claims he hasn't got anything suitable."

"Oh." Tiola rubbed her hand up and down his arm. "Is that likely? That he hasn't got one?"

"Most unlikely. He's probably got dozens, but the longer I wait the more I'll have to pay him for being moored in his bloody dockyard."

Tiola said nothing more for there was not much she could say to offer any solace.

Jesamiah kissed her cheek then offered her his arm. "Come and have a drink with me, then we'll investigate that comfortable bed you've found for us."

Smiling, Tiola nodded and re-threaded her arm through his. "Before we do so, please can we sit and talk? I have something of importance to discuss, something I've been meaning to mention for some weeks now."

Brows furrowing, echoing a sudden rise of concern, Jesamiah steered her towards a low wall bordering the well-tended front garden of a fancy house. He sat her down, sat next to her. Two lots of bad news in one day? Life was cruel.

Gravely, he said, "You are going to tell me that you are not with child after all? That it's all just weight you've put on because of the food we enjoyed in the Canarias and Azores." The disappointment stung.

Tiola watched a flock of raucously squabbling seagulls for a moment as they circled and bickered against the evening sky, then placed his hand on her already swelling belly. "I am definitely with child; I am four months gone. I am due to give birth in early January. I knew I was carrying within only a handful of days. No other woman would be aware of such a fact that early, which is why, until recently, we kept the knowledge to ourselves. Although Finch, for all his grumbling as your steward, was not blind or deaf. He noticed my morning sickness some weeks ago." She laughed. "His tempting custards and sweetmeats have been most welcome, but he really is no expert cook! Still, I believe charcoal is good for a growing child."

Moving his arm around her waist and pulling her close, Jesamiah kissed the top of her head. "What is this bad news, then?"

For a few minutes, Tiola stared out at the evening sparkle of light dancing on the dark blue sea and the array of ships at anchor in the bay. A two-masted Dutch vessel was beating outward against the wind, her wake not as straight as Jesamiah would have had it.

For his sake, she had appeared cheerful, calm and content. Quietly, privately, she fought against the anxiety that clung to her like the spores of a mould which could not be eradicated. Barbary pirates had raided the house where she had been staying, kidnapped her and the children, raping and killing the adults who were of no use to them. The ordeal of terror heightened because she had known the pirate leader, Yakub Pasha, a man who had brutalised her in the distance of a previous life. Jesamiah had come after her, rescued her and the children, but not before many had died through privation. Their deaths, and the deaths of other, dear, friends, lingered as an inflexible grief. A grief which stirred other painful memories of loved ones lost through mindless cruelty and bigotry.

For this matter, though, Tiola had to come straight out with what she had to say.

"Have you not noticed? I have not made use of my gift of Craft since that night we made love after you rescued me from those barbarian pirates."

Jesamiah wiped his hand under his nose, sniffed, shrugged. "I've been a bit busy..."

"I have not needed my Craft. We have been together, so our shared mind words have not been required, there has been no serious illness or injury among your crew and so my gift of healing has not been required." She paused, took a breath. "All of which has been fortunate because I cannot use my Craft while I am with child. To do so could harm, even endanger, the developing baby. The energy I need to summon its use could corrupt the unborn, physically, mentally or both. If I use the powers I have, a child could be born deformed or dead."

Should she add her worst fear? That a child of hers could become a vicious monster using the great power of Craft for its own, malicious purposes? Evil souls brought into the world by those who defied the laws of the Old Ways caused harm, destruction and hatred. All she said was, "There are already enough wrongly created Malevolents who need to be sought and destroyed by The Seekers."

"So, this includes not being able to mind-speak with me?" Jesamiah, too, was watching the ship. She was attempting to tack, had missed stays and her mainsail was flapping in the wind like a housemaid shaking a poorly laundered bed sheet.

"It does. For these next months I will live, and eventually give birth, as would any ordinary woman."

Ah, they had the boat under control now. *If they were my men,* Jesamiah thought, *I'd have the lot of them flogged.* He wouldn't – or would he? The mood he was in he would as likely shoot them all. He gazed at Tiola, his eyes staring into hers. There had been a time, it seemed centuries ago but was actually only a couple of years, when he had been afraid of her gift. That day when he had first witnessed what she had the ability to do; the fear which had shot through him because of it. *Never use your Craft on me,* he had said to her. Had she? Had she ever used it against him? He thought not, but had to trust her, without question, for he would never know the truth. If he did not, then that would be the end of the love they shared, for what use was love without trust? It was not easy being wed to a witch, though. Even if she was of the White, wise, Old Ones.

He leant forward, kissed her forehead. "I hadn't really noticed anything being absent so far, so I reckon I can live with it for a few more months, as long as you're not going to tell me that my husbandly rights are now also suspended?"

Tiola laughed, kissed him back, firm and inviting on the lips. "When I grow too large to be comfortable then *ais,* I might so decline. But that situation is ahead of us yet. We have time to enjoy ourselves before then."

She kissed him again, lightly on the cheek. By the Laws she could do no harm to others unless to defend her life and safety. Her very purpose was to help those who required the skills of her healing and midwifery knowledge. To bring life into the world and, when required, to see a soul safely out again, to assist with that gentle transition into the peace of Beyond. But she also knew how to curse, destroy and kill. Jesamiah had no idea of her hidden powers or what she could, if necessary, do with them. She had been particularly careful to conceal such things. And had no intention of letting him find out about them.

She kissed his cheek again. Never must he find out exactly what she could, or could not, do.

CHAPTER TWO

Almost every narrow, cobbled street and alleyway was up or down hill on Gibraltar. The cheap fleapits, and their wretched inhabitants scrabbling for a hand-to-mouth existence were squashed cheek by jowl on the flat strips of land along the shoreline alongside the wharves and warehouses; chandlers stores, sailmakers, cordwainers, taverns and brothels – everything connected to anything remotely nautical. The more respectable inns and residential buildings were ranked in tiers further up the hillside one above the other depending on their social status. The more financially comfortable Spanish-style residences had the advantage of the higher ground where the air was cooler and cleaner. Above it all – apart from the remote, windswept look-out fortress reached by a track so steep and precarious that, so the locals claimed, it could give even a goat a nosebleed – there was nothing except the sheer escarpment which gave the entire place its colloquial name, The Rock. The other advantage of high ground over the flatter shore was the view. Ideal for painters, poets and romantics. Equally ideal for keeping a sharp eye on what shipping came and went through the narrow Strait to or from the Mediterranean Sea.

Their minds set on food and drink, the view meant nothing to a few of *Sea Witch*'s regular crew: Jasper Hicks, Joseph Meadows –

everyone called him Skylark – and Ray Wheler, known as Spokesy, were making their way slowly uphill.

Only Young Jasper was bothering to scrutinise the various ships anchored in the harbour. He stopped, fists on hips, breath heaving from the climb, frowned as he watched a new Royal Navy arrival sweep into harbour, luff efficiently up into the wind and drop anchor. Impressive. Her captain must be one of the rare Navy chaps who actually knew what he was doing. Most of the vessels in deeper water were Royal Navy frigates, while scattered nearer the dockside were several merchants and a rag-tag of fishing boats. A couple of brigs were moored to the narrow wharf, unloading cargo. They would be paying a higher anchorage fee to the harbour master for the convenience of easier unloading and reloading. Wealthier owners or pushier captains?

Sixteen-year-old Jasper's concern deepened, his eyes crinkling to see better as he watched the newcomer. "Ain't that the *Bonney Chance*?" he asked as he pointed towards the vessel in question. "Looks like her."

His companions stopped walking, grateful for the opportunity to draw breath. All of them were quite capable of scrambling from the deck to the masthead without pause, but plodding up a steep incline with uneven cobbles underfoot was a different matter, although all had agreed the downward return journey would be as easy to manage as a willing whore.

Spokesy shaded his eyes, his sight not as sharp as the younger lad's. "I recognise the *Gwen Jones*. She's a Welsh merchant; a good ship, good owner who cares for his crew. I served on her several years back."

"She's not Navy, then?" Jasper asked, biting his lip and trying not to let his rising nervousness show. "Not like the *Bonney Chance*?"

"No, *Gwennie*'s a merchant."

A little further up the hill the two boys, thirteen-year-old Tom Benson, affectionately known as 'Hedgepig' on account of his short, spiky, hair, and his Spanish friend, Donréal, had also stopped to study the ships dotted below them on the dazzling blue water. Tom brought a brass telescope from his coat pocket – a present from

Jesamiah and a treasured possession. He opened it up, set it to his eye, then laughed.

"That's the *Bonne Chance*, Jasper. A Frenchie. I can see her name quite clearly. *Bonne Chance.*" He said the name again emphasising the French pronunciation. "It means good luck. I think."

Donréal took the telescope, peered, confirmed. *"Sí, Bonne Chance."* He slipped easily between languages: English, French and his own native Spanish. "It does indeed mean good luck."

Below the youthful fuzz of his first full beard, Jasper's sun- and wind-tanned skin paled. He felt sick. "Aye, 'tis what I said, the *Bonney Chance*." He said the name in its English form, *Chance* not *Shance*. "She were French; the English Navy took her as a Prize years ago."

Striding on up the hill, Skylark, *Sea Witch*'s quartermaster and second in command, grumbled at them. "Cease your dawdling and gawping, we're already late and I want my supper. So, she's the *Bonne Chance*. What of it?"

Jasper swallowed hard. "I'd know her anywhere. I were aboard her for over a year afore I decided to leave Her Majesty Queen Anne's guest list."

"Since you jumped ship and deserted Fat Anne's Navy, you mean?" Laughing, Spokesy mock-boxed Jasper's ear. "There's plenty of us who did the same, lad," he added. "And, if you were in Her Majesty's service that must have been a good many years ago."

Jasper bit his lip. Did he confess all to these men? Men he adored only slightly less than Jesamiah himself? "I were a tacker, a kid; Midshipman Hicks. I were twelve when I jumped ship. I'd had enough of the thrashings from the bloody bos'n and the taunts from the first lieutenant. I took my chance when I could, bummed around a bit, starved, learnt how to steal and fight. Then Jesamiah caught me trying to pick his pocket, shook me until my teeth rattled, then took me on as crew."

"Aye, and useless into the bargain," Spokesy jested. "You're as much of a hindrance as you are a help."

Tom had put the telescope away. "If you were even younger than I am now, Jasper, you've got nothing to worry about. It's unlikely any of the crew are the same, but even if they are they'd not recognise you now you've grown up and sprouted that curly beard of yours."

"He's right lad," Skylark agreed. "There's several of us, for various reasons, who don't want no truck with the Navy, Cap'n Acorne included. We'll keep our heads down, ourselves to ourselves and hope we can weigh anchor from this place as soon as may be."

"Which won't be soon enough," Jasper muttered as they trudged on up the hill.

Tiola had chosen a respectable inn, away from the noise and bustle of the wharves. Tucked along a side street there was a bit of a climb up the hill to reach it, but the Royal Oak had a comfortable upstairs room overlooking the harbour and the dockyard where *Sea Witch* was moored. Plus, there was a small attic room for the two boys, Tom Benson and Donréal.

Despite their preference to berth with the crew, Tiola insisted on keeping an eye on the scallywags. The inn's landlord and his wife seemed pleasant enough people, the public bar full of patrons, but not over-crowded. The food served, on her initial inspection, appeared to be properly cooked and the bedroom itself clean and comfortable. Husband and wife had tested the bed by robustly making love, but now they sat at a table in one of the inn's more private alcoves.

Tiola sipped at the glass of Madeira wine which the potboy had placed before her – wine in moderation was preferable to water for unless it came straight from a spring, water was rarely pure. Contamination came from the lead tanks it was stored in, or any manner of unpleasantries floating in it. Rare to have a water source without the addition of a dead rat or two. Jesamiah, beside her, had returned to brooding. He'd swallowed the first taste of the inn's French brandy in one gulp; his hands now curled round the stem of the glass, caressing the second.

Three men, accompanied by two boys, entered through the door, wedged ajar to allow in the cool night air. They stood, squinting into the flickering shadows thrown by candle and lamplight, the air fugged by a cloud of smoke loitering beneath the ceiling beams. Seeing them, Jesamiah stood, beckoned them over and whistled for the potboy. "Another brandy, ale for my men and lemonade for the boys," he shouted.

The potboy raised his hand in acknowledgement. The two boys scowled.

A shout of greeting from the stairway leading to the accommodation rooms upstairs, and Finch, Jesamiah's curmudgeonly but loyal steward, descended the stairs at a trot and joined the newcomers as they thrust their way through the scrum of laughter and chatter.

"Where you all been then? Buggered off when I needed an 'and to 'oist the mistress's dunnage up these bleedin' 'ills."

"Got unavoidably waylaid, mate," Skylark answered, not admitting that they had well and truly dawdled the past hour away.

"Aye, I bet y'bleedin' did."

The men nodded a greeting to their captain and, removing their hats, touched their foreheads as respect towards Tiola. Jesamiah invited them to sit. The potboy arrived with the drinks, announced that supper was on its way, and hurried off again.

"Well?" Jesamiah said after a moment of silence.

"All is ship-shape, Cap'n," Skylark answered.

Finch took a generous swallow of ale from his tankard, wiped his lips, said, "Your dunnage is stowed in yon room, Cap'n, an' I've 'anged out your gowns, Mistress. Save 'em gettin' too crumbled. Could've done wiv an 'and though."

Ignoring the grumble, Tiola smiled, "How kind. Thank you, Mr Finch."

"I've asked the landlady 'ere if'n there's a lady's maid you can make use of an' all."

"Again, thank you, but I can manage quite well without."

Finch picked up his tankard and took another generous swig, then declared, "I ain't 'avin' no cap'n's missus of mine not bein' served proper while we be marooned 'ere on this pop-cock shite-'ole."

Desperately trying to hide her amusement, Tiola did not dare gainsay him, so merely offered yet another thank you.

"What about a valet for me?" Jesamiah asked, indignant.

Finch scowled back at him. "You're quite able to wipe your own arse. An' you two young tackers stop grumblin' about leminade. It's what you 'as, an' all ye're gettin' while ashore."

"Do they drink something different while aboard then?" Jesamiah asked, drily. "I wondered where my rum was going."

"I wouldn't waste good rum on sprogs," Finch answered with an irate sniff.

Jesamiah sipped at his brandy, set the glass down, grinned. "You drinkin' it then, you old goat?"

"I drain the dregs," Finch admitted. "You got any objection?"

The older boy, Tom, exchanged a wry glance with his friend. Donréal was a skinny lad of small stature, but he had a big heart and was as loyal as a devoted puppy. He reddened slightly at the concealed lie, but kept quiet. Fortunately, any inadvertent admission about sharing an occasional sip of rum with Finch was swept aside by the landlord appearing from the kitchen with a tray laden with bowls, spoons, napkins, fresh baked bread and a tureen of goat stew.

Contrary to the expected image of the usual rotund and jolly publican, he was reed thin and dour-faced, disadvantages he made up for by being as talkative as a parrot that had been sampling the ale barrels. He served Tiola first, then Jesamiah and the two boys, while chattering about everything and nothing. Glowered at the four dishevelled crewmen before serving them also.

"You the chap who brought those children in a while ago?" he asked Jesamiah. "The ones kidnapped by them bastard Barbary Arab pirates?"

Jesamiah shook his head, lied, "Nope. I've never been to Gibraltar before. Nor had nothing to do with any children. Can't stand the blighters."

"What of these two then?" The landlord indicated Thomas and Donréal who were tucking in with gusto to their stew as if they had not been fed for months.

Jesamiah was genuinely astonished at the question. "They are crew, not children. Merchant midshipmen. Under my feet more than any use, mind."

Tiola, the boys and the four men, busying themselves with their food, said nothing.

"It was a nasty business," the landlord continued, eager to tell the story to new ears. "Over three hundred children taken; bloody Barbary pirates attacked one of them Don's wealthy houses up along the coast north of Cádiz. Butchered all the men, raped the women then cut their throats, sawed off their titties and made off with the kids – destined for rich men's bed-toys, of course. Poor beggars. But some brave sod of a sailor rescued them, blew up the pirates' ship and brought more than one hundred lucky so-and-sos back here to safety."

The two boys scooped more stew on to their spoons. Did not look up. Donréal stifled a sob, disguised it as if swallowing too large a spoonful of gravy. The numbers quoted were an exaggeration, as was much of the detail, but both he and Thomas had been among the lucky 'so-and-sos'. Both had seen things that no child, or even an adult, ought to see.

"Taking on Barbary pirates? Sounds more like stupidity to me, not bravery," Jesamiah countered.

"What happened to the children?" Tiola asked, her smile encouraging the man to keep talking.

"They are to be returned to their parents, assuming they have any. Taken a while to get things sorted, mind. They've all been up in the nunnery under care of the sisters, meanwhile. The English little 'uns are finally to be escorted home on the next ship to sail; the Frenchies and Portuguese are being sorted out, and our governor, useless fellow that he is mind you, is negotiating the return of the Spanish kids with some bigwig Don or other. Though, from what I hear, there's not going to be much gratitude from them Spanish, nor a single farthing of ransom asked, neither. Few of us here on The Rock are happy about that. I mean, kiddies must be taken care of, of course, but why waste an opportunity to squeeze blood from Spain, eh? We're at war with the beggars, after all."

Jesamiah silently agreed although he guessed Tiola would have something sharp to say on the matter were she given opportunity.

The landlord took the less than clean cloth from his shoulder and wiped at a spillage of gravy on the table, then topped up Tiola's wine glass. "Weird thing though," he said, and paused, waiting for his listeners to look up at him with expectant interest, "a coffin were brought ashore too. A coffin with a body in it."

"Ain't many coffins don't 'ave a body in 'em," Finch stated with a loud sniff, then cuffed his nose with his grubby sleeve.

"Ah," said the landlord, lowering his voice and leaning on the table, both hands pressed flat. "It was taken to the seamen's Christian church out of respect for the dead one inside, but come morning, when the good reverend came to officiate over the first prayers of the day..." he paused for dramatic effect, slapped one hand on the table, causing bowls and cutlery to rattle, "bugger me, but the coffin were empty!"

He was rewarded with incredulous, open-mouthed, wide-eyed full attention, and an accompanying indrawn breath of shock from everyone at the table.

Everyone except Tiola, who remained quietly engrossed in fishing out lumps of indigestible gristle from her stew.

CHAPTER THREE

His cravat untied and hanging loose, shirt unlaced, both boots off but only one stocking removed, Jesamiah sat on the edge of the bed, dejected, depressed and annoyed with himself and the rest of the world. He pulled off the other stocking, inspected the bruise on his left foot where a dropped keg of brandy, two days ago, had resulted in a string of cursed profanity.

"So, are you going to enlighten me?" he asked, rolling the two stockings together and turning to Tiola who stood attending her hair before the mirror set atop a low chest of drawers.

Her hair shone in the flickering candle-glow blue-black as a raven's wing. Untethered, it hung down to her hips, the fragrance of chamomile filling the room with each vigorous stroke of the hairbrush. "About what?" she said, giving three more strokes, then turned to face him, her head cocked to one side. The night chemise she wore was of French Cambric linen with delicate blonde lace along the low heart-shaped neck, cuffs and hem, the enticing shape of her body beneath visible through its fine, slightly shimmering, weave. The curved bulge of her pregnancy was beginning to show itself.

"About Maha'dun."

"What about him?" She began braiding her hair into a single plait.

Jesamiah unbuttoned his breeches, removed them and the silk drawers beneath both together, left them on the wooden floorboards along with his boots and stockings, added his shirt. He curled back the blankets and sheets, angrily pummelled the lumpy pillow. Naked, remained sitting on the edge of the bed.

Maha'dun. The most irritating, insufferable, annoying and aggravating person Jesamiah had ever met. But he had also been loyal, courageous, amusing and a good friend. A very good friend. Jesamiah had last seen him lying dead in that coffin.

He missed him. A lot.

Tiola tied a cotton thread around the base of the plait and came to sit next to her husband, caressed her fingers along his stubbled cheek. "You need a shave," she said with a smile, sniffed at his skin. "A bath would not come amiss, too."

"I had a bath last week."

Tiola laughed. "So you did. Any chance of another, *this* week?"

The irrational anger leaving him, he sighed, folded her fingers into his left hand, noticed the scars there, his missing little finger and the remaining half of his ring finger. Both shot away by Spanish cannon fire. There was no pain now, the stubs had healed well, so much so that it often came as a surprise when he realised the fingers were no longer there. Would he, before long, feel the same about the loss of Maha'dun?

He shrugged. "He loved me, you know. I was jealous because I thought it was you he cared for, but it wasn't, was it? It was me."

Tiola nodded. "I didn't think you had realised how he preferred men, not women."

Jesamiah shrugged again, an act to conceal his embarrassment. "I don't go for," he paused, "you know, *that* sort of thing. Molly boys, men with men." He exhaled again, rested his head on Tiola's shoulder. "But he wasn't really a man, was he? Not like me. He was like you. Not quite human."

Tiola chose her words carefully. "He is not at all like me. I am one of the Old Wise Ones of Craft. There are only certain ways I can die and, outside of being with child, I can control how my body functions. I can heal myself, talk to you through mind words, conceal myself in the shadows so no one knows I am there. I can mask pain, run or hold my breath for hours, hear, see, do, what no human woman can. But I cannot do harm unless it is in desperate need to protect myself. Maha'dun has many of those same abilities, but I exist because of healing and bringing the newborn into life. He exists because he," again she thought before she spoke, "because he was created as a hunter, a Seeker, of souls. He lives through death."

Jesamiah slid his arm around her waist, kissed her forehead, was not shocked or outraged by her revelation. He pointed towards his cutlass and pistol set atop one of Tiola's clothes' chests in the corner of the room. "As do I, sweetheart. As I have done, as I will continue to do. I've been a pirate since before I was fifteen years old. Pirates ain't known for their benevolence and kind-heartedness. Especially when there's yet another war raging and a chance to go legally privateering for profit. I kill, I hunt. I've lived through death."

"But you are no longer a pirate or a privateer. You are now a respectable merchant, trading in spices, wines and quality spirits. You have a new life, a new future ahead of you – us." Tiola put his hand on her belly. "A new future for this little one new-growing inside me." She moved away from him, tucked herself into the bed, pointed at the candles for him to snuff out. She knew it was not the truth. He would never be satisfied with a day-by-day repetitious, dull, steady life. He maybe would not return to outright piracy, but privateering, legal piracy? That was a different matter.

He said nothing to contradict her. There was too much of the adventurer, the risk-taker in him to remain a merchant. To sedately trundle back and forth across the Atlantic Ocean nursing a hold of cargo? That was no life. No blood-lust excitement, no challenge. Technically, he was the inherited owner of his now dead uncle's wine business, but it was Spanish and he doubted he would be able to have much access to it. Aside, he did not *want* to be a wine merchant. Not when there was a war raging and a reason to blast the guts out of Spanish shipping. He was also well aware that Tiola had evaded an answer to his original question.

He slid into the bed beside her and ran his hands upward under her nightshift, over her smooth hips, lingered over the bulge of the child then on past her waist to caress her breasts. Making love would divert his mind from another question, the one he really wanted to ask.

Why, he wanted to say, *do you talk of Maha'dun as if he is still alive?*

CHAPTER FOUR

"A bit of bad luck, I hear?"

Jesamiah looked up from trying to read the top page of a pile of papers, a scrawled tally sheet of figures for the estimated repair cost. He squinted through the fug of tobacco smoke at the fastidiously dressed young man who, uninvited, sat down opposite, and making himself comfortable, set his hat and cane on the table. He slid the empty platter which had hosted Jesamiah's breakfast of gammon and a rather tasty apple chutney, to one side.

"None of your business, Doone." Jesamiah wiped a damp ring of spilt coffee from the table with his coat sleeve and set the papers down. Pointedly did not wave the potboy over to fetch more coffee for his unwelcome companion.

Ascham Doone ignored the rudeness, called for a fresh pot. He picked up the pile of papers and glanced through the column of figures on the top sheet, raised one eyebrow. "Rather a hefty bill." He shuffled through the bundle, glancing at estimates and diagrams, his left eyebrow rising even higher. "Is all this work to repair your ship necessary?"

It was not, but Jesamiah had no intention of sharing his thoughts with this upstart.

Doone shrugged, tapped the sheaf of papers together to make a neat pile, but clumsily dropped them to the floor. He bent, retrieved them, tidied them again and handed them back to Jesamiah.

"He is cheating you, Acorne."

Folding the pages and stuffing them into his coat pocket Jesamiah glowered. He had never liked this arrogant pop-cock and did not particularly appreciate being told the obvious. "I want the job done quickly. It pays to overpay. And since when have you known about the cost of repairs to a ship?"

Ascham Doone was near the same age as Jesamiah, mid-twenties, although he looked much younger – a youth in his first flush of maturity, but there any similarity ended. The only grandson of Sir Ailie Doone, self-styled Earl of Exmoor, Ascham revelled in the position of arrogant superiority that he held, or fancied he held, over lesser mortals. A position aided by his clandestine lieutenancy to England's Spymaster General, Lord Harley, and his personal, wholly private, ambition of replacing the old fool when opportunity arose.

Doone felt in his pocket for his pipe and tobacco pouch, said as he filled the bowl with sweet-scented Virginia, "I am expected to do the accounts for my grandfather when I am at home. John Benson also handles our shipping repairs. I am surprised your mast has suffered damage, he should have spotted it whilst attending your vessel after it ran aground near Appledore – what, four, five months back?" He puffed at his pipe, sending a cloud of blue-grey smoke upward to join the drifting cloud loitering beneath the low roof beams; the ceiling boards in between were a dirty yellow. Added, "But then, I have always considered Benson to never quite stand on the right side of honesty. I would take the issue up with him, were I you, when you return to North Devon."

Jesamiah was tempted to respond that he had no intention of returning to Devon, or England. Aside from that, Benson was the most honest man he knew, and it would have been almost impossible to predict the damage after the events of that dreadful night, but he decided against wasting his breath on pointless verbal sparring with this obnoxious scut.

He did say, however, "You know perfectly well that *Sea Witch* foundered in a storm. The man who holds your leash, Harley, ensured the militia were waiting for us ashore and your own father was conveniently murdered in the fight which followed. Nor have I yet decided how much *you* were behind it all, not Harley."

Doone narrowed his eyes into mere slits. "Are you suggesting that I arranged for your ship to run aground? I find that an insulting accusation. Deliberate wrecking is a hanging offence."

Jesamiah was suggesting precisely that but staring back, his features expressionless, he shook his head, did not want to enter into an argument that he would never win against this man who twisted everything to suit his own advantage. He had better things to do this day.

The potboy arrived, set the steaming coffee pot and a cup with its dish-shaped saucer on the table, gave the surface a wipe with his cloth while Doone fished in his pocket for the necessary payment. He handed the coins over, said, "And make sure you fetch m'change, boy." He picked up the cup and held it to the opaque light filtering through the nearest dust-grimed window, assessing how clean the utensil was before pouring coffee for himself.

"Could you not have chosen a more congenial place, Jesamiah? The gloom in here is detrimental to the convivial balance of the humours."

Thinking that his humours had been perfectly balanced before Doone had moored his backside at the table, Jesamiah ignored the comment, although it rankled that Doone had additionally been too familiarly discourteous by not addressing him by his rank and surname: Captain Acorne.

"This inn is near the shipyard; I couldn't be bothered to walk up the hill to my lodging," was all he said by way of explanation.

Doone leant across the table, refilled Jesamiah's coffee cup. Continued speaking. "You will be kicking your heels on this insufferable naval outpost for a good few weeks. Gods, but these Navy officer chaps are enough to drive ye t'drink! They strut about like preening peacocks do they not? They are such…" Doone paused, pondering a suitable word for the overflowing number of Royal Navy representatives crowding the small peninsula.

Jesamiah finished the sentence for him. "Arseholes?"

Doone smiled, showing perfect white teeth. "That was not the word I was seeking, but it will suffice." He took a sip of his drink, set the cup down and leant forward slightly, glancing at who was sitting nearby. He lowered his voice. "Now, to business. These children…"

"What children?" Jesamiah did not lower his voice, nor did he lean forward.

"The ones you rescued from those Barbary pirates."

A sure sign that he was becoming annoyed, Jesamiah fiddled with the two lengths of blue ribbon which he always kept tied into his hair – for vanity, gifts for the ladies and, more specifically, to use as an effective garrotte when he needed something quick, silent and simple to use. "I rescued my wife, young Thomas Benson and his friend. I know nothing of any other children. You are mistaking me for someone else. A Navy arsehole, perhaps?"

A group of rowdy seamen entered the tavern, kicking the door wide and calling for cheap genever as they shoved their way to a vacant table. They looked like troublemakers. One seemed vaguely familiar. Jesamiah mentally shrugged, ignored them, kept his attention on the known troublemaker sitting opposite him.

Doone also paid no heed to the men, but he moved his hat and cane further away from the newcomers. Said, "Word on the street is that several months ago, Barbary pirates plundered a Spaniard's house along the coast, killed the men and raped the women – old and young – before killing them also. They then made off with the children. A valuable cargo, either for demanded ransom or to sell as rich men's toys."

"Is that so?"

Doone nodded. "People are still asking how those Arabian pirates knew where there would be undefended easy pickings."

"Are they now?" Jesamiah tipped away the coffee Doone had poured him, puddling it in the gritty sand scattered over the wooden floorboards, refilled his cup from his own coffee pot and took a generous gulp. The coffee was cold, but bloody-mindedness was not going to allow him to call for fresh, or share Doone's.

"I would guess that those Barbary Arabs did what they always do: cruise along a coast – French, Portuguese, Spanish, English – keeping watch for a promising-looking village or house, heave to, raid quick. Kill the adults, take the prettiest young virgins, female or male, and or the children. The kiddies especially, if they were looking for a particular market trade. It's how they operate." Sipping at his drink, his gaze never leaving Doone's face, added, "And you know as much about that raid as do I, Doone. You were there with me to witness the aftermath of that charnel house. You saw what those bastards had done when they killed everyone they didn't want to kidnap. But because the Spanish have a habit of grasping the wrong end of sticks, and in consequence getting very nasty about such things, I suggest you keep your mouth as firm shut as I am keeping mine. I know nothing. Neither do you."

Doone considered a moment, then, nodding agreement changed the subject. "I need someone to do a small task for me."

"Good luck with that, then."

"Well, officially, to do a task for Harley."

"Last I 'eard he were about to drop dead."

Idly flapping his hand, Doone dismissed the suggestion. "The chap drinks too much. He has gout, but his liver might function for a while longer yet."

"Particularly now that you are not around to add something ruinous to health into his port wine?"

Refilling his pipe, Doone looked at Jesamiah with a bland expression. "I agree with my grandfather. You really are an unpleasant lewdster."

Jesamiah raised his cup in a gesture of agreement. "You don't like me; I don't like you. I didn't invite you to anchor your rump at this table. You are more than welcome to get off your arse and leave me in peace."

An argument was brewing between the troublemaker sailors and an elderly gentleman; one of the sailors had knocked into the old man and spilt his tankard of ale. Understandably, the old boy was furious. The exchange between them was growing more heated. If it came to a fight, Jesamiah didn't give much hope for the old man, although his vitriolic language was quite explicitly colourful.

Ignoring the escalating disagreement, Jesamiah returned his attention to his own exchange. "Better still, Doone, get yourself aboard the next England-bound vessel and clear off."

"I think you would rather hear what I have to say before I take my leave."

"I doubt it."

The landlord strode over from behind the counter, put an end to the contretemps at the next table by politely asking the troublemakers to leave – his version of polite being to threaten them with two pistols. They left, grumbling and complaining, but wary that the landlord meant business. A further spate of complaint erupted from the old man who announced that the scum should have been made to replenish his spilt drink.

Ascham Doone turned slightly in his seat and, scowling, commented, "Be grateful for what you still have in your tankard, you miserable old apple-john."

Just to be annoyingly contrary, Jesamiah beckoned the landlord over. With one finger he brushed one of the pistols aside. "Point those things somewhere else, mate. At this fellow sitting opposite me if you wish; I'd make no objection to you squeezing the hammers home, either."

The landlord looked at the weapons in his hands as if he had no idea how they had got there. "These?" he laughed as he tucked both into his belt. "Neither be loaded, but keep the fact to yourself, eh?"

Jesamiah laughed. "I'll have another pot of hot coffee, if you please – and refill the old gentleman's ale for him."

"I'd rather be havin' a tot or two o'rum," came the immediate response.

Jesamiah nodded. "A tot of rum then. Just the one." He wasn't surprised when all he got was a muted grunt from the old boy as a thank you.

Shaking his head, the action conveying his disapproving thoughts, Doone leant back in his chair and finished refilling his pipe. "They are saying that you and your wife, if she is indeed in the eyes of God and the law your wife, informed those barbarian pirates of the whereabouts of the children." His mouth turned into a smirk. "Rumour can be such a vicious thing, don't ye think?" His words had finally gained serious attention. The smirk broadened.

It took Jesamiah an entire thirty heartbeats to calm his breathing, unclench his fists and stop himself from launching across the table to beat Doone to a pulp.

"My *wife*," he said very slowly, very distinctly, as he carefully set his coffee cup down, "was as much a victim as those others. I agree that someone tipped off the Barbary scum, but it was not she." He took several more steadying breaths. "It could as easily have been you."

"You want to be careful of insinuations, Acorne," came the levelled response. "They can get you into trouble."

"As I recall, you puked like a poisoned dog when we got to the house, then buggered off, still puking, here to Gibraltar where these cock-proud admirals coo and bow to your pretence of legal swank and political authority. I wonder how they would react if they knew you for a coward who shits his breeches as he runs? I remind you that my wife was kidnapped along with those children, and was consequently treated to abhorrent abuse. My best friend, my second in command, Claude de la Rue, the man I thought of as more of a father than my own pa, was brutally slaughtered, alongside one of my wife's own brothers. Our Spanish friends – my kindred – who owned the place were tortured then murdered. My crew and I went to rescue those we could. You did nothing. I wonder why? Because you know who was behind that blood-soaked carnage, perhaps?" Added with a snarl, "As you were also behind the murder of another friend of mine, Señora Francesca Escudero."

Doone bridled with indignation. "That is an insulting falsehood. Her unfortunate death was not of my doing. I admired the lady, and at the time she had possession of something valuable that I wanted. Her death was most inconvenient."

Jesamiah leant forward. "Not what I was told. Are you admitting that her murder was a mistake? That the man you hired was meant to kill me, but stabbed her instead?"

Doone's face reddened with outrage and embarrassment. "I admit to nothing of the sort! Your accusations about these events are nothing more than mischievous slander. Why would I want either of you dead? You, like the lady in question, are more use to me alive." That had not always been true, nor would it remain so, but Doone was not one to divulge mistakes or intentions.

He fired a deflecting salvo instead. "Apparently, a British patrol ship was attacked somewhere near here, sunk with nearly all hands. A few managed to scramble into a longboat which was found drifting. Their ship's identifying logbook and papers were with them, neatly wrapped in oilskin. Unfortunately, all the poor souls were dead. Or for you, not unfortunate at all? The longboat had no identification. It would not have come from *Sea Witch* by chance? Only it has been noted that you have no longboat on your vessel."

"There are always a lot of ships out in that sea between Spain and the north coast of Africa. Pirates of several sorts, British Navy, Dutch, Portuguese, Frenchies, Spaniards. Spaniards who are upsy-downsy at war with the English, I might remind you. And I was after the *Safeena Hamra* and those Barbary bastards who kidnapped my wife along with those kids. I've no knowledge of a British ship, but even if I had, I wouldn't have wasted time on distraction or dallying with British Navy idiots. If I'd known they were in the vicinity I'd have begged for help. My longboat was nowhere near any British dolts. Mine got smashed to splinters when I exchanged fire with those pirates we've been talking about."

In fact, the British had provoked hostility towards *Sea Witch* first and Jesamiah had not paused to offer explanation. His years of experience 'on the account' and use of his superior guns had made an efficient end to the poorly manned British vessel, despite, in so doing, that he had committed an outright act of piracy and therefore broken his agreement of amnesty. There had been a few British survivors, and against his better judgement the longboat had been lowered for their use. If they had then died that was not Jesamiah's concern. Although it was a relief.

"As an official civil service government representative, I have the ears of many influential men, Acorne. One word from me," Doone stated, "and you, your crew – and your 'wife' – will be swinging from the gallows come sunup tomorrow."

Jesamiah glared with cold hostility across the table, his nose and mouth wrinkling in disgust as if some foul stench had been wafted beneath his nostrils. "On what accusation?"

"On the other hand," Doone flourished his left hand, "a different word could see you all safe from those rumours which are beginning to float around like flotsam on an incoming tide."

"And all I have to do is this task of yours to ensure the rumours sink, eh? No deal. I have nothing to hide and there is nothing that can be proven against me, my wife, or my crew because there is nothing that requires proving." With one gulp, Jesamiah finished his coffee, pushed back his chair and made to stand, intending to leave.

Doone gestured for him to remain seated. "For various reasons I must return immediately to England. Agreement has, finally, after much heated disagreement, been achieved to repatriate the children. I leave with the English, Portuguese and French kiddies on the merchant ship *Lady Of Mercia* this evening. You, meanwhile, could accomplish this little task for me then get back here, by which time your ship will be repaired and you can sail off to whatever horizon you wish to disappear over."

Jesamiah remained seated, his features creasing into a sneer. "What is it you really want? I do not trust you, and you, as sure as an old man farts, do not trust me."

An apparently congenial smile played over the corners of Doone's mouth but did not reflect in his eyes. "Precisely so. I would not trust you with anything, but you possess talents that I do not, and I doubt anyone would remotely believe I would be out of my wits enough to consider employing a pirate such as yourself."

"Didn't know you had any wits in the first place."

"The British Government, via Harley, will pay you for your part with delivering some of the children," Doone added. "When the job is done."

Jesamiah pulled at the gold acorn earring dangling from his right earlobe. It was not his original, the one given him posthumously as a gift from his mother. This one, Tiola had acquired for him as a peace offering after one of their more torrid disagreements.

"So, what exactly, beyond the fact that you are a government intelligencer, is your role here on Gib?"

"I represent certain people of the king's government, that is all you need know."

"People like Harley?"

"No, in the public eye people like the Secretary of State, the Honourable Member of Parliament for Tregony."

Jesamiah sniffed, scratched at his chin. "No one of much importance then." He grinned at Doone's responding tight-lipped expression at the deliberate affront. "So how much, and what's the task?"

"On my part, payment will consist of the agreement that I will guarantee neither you, your woman nor your crew will be arrested for acts of piracy. And I will divulge precise details when you have agreed terms."

Jesamiah set his hat on his head and stood. "You expect me to agree to do something you personally have no balls to undertake without knowing what it is? Go take a piss, mate."

"Harley will pay you fifteen guineas to ensure the safe return of the Spanish children into the hands of their doting mamas and papas."

Jesamiah wholeheartedly wished the drink would finish Harley and his liver off once and for all. Fifteen guineas for escorting children into Spain? So, what else was there to it? Harley was a spymaster; he would not be dealing with a bunch of foreign ankle-biters, not for that sort of money.

Jesamiah answered with an outrageous figure, "Eighty."

"Twenty."

"Sixty."

"Twenty and five. My last offer, Acorne."

Ah, so there *was* more to this. "Declined."

Doone knocked the ash from his pipe then put it along with his tobacco pouch into his pocket. "There is an additional rumour circulating which could affect your woman..."

"Wife."

"And it is attested rumour, which has it that the Spanish want their property back." He pointed towards his feet. "This place, Gibraltar. They are prepared to do whatever it takes to accomplish it. Even destroy every living being here and The Rock itself if they have to. They are assembling a fleet and will lay siege. Sieges can last months. Years. I am sure you would not wish your... wife... to be caught up in any fracas and endure such deplorable conditions if you had the chance to get her out beforehand? Especially as I understand that she is in a certain condition?"

"So, this is why you want to leave in a hurry?"

For a convenient answer, Doone merely waved a hand. "The *Lady*

Of Mercia sails for England at dusk today. We are to escort the children to the respective authorities in Portugal, France and England. There are several girls and three cherub-faced boys, or so I have been informed, plus young Benson ought to be returned to his parents, do you not think? I am sure his mother and father will both be distraught to learn that you abandoned their son to the depravity of a Spanish siege? There will be no adult female aboard and I do not have any inclination to play nursemaid, therefore, your wife's supervision will be a most suitable reason to have her sail with us. I have arranged for a comfortable berth for myself, and can do so for her as well. I suggest you ensure she is aboard well before dusk. She will be in her elder brother's care once we reach England. Nothing more need be said about any other matter. If she stays here, well, I discern that you are not mindful of your own freedom, but are you to be so careless of hers?"

Jesamiah glowered at him.

"A ship is being arranged to take you and the Spanish children to Cádiz..."

"Hah! I ain't goin' anywhere near Cádiz! I'll be hanged the moment I set foot ashore!"

"The ship you sail on will carry a letter of diplomatic immunity – a truce. That means you will be safe enough. It has all been arranged with Spanish officials. You can speak the language fluently so will be the most suitable person to oversee matters. Royal Navy sea captains may occasionally be moderately good at their job, but I have yet to meet one who can speak the local lingo."

"What ship? And why not any sea captain, a merchantman maybe? All he need do is set the children ashore."

Doone stretched his arms and shoulders, canted his head to ease a crick in his neck. "And as I have already said, there is a matter which I need you to privately attend on my behalf."

Jesamiah stared at him through narrowed eyes.

"Apart from the daughters you rescued – and as far as business matters are concerned, girls count for naught – you are Señor Calderón's only surviving kindred, are you not? He was your mother's youngest brother, I believe. His death was most, let us say, unfortunate."

"Don't tell me. He was one of your spies."

"No, he was one of our informants."

"There's a difference?"

"There is a difference. His death has caused some difficulty."

"For whom? Not for me it ain't."

Doone smiled, indulgently. "I thought he had made you his partner in his wine trade? I doubt the husbands and brothers of Calderón's dead wife will take kindly to you inheriting everything."

"I don't want the partnership. They can squabble between themselves about who is to have it all."

Raising a disbelieving eyebrow, Doone shrugged. "That is a lot of potential income you are turning down, but it is your prerogative to do so. Although it surprises me that you have no concern for your now orphaned nieces being left to fend for themselves. All the same, I imagine you will need to go to Calderón's San Vincento home to declare your disinterest. Whilst there you can do something for me."

"What sort of something?"

"All in good time. Your diplomatic immunity should be adequate for such a short, personal, trip."

Should? Jesamiah did not like the sound of that.

Doone scratched at his chin. "I placed details of what I need you to privately do within those ship repair estimates when I deliberately dropped them. The content is strictly between thee and me alone."

He stood, patted his pockets to ensure he had everything safe, said, "The accomplishment of delivering the children and my additional request secreted within your pocket, shall secure your woman's safety in perpetuity."

He took up his hat and cane, walked a few steps away from the table, paused, turned. "See to it that she is aboard the *Lady Of Mercia*. I will escort her to England and deliver her to her brother. Of course, if I do not learn that you have successfully completed your private mission for me, Mistress Tiola will remain in some element of danger until you do. I know of her secret, you see. I have made it my business to discover it."

Jesamiah felt his mouth turn to dry ash, his skin grow cold and clammy. No! There was no way this bastard could know of Tiola's

Craft. No one alive knew, no one save for himself and he would die rather than tell of it, no matter the threats, torture or pain inflicted.

Doone touched his hat by way of a farewell salute. "Until then she will be under my protective wing. I suggest that you do not fail me." He cleared his throat, broadened his sickly smile, held out his hand. "Arrangements will be made for whatever ship is assigned orders to sail to Cádiz. A messenger will contact you with details in due course. Shall we agree on twenty guineas from Harley?"

Ignoring the hand, Jesamiah scowled at the man standing opposite him.

Sighing, Doone lowered his hand. "Very well, twenty and five. Good day to you Acorne. *Bon voyage,* as the Frenchies say." He nodded again as a signal that the agreement was settled and left without a backward glance.

Furious that Doone was causing his hands to shake as if they had the palsy, Jesamiah's narrowed gaze followed his departure. A possible siege? That was nothing compared to the danger Tiola could be in were her Craft made public. Witches were hanged. In some places, burned at the stake.

He felt sick.

The old man had finished his drink, rose to leave, but paused beside Jesamiah. "He be a miserly bugger that one, Cap'n. Best t'ave nowt t'do wiv 'im if'n I was you. Ta for the drink."

Jesamiah nodded, barely aware, considered calling for a large rum, reached for the coffee Doone had ordered instead. The strong, still warm black liquid calmed him a little, helped him think straight. There was no way that Doone could know what Tiola was, it had to be bluff. Had to be.

Then another, sinister, thought. Perhaps the coming child was not his? Perhaps Tiola was lying to him? Oh, what nonsense was this? Doone was a celebrated shite-stirrer, sowing doubts that bloomed into weeds within the turn of a heartbeat. But, he had to concede that the bastard was right about getting her and the boys away if there was to be the likelihood of a siege.

He finished the coffee, pulled the bundle of papers from his pocket, rifled through and found the instruction note.

• • •

Acorne.

There is a man with the name of something akin to 'Burell' residing in or near your deceased uncle's San Vincento residence. Under my orders that devil's spawn, Maharden, was supposed to have disposed of him. He failed.

For the safety of your whore, ensure you do not also fail. Kill him.

Doone

Through gritted teeth, Jesamiah held a corner of the note to the flame of one of the candles set in old bottles on the table, waited for the paper to catch, let it burn a while then dropped it into his empty coffee cup. Watched as the thing turned to ash then poured more coffee over the remains. He tipped the resulting pulp mess to the floor and scrunched it into the scatter of sand with the heel of his boot.

Whore? How *dare* he call Tiola a whore!

San Vincento. The small town where Jesamiah's friend – or maternal uncle as it had turned out – had lived before that grisly day of blood and murder. So, Doone wanted him to kill someone neither of them knew, nor, as far as Jesamiah cared, wanted to know. He had killed men when he had been a pirate. Had killed in fights, and would, no doubt, kill many more times, but there was a difference. A fight, even if the pirates initiated it, was not cold-blooded murder. He had no argument with this person, nor did he intend to start one, especially if it involved Spain and the Spaniards. If this person had indeed been known to Maha'dun then surely, he would have mentioned him? Wouldn't he? But then, there were many things the idiot had failed to mention. Tiola would perhaps know more. Should he ask her, or keep quiet?

Jesamiah rammed his hat onto his black curly hair and left the tavern. He was buggered if he was going to do Doone's dirty work. Nor was he going to ask Tiola damn fool questions. Although, if there *was* to be a siege...

Well, aye, he would rather she was safe away.

CHAPTER FIVE

"Are you completely brain-coddled?" Tiola admonished, staring at Jesamiah with intense incredulity from the window seat, the sewing she had been attending fallen, abandoned, to her lap. "I have no inclination whatsoever to return to England. Especially not with Ascham Doone! It is an idiotic suggestion."

"No, but this will be for the benefit of those children that I – we – rescued, won't it?" Jesamiah had decided to only mention Doone's warning about a possible siege, and that Tiola's role in returning the kidnapped children to Portugal, France and England therefore made sense. Except, he'd miscalculated. Even without her gift of Craft, Tiola could always seize on anything that he hoped to keep hidden from her.

He shrugged, said as casually as he could, "Well, I did wonder that as I've nothing better to do for a few days, I might think about assisting with repatriating the Spanish kiddies. Especially as, Calderón being my uncle, most of them are my cousins."

On the walk back from the tavern, it had occurred to him that to go to Spain might be of personal benefit, although he was unsure how or why that could be so. Maybe it would emphasise his part as a rescuing hero? Strike a favourable light and get this ridiculous threat of Spanish animosity towards him removed? Pat him on the back, rather than put a noose round his neck? All that, he had intended to keep to himself, though, along with the other thing Doone had wanted him to do. Being hired to kill someone was not the sort of thing Tiola would approve of. But as he had no intention of fulfilling that particular request of Doone's, there was no need to mention it anyway.

He tried explaining again. "With nothing much to do, I'll end up as mad as a salt-crazed mariner if I hang around here for the next several weeks."

"So, *you* take the children to England then."

"Tiola, I can't do the Spanish *and* the other kids!"

"So, Doone has arranged two ships? One to go to Spain, one to sail elsewhere? Why? Why not just the one voyage? What else has he in mind? You have agreed to work for him, haven't you?"

"No. The British Government, the Admiralty – I don't know what bloody department – have spent these past weeks arranging to repatriate the children. Not Doone."

Tiola folded her arms. "Oh, Jesamiah you can be such a dolt at times. Ascham Doone pulls too many strings, you know he does. And what care does he have for the children? For anyone, come to that! He is not being honest with you."

Jesamiah responded as he usually did when backed into a corner: he lost his temper. "And here is me thinking you *are* concerned for them? Obviously not. We'll leave their parents to grieve for yet more months than have already passed, shall we? Let them think they are dead, gone forever! I cannot risk you being caught up in a siege and I cannot sit around here."

"You are missing my point," she snapped back. "Is a siege really likely? I don't think so. You've said yourself, often enough; the Spanish have few ships and those they do have are rotting hulks. How can they lay siege? Aside, I do not want to be at sea. I like it here; this is a comfortable room. And do you have no interest in keeping your wife company, of rubbing my back when I spew into the piss-pot of a morning, of…!"

"You will be safer in England!"

Tiola rarely raised her voice in anger. When she did, she could roar like an aggrieved tiger. "Safe? Aboard a ship with Ascham

Doone? The bastard who raped my maid and was the cause of her throwing herself into the sea to drown because of it? I'd rather face a siege than be in the company of that man! You can forget your silly plans Jesamiah Acorne! You can forget all of it, children or no children!"

In an attempt to calm himself, Jesamiah exhaled slowly. He really did not fathom women on occasion. "Had the rot not been found we would not be here in this room, we would be at sea, so what is the difference?"

"The difference is, aboard *Sea Witch* I would be in my own cabin with my own things, aboard a vessel captained by someone whom I knew, where sailing is concerned, to be capable and competent." Under her breath, she muttered, "Ashore, however, capable or competent is rarely the case."

Twice, Jesamiah opened his mouth to make an answer, twice, thought better of it, then spread his arms in a gesture of utter bewilderment. "But you haven't got many of your own things here! A few gowns in the closet, your medicine chest, that sewing, some trinkets and personal bits and bobs. Most of it has been packed away and stored in a warehouse, along with everything else that belongs on my ship." Concluded, "At some expense, I might add." The bit about being incapable ashore, he ignored.

Tiola sucked at her finger, realising she had stabbed herself with the needle; she inspected the linen to ensure she had not spotted blood on Jesamiah's shirt, then threw the thing to the floor, not caring how much it became spoiled. She was tired and grouchy, partly from the pregnancy, partly, a residue from the nightmare of being a prisoner aboard the Barbary pirate ship, the *Safeena Hamra*. The energy of Craft that she had used to protect the children, and herself, had drained her mentally and physically. Had she not been so exhausted she would have restricted her womb from conceiving a child on the night after Jesamiah had rescued her, would have waited to release her fertility with her next cycle. But she had slipped up, and what was done was done. The result was extreme tiredness. She looked at Jesamiah. He must never know, must never discover that she controlled her ability to conceive or not, that until now she had suspended the begetting of a child. He must never know how she had used her Craft to destroy the Barbary ship and its crew. Nor that several weeks before, she had slaughtered a woman of Maha'dun's own Night Walker kind by the use of fire – a lightning strike deliberately guided to the right target. If he knew any of this dark side to her ability, if he ever became aware of these other powers... Aside all that, she was frightened of Doone. He had an evilness about him which she had not been able to uncover, and without her Craft she would be vulnerable to his nasty little narcissistic games.

"I am tetchy," she said with a sigh. "You will need to indulge me while I carry this child. I do not want to return to England on an unknown ship with unknown men."

"You'll not be with unknowns. I'll send Finch with you, and Tom Benson and Donréal, seeing as we have taken over responsibility for the lad. I cannot risk either of the boys remaining here in case there is a siege. Not that the Spanish are competent at sea-based sieges, but I'm not prepared to risk it." He sat on the bed, rubbed his hands over his face. He looked drained, as tired as she felt.

"You're not safe with Doone, Tiola, I know that, know it very well, but you *will* be safer with your brother Carter – I loathe the chap, but he cares for you, I have to grant him that. And do you really want to leave those children, the ones you were imprisoned with in that stinking hold, to face more fear and uncertainty? See them endure a sea crossing without someone they can trust to reassure them?"

Should he mention that Doone had hinted that he knew about her Craft? No, Doone was all bluff, he was sure of it. Said instead, "I think he intends to stir some trouble about us not being legally wed. He hinted about our union not being blessed in a Christian church. I don't see your brother taking that sort of information calmly. He'll listen to you, though."

"So, first thing in the morning you obtain the necessary papers and we pay a priest to officially marry us."

"I can't. We can't. Your ship sails this evening."

"Doone is not telling you the truth, Jesamiah. He is plotting something at your expense."

Jesamiah ran his hand through his hair. Stupidly, he suddenly felt like weeping.

"Don't you think I know that?" He gulped as tears welled in his eyes, choked his throat. "I don't want you anywhere near Doone, but equally, I want you away from here. To be with your brother in Devon, where you and the baby will not get hurt."

Tiola was quiet a moment, deep in thought. "And the children? Do you think he will, intentionally, not see them returned to their homelands?"

Doone would not be so foolish, but Jesamiah leapt on the suggestion. "He, and his grandfather, make their money from smuggling and the slave trade. Add that I suspect he might have somehow been involved in the organisation of kidnap..."

Tiola gasped. "He was behind it?"

Jesamiah spread his hands, truthful for once. "I don't know, sweetheart, I have no proof, just a niggling suspicion. He, or at least his grandfather, knew Yakub Pasha, of that I am certain." He sighed, dropped his hands to his sides. "No, not certain. Highly suspicious, perhaps? But he was genuinely shocked and upset when we saw what had happened at that house."

Quietly thinking, Tiola sat still. Then she nodded. "So, someone needs to keep close eye on those innocents?"

By way of an answering acknowledgement Jesamiah stood and enfolded her within an urgent, desperate embrace.

She looked up, kissed him. There was a lot more that he was not telling her, but he was right, she could not abandon the children. She sighed, a sound of reluctant resignation. "I suppose I had better speak to the boys then, tell them to pack their belongings? They are not going to like the news."

An apologetic half-grin. "I've already told them. They are not delighted, but I pointed out that sailing to England would be better than kicking their heels against a brick wall of nothing interesting to do here."

Tiola glanced around the room at her meagre possessions. She hated packing; it was such a chore. "I wish," she said, "that we had our own house where everything could stay put."

Holding her close, Jesamiah could not answer. That was one wish he would find it hard to help her achieve, but something that he would need to face one day, and one day soon.

"I promise you," he said, resting his chin on her head, "that I have no intention of doing anything for Doone. I'll make my own arrangements about the children." Added to himself, *and see what's what at San Vincento in my own way, in my own time*.

Tiola refrained from saying aloud the thought which ran through her mind.

Ais, but you rarely keep your promises, do you?

CHAPTER SIX

As Jesamiah had feared, not one of his regular crew was happy with his decision to assist with escorting the children to Cádiz. It did not help that they had already heard various rumours, one of which was not what he had expected and he was finding it difficult to convince them of a firm denial.

"Why," he snapped, thumping his fist on the dockside tavern's old barrel serving as a table, "would I be wanting to go to England aboard the *Lady Of Mercia* with Ascham Doone? Who told you this nonsense? There's not a firkin of truth in it!"

"You were seen chatting like best mates with him not long since, and you are sending the two boys," Spokesy piped up, his face crumpling into a glower of iron-hard resentment.

"And yer wife is goin'," added Bert Moody, "so it's a good wager you be goin' too in'it?"

"Aye, you're getting' yer arse out o' 'ere an' leaving us to bloomin' gawd knows 'ow many bloody months of a bloody Spanish siege," Nick Partridge, 'Grousy', grumbled. "Leavin' us 'ere to rot."

Give me strength, Jesamiah thought. "Will you all listen? My wife and the two boys are going to England with the children, and aye, yes, in case there is a siege. Which, actually, is very unlikely. Have you ever known the Spanish to be clever enough to organise anything of a nautical nature successfully? Do you seriously think they would be able to stop *Sea Witch* leaving harbour when it's time for us to sail? But I am *not* going with my wife. I am *not* going to England. Do you really believe I would abandon my ship – even if I couldn't give a rat's turd about what happens to you ungrateful lot?"

"But you *is* goin' to Cádiz."

"Yes Bert, I is – am. Cádiz is not far away. The children being returned there are the nieces, cousins – kindred – to a man I admired and who was my mother's youngest surviving brother. A man who was brutally murdered along with our quartermaster. Someone tipped the wink that those children were at a house with a suitable anchorage. I intend to go along the coast to San Vincento and have a go at finding out who that someone was. Is."

"And what about Doone?" Spokesy asked.

"What about him?"

"You trust him with your wife?"

Jesamiah narrowed his eyes, rested his right hand on the pistol butt protruding from his belt. "No, Spokesy, I do not, but I *do* trust my wife."

"And how do you intend to find this 'someone' you speak of? Seems to me you'd 'ave better chance of findin' one o' them tulip flower bulbs in a six-month stinkin' pig pen."

Jesamiah shrugged. "I've no idea Bert. I'm open to suggestions." He looked, pointedly, from one to another. No one answered. "So, I'll just have to make something up as I go along, won't I?"

"What is to happen to us?" Skylark asked.

A few men muttered the same question.

"Finch is already seeing to Mistress Acorne's dunnage. He and young Jasper will be accompanying her back to England."

There came several murmurs and growls of disapproval. Jasper Hicks was the youngest of the regular crew.

"No disrespect, Cap'n," Spokesy said, with an obvious edge indicating the opposite, "but how do you figure old Finch and a young lad like Jasper will be able to protect Miss Tiola if need be?"

Jesamiah poked his tongue at a molar tooth that was loose. He had been intending to ask Tiola to pull the darn thing out. It wasn't painful, just annoying. "I'm sending Finch because he's a good steward and he'll keep an eye on the necessaries for my wife. And sending Jasper because he's been blatherin' about a ship he decided to abandon a few years back. As for Doone, you reckon my wife will need protecting, then?"

"I do. Doone's a nasty piece of work."

Massaging his cheeks and chin with his fingers, Jesamiah was thoughtful for about half a minute, finally said with a single nod, "I agree with you Spokesy. He is. You'd better go an' all then. And God help you if you fail to keep my wife safe."

"Fair enough by me," Spokesy responded. "My ma lives in Dorset, Weymouth; might be nice to see her and m'sisters again if'n it's all right with you for me to visit?"

"Once my wife and the boys are safe at Appledore with her brother I have no objection at all. As long as you're there to meet me by, let's say, early October."

"If you're not?" Spokesy queried.

"I'd bloody better be, but if not, you stay put and wait for me. My wife will take charge and keep you informed." It occurred to Jesamiah that if he was dead, killed by means natural or foul, they could be waiting a long time, but once the babe was born Tiola would have her gift back and would know what had befallen him. He swallowed hard. That would mean he would never see her again, or his child. Best not dwell on it. "Anyone else want to leave? I'd wager the captain of the *Lady Of Mercia* will take on extra crew."

A couple of the men shrugged, uncertain. A couple more, keen to get away, but reluctant to say so, exchanged glances.

Tactful, Jesamiah added, "Those who want to leave here fetch your dunnage now, and get yourselves to the quay. Ask to sign on as crew. Or find yourselves another ship if that's your preferred inclination. Same applies about meeting up in Appledore if any of you decide to join me again. He looked at Skylark. "Has everyone been paid what is owed them?"

"Aye Cap'n, they have."

"Well, off you all go then." Jesamiah kept a congenial smile on his face as the men he'd ordered to escort Tiola and eight others left the tavern.

"Good riddance to a couple of 'em," Bert Moody said. "Lazy luggers never pulled their weight."

"Like you do, you mean?" Coffee quipped – 'Coffee' for the colour of his skin and his Hindu name the crew had corrupted into 'Coffee' as something more familiar to pronounce.

Bert sent a rude gesture in his direction.

After a few general comments and opinions – not all of them useful or supportive – Jesamiah looked direct at Skylark. "Getting back onto Gib is going to be my main problem, but I'll manage it somehow. As my quartermaster and second in command, I'm putting you in charge of everything that needs being put in charge of. Everything that needs repairing or tarting up must be repaired and tarted up. Worn sails patched or replaced, guns inspected, scuttlebutts cleaned – and get their lead linings removed and fitted with copper like Tiola has been telling us to do for weeks now."

"Lead's longer lasting," Bert Moody said.

"Aye, an' it'll last longer than you, Bert," Jesamiah shot back. "My wife informs me that lead will rot your insides, causin' your balls and cock to shrivel up and drop off before next winter sets in." Tiola had said no such thing, apart from emphasising the dangers of lead poisoning.

More sailors die from lead-lined water butts than they do of scurvy, she had argued several months ago.

Not much we can do about scurvy, Jesamiah had answered. Her response had been forthright, informing him that were he to improve the shipboard diet to include more vegetables and fruit, the fresher the better, not only would any existing scurvy be cured, but it would be completely gone.

A healthy crew, she had insisted, *is a more efficient crew.* And had proven her point by ensuring the men had as much nutritious food as possible for their daily rations, even though several grumbled at the sour taste of lemon or lime juice, and the boredom of cabbage. Few aboard *Sea Witch,* however, became ill and not one of them showed any sign of scurvy.

Jesamiah ploughed on. "I expect *Sea Witch* to be as ready as can be as soon as possible. Then we can make sail and get the fok out of here as soon as I get back." He paused, looked eye to eye at each and every one of them. "If I'm not back by, let's say the first week of October, Skylark will take over as captain and sail *Sea Witch* to Appledore. John Benson has the accounts for my affairs. He'll see you right for any financials, and my wife will know what to do. How long to wait for me."

"Assuming there ain't no bloody siege keepin' us locked in." That was Grousy again.

"A siege will be of little consequence to us. It'll not be the first time we've had to fight our way out of a tight spot," Jesamiah insisted. "Our cannon against a couple of hull-rotten Spanish sailboats which wouldn't even make efficient fishing tubs?"

That seemed to win them round, for there came a lot of laughter and a lively discussion of the best tactics to use against a Spanish galleon attempting a blockade.

Jesamiah pulled his gold fob watch from his pocket – he'd stolen it from someone years ago, and guessed they missed it, for it was good at keeping the time, even at sea. He tucked it back into his waistcoat. "Right then, time's getting short. I've got to see my wife aboard the *Lady Of Mercia*."

As an afterthought, he added, "I've arranged with the bank here for the dockyard bill to be settled on my behalf. Check the bloody invoice first, though, Skylark." He felt in his coat pocket, pulled out a pouch that chinked enticingly and tossed it to his second in command.

"That should see the lot of you all right until I get back from Spain. Don't drink it all in one go."

CHAPTER SEVEN

Jesamiah put his hand on the arm of his curmudgeonly steward and nodded over his shoulder at the two boys who were trudging dejectedly behind them. "I'm relying on you, Finch, to keep close eye on those two scamps; and on m'wife."

Finch nodded, stopped walking and set down the heavy chest hoisted to his shoulder. Hands on hips, he regained his breath before answering, "Be expectin' us then, will them aboard this 'ere *Lady Of Mercy*?"

"*Mercia,* it's an old Anglo-Saxon place in the English Midlands, and aye, they will. I didn't trust Doone to see to necessary comforts; I met the captain earlier this afternoon, took him a couple of bottles of brandy. He's arranging a cabin for Tiola and suitable quarters for the children."

"It'll be squished for space, an' noisy with their chitter-chatter, but I guess I'll cope wiv it."

Jesamiah slapped Finch on the back. "Course you will! Though this cabin had better be worth the sovereigns I had to line the captain's pocket with. I doubt he's ever seen as much silver in one handful. I've also paid passage as passengers for you, Jasper and Spokesy. You're Mistress Tiola's servants and your priority is keeping watch where a watch is needed, not crewing for some unknown captain. Mind you do so. I'll dock any future specie from you if you as much as spend one hour drunk below deck."

Finch glowered at him. "You should've left the bargainin' to me. An' I'll need silver to ensure things stay as you meant 'em. An' for vittles an' such."

Solemnly, Jesamiah removed a leather pouch of coins from his pocket and passed it to Finch, his stern expression clearly indicating that the money was not to be squandered.

Shoving the pouch securely into his own pocket, Finch bent to pick up the heavy seaman's chest again, grunting at the ache in his back.

Jesamiah suppressed a grin and, gently pushing the older man aside, hefted it onto his own shoulder. "Spokesy and Jasper will be there to help, and don't let those two lads idle their time. Once in England I've given Spokesy permission to go off and visit his family in Weymouth. You got anyone you want to show you're still alive to?"

Finch sniffed, then spat a glob of chewing tobacco onto the cobbles. "I 'as fam'ly, a wife, but I've no bloody intention of seein' if she's pushin' up the daisies in case she bloody ain't."

Jesamiah laughed.

Finch changed the subject. "This 'ere *Lady Of Mercy,* she shipworthy?"

"*Lady Of Mercia*. As far as I can tell, aye."

"An' the captain? Know the ropes do 'e?"

"He seems to."

"An' what about Doone?"

Jesamiah shifted the chest to his other shoulder. "What about him?"

"What if I ain't 'appy with somethin' 'e do or don't do?"

"Hold your tongue and temper until night falls, wait your chance then shove him over the side. I believe a deck can get mighty slippery in the vicinity of Biscay and Finistère."

"If you do any such thing, Mr Finch," Tiola said, emerging from a haberdashery a few stores ahead, her arms laden with brown paper-wrapped parcels, "I will never talk to you again."

Finch touched two fingers to where a forelock would be had he enough hair to form one. "Figure o' speech ma'am, nowt but a figure of speech." He hurried forward to relieve her of the packages, called to the two boys: "Oi, you two slug-a-slops get yerselfs 'ere and take these parcels. Shift yer arses. If you shuffle along much slower yer boots'll grow roots an' cling fast to these ruddy cobbles forever."

He didn't receive a response, merely a sour glower from Thomas.

"Now listen to me," Jesamiah said, stepping in front of the boys, and setting the chest down onto the cobbles. "I've seen funeral processions appear more cheerful than you two. I can't risk my wife, or the both of you, getting tangled up in a possible siege which could last months, years even. For one thing, Tom Hedgepig, your ma would never forgive me. Your pa would understand, but not she."

Thomas looked even glummer. Muttered, "I know you are right, sir, but I do not want to leave you, the crew or *Sea Witch*."

"I know you don't, but what has to be, has to be. Aside from that," Jesamiah continued, "I trust Jasper, Finch and Spokesy to keep a watchful eye on Tiola's well-being; they're good, loyal, men but they like their drink, and with a skinful they can get as pissed as Bacchus. I need you two, therefore, to keep an eye on them. I *think* I can rely on you as my acting lieutenants? Can I rely on you?"

Grasping at the offered straw, Donréal answered immediately. "You know you can, sir."

"Tom?"

A little more reluctant than his friend, Tom nodded. "Aye sir. Acting lieutenants?" He shrugged, nodded. Liked the idea. "Aye, you can rely on us."

Jesamiah ruffled both boys' hair. "Good lads." He hoisted the chest to his shoulder again. "And when I get to Devon with *Sea Witch*, after we've sorted this mess here, I will be expecting both of you to report sharp aboard again. Understood? Go on with you, assist Finch before he starts up with more grumbling."

Tiola smiled at her husband. "That was neatly done, my luvver."

"Aye, well, it's always easier to let men – and boys – think they're being given an important job to do. Carrots are better than sticks most of the time."

CHAPTER EIGHT

The warm Moroccan wind was gusting from the African coast, swirling particles of sand as it swept in across the Straits. Lit by the last remnant of what had been a magnificent sunset, boisterous waves skittered and raced each other, looking every bit like the prancing white horses they were named for. Tiola's eyes were watering; she told herself that it was the sting of the wind, but knew it was not. She wiped the stray teardrops away from her cheeks, willed herself not to openly weep. Jesamiah was watching from the quayside; twice he had raised his hand to brush away hair from his face. Was he fighting tears as well?

The activity aboard the *Lady Of Mercia* was intense, men darting about preparing to weigh anchor and make sail. Merchant men, some rough old salts, some wet-behind-the-ears foremast jacks. Tiola hoped the apparent confusion was temporary, otherwise they might not make it across Biscay. Compared to *Sea Witch* she found it odd to have fewer men around her than she was used to. Pirate and Navy ships needed the men to work the vessel and the cannons, the manpower to manoeuvre quickly when action was imminent; merchants relied solely on storage space for cargo, fast speed and ultimate efficiency, so operated with as few men as possible. The brig, *Lady Of Mercia,* was a vessel with two square-rigged masts and had twenty-and-six men as crew, including the captain and sailing master. For this voyage, a portion of her cargo was human – the children. Apart from two young boys, all were girls: nine to go to Lisbon in Portugal, ten French girls, one with her two brothers to be delivered to Roscoff, and nineteen girls to be returned to Falmouth in England.

They were all standing together, leaning over the rail to wave farewell to the dockside workers – not that any of those busy men, beyond one or two, noticed passengers, especially children. They saw ships drop or weigh anchor every day, held little interest in who was aboard unless a chance to earn extra money was involved.

Tiola glanced towards the girls. Tom Hedgepig and Donréal had taken charge, keeping them together like eager sheepdogs mindful of a skittish flock. Tiola suspected that Tom's enthusiasm was because he was trying hard to impress one of the older girls – Harriett, a young lady of about fifteen. She was Cornish, moderately educated, and would probably have fetched a high price for the Barbary pirates. Tiola smiled to herself. Tom was on the cusp of awakening to the allure of pretty young maidens. Ah, the innocence of children! Alas it all too soon vanished when whiskers started to sprout, a voice deepened, or for girls, a bust began to develop and monthly courses began to flow.

The captain was vociferously reprimanding a crewman for not coiling a rope down correctly, his harsh words bringing Tiola back from her reverie. Captain Ash seemed the sort of man who knew what he was doing, was not one to tolerate fools, slackers or layabouts. His berating concluded, he strode towards the men clustered near the capstan.

"So why the delay?" he barked. "Get those pawls set and yourselves sorted for Christ's sake. Do I need to hold your bloody hands to get us under way? You there..." Then he saw Tiola standing at the mid-ships rail and touched his three-corner hat with a right-hand forefinger. "Begging pardon for my language, ma'am, I did not notice you."

Tiola sent him one of her warmest smiles. "That is perfectly all right Captain. My husband is also a sea captain, I am therefore familiar with a sailor's," she laughed, "shall we say, verbal indiscretions?" She broadened her smile. "I would ask you to convey to the men to mind their language near the children, however."

She thought it prudent not to mention that many of the girls were fisher-folk offspring and were probably aware of as many profanities as these men. One of her aims, while on this voyage homeward, was to attempt to instil as much useful education as she could into their young minds: sewing, literature, geography. Moral standards. For the former, the packages she had brought aboard contained bolts of material, needles, cotton and embroidery silks. Each girl, she was determined, would go home with at least one new best Sunday dress to wear and something better than the ill-fitting makeshift dresses the Gibraltarians had provided. Another package had chalk and slates; another, books. At the very least she could teach the children the alphabet and to write their own names. The two young brothers were but three and four years old, too young for formal lessons, but Tom and Donréal could teach them something useful – knots or simple sailing skills perhaps? If nothing else, daily lessons would while away the time.

Captain Ash nodded to her in agreement about the indelicate language and hurried after a crewman who was about to uncoil a rope he ought not to be touching.

"One is to trust," a voice said, unexpectedly, at Tiola's elbow – startled, she realised that Ascham Doone had joined her – "that most of this meagre crew know enough to keep us afloat. I am uncertain whether a voyage with incapable men will bring us the comfort we are accustomed to."

Tiola forced a smile. "Perhaps, then, it is just as well that I am accompanied by three of my husband's men? They can be called to assist if required."

Doone raised one eyebrow. "If those three skivers are all I know them to be, then I doubt they will be sober enough to be aware of whether it is night or day, let alone be of any use to anyone. I am surprised Acorne is paying for their passage," he said, nodding towards where Finch, Spokesy and Jasper were lounging against the rail forward along the deck. "Or is he pleased to be rid of them?"

"They are trustworthy, and they are still in my husband's employ, Mr Doone." Tiola did not add that the other men Jesamiah had released had taken themselves off somewhere – probably to brothels – rather than sign on for work as crew.

Doone shrugged, clearly sceptical. "And those two boys who are bragging among the girls? Are they also trustworthy?"

"They are becoming young men, and a little harmless showing-off towards the fair sex has never harmed any young lad. Did you not accomplish your share of boasting at their age?" She was tempted to add that he excelled at bragging, so must have practised during his early youth. Or had he taken specific lessons in the art of arrogance at college?

When he made no answer, she added, "As you are aware, Gibraltar may soon face a siege. My husband thought it best for Tom to return to Appledore."

Ascham Doone narrowed his eyes to observe the two lads. Thomas Benson appeared to possess as much swagger and self-opinion as did his father. John Benson was Squire of Appledore and Northam, and liked to ensure that everyone knew his position of authority. And his expanding wealth.

"The lad, Donréal? He is somewhat of a conundrum. He reminds me of someone, I cannot place who. He has a distinct shape to his face. Do you know his parentage?"

Tiola said nothing. A moment passed. Several of the *Lady Of Mercia's* crew were stamping around the capstan hauling in the anchor cable, the *clank, clank, clank* reassuringly efficient.

"Loosen mains'l'," Ash roared. Canvas banged and flapped as the men grappled with the disobliging sail. From somewhere forward a voice called, "Anchor's aweigh, sir!"

Men were scurrying about from one task to another as if they were trying to achieve three different things at once. Loud squeals from the children as the ship began to make way and leaned over, a cascade of spray bursting over the rail. Tiola stifled a laugh as Tom removed his jacket and placed it around Harriett's shoulders – she was a good two years his elder, but he had the making of a fine gentleman. The yards were squealing as men hauled, the sail filled with wind and *Lady Of Mercia* gathered speed, heading for England as eager as a homing pigeon. A pity that Tiola could not join in with the children's excitement. She waved to Jesamiah on the dockside, bit her lip as he raised his hat in acknowledgement.

"Ah, I have it," Doone announced. "The boy reminds me of Señora Escudero."

"I do not know the lady," Tiola answered brusquely. Untruthfully.

"No? Acorne does. They were lovers. She is dead, killed a short while ago in Bristol. It was she who saved your husband from the gallows."

"Then I thank her soul for her intervention, and trust she is at peace with her God, but if she and Jesamiah were lovers, it would have been before I met and married him." Another lie.

"Of that I am not so certain. Do you not think the boy has traces of a likeness to Acorne?"

Everything aboard was banging and creaking as the brig plunged into her course, the anchor was catted securely home and Gibraltar was already some way distant. Tiola bunched her fists, annoyed that Doone had robbed her of the last moments of waving farewell to Jesamiah.

"I can tell you, sir," she snapped, "I have no reason to doubt my husband's fidelity, have no call to speculate on Donréal's parentage and am not prepared to listen to your insults. Good day." Gathering her skirt to a height not entirely respectable, she marched, as steadily as the rolling deck permitted, to join Finch, Spokesy and Jasper. They could see by her expression that she was furious.

"If the bugger vexes you, ma'am, I'm sure we can do somethin' about him. Permanent like," Finch offered.

Tiola relaxed, laughed. "Believe me, at this moment it would not take much for me to do something about him myself!" She fell quiet as she watched the foresail fall and the wind fill it. *Lady Of Mercia* was racing now. Tiola looked towards Tom and Donréal, the two of them laughing and larking about, turned her attention towards Doone then back to the boys, her lips thin, expression grim.

"Gentlemen," she said in almost a whisper, "it is in my mind that Doone has a particular interest in young Donréal. I would ask you to ensure that at all times one of you keeps him within your sight. I stress, at *all* times."

"Is he someone special?" Spokesy asked, out of curiosity.

"He is, although he is of no value to anyone save his kin." She could not say that Donréal was indeed the son of Francesca Escudero, one of Jesamiah's lovers, a woman whom Doone, possibly, had ordered killed because she too was a spy – Lord Harley's best intelligencer. Nor could she say that the boy had been sired by Jesamiah's father. No one besides herself and Jesamiah knew that. But why Doone had interest in the lad was another question entirely.

One that, as far as Tiola could see, did not possess a reasonable answer beyond his penchant for spite.

CHAPTER NINE

Hands thrust deep into his pockets, a frown just as deep creasing his brow, Jesamiah had watched the *Lady Of Mercia* set sail, biting his lip to stem any outburst of criticism. Weighing anchor was being sloppily done, but then, Jesamiah reasoned, he was used to the experienced competence and efficiency of his own men. Some of the captain's orders had been carried by the wind over the several hundred yards distance. Or, at least, Jesamiah fancied he'd heard them. With familiar orders and tasks, maybe the words had merely been in his head? The canvas cracking and thundering as the sails were unfurled was real enough, though.

Released from her tethering anchor the vessel gathered speed and dodged across the wind. There was another scurry aboard; round the yards came and with more canvas bowing like the belly of a woman heavy with child, the *Lady Of Mercia* canted over, her gunwale awash. Was that children's laughter he heard? The vessel righted herself and thrust forward, sweeping aside the churning spindrift. Jesamiah fancied that he could hear the squealing of the blocks, the groans and complaints of stays and shrouds. He knew every sound, but those would be different from the ones he was used to – the same words of the same song, but sung to a different tune. The *Lady Of Mercia* would not possess *Sea Witch*'s sweet timbre.

The distance between them increasing rapidly, Jesamiah took his telescope from his pocket, extended it and put the brass instrument to his eye. He saw Doone standing next to Tiola and purposefully focussed on her face. A little too far to clearly judge her expression but he formed a smile as he saw her toss her head and walk away.

"Good girl," he muttered, "stay well away from the bastard."

The crew were preparing to tack. Jesamiah collapsed the telescope and returned it to his pocket. No use watching now; Tiola was too far away. He gulped down tears.

"God speed," he murmured as he raised his right hand in a farewell salute. It could be weeks before he saw Tiola again.

"That's her gone, then."

Jesamiah whirled around with an indrawn breath of alarm, his hand dropping to the hilt of his cutlass – he hated people coming up behind him – looked direct into the amiable, blue-grey eyes of a cleanshaven man in his early forties.

Removing his hand from his cutlass, Jesamiah growled, "Richie Tearle. I was wondering when you might bob up again, like a turd that will not swill away."

The man grinned, held out his hand for Jesamiah to clasp and shake – a fairly new, fashionable custom that was rapidly spreading through men of the gentry, and much to the dismay of some of them, even among the better class of women. "I'm heading for a drink and something to eat," Tearle said. "Care to join me?"

Jesamiah did not particularly want company, but to sit on his own would only lead to brooding and getting drunk. And that would set a standard for every day that was to follow. Not a good idea.

"The Anchor is not far off," Tearle said, indicating the way. "William, the landlord, is a friend of mine."

With the suspicion that Tearle knew too many friends in too many different ports, Jesamiah shrugged acceptance. Dubious 'friends' aside, one tavern was as good as another.

"I'm surprised you were not aboard the *Lady Of Mercia* as well," Tearle said, falling into step beside Jesamiah. "Though, I can understand why. Ascham Doone is a man to be avoided where possible."

"Yet you work for him."

"No, I work for Harley."

Jesamiah snorted disbelief. "Whoever you work for, you are still a spy."

"An intelligencer."

"Same thing."

"Not quite."

Intelligencer. Informer. Spy? They all added to the same answer: someone who sneaked around gathering information about other people who were also in the business of sneaking around for one reason or another.

With dusk settling in, the lamplighter was solemnly making his way up the main cobbled street, heading away from the rowdy bustle and noise of the dockside workers and sailors filling the wharfside brothels and taverns. Businesses – barbers, candlemakers, apothecaries and taverners in particular – were obliged to place candle lanterns or smoking tar-torches outside their doors from dusk until ten of the evening, except when a full moon was bright enough not to warrant the provision of additional light. Time Callers, men or women who shouted the time taken from the church clock for specific daily events such as morning mass and the night curfew, would traipse the streets when it came for the lighting to be doused, with the night watch patrolling in their wake to ensure the streets remained safe and deserted. Except, of course, the bribery of a few coins, free drinks, or the complimentary service of a woman, caused many a blind eye to be conveniently turned.

The wealthier residential areas, however, were usually emptied of stragglers and strangers by the coming of night, for theft, burglary and assault were common and those who could afford night-time protection were obliged to pay for it. Their money also carried the additional provision of a variety of civil amenities: night-soil men who, come daylight, collected the overnight human waste from chamber pots and buckets; men who cleared animal dung and strewn detritus from the cobbled streets – and the lamplighter, a curmudgeonly, elderly man who detested his wife, his job and everyone and everything in between. Jesamiah nearly collided with his ladder and received a torrent of blasphemous abuse. He recognised the vitriol, and the voice.

"You could show a little more respect to those who bought you a bloody drink!"

The lamplighter, the old man from the tavern, glowered back at him. "An' you could mind where you're bleedin' goin'!"

Jesamiah muttered something equally as abusive.

"Good evening to you, Mr Tuffnell," Tearle intervened, touching his hat. "A fine night, I perceive?"

The lamplighter scowled back at him. "Fine night fer what? Makin' a bleedin' nuisance of yersel', or fer annoyin' me?"

"Cheerful chap, ain't he?" Jesamiah observed as they strolled on.

Tearle nodded, laughed. "He has his uses." After a few minutes of silence, queried, "I'm curious. Are you not concerned by one of those frigates at anchor in the harbour?"

"Should I be?"

Tearle turned his attention momentarily to a blue-eyed blonde partially displaying her assets as she leant against the wall outside what appeared to be a better class of brothel. He smiled at the girl, winked. Said, regretfully, to Jesamiah, "A pity, I'm a bit busy at the moment... Anyway, the *Bonne Chance*. Her present captain is Edward Vernon."

That pulled Jesamiah up sharp. He was ahead of Tearle; he turned on his heel, stared at the man. "What? Vernon is here? On Gib?"

Tearle nodded. "He is. Of course, he might have forgotten that not long ago in Nassau you attempted to blast his ship to pieces, and made him look an incompetent fool into the bargain."

Jesamiah responded with what he saw as a reasonable justification for the action. "He was trying to commandeer my ship!"

"He lost his commission of command in the Caribbean because of you, and regards the *Bonne Chance* as a step downward for his career."

Jesamiah shrugged. Walked on. "That ain't no concern of mine." He kept quiet about the vessel itself. His run-in with a previous captain of hers had been a long time ago. Unlikely that she still had any of the original crew. At least, he hoped so. The disgruntled Vernon was the much bigger worry.

They were ahead of the lamplighter, so the steep, cobbled street was in shadowed darkness, save for the flickering spill of lantern and candlelight from a few, as yet unshuttered windows. Two men, puffing slightly and walking faster than Jesamiah and Tearle, pushed past, disappeared into the darkness ahead.

"Captain Vernon is probably not too impressed with his latest orders, either," Tearle said, following in Jesamiah's wake. "I guess he won't be too pleased at playing nursemaid to a bunch of Spanish children."

Jesamiah spun round again. "What?"

"Ah." Richie Tearle thrust his hands into his coat pockets, nodded understanding. "Doone didn't tell you which ship – which captain – was to take the children to Cádiz?"

"He said he'd send me a message." A resentful scowl of comprehension swept over Jesamiah's face. "So, you *are* Doone's messenger boy? Not bloody surprising he didn't want to tell me himself, the bastard."

"For what it is worth, I repeat, I am not Doone's man. I do not carry messages for him. I assumed you had already been told."

"No, I hadn't. And that settles it. I'm having nothing to do with any of it." Jesamiah glowered at Tearle a moment then continued up the hill, on the edge of announcing that he didn't want company after all. He had a slight prickle of conscience about the children, and what he had – hadn't – told Tiola... Damn it all, he'd stay in Gibraltar, get *Sea Witch* seaworthy as soon as possible, sail for England, sort Doone out once and for all then return to the Caribbean.

The two men who had walked past stepped out from a recessed doorway several yards ahead, both with aimed pistols. One of them, as he came forward into the dim light from a partly shuttered window, Jesamiah recognised from the group of rowdy seamen who had been in the tavern that morning.

"Was Doone, this morning, aware of what ship was to take the children?" he asked Tearle.

"Possibly not, but I told you, I do not work for the man, so I would not know."

Jesamiah snorted. Oh, Doone knew all right! He knew damn well that under no circumstances would Jesamiah get within a hangrope's length of Edward Vernon. That unnecessary swapping of hat and cane from one side to the other? A signal to these troublemakers? *This is the man I wish to mark*!

Jesamiah was suddenly aware that there was someone behind him – not Tearle, someone else.

"Tearle?" he called, keeping his gaze firmly on the two men with raised pistols. "Tearle?" he repeated. No answer. He could hear the lamplighter's wheezing breath a distance off down the hill, but he would be of no help in a confrontation. A heartbeat pause for Jesamiah to decide what to do. Run? With two pistols pointing straight at him? He glanced at the nearest front door. Worth hammering on it? No, he'd be shot before he even reached for the brass knocker. To each side of the white-limed doorstep, a round terracotta pot of red flowers – incongruously, he wondered if Tiola would know what they were. He vaguely remembered her talking about them when they were together in Cape Town those years ago. Gernimums, or something like that.

One of the assailants steadied his aim and squeezed the hammer of his pistol... Jesamiah dropped to one knee, rolled, as the buzz of the shot thudded a foot away into the wall of the house, sending brick dust puffing out into the evening air. Where had Tearle disappeared to? As Jesamiah came up to his feet he lunged for the nearest flowerpot and hurled it at the two assailants ahead of him. It smashed into one man's head with a satisfying crunch – he staggered, overbalanced, fired the pistol in his hand as he fell, the shot spinning harmlessly into the other flowerpot, shattering it.

Snarling, fists raised, Jesamiah made for the other man who raised an arm to block the double punch heading his way – one to the belly, one to the jaw – except the man lurched aside and the punch went wide.

Jesamiah heard, felt, movement directly behind. Where *was* Tearle? He turned slightly, remembering the third man.

The butt of a pistol. A sharp jolt against his skull...

CHAPTER TEN

Richie Tearle was aware of someone leaning close over him and of a calloused hand patting, none too gently, at his cheek.

"You goin' t' wake up, mate?"

Tearle opened one eye, closed it again as the world spun by.

"That's some lump on yer 'ead," the voice said, leaning in even closer. "It be a wonder them from the Frenchie frigate didn't drag you off an' all."

Tearle opened both eyes, took a slow, deep breath to swallow down the threat of vomit – a natural reaction to an olfactory objection to the lamplighter's too-close stink of sour breath and body odour. Tearle looked straight into the whiskered face and scrutinising eyes of Mr Tuffnell.

"And how would you be knowing who they were?" Tearle asked, as with a groan he hauled himself to his feet, grateful for Tuffnell's steadying hand as he wobbled slightly. He peered up the street to where he had last seen Acorne, saw nothing except two shattered terracotta pots and a scatter of earth, leaves and red petals.

Tuffnell, satisfied that his temporary charge was not going to keel over, retrieved his ladder from where he had propped it against a wall and set it against the next unlit street lamp. Began to climb. "I recognised one o' them whoresons. Same booger I 'ad a run-in wiv earlier t'day."

"French frigate?" Tearle was puzzled; there were no French vessels anywhere near Gibraltar. "Ah, you mean the *Bonne Chance*?"

"Aye, that be 'er."

A door opened at the house which had once boasted two intact flowerpots of geraniums. A man stood in the light streaming out into the street, a duelling pistol in each hand, a frightened manservant a few paces behind wielding a stout wooden club.

"What is happening out here? What is all this? Answer me or I will shoot!" The man took a tentative step forward, waving the pistols with a pretended air of menace.

"'S'all right, Sir George," Tuffnell called. "This gent'man saw orf a couple o' ruddy thieves tryin' t'set upon me. I be grateful to 'im."

The question of why thieves would attack a lamplighter who had nothing to steal except for a canvas bag of tallow candles, a slow match, a tinder box and a ladder, clearly did not enter Sir George's head. He lowered the pistols. "I will have to report this," he announced. "We cannot be having this sort of thing in this street; it is a quiet area. I have women and children withindoors."

"Best keep them there then, sir," Tearle responded, retrieving his hat from where it had fallen. "Just in case there's more of the gang hanging around."

Sir George immediately saw the sense of that, and gestured with one pistol for the servant to return indoors, hurried after him, slammed the door shut and thrust the bolts home.

"'Is wife'll be in 'igh dudgeon when she discovers them damned flowerpots be spoiled," Tuffnell wheezed through a bark of laughter as he descended to ground level. "Bleedin' things are a ruddy nuisance; I catch me ladder on them pots every bloody night." He sniffed loudly. "I reckon them were press, them boogers 'oo took 'im." He looked Tearle up and down, his gnarled old face crinkling even more like a crumpled walnut. "You be too old fer what them wanted, eh?"

The sound of feet and voices approaching from further up the hill distracted Tearle from making any indignant answer.

"You best be goin'," Mr Tuffnell suggested. "That'll be tha Watch, an' once they start their ruddy questions they don't know 'ow t'stop. I'll tell they t'piss orf."

"That's mighty helpful of you, sir," Tearle said, although his brows were furrowed in puzzlement. "From what I've heard, such niceties go against your usual better nature?"

The old man loosened a brief cackle. "Better nature? Nay I ain't got any o' that nonsense in case me old crone o' a wife finds out 'bout it. Don't want 'er t'get a wrong impression. If'n y' want t'see yer friend agin, though, I'd 'as git yerself to that there *Bonney Chance* afore she sails." He gobbed a generous dollop of tobacco spittle to the cobbles. "I don't hold no truck wiv them bastard press gangers. They took m' son three year back. Never seen 'im agin. Least, that's what I were tol'. 'E might've just upped an' buggered orf. Cain't say as I blame 'im."

Tearle had heard no rumour of press gangs out looking for additional crew. Nor had his government contact made any mention of an ambush. Knowing that Acorne would never voluntarily go aboard that particular frigate, the agreement had been for Tearle to get Acorne drunk and haul him, well inebriated, aboard the *Bonne Chance.* If that interfering Doone had made other plans... Damn, damn the man!

Tearle felt in his pocket for some coins, handed them to the old man. "For your trouble," he said, "I'll buy you a drink next time we meet."

"Chance'll be a fine thing," Tuffnell grumbled as he thrust the coins deep into his pocket. He moved his ladder to tend the next lamp. He sniffed, wiped a glistening dewdrop from his nose with the back of his hand, chuckled, as he started to climb slowly up his ladder, muttering to himself, "Tha's fortunate. No need t' bother wiv passin' damned fool messages on t' that Acorne fellow now. An' if Doone wants 'is money back fer payin' me t'do it, he can go bloody whistle."

Richie Tearle trotted down the street. He had his own dunnage and Acorne's to collect, then he had to get aboard *Bonne Chance*. He turned once to raise a hand in farewell to Tuffnell, but the lamplighter was busy placing a new candle inside a glass lantern.

CHAPTER ELEVEN
AT SEA

He was aboard a ship. That much was plain by the sounds filtering down from above. A ship weighing anchor. Jesamiah knew the rumble of the capstan, the *stamp, stamp* vibration of feet and accompanying grunts of men as they worked to bring in an anchor with its sodden, weed and slime-encrusted, heavy cable. Fettered by the ankles, lying on his back, he was uncomfortable and had a pounding headache. He tentatively moved. Abandoned the idea as his dizzy head swirled even more uncomfortably than the dull ache of his stiff back. He wore no coat, waistcoat or cravat. No boots, and from the cold of his feet, his stockings had gone as well. They were new, expensive, finely knitted silk. *I'm surprised they left me m'shirt and breeches,* he thought, wincing as the pain from the back of his head shot across his skull to throb behind his eyes. Which he kept closed, partly from the discomfort, partly from a reluctance to discover exactly where he was. The sounds, though, he could not ignore.

The tumble of bare feet on the deck above, the clang of a ship's bell – two rings, pause, two rings... What was that? Ten of the evening or six in the morning? He had not eaten but was not particularly hungry, and his bladder was not full, so maybe he had not been unconscious for long? He opened his eyes. All was dark except for the distant glow of a lantern. Night then. Early morning daylight would have filtered down through the hatches. He closed his eyes again, a defence mechanism; if he couldn't see it, it might go away. More questions flooded his mind. What ship? Where bound? What had happened to Tearle? The bastard must have run off the moment he realised those buggers had been the press. So much for friendship! Although, Jesamiah reasoned, Tearle was no friend, especially if the sod worked for Doone. Or Harley. Or both of them, or anyone else, come to that.

More familiar sounds and recognition of movement. The anchor was aweigh, the vessel, released from her tether, sidestepped across the wind, heeling to larboard. Sails would be tumbling from their restraints – he heard the rumble of loosened canvas. Fores'l, mains'l. Recognised the sound of their grumbling and straining as the wind drove the ship forward. The yards would be swinging and creaking, men hauling at the braces, trying to keep that great strength flapping above them tamed and under control. The ship heeled again. Then she steadied. White water would be foaming along her hull, spray crashing over the bowsprit, engulfing the figurehead – what figurehead? Jesamiah tried to muster his memory. What Royal Navy vessels had been at anchor? *Triton, Fortitude, Godolphin – Bonne Chance*. He discounted the numerous merchantmen and fishing boats; they did not press innocent men into service. He swallowed down a desire to vomit. Nauseous, not from the movement of the ship, but from anger – and more than a little bit of fear. Where was Tearle? Doone's man – for all his protestations. Had the pair of them planned this? Hah, a bloody good way of ridding themselves of someone they didn't want pesterin' or pokin' into their business! Shite... and Doone had Tiola! If this was the man o'war that had been anchored on the far side of the harbour – HMS *Royal George,* Jesamiah thought she was – if this was her... He felt his body start to tremble. If this was *Royal George,* he would never see freedom again. Never see Tiola, the child she carried born into life, or *Sea Witch...* Someone was coming. A lantern light bobbing down the hatchway ladder, the sound of booted feet. A moment later a foot kicked Jesamiah's ankle, none too gently.

"This is 'im sir, the gorbellied malt-worm." Another kick to Jesamiah's ankle, the rattling of keys and the leg shackles were released. Jesamiah stayed where he was, prone, eyes closed. A mistake.

"Up, you lazy pignut. Up on yer feet!"

Jesamiah opened his eyes, winced as the light from the lantern being held a few inches from his face pricked at his eyes. No kick this time, but a bosun's rattan cane, rapped hard across his shin. It hurt. He growled beneath his breath, not quiet enough, for another blow fell across his spine as he rolled over onto his knees.

"Get up!"

"I'm bloody trying!" Too late, the annoyed words left Jesamiah's mouth and another blow fell across his shoulders.

A different voice: "That'll do, Mr Almitty, the fellow's trying his best."

"Beggin' yer pardon, Lieutenant, but he ain't tryin' at all."

"I said that'll do, bos'n. Come on you, on your feet."

Inhaling, painfully, Jesamiah stood, forced his aching, protesting body to straighten up. No use in courting further discomfort from that cane.

"Are you certain this is the man, Buckeridge?" The officer, the first lieutenant, motioned for the sailor holding the lantern to step forward again.

Buckeridge complied and thrust the light close to Jesamiah's face, his own visage peering as close. His breath stank of sour ale and onions.

"Aye, sir, this be 'im. Never forgotten 'is face I ain't."

Jesamiah kept his gaze fixed firmly on the lieutenant. "I have no idea who this man thinks he remembers, but I have never seen him before this morning when he was making a nuisance of himself in one of Gibraltar's more respectable taverns."

The bosun, Almitty, raised his cane again. "You speak to Lieutenant Coffney when you're spoken to, maggot-pie." The cane thwacked against Jesamiah's arm. With fortitude, he ignored the blow, but stored the memory away.

Coffney stood with his hands linked behind his back. "Buckeridge here," he nodded towards the sailor holding the lantern, "says that several years ago you murdered some Navy men while they were ashore at Ponta Delgado in the Azores. Men who served aboard this vessel. He witnessed you doing the foul deed."

His eyes narrowing, mouth puckering, Jesamiah tipped his head back a little. Enlightenment dawning, he opened his mouth slightly, nodded once. Ah. Buckeridge had been a tar aboard HMS *Bonne Chance* that time in the Azores. At least this was the right ship, although given the circumstances the fact was not much comfort.

Interpreting the signs correctly, Coffney nodded. "I see you are suddenly remembering?"

Ponta Delgado, the Azores. 1710. Jesamiah had been aboard *Mermaid* under the captaincy of Malachias Taylor, sailing, as it had turned out, as pirates although he'd been under the impression that they'd been granted a Letter of Marque and were trailing the enemy – the Spanish – legitimately as privateers. For a short while they had sailed in consort with *Barsheba,* Henry Jennings' ship. Jennings had, since then, retired from the sea and was now the vice-governor of Nassau, New Providence Island in the Bahamas – when he wasn't coercing Jesamiah into doing some underhand, dangerous task that he did not want to do himself.

Sailing with Malachias and Henry had been good. Good days filled with adventure and the freedom the sea offered without any of the responsibility. Good days except for one inconvenience. Charles Vane, one of Henry's crew, who had made it his task to ensure that he and Jesamiah had no liking for each other. There had been several altercations between the two of them, fights that these years later, with Vane now the captain of his own pirate craft, Jesamiah went out of his way to avoid. A sensible precaution on Jesamiah's part, for it was an odds-on bet that one day Vane might win a bout of fisticuffs between them.

In the Azores, Jesamiah had, foolishly as it had turned out, assisted Vane when he had been set upon by a gang of unruly Royal Navy scum from the *Bonne Chance*. The Navy had come off the worst, with several dead. Unfortunately, their captain had then been obsessed with finding the killers, and Buckeridge had recognised Jesamiah. Given his ability to think quickly and promote a believable lie, the 'misunderstanding' had soon been cleared up. Or so Jesamiah had thought.

He smiled, spread his hands wide. "I'm beginning to remember. This troublemaker accused me of murder some few years ago. I denied it then, as much as I deny it now."

"I saw dead men an' you with a bloodied weapon in your hand, you scumbag murderer," Buckeridge hissed.

"And as I recall, I explained the circumstances more than adequately to your captain then, as adequately as I am explaining them now. I was defending myself – and those Navy jacks – against the man who was the killer. I told you, and your captain, that Charles Vane was the one you wanted. Not me."

"You was wearing them molly boy blue ribbons and an acorn earring; I recognise that an' all," Buckeridge added. His breath truly did stink.

"Aye, I was... am." Jesamiah touched the two ribbons wound into a strand of hair and then the earring dangling from his earlobe. "I ain't no molly boy and this is my lucky charm, I ain't ever without it, though this one is not the one I had those years ago. That one, as I told you, was part payment of money Vane owed me. I still ain't got the rest of it from the bugger."

Lieutenant Coffney cleared his throat with a harrumphed cough. "You deny this accusation of murder, then? And, I insist on asking, given that Vane is synonymous with a brutal pirate of that same name, were you, are you, a scum pirate?"

"Vane is committed to piracy. I sailed, then, as a legitimate privateer against the Spanish. And aye, I most certainly deny this accusation. Though to an extent I must thank Mr Buckeridge here. Had he not turned up, Vane would have gutted me as swiftly as he'd disposed of those other poor souls. I'll readily sail aboard a Navy ship that's prepared to go after Vane to hang the bastard."

"You ran away!" Buckeridge objected, his face puce with anger.

"I did not. I was chasing after Vane, who *was* running away." Total lies, but Jesamiah knew that this man, Buckeridge, had held no proof then, held even less – apart from an obvious grudge – now.

"What do we do Lieutenant?" the bosun asked. "Do we chain this liar, interrogate him more thoroughly? Buckeridge here went to a lot of trouble to bring him aboard to face the justice he deserves..."

Did he now! Jesamiah filed the sliver of information away into his memory.

"Indeed, a lot of trouble to cause trouble," Lieutenant Coffney said, cutting the bosun short. "There are two sides to this story and it is not in my authority to judge which side is the right, or wrong of it. It is up to Captain Vernon to decide what to do."

Vernon? Ah, that confirmed it. This was *Bonne Chance,* although Vernon was the last person Jesamiah wanted to tangle with.

"You are a sailor you say?" Coffney queried. "What vessels have you served aboard?"

Maybe best to keep quiet about the pirate ships, Jesamiah thought. He touched his right forefinger to his forehead by way of a respectful salute. "I was aboard the privateer *Mermaid,* sir, but I moved on to a variety of merchantmen. Mostly English, some Dutch. I was with *Duke,* captained by Woodes Rogers on his circumnavigation of the world." When Jesamiah lied, he did it well, using untruths that sounded credible. If he was asked questions, he had read Rogers' and his navigator, William Dampier's, published accounts of the voyage enough times to make plausible answers.

He achieved the desired effect, because the lieutenant looked suitably impressed. The result somewhat compromised when Coffney then asked, "That voyage was some while ago; in what vessel did you last serve?"

Jesamiah had to think quickly, needed a persuasive, but fictional, response. "The *Daisy Anne,* a Cornish lugger, shipping tin and copper from Falmouth to Gib. I didn't sign on for another voyage. Didn't think much of her bos'n."

Ignoring the implied insult, the lieutenant asked, "What experience have you?"

"Topman, helmsman, gunner."

"Gunner? Aboard a merchant?" Almitty's snort was derisive.

Jesamiah looked at him witheringly. "We got plenty of practice at the guns aboard *Duke* when fighting the Spanish." Touched his forehead with one finger again, added as a sarcastic afterthought, "Sir."

Lieutenant Coffney waved a hand to silence the bosun from making a reprimanding response. "Your name?"

Jesamiah was expecting that question. Had no intention of supplying a truthful answer. "Oakwood." He'd used the name before, when delicate situations required it.

The lieutenant followed with, "Until we decide what to do with you, Oakwood, are you willing to work as crew?"

Almitty jumped in with a disapproving answer. "With respect, Lieutenant, this man may well be unreliable and dangerous."

"That he might, Mr Almitty, but I have no wish to fetter a man who may be innocent of charges laid, possibly incorrectly, against him for a crime committed almost a decade ago."

Almitty and Buckeridge both scowled; Jesamiah huffed quietly to himself. Doone had arranged all this hadn't he? Tip the wink to Buckeridge, get Vernon to hang him on a charge of murder? Oh, nicely done Doone, you bastard! If he ever found out that Tearle was a party to this... On the starb'd side of things, Doone wanted that private job done. Another murder. So why put him in this situation? Didn't make sense. Could it be...? Jesamiah hadn't had any intention of voluntarily coming aboard *Bonne Chance* – nor of doing Doone's bidding. His own alternative plan had been to lie low, get himself aboard a ship bound for England, collect Tiola, get back to a repaired *Sea Witch* and then disappear to the far side of a convenient ocean. It hadn't been a good plan, admittedly, but he'd not had much time to think of anything better. The flaw in it all was that Doone, and Tearle for that matter, would have guessed his intention even before he'd thought of it. All this nonsense was a way to ensure he was aboard this ship. Bastards.

As he now appeared, albeit unwillingly, to have become a government intelligencer set about government intelligencing business, surely Vernon would not dare hang him, no matter how many charges of murder or destroying Royal Navy ships were laid at his feet? He was safe. Wasn't he? What if he wasn't?

Jesamiah formed a pleasant smile. So, he was here against his better judgement and there was little he could do about it. But he had no intention of rolling over to placidly play Doone's manipulative game. He made his own rules. "Well, Lieutenant, sir," he said, "as it happens, I were intending to sign on as crew to whatever vessel would have me, before your ruffians beat me to the opportunity."

Buckeridge and Almitty growled in quiet unison.

Studying Jesamiah a long moment, the lieutenant eventually nodded, said, "I am not convinced that I believe you, on any of this, but you might as well earn your keep while aboard, and until I have opportunity to raise the matter with Captain Vernon. Mr Almitty, add this man's name to the ledger. Set him to work where appropriate."

"I would appreciate the return of my personal things. Before I was attacked, I had good clothes and my father's weapons. Whoever stole them," he looked pointedly at Buckeridge, "must return them."

The lieutenant scowled, disapproving. "'Stole', Mr Oakwood is a contentious word. I'd rather allude to 'safe keeping'. I am sure Mr Buckeridge can discover where these things have been stowed, and will return them to you. The clothes at least. I will personally take care of any weaponry that would not be appropriate for a mere sailor." He turned to the bosun. "See to it bos'n."

"Very good, sir, but..."

"No buts, Mr Almitty, Buckeridge. No buts from either of you. And you, Mr Oakly, remove those ribbons from your hair. We permit one earring and discreet tattoos but not unnecessary fripperies." Coffney dismissed the men with a curt nod, turned on his heel and retraced his steps to the ladder leading to the upper deck, paused, looked back. "However, Mr Almitty, should he slack in any duties, you have my permission to flog his hide raw. Do I make myself clear, Oakly?"

Jesamiah again touched his finger to his forehead, began unlacing his ribbons. "Oakwood, sir. Aye, sir, quite clear, sir."

Almitty's expression could not be described as anything except wickedly calculating. "Foremast topm'n suit you, eh, Oaky?"

Topmen, the most agile and experienced men of a ship's crew – technically the 'sailors' named for their skill with handling acres of canvas sails. They had to be fit and fearless; men able to climb, or descend quickly in all weathers, night or day. Men who needed to possess no fear of working along a swaying yard under conditions which could cause death at any moment. For an unskilled or nervous man, 'could' often became 'would'.

"Suits me fine," Jesamiah answered as he shoved his ribbons into his pocket, thought, *But only as far as Cádiz.*

CHAPTER TWELVE

"Captain?"

Edward Vernon looked up from the letter he was writing, annoyed at being disturbed in the sanctity of his Great Cabin, but half expecting it. They were not long under way and there was always uncertainty during the first hours of making sail. Especially where his dithering second lieutenant was concerned. A young man of nineteen years old, he had the prospect of a good future ahead of him were he only to apply himself, but Lieutenant Lancelot Lande well-earned his nickname of 'Three Ells', for his name, his general uncertainty and over-used, 'Look Lively Lads' the latter two of which the bosun, Almitty, seized upon to make use of his cane. Not that Vernon disapproved of genuine discipline – far from it – but unnecessary brutality soured the men, and there was a loyal, hard-working crew aboard *Bonne Chance*. Despite the sadistic nature of 'Gawd Almighty', Mr Almitty.

Lande entered, did not stoop low enough beneath the overhead beams and knocked his hat off. He blushed, retrieved it and stood smartly before Vernon's desk, which even after this short time at sea was already littered with cluttered paraphernalia.

"My apologies for interrupting your solitude, Captain. Writing to your lady wife, are you? I will do so to my dear mama, if ever I find the time. Not that she appreciates letters pertaining to a nautical bent, but..."

"Yes, Mr Lande, I pen a paragraph or two for Mrs Vernon at the close of every day. How may I help you?"

Mr Lande twirled his hat between his stubby fingers. "Well, 'tis a tad unorthodox, but there's a chap aboard, a passenger bound for Cádiz. He is something to do with the children."

Vernon focused on the hat. How many times had he told Lande not to wear the thing below deck – for the reason shown. Low ceiling beams and the height of men were incompatible. Hats got knocked off, and looked comical in the eyes of the crew and undignified for the officers. Ignoring the hat issue, he said, "The children, and their escort, are of no consequence to me Mr Lande. I have made it quite clear that they are to remain below and out of our way. Fortunately, it is but a short voyage to our destination. I estimate, twelve, sixteen hours at most if wind and weather suit?"

"Aye, indeed, sir."

"So, what is the problem? Everything is in order, is it not? Where is Mr Coffney?" Vernon faked a smile, despite his irritation.

"First Lieutenant Coffney is busy, sir, with an incident concerning one of the men."

An incident? Something I should be informed of? Vernon wondered, then dismissed the thought. Unlike Lande, Coffney was a capable officer, and obviously the matter was of no large consequence, else he *would* have been informed of it.

"I am more than content to leave our passage and those children in the capable hands of yourself and Lieutenant Coffney." Vernon indicated his letter. "So, I would very much like to finish this paragraph and then seek my cot. It is, after all," he extracted a pocket watch from his waistcoat, flipped its gold protective case open and studied the hour. "It is approaching a quarter less eleven of the clock. Should these children not be snuggled in their blankets, and asleep?"

Lande did not return the smile. "I think they are, sir. I apologise for the interruption, but it is not about the children. Least, I do not think it is. Mayhap it will wait until morning? Although he was most insistent."

"He?"

"Our passenger."

"Is it, then, important?"

"The gentleman said it was."

Give me strength, Vernon thought; said with patience, "Who is this gentleman? What does he want?"

"What he wants I do not know, sir, but he said he requires to speak in private with you as a matter of urgency. He made the request to Lieutenant Coffney as soon as he came aboard, before we sailed."

"And you have only now brought the matter to my attention?"

"Aye, sir. We were busy getting under way and Mr Coffney did not wish to disturb you."

"But you feel I may be disturbed now?"

"The gentleman has been most persistent. He says it is government business."

Vernon pursed his lips. So, this was the government representative for these blasted children? As a captain, Vernon considered that he was perfectly capable of delivering them to their devoted parents without some fop of a government attaché interfering. He sighed. Could there be more to this mission than he perceived?

"I had better see him. Please show him in, Mr Lande."

Lande gestured a salute, made to replace his hat, thought better of it and tucked the thing beneath his arm. "Very good, sir."

Vernon returned to his letter, heard someone enter, did not look up but continued writing.

A soft cough.

He finished the sentence, placed the quill pen in the inkpot, dusted the letter with sand, then sat back in his chair, folding his hands over his stomach. Looked at a cleanshaven, well-dressed man of about his own height of four inches under the six foot, but a little stouter of build. Hat tucked beneath his arm, he made a slight, respectful bow. Vernon noticed that his hands were work-worn and bore a slight trace of tar beneath the nails. No rough sailor, but a man who knew work when required?

"Good evening to you, sir," Vernon said, congenially, but with a little curiosity to his tone. "How may I be of assistance?"

The man smiled. "I was wondering if you might know where my assistant might be? We were to meet aboard in order to deal with the, er, Spanish matter. But I have not yet managed to locate him?"

Two passengers? That was the first Vernon had heard of it.

"I was expecting just the one government representative. A Mr Doone?"

"Forgive me, Captain," the man smiled, indicated whether he might take a seat. Concealing his reluctance to agree, Vernon nodded and the man drew up a chair to the desk. Sat. Crossed his legs at the knee. "I am Richard Seymour Stanbridge Tearle. I work for various government departments by assisting officials as, when and where, required. At present, the Spanish children are to occupy my attention. The young ladies, well, little girls, in my – our – present care are made comfortable and content enough, thank you for asking, although they, understandably, remain frightened and uncertain."

Vernon had made no such direct enquiry. He noted the subtle rebuke that he ought to have done.

"The kiddies were most sorely treated, and saw things which even we, as grown men, would baulk at. Rape, murder, butchery, wickedness," Tearle added.

"But returned to their kindred they will soon fare better?"

Tearle hesitated, then said, "Several of the girls are now orphans, but I believe so, aye, although the many weeks between their kidnap, and now, has been insufferably long for them. Diplomatic negotiations, alas, always seem to take an interminable time where government officials are concerned."

With that, Vernon was inclined to agree, but not knowing precisely who the 'government officials' were, judged it politic to remain silent on the matter. "So, what may I do for you Mr Tearle? I have no knowledge of a second passenger aboard my vessel. This Doone, fellow?"

Tearle scratched behind his ear. "I believe there may have been some sort of misunderstanding. Mr Doone has returned to England with a second batch of the kidnapped children. I was unaware that he was supposed to be aboard *Bonne Chance*." Tearle kept a friendly smile to his face, though inside he was seething. *So,* he thought,

Doone was supposed to be here, not me or Acorne? Had manipulated orders and ducked out of this mission? Bastard! Said aloud, "I will be frank, Captain; there is more to this mission than just delivering children. The man who is supposed to be accompanying me has gone missing, and not, I fancy, by his own choosing."

Vernon raised an eyebrow. "Explain?"

"He and I were set upon by some of your crew who were intent on pressing us into service. I managed to extricate myself, but my companion... The King's Government will not be overly enthusiastic with their representatives being thus manhandled. And, the last I knew, Colonialists – and government officials, of course – are most stoutly exempt from forceful employment into the King's Army or Navy."

Vernon's erstwhile semi-congenial expression faded into one of marked displeasure. "Are you accusing me of lawbreaking, Mr Tearle?"

Richie Tearle spread one hand, apologetically. "Not you personally, Captain Vernon, but whoever you sent out to obtain men to press into service, most certainly have."

For several heartbeats, Edward Vernon stared, coldly, at the man sitting before him. Finally, he said, "I sent no one out this evening. I do not approve of pressing men, unless there is a desperate need. Willing volunteers are better workers. Pressed men are naught but a useless liability. To my knowledge, none aboard this vessel has been pressed."

"Beg pardon, but I was witness to his abduction. As was the Gibraltar lamplighter who recognised your men."

Briefly Tearle explained the circumstances. When he had finished, Vernon appeared suitably annoyed. "Then we must look into your claim, Mr Tearle. The name of this Colonial Government official?"

Tearle smiled slowly. He was looking forward to seeing Vernon's expression. "Acorne. Captain Jesamiah Acorne."

The result, a mixed colour of purple and red outrage suffusing Vernon's countenance, was most rewarding.

"Acorne?" He spat with terse contempt. "That pirate, Acorne, *dares* to be aboard *my* ship?"

Tearle broadened his smile. "He is no longer a pirate, but, as I have stated, in the employ of the government. We are well aware of your, shall we say 'animosity' towards each other, but his services are essentially required for this particular mission."

"Services?" Vernon rasped through gritted teeth. "Services that are not required or approved by *me*. If that miscreant has set foot aboard *Bonne Chance*, then by God, sir, I will make no hesitation in hanging him."

Tearle tilted his head to one side. "In which case, Captain, I'm afraid on return to any British port you will be immediately arrested and court-martialled for insubordination against admiralty orders."

"I have received no such orders."

"Ah..." Tearle reached into an inner coat pocket, withdrew a sealed fold of paper, handed it with solemnity to Vernon. "I did request to speak with you when first I came aboard, but I was rather robustly dissuaded." He sat back in his chair, folded his arms while Vernon broke the seal and read, his brows furrowing deeper as he scanned the words writ there.

Vernon looked up, tossed the orders onto his desk, waved his right hand at them. "You know what is in here?"

Richard Tearle nodded. "I do. We are to deliver the children, but take every opportunity to ascertain whether this rumour to besiege Gibraltar has any credence to it."

"And no one, aside ourselves, is to learn of this undertaking?"

"No one. If the Spanish were to realise that we hope to find out what we can about their plans we are all dead men. If some of the English Jacobites also discover it, come to that."

"And Acorne is essential to this?"

"He is."

"Why?"

"He speaks Spanish, for one, although I am not really at liberty to divulge more. But I suppose I can let slip..." he paused, massaged his chin as if in thought, then continued. "Let us just say that, in this instance, we cannot endanger the Royal Navy, but Acorne is expendable."

Vernon mulled the words over a moment. Nodded understanding, indicated the orders. "So, he is a spy. Fair enough.

And the innocent delivery of these children is but a diplomatic smoke screen?"

"It is. Whilst we are administering to the children, Acorne can be undertaking our true task."

"And if he is caught?"

Tearle shrugged. "That would be unfortunate, but..."

Vernon nodded. The 'but' suited well enough. "So, assuming Acorne is aboard, what, Mr Tearle, do you suggest I do about him? I will not bring myself to be pleasant to the man."

Tearle grinned. "I suspect he has no wish to be pleasant to you, either, Captain. He is a strong young man, and possibly, if he is indeed among your crew, it would be the most suitably discreet place for him. Given your assurance that there are no pressed men, I am wondering whether that little charade of abduction was a mere ploy to get Acorne aboard? Whoever was behind the idea, whatever the motive or manner of doing it, now it is done I would imagine that Acorne would be most content were he not to be recognised."

Tearle allowed the captain to consider things, then added, "And it is but a short voyage for blind eyes not to see things. However, I would beg the favour that you grant me permission to explore *Bonne Chance* in order to find the fellow? Perhaps you could put the word round that I am your guest and have your permission? We can say I have a personal interest in the construction of model ships, and wish to create a likeness of this vessel?" His smile broadened. "The first part is true, the second, well, not so accurate."

"As long as you do not upset my carpenter, Mr Baker."

Tearle smiled. "I will seek his expertise with the utmost delicacy."

Vernon nodded once, grunted acceptance of the proposal and retrieving the orders, stood, opened the glass door of the lantern dangling on his desk and held one corner of the dispatch to the candle within. Once the flame took hold, he opened one of the stern windows and dropped the burning paper into *Bonne Chance*'s foaming wake.

It was, after all, as Tearle had said, only a short voyage to Cádiz.

CHAPTER THIRTEEN

By morning the wind had become capricious. *Bonne Chance* had to wear ship several times during the night and had, by necessity, run much further out into the Atlantic Ocean than her sailing master, Mr Sawyer, had intended. Which meant more work for the crew, and a longer voyage.

Mr Almitty, the bosun, was a regular pain in the buttocks, but the only real annoyance for Jesamiah was Buckeridge. Jesamiah stayed out of his way as much as he could, but on a frigate not that much larger than his own *Sea Witch*, staying out of the way was not easy, especially as the wretched man seemed to be making it his business to stay *in* the way whenever Jesamiah was not aloft. Jesamiah's – Oakwood's – plan was to do the work required of him efficiently, keep his head down, not draw attention to himself and skip ashore as soon as he could. He ought to present himself to Vernon, make a clean breast of who he was and why he was aboard, but what if the resurrection of this murder charge had been Vernon's idea? Except, that sort of malicious underhandedness did not fit well with Vernon's reputation of being a stickler for rules, fairness and justice. And Vernon knew his stuff, unlike many another captain who had paid for the privilege of rank but had no idea whatsoever about ships or sailing them, Lieutenant Lande, one among them. Vernon *did* know ships and sailing, and he cared for his men, which is why they worked well for him. Trumping up a hanging charge was not in his nature. Even so, Jesamiah was reluctant to make his presence known. He was stuck between the proverbial rock and a hard place – or in this case, The Rock and Cádiz – and hoped to the High Heavens and the Seven Seas that luck would stay with him, the weather would improve and they'd get to Cádiz as quickly as possible. Watching the horizon from the maintop as dawn had lazily filtered in, however, he had not much faith in the fickleness of luck. A feeling which rapidly deteriorated as some while later his bare foot stretched down from the ratlines to touch the wooden deck.

"Yon bos'n will complain that you're too fat and too slow."

Jesamiah stepped down from the last rung of the tarred rope that formed the ladder attached to the shrouds. He wiped his sore hands on the seat of his breeches. "You tend to turn up like a wet Sunday, Richie Tearle. What sort of shite are you goin' to spin me this time?"

"I'm wondering if you can suggest any area of the working of this ship that may be of interest to me. I have a hobby of carving models. I like to study the intricacies of the real thing whenever I can."

Jesamiah stared at him, twisted slightly to allow two sailors to get past. "Is that so?" he answered, loudly. "Try the bilge. I reckon that'd be the best place for you."

"Keep your voice down," Tearle whispered. "Models are a cover I've devised so that I can roam freely around the ship."

"I ain't interested."

"So, I can keep an eye to your safety, you dolt."

"Not done a very good job so far, 'ave you?"

"Ssh! I've cleared things with Vernon. As long as you stay out of trouble, and out of his way, he'll ignore your presence aboard."

Jesamiah sighed, lowered his voice. "I could've quite happily helped him out by staying ashore."

"But that wouldn't have got you to Cádiz."

"I don't want to go to Cádiz."

"Yes, you do. You need to help me."

"Do I?"

"Aye. I need to discover what the Spanish have planned – are they capable of besieging Gibraltar..."

"I can tell you that without going to Cádiz. No, they are not."

"And you have this information from… Where?"

"From experience."

"But nothing recent. You have no idea how many ships are in harbour at Cádiz?"

Jesamiah made no answer.

"Your dislike of the Spanish, is, let's be truthful, purely personal."

Again, no answer for there was not one that Jesamiah could give.

Tearle waited a moment, continued. "Discovering Spanish intentions is a bluff to keep Vernon's nose out of more important things. We want you to accompany the children – most of whom are your kindred via Calderón's deceased wife, I believe, in addition to his own orphaned daughters? You will travel northward from Cádiz with them to San Vincento, Calderón's home. You have legitimate reason to do so as you are, I believe, a partner in his wine trade business?"

Jesamiah merely grunted.

"We need to ensure that certain documents and papers of your uncle's do not fall into the wrong, Spanish, hands."

"We?"

"I."

Another grunt.

"Calderón was one of our – my – informers. I must make sure there is no damning evidence left anywhere. You have a legitimate reason to be there, know the place and can speak the language. I'm not familiar with any of that. Besides, surely you do have an interest in ensuring that your nieces are safe?"

"Aye, I do, but I'm not doing anything or going anywhere until I've had all my possessions returned." Jesamiah indicated his minimal clothing. "I want my clothes and my weapons. Immediately. I've asked for them, but they've not been returned."

"I have your dunnage from the inn stowed alongside my own. I doubt you'll get your pistol and cutlass returned, though."

"You find them and take responsibility for them. But I want my knives now."

Tearle unbuckled his belt, removed a leather sheath, drew from it a short, but lethally sharp, knife. "Will this suit you?"

Jesamiah took it, lightly ran his thumb along the blade, sucked at the resulting thin line of blood. "Aye, for now."

"As for the rest, I'll see what I can do."

"You do that, or I might just start spreading rumours about you not having a ha'penny worth of interest in models. Sailors don't take to spies."

"I've already told you, I am not a spy."

"Aye, and the sun shines at midnight. I suppose you also want me to kill this fellow who's at San Vincento?"

Tearle cocked his head to one side, not understanding. "What fellow?"

"Someone Doone wants dead."

Tearle laughed. "Oh, so he's already commandeered you, has he?"

"He's asked me to dispose of someone called Burell. I've no intention of complying."

Shaking his head, Tearle pursed his lips. "I don't know of a Burell. We know the Doones trade – did trade – wine and other commodities with Calderón, but we do not know all their contacts."

"There you go with that 'we' again. You mean *your* string-puller, the Spymaster General?"

"Burell?" Tearle repeated, ignoring the jibe. "So the Doones have fallen out with someone have they? Interesting."

"Not to me it ain't."

Tearle just smiled.

"Vernon know about any of this?" Jesamiah asked, to break the silence.

"He does not. He has his own orders."

About to ask what they were, Jesamiah clamped his mouth shut as Almitty stepped into view, and kicked at his ankle.

"You there! Maggot-dung, get back to work!"

Tearle spread his hands apologetically, smiled at the bosun. "My fault! I'm making a start on asking all the crew about this vessel. With the captain's express approval. I wish to make a model of her."

"Well, the cap'n ain't here and this louse ain't workin', so you can go an' ask elsewhere." Almitty turned with the intention of having a second rant at the new, annoying, sailor. But Jesamiah had gone, was heading for the below deck world of semi-gloom, creaking timbers and the hope of soon being summoned to breakfast.

CHAPTER FOURTEEN

Jesamiah's shoulders and thighs were aching, his hands sore from the hard work of fisting and hauling canvas, and climbing and descending the shrouds. Despite the protests from his body, and his surliness towards Tearle, he was enjoying the work up in the tops. As the captain of *Sea Witch,* he'd rarely found need – or time – to climb the masts, except for rare occasions when he wanted to see for himself what sailed – or didn't – in his wake or on the horizon.

These few hours after dawn, he was hungry, and had a feeling that the forty and five minutes allocated for breakfast might get rudely interrupted. Although, as it turned out, that would maybe not be a bad thing: the salted porridge served up was not too bad if you didn't mind solid, semi-cooked, or partly burned lumps, but the dark rye bread tasted more like sawdust than bread, although at least the flour was fresh provisioned so there were few weevils incorporated into the hard dough. Listening to the patter of conversation from the men of the mess group he'd been allocated to, he sucked at the hard bread crust, the thought crossing his mind that even Finch was a better cook than whoever had responsibility in the galley here. The one benefit, his first bite of the bread had dislodged the loose molar tooth. There was a bit of blood, which he dabbed with a kerchief and swilled with ale, and he'd be poking around with his tongue for a while until he grew used to the resulting gap.

He looked up as Buckeridge sat himself at the table opposite and called out, "Oaky. Your dunnage 'as been put in a spare sea chest. Bos'n's chalked yer name on it. If you're able to read it. It's with those belongin' to y' sour-faced mess mates."

"Mr Oakwood, I think, to you, mate. I trust everything of mine is there? All the same, I thank you for your trouble, but don't make a habit of helping yourself to what isn't yours in future."

Buckeridge got to his feet, a growl in his throat, his fists bunched. "You accusin' me of thievin'?"

Leisurely, Jesamiah retrieved Tearle's knife from where he'd threaded the sheath onto his belt. Balanced the blade in his right hand a moment then threw it, with deadly accuracy, to thud into the wooden deck support no more than an inch from Buckeridge's shoulder.

Lieutenant Lande was not far away; he turned abruptly at the sudden descent of awed silence. Jesamiah smiled, rose, retrieved the blade. Touched his forelock in Lande's direction. "Dropped my bread knife, sir. Sorry, sir."

Throughout the deck, talk resumed.

The sailor sitting alongside Jesamiah held up his hand, offering his palm for Jesamiah to slap with his own. "I'm Tyburn, from London. You've made an enemy there," he said. "You'll 'ave t'watch that one; 'e's 'and in fist with Gawd Almighty, our bloody bos'n."

"I can look after myself," Jesamiah answered, then added with a smile as he tapped the hard bread on the tabletop, "not sure I can say the same about looking after m' teeth, though."

His mess mates laughed appreciatively.

"I'm Walnut, on account of my name being Walter Nutt." The man seated next to him congenially offered his palm.

"We weren't supposed t'be so long at sea. Should've been anchored in Cádiz by now. But no, we're half bloody way to the Americas!" another man next to Tyburn grumbled.

"That'll do, Featherstone," Mr Lande reprimanded, overhearing as he came up to the table. "Just get on with your food without voicing incorrect opinions."

Jesamiah said, without thinking, "We're nowhere near the Americas. We're not even a quarter of the way to the Azores, yet."

Featherstone rounded on him. "Oh, so you know of these things? Know about navigation, compass points and such stuff, do you?"

Jesamiah shrugged. "As it happens, aye, I do. And with respect, Mr Lande, sir, should someone not have drawn attention to that distant sail, three points off the starb'd transom, that I spotted when I were sent atop half-an-hour ago? I can't tell without a bring-it-close, but to my reckoning she looks like a Spaniard following in our wake. Might be nothing, of course. But so far, I've never known a Spaniard I can trust." He sucked at the hard bread as Lande scurried off to see for himself if this sailor had spoken the truth.

"You made that up to get rid of Three 'Ells, did you?" Featherstone asked, impressed, despite his previous hostility.

"Nope. She's been in our wake since dawn. Probably long before that. Maybe since we left Gib."

"How'd you know she'm a Spaniard?" asked one of the other men, a big black man known, as Jesamiah had already discovered, as 'Curly'. The name given for some unfathomable reason, as the man was as bald as a cannonball.

"Seen enough of 'em," Jesamiah responded. "I sailed round the world with Woodes Rogers. We came back with our hold full of treasure."

Featherstone snorted. "So why you 'ere then, not lording it in some fancy mansion, with servants and such?"

"Leave it out, Feathers, he's on our mess, one of us. Stop yer jibing," advised the gun captain, Longjohn – Mr John Long.

Laughing, Jesamiah reached for his tankard of watered ale. "I don't mind. Takes a while to accept a new face. The bloody sponsors took half of the total Prize, King George took the rest. Even Rogers was left nigh on a pauper. Why else d'you think he accepted the position as Governor of the Bahamas? A godforsaken spit of land riddled with crabs, sand flies and bloody pirates."

He did wonder, as he sipped the ale, what these men would say were they to discover that he had been one of those 'bloody pirates' for many years.

Relieved of duty for a while, Jesamiah found the sea chest and inspected its contents. Boots, stockings, coat, hat. A coin pouch with less than half the amount originally in it. Nothing else. He'd need to find the pocket watch; it wasn't especially valuable, but that was not the point. At least Buckeridge – he assumed the thief was Buckeridge – had only pinched the unimportant stuff. The several gold and silver coins which he always had with him when ashore were still sewn into the lining of his coat. He stowed the chest, headed to where he hoped he could find a quiet corner to rest a while.

His body ached and his hands throbbed – *fat,* Tearle had said. He wasn't fat! Was he? He ran his thumb along inside his belt. Not fat. Expanding a little, perhaps? Not fat. He dismissed the ridiculous suggestion. Tiola would have said if he was putting on weight, and she *hadn't* said. Had she? He grinned. Hah! It'd be her doing the expanding these next months!

Now, if he could find somewhere to sit himself down, make it look like he was doing something useful... He noticed a coil of knotted rope. That would do; he'd pretend he was sorting out the tangle. He made himself comfortable on a pile of old canvas sacks, picked aimlessly at the cordage, felt his eyelids drooping... Jerked awake fifteen minutes later as urgent drumming thundered through the ship.

"Beat to quarters! All hands! All hands!"

"What the...?" Jesamiah was no Royal Navy sailor, had no idea of Navy routine or orders, but he knew enough to guess what 'beat to quarters' meant.

"Christ," he muttered, "we're not going to take on that Spaniard, are we?"

CHAPTER FIFTEEN

As he came up through the hatchway into the fresh air, Jesamiah looked vaguely surprised at the activity up on the quarterdeck. Nets were being rigged, a protection for the officers against flying splinters of wood and the jagged ends which could be as sharp and deadly as arrows. They rarely bothered with such precautions aboard a pirate vessel. Below deck, hammering and banging accompanied the unbolting and removal of bulkheads and screens, taking cabins apart and shifting the furniture and unrequired or valuable belongings from the officers' quarters down into the hold.

Jesamiah half-saluted Lieutenant Coffney who was striding towards the quarterdeck. "Beg pardon, sir, what station will I be wanted in?"

Longjohn was coming in the opposite direction, a young boy trotting in his wake. "You'll be with us mate; 'Topside Tom' is our gun. Gun number three over to starb'd."

Other youngsters – the powder monkey boys – were scampering about the open deck, spreading sand around the wooden gun transoms to give sure footing for the gunners. Once the cannons were run out the boys' task would be to fetch the pots of gunpowder up from below. Many of these boys were only nine or ten years old, with dreams of becoming able seamen one day. A few of them were aboard because their families had been too poor to feed and clothe them; the rest were orphans or street urchins. Most would never reach maturity, let alone the status of able seaman. A dangerous life, fetching and carrying gunpowder, but a better life than starving in a filthy street.

Jesamiah was used to boys aboard, although those on his own ship were older, eleven or twelve. Neither was the loading of the guns unfamiliar, although, again, he hadn't taken part in the process for many a month around. It was not the sort of thing anyone who had ever fought in a sea battle would forget, though. Nearly all the men had stripped off their shirts and were wearing only loose-fitting trousers. Jesamiah pulled his own shirt off, stuffed it with the bundle beside the wooden box of shot. He knew of some pirates who fought entirely naked except for a cloth bound around cock and balls – some didn't even bother with that. Being bare skinned could be the difference between living and dying. It only took one, small, apparently insignificant thread to enter into a wound for it to suppurate and induce fever, with death following hard behind.

Stripped to the waist he waited, attention focussed on Captain Vernon who stood almost motionless on the quarterdeck, hands clasped behind his back, gaze locked on the Spaniard. Jesamiah snorted quietly to himself. At least that meant Vernon's mind was busy with other things and might not notice his presence here.

"Ship cleared for action, sir!" came the call. Jesamiah automatically almost answered, too used to giving orders. Stopped himself in time, watched Vernon acknowledge with the briefest of nods.

Clearing had taken fifteen minutes. Jesamiah couldn't resist a wry smile. His men aboard *Sea Witch* were quicker than these Navy chaps. They would have cleared away in ten.

Bonne Chance was moving forward at steady, unhurried knots, her lower sails being clewed up to expose the length and width of the deck for a clear view. The handful of marines aboard were assembled near the bow, muskets loaded and primed, ready to receive their specific orders of where to go – usually up in the tops in order to shoot more efficiently onto an enemy deck. They were a smart lot, though why they wore those bright cherry-red coats Jesamiah could not reckon. His father had been in the marine Holland Regiment for a while; had, or so he boasted, been a close friend of John Churchill, a young fellow officer who went on to become the first Duke of Marlborough. Jesamiah had never totally believed that the friendship was true; his father's claims had never been reliable.

Musing on his childhood history lessons with a tutor who'd had a passion for warfare and military matters, Jesamiah dredged up what he remembered about the formation of regiments. In 1702 six regiments of marines and six sea service regiments of foot had been formed for the War of the Spanish Succession, their most significant achievement being a successful assault on Spanish-held Gibraltar, although it had been sailors of the Royal Navy who had eventually captured The Rock itself. After the Treaty of Utrecht in 1713, four of the regiments had been redeployed as line infantry, these men aboard *Bonne Chance* being from the Gibraltar Foot. Jesamiah grinned to himself. By 1713 he'd been at sea for several years aboard *Mermaid,* serving with a pirate crew under Captain Malachias Taylor, for some of that time, as legalised privateers, fighting against the French for Queen Anne. They'd all expected pardons for various misdeeds come the signing of that treaty. The pardons had never materialised. In consequence, illegal piracy had escalated.

He scratched at an itch beneath his chin. Those early years had been when he'd first encountered *Bonne Chance* and that unfortunate episode of her murdered crewmen. She'd had a different captain then; Jesamiah tried to remember his name, couldn't. He should have recognised Buckeridge – that one face in the tavern had nudged a memory, but not clearly enough. He would probably have to do something about Buckeridge before too long. With any luck this Spaniard might oblige, save him the bother.

Tearle appeared, leant his arms casually on the rail, looking in the same direction they all were. Jesamiah joined him, said, for the benefit of others within hearing, "You all right, sir? I suggest you get yourself below. Maybe keep an eye on them children aboard? I expect they'll be a bit fearful?" An innocent enough statement, but with a significant meaning that Tearle had outstayed his welcome as far as Jesamiah was concerned.

"I'm just curious, sailor." Tearle pointed to the furled sails. "Should they not be full down? Getting us away?"

Moving closer, Jesamiah answered, clear and loud, "Well it's like this..." then lowered his voice. "Why's a Spaniard threatening us? Ain't we got special clearance because of the children?"

"We have. But obviously that captain hasn't read the same diplomatic orders as Vernon has."

"So why don't we heave to and explain?"

Tearle gave Jesamiah a withering look. "Probably because they'll shoot first, talk second?"

"You do realise that ship's been following us since we left Gibraltar, don't you?"

Tearle didn't know. "You sure?"

"She followed *Sea Witch*, at a discreet distance, as we came into Gib's waters. So, she were hanging around there then, and now she's here? Bit coincidental ain't it?"

"Might not be the same ship?"

Jesamiah snorted. "Oh, I'm fairly certain that she's the same ship. I'm just hoping she isn't the one I think she is." He paused to let the information sink in. "And if she has intentions of an altercation with us, I'd be asking m'self why. Maybe, we're not supposed to reach Cádiz in one piece?"

"But we have children aboard! *Their* children..."

"You working with us or him?" Featherstone called testily from the far side of the gun.

From the next gun, Buckeridge sneered, called, "You won't get no work out o' that lyin' bastard."

Jesamiah ignored the insult and acknowledged Featherstone with a raised hand. Said to Tearle, "I hope that satisfies your curiosity, sir, but now I really do suggest you get below. Keep an eye on them kiddies, mebbe?"

Tearle nodded, walked away towards the quarterdeck, not the safety of below. Jesamiah wanted to ask him more about the safety of the children, but had to trust to Vernon's capabilities to issue sensible orders, for at this moment he had other things to concentrate on. That Spaniard, by the look of her, had every intention of bettering the English Royal Navy.

It was always the waiting that shredded men's nerves. The watching an enemy ship come closer and closer into range – or as a pirate, prowling nearer and nearer to a Prize. Predator or prey it made little difference where a fight was concerned. Before long the quiet sea would become a hell of blood and gore and death. Only the lucky ones survived. Jesamiah looked up at the set of the sails, studied the yards braced round, at the anxious faces of men, most of whom had their full attention on their captain.

Why do you men do this? Jesamiah thought to himself. "What reward do you get for the possibility of being blown to bits?"

"Why? For king, country, glory and fame."

Jesamiah hadn't realised that he'd spoken aloud.

"With maggoty food and constant damp clothing thrown in for good measure," Featherstone continued, sarcastically. "That's why. It's a better option than rotting in Newgate."

"It's better'n army," Curly added. "All dat marchin' about? I'm not wantin' none o' dat."

"Army gets the pick of more women than we do," Featherstone pointed out.

"Aye, and more chance of the cock-pox from them!" the gun captain, Longjohn, added.

They all laughed agreement, although Jesamiah couldn't resist commenting, "Pirates get the women, the rum *and* the treasure."

"And the noose," Featherstone countered.

"What d' you know o' pirates?" Curly asked, suspicion creeping into his question.

Jesamiah grinned. "There's a fine line drawn between privateering and piracy. I reckon Captain Woodes Rogers didn't always stay on the right side of it."

"What's all this chatter?" Almitty's cane rapped down on the cannon with a resounding clang. "Stow it or I'll have you all on bilge duty for a week. Keep control of your gun crew, Mister!"

"Aye, bos'n."

"I'll stow you one o' these days," Curly muttered.

"Men!" The call came from Lieutenant Lande who had moved to

the quarterdeck rail and raised his voice so most could hear. "We'll be relying on you gunners today. Relying on you to put short work to this scamp dogging our tail. We'll load in five minutes, but not run out yet. Make your shot count, and may *Bonne Chance* live up to her name! Good luck and look lively, lads!"

Jesamiah winced. Aboard a pirate ship it was bad luck to verbally wish good luck. He touched his acorn earring, noticed a few men scratching a stay, three of the powder monkeys scurrying in a circle, widdershins. All to reverse the unfortunate blunder.

Jesamiah peered out over the rail. The Spaniard was closing, but he reckoned ten minutes not five before any shot would be anywhere near a sighting range, though he did admit to himself that it was not so easy to judge from down here in the waist. Were he up there, on the quarterdeck...

Take your time, Vernon, he thought. *Let them come to you. They'll do so soon enough.*

CHAPTER SIXTEEN

"All guns! Load!"

"Here we go!" Longjohn announced, giving a mock cough. "Our Lieutenant Coffney, good old Coughdrop, has got his eye on the game!"

"Aye, an' if Groggy stops a shot, Coughdrop will be in for a hike up to acting captain."

"Groggy?" Jesamiah queried.

Longjohn explained. "Cap'n Vernon always wears coats made of that grogram cloth, earning him his nickname. We call his bloomin' awful watered rum 'grog' an' all."

"Watered rum's better'n none," Curly proposed.

"French brandy's even better," Jesamiah said, added, "or Spanish cognac. Maybe they'll have some aboard the Spaniard for us to make use of when we take her as a Prize?"

"I'll drink t' that!" Feathers responded with an approving nod.

"Got to take 'er first," Curly reminded them.

Each great gun had its own group of attendants, a specific gun crew who worked as a team. Once the fight began they would be oblivious to what was going on around them, no matter the noise, the death and destruction. On Coffney's order, the heavy securing breeching ropes were cast off, freeing the guns for loading. The muzzle plugs – the wooden tompions – were removed, the charge taken from a powder monkey, who had carried a previously prepared canvas bag of gunpowder from the safety of below deck where the powder barrels were stored behind curtains of wet canvas, the cartridge bags shaped and sized to fit the guns. The boys were breathless from running, excitement and the first stirrings of apprehension. Mr Featherstone rammed the charge into the muzzle and tamped it home with two sharp taps for luck and to wedge it in place. Walnut pushed in a wad of cloth, canvas, oakum and old rags to secure it. The balls did not always precisely fit, made smaller than the size of the gun barrel, so the wads took the extra space and ensured that the ball, when the gun was fired, would have maximum pressure behind it. The ball itself went in next, Tyburn rolling it down the slightly elevated barrel, all done with deliberate care and calm, in no haste. Haste would come very soon when every second counted; haste, but still tempered by care and calm.

Waiting. That was always the worst. Jesamiah found it almost unbearable standing here beside the gun carriage – the waiting was always bad enough, but here he was not in command, here he had to wait for someone else to give the orders. And what if that someone was not as competent, not as skilled as himself? He glanced towards the quarterdeck, shook his head, thrust that thought aside. Vernon was a capable man; he knew his business. On the other side of the coin, the way pirates fought – for themselves, their freedom and the possible reward of treasure – was different from the regimented discipline of the Royal Navy. By now, a pirate ship would be awash with noise, the drumming of whatever came to hand on rail or stay or mast, the screaming and shouting: *Death! Death! Death!* Here, everyone was quiet, no talking, no unnecessary noise permitted lest orders could not be heard. Jesamiah found the quiet unnerving.

"Open ports!"

A moment later, "Run out!"

Jesamiah hauled with the rest of the gun crew, running the cannon up the slight slope of the deck as *Bonne Chance* heaved herself over a particularly large roller coursing under her keel. Jesamiah caught his breath at a glimpse of the fast approaching enemy, a different angle from what he was used to – full view from the quarterdeck. Fear knotted in his belly.

A dull *bang*, and a *whoomph* of displaced air, followed a few heartbeats later by a single splash. The Spaniard sending a sighting shot to gauge the distance between the two ships. Another bang, another shot which fell short. The third shouldn't, wouldn't.

Jesamiah had a chance to peer out at her, his stomach cringing as his previous assumption was proved to be correct.

"That's the *Santa María del Bartolomé,* all right," he said. "Seen her several times over the years." He didn't add that twice, aboard *Sea Witch,* he'd had two close encounters with her. Both times he had made a run for it, knowing that the *Santa María del Bartolomé* was one of the few Spanish ships to get the better of the English – or pirates. Twenty-four guns and well crewed with an experienced captain. Of all the Spanish fleet, this was the only one you did not want to tangle with.

From the quarterdeck: "Gunners! Lay for their masts, let us cripple her then take her as a Prize! Run out!"

The target was a quarter-mile distant, coming up almost parallel.

The guns rumbled on the wooden deck as they were run out, the gun captain, Longjohn, responsible for their sighting and aiming, his experience taking into account the wind direction and the mood of the sea.

"Fire as you bear!"

Gun by gun, from the waist, from stern and bow chasers, from the confinement of the gun deck below, the deafening roar of cannon fire, the scream of shot, the squeal and creak and protest of wooden wheels as each gun lurched inbound, each man straight away about his given job, Jesamiah leaping forward, dipping a sheepskin sponge on a pole into the bucket of sea water at his feet, then ramming it down the hot barrel to extinguish any smouldering debris or hot embers left in the bore.

Longjohn, wearing a fireproof glove, thumbed the vent hole to minimize air or gasses rushing in or out, which might fan any ember back to life. Featherstone rammed in the next lot of wadding and a new powder bag, Tyburn loaded the shot. Walnut followed quickly with another lump of wadding.

"Two, six... heave!" Longjohn called and all the gun crew pulled on the ropes to run the gun back out. Longjohn bent and sighted along the barrel – no need to use the handspikes to position the cannon further right or left. The gun crew stepped back a pace, Longjohn judged the point of the ship's roll to be right. Curly, the assistant gunner, inserted a goose quill priming tube filled with gunpowder and quickmatch into the vent, then blew on the end of a lighted fuse of slowmatch attached to the linstock, a long stick that he touched into the touchhole where it lit the priming tube and the powder bag. Immediately, the ball and wadding tore out of the barrel with a noise loud enough to wake the devil, and the fired gun hurtled backward in a cloud of acrid smoke, the breech rope checking it from too much of a recoil – a strong rope made fast to ring bolts attached to the bulwarks, with a turn taken around the cascabel, the knob at the rear of the gun's barrel.

The noise, smoke, recoil... Ears ringing, throat choking – run in, sponge out, reload, run out, fire. Speed and accuracy essential. The average rate of fire for British ships was a broadside every three minutes, faster for well-trained crews. Jesamiah's crew could achieve almost half that rate.

No time to feel fear, to think, question, consider. Only time to do, and do it with quick, accurate efficiency.

But the Spaniard was also firing, and closing the distance, as intent to take the Englishman as a Prize as the Englishman was to take her. The Spaniards would be following the same drill: sponge out, reload, run out, fire. Her shot, grape and langrage, slamming into *Bonne Chance*, tearing great holes in the canvas sails, ripping apart the rigging. Round shot: a direct hit to one of the gun ports on the gun deck almost directly below the gun Jesamiah was working. Then another shot tore through the bulwark, taking out a stern chaser on the quarterdeck, tearing through the wooden gunwale, the protective netting pinging apart, smashing into the gun itself and killing the entire gun crew. Screams, cries, blood, bone and gore filled the ship. Too many men dead, or not far from it. The Spaniard was larger, had more guns, more men. Was relentless. Was, as Jesamiah had known, nigh on invincible.

Smoke everywhere, clawing at lungs, stinging eyes that poured tears. No time to think about or grieve for the dead. Only time to concentrate on running in, swab, reload, run out. Fire.

A gun crew further along the deck yelled a cheer as their shot struck home, gouging at the Spaniard's midships rail, sending up a large fountain of jagged splinters.

The Spanish were as adept, apparently intent on disabling not destroying. A direct hit. *Bonne Chance*'s top mainmast wavered, creaked, then crashed in a tangle of rigging and canvas. Doomed men, red-coated marines and sailors caught on the ratlines, tumbled towards the sea with desperate cries, arms and legs windmilling. They were the fortunate ones. They would drown quickly. Two poor men landed with sickening thumps on the deck, their bodies broken and ripped apart, but life lingering. For a while.

Among all the noise, more ominous whistling sounds coming nearer to the British ship, the heavy crump of round shot striking home. A length of splintered gunwale flew into the air, somersaulted, spiralled downward... Jesamiah looked up, saw it hurtling direct towards him. He stepped back, tripped, flung out his left arm to save himself. Heard and felt the snap of bone, felt a sharp, deep agony in his right thigh. An instant later, as he toppled downward his head made hard contact with the front wheel of the gun truck. Knew nothing more.

CHAPTER SEVENTEEN

Jesamiah was aware that he ought to wake up, but there was too much pain throbbing through his body; a little less painful to stay asleep. Only a little, mind.

His left forearm was broken, of that he was muzzily aware. His head and the left side of his face hurt as well. And his right thigh. That hurt even more. Lying there, crumpled against what remained of the shattered bulwark, he wished they would all stop running and stamping about, leave him alone to sleep. And if one more bloody fool kicked him, he'd... Do nothing because he couldn't be bothered. All he wanted to do was sleep.

The fellow draped across his lap was also a nuisance. He was heavy, stank of acrid smoke, human sweat and waste. *Move yourself. Get off me.* Jesamiah thought he'd said it aloud, but as he couldn't hear his own words and the man didn't attempt to shift himself, perhaps he'd only thought it.

He forced his eyes open. Was that smoke or was his sight blurred? Everything had a red tinge to it. He moved his left arm, caught his breath. Not good. Definitely broke. Raised his right arm to his face, squinted through one eye at the blood on his fingers. Realised that his cheek was slashed open. He looked down at the blood on his naked, grimed chest, assumed it was his own. All of it?

If so, there was one hell of a lot covering him. Where was it coming from?

"C'mon mate, get off m' bloody legs, let me try to get up." He hefted his uninjured knee; the man toppled to the right. Jesamiah remained still, staring at what was left of Walnut. Most of his chest and left side was gone. That at least explained the blood. Longjohn also lay dead, his legs shattered. Tyburn sat, slumped, nearby. He looked all right until Jesamiah realised that he had a bloody, holed mess instead of a stomach. Half the gun crew. Dead.

He looked at his right leg. There was a shaft of wood, maybe six inches long, sticking out of his thigh. Not much blood, surprisingly, but then the wood was plugging what seemed a sizable hole. He tried moving his leg. Bad idea. Passed out.

Five, ten minutes later? More? He came round, muzzy, confused. There was still fighting; he could see the occasional flash of gunpowder from fired pistols and muskets. He watched two men slash half-heartedly at each other with blood-caked swords, two more men trading blows with fists and feet. Odd that there was no noise. He closed his eyes, let them get on with it. He wasn't Royal Navy. This wasn't his fight. He hurt. Badly. In more than one place. He drifted back into unconsciousness.

"You ought to wake up. Sleep's not good."

"Piss off."

"If I did that, you would stay asleep. Sleep is not good. You need to wake up."

Through the swirling and thudding haze fogging his brain, Jesamiah took several deep, slow breaths. His ribs were hurting as well now, but at least the blood seemed to have stopped dripping from his cheek onto his chest. When he touched his face again, the blood felt sticky beneath his fingers. *Best stay away from mirrors for a bit. I bet I look a right sight.*

It occurred to him that the voice in his head telling him to wake up had sounded very much like Maha'dun's. He could also smell sweet tobacco smoke, not the foul, choking stuff hanging in the air from cannons and firearms. Maha'dun had liked to smoke cheroots. Jesamiah had lost his temper with him once, after catching him smoking below deck. *Bloody dangerous to smoke those damned things of yours with all this gunpowder around,* he thought. He opened his eyes, expecting to see Maha'dun squatting beside him. No one there. Of course he wasn't! Maha'dun was dead. Ah. Perhaps he was dead too?

He moved, sucked in his breath. Nope, not dead, or if he was, death must be a damned lie, for every inch of his body either ached, throbbed or downright hurt.

They'd stopped fighting now. Everyone was either bunched together, waving arms and arguing, or slumped, breathless, defeated. The Spanish people were the ones standing around, the English were the ones gesticulating, arguing. He snorted. The Spaniards wouldn't take kindly to being shouted at. So, *Bonne Chance* had been boarded? The bigger, more powerful Spaniard had got the better of the British Navy. Hah! That must be a first! Apart from this particular vessel, Spanish ships were not noted for their effectiveness at sea. Vernon would not be taking kindly to the situation. Jesamiah peered towards the quarterdeck, watched Vernon ranting, getting nowhere. He needed someone who could speak the lingo.

I can do that, Jesamiah thought. *Ain't bloody goin' to, though, since no one's bothered to ask me nicely.*

Sleep was still nagging at him. They had to be whispering, for he could not hear anything. Why were they whispering? He closed his eyes again. Dozed.

Someone was shaking his arm. The non-broken one, but it still hurt. He swore. Quite prolifically. He roused. Looked into the eyes of a frightened girl. Swore again under his breath, then mumbled an apology.

That was odd, she was clearly talking to him for her lips were moving, but he couldn't hear a word.

"*¿Qué?*" he said, "Spoke up." Where had she come from? Did the Spaniards use girls for powder monkeys? Something else was not right. Had he said *spoke* up? "Peak up," he repeated. That wasn't right either.

He heard, very faint, very distant, in distraught Spanish: "¡Capitán Acorne, Capitán Acorne, please wake up! ¿Uncle Jesamiah? Please. We need you to tell these men that we have been well looked after. That you rescued us, that we are being taken home."

"What?" Jesamiah peered into her drawn and pale face. Repeated, but also in Spanish this time, "*¿Qué?*"

The girl responded with another flow of hurried Spanish. "The Spanish men think that Capitán Vernon is responsible for kidnapping us. I've tried to explain, but the Spanish capitán will not listen, and he is determined to hang everyone, and it is awful, and you need to wake up to tell them. ¡Please, Uncle Jesamiah, wake up!"

Jesamiah could not hear a word of what she said.

"Can't see a bloody word," he muttered, groggy, concussion muddling his speech. Trying to convince his fuddled brain to concentrate, he gathered his thoughts, realised that this was his maternal niece, Calderón's eldest daughter. Caterina? Catalina? Was that her name? Twelve years old. Thirteen, maybe. One of the children he'd rescued from those Barbary pirates. "I can't hear anything and I can't get up. My arm's broke an' I've been stubbed. I mean stabbed."

The girl's face fractured into creases of despair, tears rolled down her cheeks. "¡I do not understand!" she sobbed in Spanish. "¡I speak no English!"

Why can't I hear anything except this ringing in my ears? Jesamiah wondered. Then, *What's the Spanish for I need help*? He snorted. *What's the Spanish for I've forgotten how to speak bloody Spanish*?

He closed his eyes to shut out the men gesticulating wildly at each other, the sobbing girl and the nauseous feeling lying like a lump of lead in his belly. His head thumped, his arm ached, his leg throbbed. Everything hurt.

I'll sit here and quietly think about things, he thought as he drifted back into unconsciousness.

CHAPTER EIGHTEEN
LISBON, PORTUGAL

The *Torre de Belém* – the Belém Tower – was the first or last fortification that sailors saw when arriving or leaving Lisbon. Built of limestone, its bastion terrace with its Moorish turrets and cupolas, and the four-storey tower above had seen the coming and going of many a vessel since its sixteenth-century construction on the northern bank of the Tagus River. Two hundred years old, young compared to some structures: the Roman Colosseum, the Great Pyramids, the Stone Henge in Wiltshire, England. Indeed, to Tiola herself, for her soul had existed through many generations passing as reincarnation from grandmother to granddaughter.

She stood marvelling at the intricate architecture, admiring how the creamy-white stone sparkled in the bright sunshine and the shadows of the rippling river water played upon its walls. How much of it was the original design, how much of it had been added through the years she did not know, nor was there anyone to ask, for the dockworkers were busy and the soldiers manning the fort showed a distinctive air of disdainful uninterest. She had never been to Lisbon before, nor even Portugal for that matter, but she could feel in her veins the past excitements of this place. From here, from beneath this very tower, Portugal had expanded its nautical trade, her adventurers and explorers had discovered the new – to them –

civilisations of India, Africa, the Americas and the still relatively unknown Far East. Vasco da Gama, Columbus, Ferdinand Magellan: had they all known this river, this city? Sailed away, wondering if they would return home?

Tiola sighed. Given the destruction and genocides, in the name of Catholic Christianity that explorers such as these had caused, she wondered, as she threaded her way carefully through the hustle and bustle of such a large port, whether those voyages should be honoured or condemned.

Had Jesamiah been here, she wondered? She had never talked to him about the various places he had seen, where he had been, what he had done – although, for some of them it would maybe be advisable not to know. She smiled to herself. As a young man it was more than likely that, wherever he had been, he'd got up to mischief of one sort or another. In a brothel, probably.

"I'll describe Lisbon in my next letter to him," she said aloud. "If he has been here, he will be able to picture everything in his mind; if he hasn't it will be something new to amuse him."

She had already written a couple of letters, addressed to him care of the tavern in Gibraltar, telling of the voyage so far, and of how much she loved and missed him. The correspondence had gone ashore with Captain Ash's dispatches, and Doone's post. Whether any of it would get to where it had to go was highly debateable.

Reaching the streets, she concluded that she rather liked Lisbon, but maybe this was because she was ashore, alone, and Ascham Doone was, mercifully, elsewhere. The Portuguese children were now safely with the authorities, although she hoped that they would be returned swiftly to where they belonged. There was no guarantee of it. That the children could be sold as cheap labour was possible, but there was nothing Tiola could do to prevent that happening. Dealing with the Portuguese was Doone's responsibility. She suspected that his apparent concern for the children's welfare was a convenient excuse to make acquaintance with those he needed to meet in order to attract lucrative trade for the various pies he had his sticky fingers poked into. He was taking luncheon with the British Envoy in Portugal; she had been invited by Doone to accompany him, but had declined the offer. She was glad, for she was enjoying this rare chance to explore a beautiful old city, and was determined not to allow anything to spoil it. Not even Ascham Doone.

Beyond the noise of the harbour, and despite her inability to use any of her Craft, she could instinctively feel the presence of the past lingering within the streets: the echoes of laughter, of voices chattering genially or arguing ferociously, of mothers singing to their infants, men feigning bravado or crooning their love to a pretty girl. The distant whispers clinging to the white lime-washed walls and spilling from flower-festooned iron-railed balconies – the past tumbling, higgle-piggle, with the present.

She bought herself some fresh fruit from a tucked-away stall and nibbled at it as she strolled up the steep and tangled cobbled streets, wiping sweet juice from her chin, licking it from her fingers. She smiled; how her old nurse and guardian, Jenna Pendeen, would have scolded her – twice over. Young ladies did *not* devour such messy food in public, nor did they wander alone without a suitable escort or chaperone. Dear Jenna. She had been shot, dying instantly; the blame, falsely, put on Jesamiah. Jenna was at peace on the Other Side; a kind, gentle lady despite her over-intense sense of protection towards her young ward. Had the dear lady achieved her way Tiola would never have had anything to do with Jesamiah, let alone wed him. But deep, meant-to-be love was occasionally beyond the sense of reason.

From a small tavern, the singing of what sounded like an emotional folk song drifted into the street. An elderly lady was sitting on a stool at the entrance; she smiled, stood, beckoned Tiola inside and showed her to a table. Almost immediately a dish of baked food was placed in front of her with a small glass of Lisbon's famous port wine. The food smelled – tasted – delicious. Salted cod baked in herbs and breadcrumbs. Another song, delivered by a young woman who, undoubtedly, was the daughter of the older one. Tiola had no idea what the words meant, but it was clearly a ballad about a sailor going to sea and not returning; a song of love and yearning, of hope that one day he would come back. The song struck Tiola's heart. As it ended, she wiped away tears.

Brushing them aside, she applauded along with the small audience, put what she hoped was appropriate payment on the table and left, heading back downhill. She came to the open side door of a church; on impulse, pulled her lace shawl respectfully over her head and entered.

A medieval building, surprisingly light and airy inside, with slender columns that reminded her of palm trees, although up to an ornate ceiling instead of a clear, blue Caribbean sky. Everywhere she looked were motifs representing the sea: sailors, ships, strange beasts and foreign lands carved on the walls or columns lining the nave and side aisles. She thought again of Jesamiah. How, where, was he? It felt strange not to be in intimate contact with him through their shared mind words.

She had known of his presence, but not the man himself, for millennia. Their paths had often crossed, but their true identities had remained unknown to each other, as the waves of time had undulated through the shifting patterns of eternity. They had finally met a handful of years past when the love that had been dormant burst into flower like blossom on a tree on the first sun-filled day of spring. Love of souls finally united; true, deep-rooted soul-bound love.

She smiled as she found a bench in a quiet corner, seated herself and stared up at the ceiling, decorated with carvings that resembled lengths of rope and sailors' knots. She pictured Jesamiah fashioning several of the real thing with the ease of practice, her own fingers following the formation of a complicated knot that he had once tried to teach her – an intricate thing that she had never quite mastered. Soul mates: their hearts, minds and lives entwined. *Ais*, sometimes they argued; two people of intelligence and passion would never always see things eye-to-eye, but sometimes differences of opinion strengthened love and respect. And the making up was always pleasurable.

She missed him beside her, with her. Missed his quick laughter, his occasional idiotic absurdity, missed his formidable anger when something offensive outraged him. Their first proper meeting had been in Cape Town, South Africa – at least, the first meeting that *he* had been aware of. They had 'known' each other in what he had taken to be instances of imaginative fancy during times of acute stress. She had been young, inexperienced, her Craft not fully fledged, but those times of his stress had touched her gift of empathy and they had mentally connected. Her own traumatic ordeal in her present life had been from the hands of her abusive father – or at least, the man believed by others to be her father. Remembering, unexpected tears dripped onto her hands, unbidden thoughts crowding into her mind as if a floodgate had been breached.

Jenna Pendeen, who had not hesitated to grab what she could of warm clothing, coin and her mistress's jewels on that awful night in Cornwall. Jenna, who, without raising a question or expressing a doubt, had bundled Tiola and herself into woollen cloaks and stepped aboard a smuggler's lugger to be safely taken to who knew where. Eventually to Cape Town, a long, long way from Cornwall. Had it not been for Jesamiah they would, perhaps, still be there, with Tiola wed to the Dutchman who had wanted her as wife. He was also dead.

Too many, far too many, were dead!

The alternative to fleeing Cornwall had been to stay, to risk the mob that had dragged Tiola's mother away and hanged her. Had Jenna hesitated, had she not done as Mother had instructed... Tears were more than trickling down Tiola's cheeks. She wanted to sob aloud, wanted to scream, to shout, just as she had wanted to shout and scream on that night of abuse, horror and fear.

"Take her, Jenna, take my only, precious, daughter. Hide her, keep her safe!"

Her gaze fell on a statuette of the Madonna, the tender, adoring mother cradling her newborn child, and her thoughts went to the Christian belief of a mother heavy with child having to journey many miles, close to her time. The mother, risking all to give birth, and the dangers that followed that child from cradle – crib, a manger in a stable – to the cruelty of crucifixion and a lonely grave. Did the Madonna know, from the beginning, what would eventually become of her son? Did all mothers live in fear for the safety and well-being of their children? How many mothers willingly sacrificed themselves for the lives of their offspring? As her mother had done for her.

"Mama! Oh, my Mama!" Emotion overwhelmed her, and Tiola fell to her knees, her hands clasped, fingers linked, pressing against her lips to hold back the sound of despair that was choking into her throat. She could see, smell, her father's blood puddling on the wooden bedchamber floor, the spatters marking her nightgown, dripping over her hands, dappling her face, the walls, the rumpled sheets and blankets. Her mother, white-faced, clasping that bloodied blade.

"Take her, Jenna, take my only, precious, daughter, hide her, keep her safe!"

A hand on her shoulder, squeezing gently. "Lady?"

Tiola started. Looked up through tear-blurred vision at the boy standing, concerned, next to her.

"Lady?" he repeated in English, although his voice had a trace of his native Spanish. "Are you unwell? Shall I fetch assistance?"

Tiola forced a smile, wiped at the trickle of tears with the edge of her shawl. "Thank you Donréal, I am quite well, merely a little melancholy." She placed her hand on his proffered arm and rose to her feet, brushed at the creases in her skirt.

"I saw you enter," Donréal explained. "I'd come in to offer a prayer to God for my Mama's soul. I am anxious that she is resting at peace."

"I am sure she is, my dear," Tiola answered, touching her palm to his young face. "She was a good woman, a devout Catholic and a child of her God. He would have welcomed her into his arms."

Was that a lie? Tiola had no idea what sort of woman Francesca Escudero had been. That she had seduced Jesamiah, was involved with the English spymaster, and for all Tiola knew, with Ascham Doone and the entire Doone Clan as well, all of which reflected poorly on the woman's character. But then, Jesamiah had possibly just as much seduced her, and maybe the woman's intelligencing had been for good purpose. Whatever the truth, it was of no consequence to the boy.

Tiola took his hand in her own and started walking towards the open main door where bright sunlight was streaming in. "Where are the others? You are on your own, are you?"

She kept the slight edge of annoyance from her tone as she looked sharply around. The church was not busy, but there were enough people within, in groups or as solitary visitors. Was that Doone? She caught her breath, tightened her grip on Donréal's hand.

No, a man much older and stouter; she was seeing things that were not there. Doone was busy elsewhere for goodness' sake! What was the matter with her this day!

"Jasper, Tom, Mr Finch not with you?" she asked.

"No, Lady, I..." the boy looked down at his feet, bit his lip then looked up again. "It is not their fault. I deliberately lost them. I do not need nursemaiding."

"I don't suppose you do, but Mr Doone is not a man I trust where you or your mother are concerned."

"She taught me well how to look after myself."

Tiola's smile was grim. "*Ais*, I expect she did, but part of looking after yourself is knowing that you have others you can trust to cover your back."

"Why are you so worried, Mistress Tiola? Is it because Mama was murdered and because she worked for Master Harley in London?"

Ah, the innocence of children!

"Partly, yes," she admitted. "Your mother was..."

Donréal pointed towards the nearest pew, indicated that perhaps they should sit. Curious, Tiola obliged him.

He took a little while to gather his thoughts, then, looking direct at her said, "As you know, my real name is not Donréal. I am Leandro. Mama kept my identity hidden, for there are those who wished her harm. My real father was Captain Jesamiah's father, although I was given my stepfather's name of Escudero." He smiled. "But you know all this?"

Tiola nodded. "I do. Your mother married your stepfather because Jesamiah's father already had a wife. Dona Sofia Molina, the elder sister of Antonio Luis Calderón. I also know that 'Leandro' is two years older than is 'Donréal'; presumably this was to conceal your identity further?"

He studied his hands, clamped now between his knees. "My mother thought it safer for me to live as Donréal," he shrugged, "although I confess, I never understood why, and now that she is dead, I will never know."

"I suspect that she had secrets to keep safe about your real father. Secrets that others wanted to force from her. She had to keep you safe in order for you not to be used as a means to threaten her.

Maybe one day you will learn the truth." Tiola rose, offered him her hand. Secrets that Jesamiah knew as well, perhaps?

She shrugged the thought aside. If he did, they were not for her to know. "Come, let us return to the *Lady Of Mercia*." She glanced around at the ornate carvings, the cheerful beauty of the sunshine pouring in through the stained glass windows and the rainbow colours dancing on the stone floor. At the religious statues, the opulence, the overwhelming spirituality and the cloying aroma of incense that was, of a sudden, becoming oppressive because none of this was her faith or belief.

"Churches are good places to sit in quiet reflection, but they can so easily sadden the heart. You are free to live as you wish now, as Donréal or as Leandro. Either way, you will be loved and cared for by Jesamiah, your half-brother, and by myself, his wife."

"But perhaps we will not tell any of this to Master Ascham Doone, *sí*?" the boy said with a slight chuckle. "I think he has no liking for your husband, nor for my dead mother. Mayhap knowing too much will startle him unnecessarily?"

"It might," Tiola said, "but then it might startle him to the degree that the wretched man has a heart seizure and departs this life to leave us in peace."

"Madam!" Donréal said, shocked but with a hint of laughter. "Was that not a scurrilous thing to say!"

Tiola laughed. "*Ais*, it was, but it felt good to say it."

CHAPTER NINETEEN

The plan was to spend no more than the turn of the tide in Lisbon harbour, but the *Lady Of Mercia* was a merchant ship and she had wool to trade for sugar, a commodity in short supply. The Portuguese King, Dom João V, had busied himself targeting, among other groups, the Brazilian planters, most of whom were Jewish. More than a few British merchants had not helped the situation by smuggling out of Lisbon Jewish families seeking refuge from the Inquisition. Add to that, there was speculative tension in the air: would Portugal remain neutral, or join with Spain or England in this latest spat of hostility between the two nations?

Soldiers stared suspiciously at Tiola and Donréal as the two passed near the Belém Tower heading back to the ship. Every foreigner about to leave port was regarded as a potential aide to the hated Jews. Tiola wondered if she should cover her head and act demure as a group of four off-duty uniformed men leered at her. They were leaning against the harbour wall, worse the wear for drink. Ordinarily, she would have cloaked herself with her Craft as a means of discreet protection, but could not. Two of the soldiers stepped unsteadily into her path, one grasping her arm saying something in Portuguese which she did not understand, but could guess by his smirk and the bulge in his breeches. She attempted to shake him off, but his grip tightened. Another man was behind her, his breath stinking of strong alcohol.

"Run to the ship," she urged Donréal. "Fetch help."

Donréal hesitated, unsure whether to obey or stay to defend her as best he could. Hesitated a moment too long. One of the soldiers struck at the boy's face, sending him reeling against the corner of the buttress wall.

Tiola shouted alarm, pitching her voice high, hoping someone from the *Lady Of Mercia* would hear above the noise of the harbourside. From behind, a hand clamped over her mouth, the man's other hand groping at her breasts. Tiola bit him, hard. He yelped, moved a step backwards, slightly releasing his hold on her. Taking advantage, she spun around and jabbed a finger into his eye and rammed her knee into his groin. Another soldier clawed his hands into her hair, scattering her pins and combs which rarely stayed in place at the best of times. Grasping her loose tresses, he dragged her aside; two others, ignoring their comrade who was doubled over clutching himself and mewling piteously, grabbed at her flailing arms. One of the assailants, laughing drunkenly, ripped her bodice, exposing her undershift. She screamed, kicked with her feet, but she wore only soft, doe-hide shoes, barely more effective than fur slippers would be against a soldier's knee-high leather boots. One of the men slapped her face, hauled her upright as she began to sink to her knees, his hand drawing back for a second blow.

A pistol shot. Angry shouting, roared orders. Fists striking against flesh. As quickly as they had descended on Tiola the men backed away from the newcomer laying into them with outraged fury.

"What is this disgrace? How dare you attack an Englishwoman! Be gone with you before I decide to report you to your superior and have you all flogged!"

Never would Tiola have thought it possible to be grateful to Ascham Doone. She tugged the shawl from her head, scattering the last of her hairpins, watched him stride after the fleeing soldiers with all the authoritarian pomposity that he possessed. A second, elegantly dressed, man was alighting from an open carriage, and was immediately flanked by two uniformed servants who had descended from the back step of the carriage – slaves, for they were black men.

Tiola sank to the ground, her arms wrapped around her waist, breathing deeply, trying to calm herself. Dreadful memories tumbling into her mind of the horror of being aboard that Barbary pirate ship, where brutal assault and rape had been a constant threat.

"Are you harmed Mistress?"

She looked up at the stranger who was offering his hand to assist her to rise. She managed a weak smile, took the proffered hand and climbed unsteadily to her feet. Found that she was trembling. Managed to say, through chattering teeth, "No, sir, I am unharmed I think, just shaken."

"Glad I am to hear it." Ascham Doone said, as he returned to her side and also offered his hand to steady her. He indicated the stranger. "This is the British Ambassador." But Tiola did not hear him, she had broken away, was running to Donréal, slumped against the wall.

The sun sparkled on the rippling river, the glare of white stone, and a red slick of trailing blood. Tiola knelt, cradled the boy to her, stroking back his blood-matted hair, crooning to him as a mother would to her child. There was nothing more she could do, even had she the use of her Craft.

Donréal was dead.

CHAPTER TWENTY
AT SEA

Tiola opened her eyes. Was it her vision, or had the world around her turned into a whirlpool? Closed them again. A sick feeling clung like an undigested meal in the pit of her stomach. She was abed. Something cool and damp was soothing her forehead; she raised a hand to irritably brush it away. It disappeared at the same instant as a girl squeaked.

"Oh, ma'am, you startled me!"

Again, Tiola opened her eyes. Her bed, her small box-like private cabin to the side of the captain's cabin assigned for her and the children aboard *Lady Of Mercia*. They were at sea, the ship making headway through a swell that was, by the feel of it, threatening to become a rough tide. Biscay? Surely not? Surely, she had not been unconscious for that length of time? It occurred to her, slightly bizarrely, whether the real Lady of Mercia, whoever she had been, had been a mother, had borne children. A lump of grief clamped in her throat as her memory jolted to the present. Donréal...

With a groan – her head ached – Tiola sat up, the girl moving quickly to pluck a spare pillow and prop it behind Tiola's back.

Glancing down, Tiola could see that she was wearing only her chemise. She moved her feet. No stockings. Felt, surreptitiously, between her legs. Thank the goddess of childbirth, no stickiness, no blood. She had not lost the child.

"Who put me to bed?" she asked, concealing as best she could the worry that she had no recollection of it.

"I did ma'am. Master Doone carried you aboard, you were in quite a swoon. Captain Ash directed that you be put to bed and I offered to take care of you. We've all been that worried, ma'am, these past hours."

Closing her eyes again – the blurring of her vision and the swaying motion was not just the ship – Tiola took several calming breaths. "And Donréal?"

The girl did not answer immediately. Very quietly, the tremble quivering in her throat, she answered, "They brung his body aboard. Master Doone said as we would bury him at sea soon as you be well enough. The captain were all for leaving them Portuguese to see to him, but Master Doone insisted."

The uncharitable thought of wondering why Doone should care chased into Tiola's mind, but she as swiftly sent it away. Asked instead, "And you are from Cornwall, are you not?"

"*Ais*, ma'am, I be from a fishin' village by along St Ives. I were in service at the big 'ouse, but I be down the village when them pirates come. Killed the men an' took us'n maids. We thought the worse 'til you an' Cap'n Acorne come."

Her lip quivered as she tried to stem threatening tears. In her anxiety she had slid into the Cornish accent that she had previously been masking. "I 'as a lot t' thank thee an' 'im fer, ma'am, tho' I doubts I be 'avin' a job t' be back to now. My lady, she be as fussed as a broody 'en lookin' fer a secret nest t' lay eggs in. I as suspec' I be not suitable fer 'er now. She be no believin' them pirates didna touch us. If'n it be tha' I be needin' work I'd as not worry. I 'ated it there."

Tiola guessed that this was not the whole truth, but did not query anything. She reached out and patted the girl's hand. "We will worry about that later; there are other things to concern us right now. Your name is Harriett is it not? Harriett Blackthorne?"

"*Ais*, ma'am, but I prefer Hetty."

"Hetty it is then. Have you kin? Mother, father?"

The girl shook her head. Took a breath and remembered to revert to the more appropriate speech cadence of an educated lady's maid. "No ma'am. Ma died six year gone, Pa sent me to service when he remarried; his new wife didn't want me around as she weren't much older than I be. Mind, I as wager she be changin' her tart's mind about me now the childer have started coming. Two already an' a third on the way, or so I las' heard."

Ah, Tiola thought, *so no love lost between the two then. Jealousy on both sides, perhaps*?

Hetty was tall, already well-formed in a womanly way, although she could not be much older than fifteen. She had already made use of the material Tiola had brought aboard by fashioning herself a dimity gown to replace the ill-fitting, plain dress that the nuns, looking after the children on Gibraltar, had provided to replace the clothes that had been torn and soiled aboard the Barbary pirate ship. Tiola had noticed, these few days at sea, that the girl's fingers were quick, her stitching neat – as neat as her personal appearance. Hetty had combed and pinned her fair hair as well as she could, kept herself as clean and tidy as was practical and possible aboard a merchant ship. She spoke well, although her Cornishness often slipped in. Had shown herself to be capable and reliable. A pleasant young lady with the prospects of becoming a suitable wife for someone one day.

"I'm that sorry about Master Donréal," Hetty said, biting her lip and rubbing her thumb over her knuckles. "I liked him, he were a gentle lad. I wish I'd have warned him."

"Warned him?" Tiola cocked her head to one side.

The girl reddened slightly. "Oh, nothing, ma'am. Just warned him to be careful in a strange place."

"Perhaps I should have been more careful, too," Tiola answered as she folded the bed covers back and swung her legs from the cot. "Pass me my clothes please, my dear."

"Should you be getting up? Master Doone said because of the child you carry you need rest."

"And does Master Doone know more than I about what is best for me, do you think?"

Hetty risked a tentative grin. "No ma'am, I guess he don't."

"Then help me dress and let us be seeing about what is more

important than me lazing unnecessarily abed. Better to be doing, rather than thinking."

And grieving, Tiola thought to herself. Then, *How am I going to tell Jesamiah? Where is he, what is he doing*? She missed him all the time, but suddenly she missed him so much achingly more. She wanted to feel his arms around her, his calm reassurance.

She took a slow, deep breath. Repeated aloud: "*Ais,* better to be doing, than thinking."

Finch was waiting for Tiola on deck, sitting hunched and dejected on a pile of old canvas. He hurried to his feet as she approached, his face grey and drawn, his woollen cap clutched in his agitated hands.

"Ma'am? I'm that sorry, ma'am. I lost sight o' 'im. I failed you, the lad an' Cap'n Acorne. I jus' lost sight o' 'im. The lad were there one minute, then 'e were gone. I..."

Tiola rested her hand on Finch's arm. "What occurred was not your fault, Mr Finch. Donréal had wanted to visit the cathedral alone in order to pray for his mother. His death was at the hands of those soldiers, it was not your fault. Nor mine." She squeezed his arm, although she was not quite convinced of the accuracy of the latter. "Where is Thomas? I would speak with him."

Finch nodded forward towards the bow. "Young Hedgepig be up yonder."

Thomas Benson was sitting, hunched miserably in the lee of the wind, his knees drawn up, head cradled into his folded arms. Tiola seated herself next to him and, gently sliding an arm around his shoulders, drew him into an embrace. He buried his face into her cloak and sobbed silently.

She let him weep. Tears were for the release of grief. It occurred to her, suddenly, incongruously, that she had never shed tears for her mother, back then, when she had hanged. Perhaps she should have done? Perhaps, if she had, this grief that was now burdening her would not weigh so heavy? But fear and uncertainty, then, had been the priority, not tears.

"He was my friend," Tom eventually mumbled, as he wiped at

the snot dripping from his nose with the back of his hand. Tiola withdrew a linen handkerchief from her coat pocket, gave it to him.

He blew his nose, passed the linen back to her. "We had plans to do so much together. Go adventuring, sail the seas, capture pirates. Make our fortunes."

"There will be other plans, my dear, with other friends. Perhaps even better ones, or ones that are equal. And the exciting things you did do together need never be forgotten."

Finch re-appeared, offered a glass of brandy to her. "Cap'n sends you this ma'am. Says it'll do you good."

Tiola took the glass, and a small sip, the comforting taste warming her throat and stomach. Gently she peeled Thomas' tightly gripping fingers from her waist and put the glass in his hand. "Just a sip, mind," she said, "we have things to do and we must be sober for them."

Thomas nodded, took a small sip only, and gave the glass to Finch.

"Cap'n also asks if'n you're ready to do as necessary, ma'am. Shall I tell 'im aye, you are?"

Tiola nodded. "If you would, please, Mr Finch."

Finch turned away. Saw no reason to waste what was left of good brandy.

CHAPTER TWENTY-ONE

Standing at the taffrail, the stern of the ship, Tiola gazed at the spot where ten minutes before Donréal's body, sewn into a canvas shroud, had with reverence and dignity been slid over the side of the ship. The crew, passengers and all the children had stood silent, heads bowed, while Captain Ash had read a passage from the Bible and led the recital of the Lord's Prayer. Donréal and his mother were of the Catholic faith and this was no Catholic funeral, but at sea burials had their own tradition and, regardless of an individual's belief, Tiola knew that it made no difference what was, or was not, spoken once the soul had departed the host body. The Beyond was the Beyond; to the dead it was a new existence within the embrace of peace, to the living it was a promise of Paradise or a threat of Hell, with a multitude of various connotations in between depending on culture and creed. Prayers, rituals, burial, cremation or whatever were methods of practical disposal, the how, where and when mattered only to the living in order to bring comfort at a time of immense sorrow, grief and, sadly all too often, to allay regret or guilt.

With her Craft, Tiola would have seen Donréal safely across from Life to Beyond, but for now she had only her human side of emotion to rely upon, and guilt was making its unwelcome presence felt. Had she not gone ashore, had she not walked so close to the soldiers, had she not been preoccupied by the resurgence of her own fear and grief... She inhaled a slow, deep, breath and brushed glistening tears from her cheeks. Dwelling on what had been done, or not done, would serve no purpose. Donréal was with his mother and he was safe, of that Tiola was certain. Nothing else really mattered.

Ascham Doone came to stand beside her, not close but near enough to talk quietly. He smelled of pipe tobacco, Spanish brandy and a fragrance Tiola was unfamiliar with, an aroma that reminded her of the sweet scent of daffodils after a gentle rain had washed everything clean.

"A sad situation," he said.

Tiola continued gazing at the spot where Donréal's body had disappeared. The white, churned path of the *Lady Of Mercia*'s wake was rapidly lengthening, the burial place receding. Captain Ash had got under way immediately, not wishing to lose any more time or daylight beyond what was necessary, especially as black clouds were building along the western horizon.

"Sad indeed," she answered brusquely, thinking Doone's understatement was somewhat trite and probably not genuinely meant. To compensate for her uncharitable thoughts, she changed the subject. "That is a pleasant perfume you are wearing. I am not familiar with it?"

Doone folded back the froth of French lace that showed beneath his velvet coat cuff, exposing his wrist. He held out his arm for her to sniff. "'Tis what they call *Eau de Cologne*, from Obenmarspforten in Germany. Made, so I have been informed, by Heir Giovanni Farina. Nearly all royal houses in Europe have vials of it. I acquired some while we were in Gibraltar. Expensive, but satisfyingly refreshing. Had I known we were to be sailing home together I would have purchased you a vial, perhaps as a gift of truce?"

She disregarded the truce reference. "It is indeed pleasant. But is not Farina an Italian name?"

"The man is Italian, yes, but he resides in Cologne, a German city on the Rhine where there is a major trade harbour. The region provides very fine wines which my grandfather delights in, although I have always preferred a French grape myself. That incident ashore should never have happened, although I beg forgiveness for remarking that you should not have been wandering unaccompanied."

"No," came her reply, "it should not, but I was not unaccompanied. Donréal was with me."

"An orphan child?"

She ignored that as well. Said instead, "I would not have expected danger in such a public place. Had we not sailed so soon I would have lodged a severe complaint with the Portuguese authorities."

He turned to her, spread his hands to emphasise his sincerity. "My dear lady, I have already done so. The gentleman with me, the British Ambassador, will see to it that those men are identified and flogged."

"Flogging them, Mr Doone, will not bring the boy back to life."

"No, it will not, but mayhap it will ensure that they, and others, will think twice before behaving so abominably again. Example is an excellent deterrent."

There were several responses Tiola considered making but none were complimentary.

"I do wonder, however," Doone continued, "whether the boy shouldn't have been sent to the loving embrace of God with his own name to follow him?" When no answer was forthcoming, he expanded his thoughts. "Will the father be able to find the lad's eternal spirit in God's Paradise, if the boy carries no correct name?"

Deliberately, Tiola misunderstood. "God, the Father, knows all by however they are named, but I know not what you allude to? The boy had a name. Donréal." She raised a slight smile, conceded, "Though I grant there was, apparently, an unpronounceable jumble of other Spanish names to go with it. They have a list as long as a Catholic prayerbook where personal titles are concerned."

Bowing his head, Doone acknowledged the subtle chastisement, spoilt the apparent contrition by saying, "I suppose a name is not so important as there will be no gravestone marker for the lad, although Captain Ash has, rightly, entered him into the ship's log."

Tiola waved her hand towards the sea, curling her fingers as if to indicate scooping the ocean into her grasp. "Donréal will require no marker Mr Doone. The sea, Tethys herself, is an adequate memorial for the remains sent into her water-world realm."

Doone was puzzled. "Tethys? I have not heard that name before."

"The folklore spirit goddess; the omnipresent queen of the sea."

"Ah, superstitious nonsense."

"Not to sailors or those who can hear the secret whispers."

Not wishing to pursue a subject he knew nothing about – or cared to know about – Doone said, "All the same, is there kindred we should inform? Is there someone I should contact? He *was* Señora Francesca Escudero's son was he not? Is the father known? Grandparents who need to be notified, perhaps?"

"All are questions I cannot answer, sir. And are questions that you have no authority to be asking."

Waving a hand dismissively, Doone qualified his statement. "I merely wish to be of service, madam."

"You had no liking for Señora Escudero, Mr Doone, so I find it incomprehensible why you should so continuously be interested in her."

Doone acknowledged her observation with a slight nod of his head. "You are perceptive regarding my feelings towards the lady in question, yet I stress I am merely trying to help. The boy, if he was indeed the woman's son, may have held vital, secret, information. The señora was a known, and believed to be dangerous, spy. A threat to British security for we were never certain whether she passed sensitive intelligence to the Spanish."

"Which is why you had her murdered?"

"My dear lady," Doone laughed, "you have been listening over much to the lies of that pirate rogue of yours. The señora's death was not of my doing. I perceive, however, that you also may have held a dislike for her? Perhaps for personal reasons? She was with child, but it did not survive birth. I have heard that the child was, forgive me, there is no delicate way of saying this, it is believed that your – if I use the word 'husband', I use the term loosely – that your husband was the father. Mayhap you arranged her murder through understandable resentment?"

Outraged – because it was true about Jesamiah, and the truth, for all her attempt at understanding, hurt – Tiola raised her hand, about to slap Doone's face, but he caught her wrist, stepped nearer to her, the cologne smelling sickly sweet and causing her to feel suddenly nauseous.

"It is my responsibility, madam, to discover all I can where matters of government intelligence are concerned. Acorne had a relationship with the woman; it is possible that they shared more than a bed. That they were working together?"

"That is absurd!"

"It is unlikely, but not impossible. At the very least she may have divulged to him the true identity of a spy whom we, shall I say, recently 'mislaid'. By the name of Chesham. Have you heard of him?"

"No. Should I have done?"

Doone shrugged. "'Tis no great matter, but the fellow was important and he disappeared. Word was that he died. Until I see indisputable evidence, I do not believe 'word'."

"I cannot help, nor, I imagine, can my husband."

Doone felt in his pocket for his pipe and tobacco pouch, sighed. "I do so dislike untied ends. The señora's son might have known, but if, as you say, he was not this Donréal, then I do not know of his whereabouts."

"Perhaps he, too, is dead?"

"Perhaps? I suspect he is, madam." Doone pointed with his pipe towards the ship's wake, "I suspect he is."

"Then let us leave the subject, sir, and desist with the insults."

Doone looked genuinely offended. "Insults? No, mere conjectures based on observations. Politics and power, Mistress Tiola, sit together like a hand in a glove, but both, to be effectively made use of, require knowledge in order to work the falsehoods and sleight of hand to best advantage, and I dislike not being in possession of knowledge." Doone touched his hat, gave a slight bow. "I truly do not wish to offend, and I am sorry about the boy, but these things happen."

Tiola suppressed a derisive snort, snapped: "Was your mother proud of you as a child, Mr Doone? Did she fear for your apparent lack of sensitivity, or did you learn how to be so insufferably indifferent when you studied at your educational college of law?"

Doone missed the implied sarcasm. "My mother? My mother did as she was told and kept herself to the home and her wifely duties. She died in childbirth when I was eight years old."

What a blessing for her, Tiola thought as she walked away. *The poor woman was saved from suffering the arrogance and bullying of you and your grandfather.*

Gathering her cloak nearer against the rising wind and the rain that was beginning to fall, she walked quickly across the quarterdeck and descended the companionway steps into the waist. The crew were busily adjusting the great sails, hauling on yards, preparing for the bad weather that was looming nearer. Hetty had already ushered the children below and re-emerged to chide her new mistress for lingering in the cold and wet. She ran forward suddenly, shouting and waving her arm. "Ma'am! Look out!"

By instinct, Tiola sidestepped as something – a belaying pin – fell from on high and clattered to the deck, missing her by the width of a cat's whisker.

Doone was at her side, one hand on her arm, moving her another few feet, the other pointing angrily upwards. "That man! Yes, you! You dropped that deliberately! I shall see you flogged for this!"

"He did nothing of the sort," Tiola scolded back, wrenching herself away from his hold. "It was an accident, I am unharmed and the running of this ship is none of your business, Mr Doone." Seething with fury at his unnecessary and unwanted intervention, and from the blood-rush of fear at what could have been an ugly injury, she moved away from him, ushering Hetty ahead of her.

Doone hurried to catch her up, grasped her arm.

"Madam, my dear, I have only interest in your well-being and safety. I spoke out of turn, from alarm. Forgive me."

Tiola's only response was to shake herself free of his grip and to continue on her way.

CHAPTER TWENTY-TWO

Tiola seated herself on the stool in her cabin to the side of the Great Cabin, where the children were settling to bed. It had been generous of Captain Ash to forgo his own quarters for the sake of his passengers, and Tiola was grateful for this small bit of privacy, although 'small' was indeed the correct word. She patted the cot beside her, inviting Hetty to sit.

"Now then," she said, keeping her tone calm and low, for she had no desire to alarm the girl, "we do need to talk. You shouted a warning before there was anything to warn about. Are you aware that you are Fey?"

Hetty looked both alarmed and frightened. "Oh no ma'am, I'm perfectly clean and healthy! I ain't got no spots nor rashes, lumps or bumps. No coughing or anythin' like that!"

Tiola laughed. "No, my dear, this has nothing to do with the state of your health. For how long have you perceived danger in your mind?"

The girl clasped her hands together, her knuckles white. "I don't know what you mean, ma'am."

"You saw that belaying pin fall before the sailor dropped it."

"Oh, I don't think so ma'am. I saw it falling..."

"And you have seen other such warnings."

Again, Hetty denied it. Tears were brimming in her eyes. "No, I assure you I 'aven't!"

Reaching forward, Tiola took one of the girl's hands in her own, held it loose but firm. "You do not need to hide your gift from me, my dear, for I too have a little of the Fey within me." A slight distortion of the truth, but Tiola was not about to divulge the full extent of her abilities.

Hetty stared at her lap. One tear escaped and trickled down her cheek, followed by another. "I don't know this word 'fey'."

"It means to be able to 'scry', or see into the past. Or, in your case, the future."

Mute, not daring to speak, Hetty nodded, once.

"Have you been blessed with this gift for a long while?" Tiola prodded, gently, needing to know but hesitant to pry.

Hetty looked up sharply, her face reflecting a mixture of emotion, shock, embarrassment and fear. In her agitation her Cornish accent leapt to the fore. "'Tis no blessin' ma'am! It be a curse! My mam did scold me when I were a tacker, tol' me not t' tell tales, an' if God caught me, He'd as throw me t' Ol' Nick's fire. I couldna stop seein' things, but I as 'eld m' tongue an' larned not t' go clackin'."

Tiola squeezed the girl's hand, reassuringly. "Your mother was quite right about keeping this to yourself, because folk do not always understand things they do not..." Unable to think of a suitable word, she shrugged, smiled, "Well, things they do not understand."

Hetty sniffed, nodded. "Folk do look t' me queer when I've forgot an' said things. You'd 've thought they be pleased t' know 'bout danger. But they ain't. An' I be afeared of bein' thrown t' the fire."

"That is not going to happen, my dear, but you must, indeed, be discreet. How far ahead do you read the future, see things that have not yet happened?"

It was Hetty's turn to shrug, reluctant to speak openly. Tiola waited, patient, for her to find her confidence.

"Sometimes," the girl finally admitted, "I see only a matter of heartbeats, other times, days, weeks or even months." She blushed, looked down at her hands again, muttered, "I see you, ma'am, very big with child."

Tiola laughed and patted her belly. "Well as I am several months gone, it does not take a seer to assume I'll be quite big very soon. I do hope you see the great, fat, me waddling about in a favourable light, though, and you'll not agree about my ungainly state with my husband when we meet with him again in England!"

Hetty blushed. Captain Acorne was immensely handsome, and although she had barely had anything to do with him during those few days between rescue and dropping anchor in Gibraltar harbour, she had fancied herself in love with him.

Misinterpreting the blush for delicate embarrassment about the intimacy of conceiving a child, Tiola's smile broadened. She leant forward and placed a light kiss on Hetty's cheek.

"Even without the gift of Fey, I feel that we are going to be good friends for a long time, my dear. Especially as we now have each other's secrets to keep safe. Now, go see to the children, settle them to their beds while I finish the next letter I intend to send to my husband. He will be most pleased that I have found a new friend."

It will balance the difficult news about Donréal, she thought. She had already explained that sad news, her tears splashing the paper and smudging the ink. Her bundle of letters would be sent on by packet ship from their next port of call, Roscoff in France, although when, if, Jesamiah would receive them was dubious conjecture.

At least, however, she was spared the heartache of having to write to inform a mother or father of such grievous news.

CHAPTER TWENTY-THREE
THE BAY OF BISCAY

Hetty held up the dress she had just finished sewing. The last of the dimity; there had been just enough material left to fashion a simple dress for one of the smaller girls. There was now only the linen and light-woven wool that Tiola had purchased in Gibraltar to use up. Hetty cocked her head to one side; the left sleeve of the dress was a little crooked but it would suffice. Most of these children were used to hand-me-down rags, had never enjoyed the delight of new clothes that no one had ever worn before. A few skew-whiff stitches would not be noticed.

She looked up as Tiola stirred in her bed. She had been asleep this past hour, Hetty keeping quiet watch while sewing. It had been a busy day. Bad weather had followed in their wake since Lisbon, although until this afternoon, never quite catching them up. By mid-morning, the *Lady Of Mercia* had been pitching and rolling as if demented. Sunday morning service, conducted by the captain up on the open deck, had been brief. A hymn, accompanied by one of the crew on a scratchy old fiddle, the Lord's Prayer and that had been it. The crew had been in their Sunday Best, with Miss Tiola, herself and the children wearing their new or cleanest clothes, but when the rain had come lashing in Captain Ash had sensibly proclaimed a quick 'Amen' and sent everyone about their day. The rain had persisted since then, and now there was thunder grumbling and rolling around the grey, sullen skies.

She liked Captain Ash, a kindly man with a sense of humour and several children of his own 'back home' in Weymouth, Hetty had discovered, where a wife and an elderly mother also awaited him. It had turned out that Mr Wheeler, Spokesy as everyone called him, knew Captain Ash for he also came from Weymouth and had family there. Hetty liked Mr Wheeler, a quiet-spoken man who had carved little wooden poppet dollies for each of the girls, and soldiers for the boys. For her, for Hetty, he had fashioned a wooden rosebud. She'd never had a present before; this little, exquisite carving, she vowed, would remain a lifelong treasure.

Thinking of a captain, Hetty smiled as she trimmed off a few trailing threads. Now there was someone she *could* lose her heart to: the captain of the *Sea Witch*, Captain Jesamiah Acorne, were he not Miss Tiola's husband. Even musing on his name made her innards catch and flutter. She would never forget looking up from that desperate, dark, stinking hold aboard that Arab's ship and looking directly into his eyes as he had peered down at the captured children. No, nor the feel of his hands about her waist as he'd helped her to board *Sea Witch*. That had been just before the pirate ship had exploded – their gunpowder had caught, apparently, killing every one of those foul bastards. Strange, though, Hetty had thought that she had caught a glimpse of Miss Tiola silhouetted against the ball of flame, almost as if she had been controlling that burst of fire, for it had seemed to come from Miss Tiola's outstretched hands. Hetty tutted at her silliness. All fanciful nonsense. Miss Tiola had been beside that man, the one they called Maha'dun, trying, in vain, to save his life, for he had been shot. The other man, Mr Doone, was a different matter. Him, she did not like at all. Pompous, arrogant and stuffed with his own self-importance. 'Full of piss and wind,' Mr Finch often said of him.

Mr Doone had grumbled and complained when he had discovered that *Lady Of Mercia* was heading direct for Weymouth, not Falmouth as he had been led to believe. Lisbon, Roscoff and Weymouth: these were their three ports of call, Captain Ash had insisted, adding that if Mr Doone thought different, then he had been misinformed. That he would find an alternative vessel at Roscoff, although there might be some delay in doing so. Which had made Doone grumble even more. It seemed that he was in a hurry for some reason, but tide and weather were not always compliant where sea travel was concerned. Especially in the heaving waters of Biscay.

Setting the dress aside and ensuring her needle, thread and scissors were tucked safe away in the sewing basket, Hetty rose and tiptoed to the bed, steadying herself against the roll of the ship by keeping one hand on the wooden bulkhead wall. Was Miss Tiola awake, or merely dreaming? Dreaming, surely, for she was restless, mumbling slightly. Words that were not coherent. Hetty sighed, wished she could do something to allay the disquiet that was haunting this lovely lady. Miss Tiola was kind and gentle, did not deserve these nightmare visitations that had been stalking her ever since they left Gibraltar, and had grown worse after Lisbon. Donréal's tragic death and that awful man, Doone's frequent tactless remarks, were not helping matters.

Hetty sat down again, stared out of the salt-grimed window at the rain lashing down, hissing and burbling into the tossing, grey sea. It would be dark soon; her own distorted reflection was growing stronger in the small panes of thick glass, the stormy evening beyond closing in. Not for the first time she wished that the *Lady Of Mercia* could boast a ship's doctor or physician aboard, but alas, there was neither. All she could do for Tiola was sit here and be ready to offer comfort when she awoke – and a tot of the brandy that the captain had generously sent from his own supply, although she had, secretly, partaken of a few sips herself.

Lightning flashed a distance away, turning the blackening sky a lurid purplish-pink. Hetty's only comfort was that she'd had no dire visual warnings of the ship sinking or anyone drowning. She did have nagging misgivings about Roscoff, though why, she had no idea.

Her visions of the future troubled her, for they were always warnings of accidents, illness or coming calamities. One reason why she had, from a young age, learned to keep quiet about them. Even at six years old she had understood that people did not want to hear of doom or death. It had only taken one person to mutter that the child brought evil for her to keep her mouth trimmed shut. What puzzled her was the infrequency of the important stuff – why had she not seen that wretched Barbary pirate ship and the misery it had brought? There again, if that kidnapping had not happened, she would still be working her fingers to the bone with that wretchedly miserable woman in Cornwall. And she would not have met Miss Tiola.

Her unease about Roscoff, however, was like an itch that she could not reach to scratch. Perhaps her misgivings were nothing more than at Roscoff they would need to find another boat?

One not so well manned or captained as was the *Lady Of Mercia.*

CHAPTER TWENTY-FOUR

Dreams haunted Tiola's sleep, for they were memories of the past, re-awakened by some mischief of malevolence that had burrowed like a teredo worm into her soul. Dreams of fearful events that she would rather have kept buried, or forgotten, but dreams that insisted on being remembered.

Night. Cold. A wild wind moaning down from the Moor. The rain had turned to snow. Tiola snuggled into her bed, warmed by woollen blankets and a goose-down quilt, listening to the raised voice of her father seeping up from the kitchen two floors below. His fierce words were always spoken loudly, the volume increasing with righteous indignation. In church of a Sunday morning, none in the congregation ever dozed during his delivered sermons.

In her dream she, the child, wrapped the quilt around her shoulders and went to the window, watched her father walk with long, purposeful strides towards the village, his boots leaving dark prints in the settling snow; the antithesis of King Wenceslaus of Bohemia, setting out to deliver cruelty and denouncement, not charitable benevolence. Heard, immediate as is the way with the discordant shifting patterns of dreams, the blood-stirred shouts of men and women; saw the bobbing lights of smoke-streaming tar torches, and then the blaze of a fire up on the cliff height. Red, orange, yellow with black smoke mounting into the night sky against the white flutters of snow. The acrid smell of burning fat and flesh penetrating deep into her sleeping mind. She stirred, mumbling her fear, her horror.

Heard the screams drifting on the gusting wind, an old woman's pleas for mercy. Her own screams choking in her throat. Mercy? The Reverend Garrick had no sense of the word, nor did the villagers when their blood was raised by the false claims of a man they looked up to and respected, despite their fear of him and their wariness of the Church and the retribution of God.

The Reverend's word was law in their eyes, for he was educated and learned. The nearest magistrate was more than twenty miles away in Truro; the Reverend Garrick was all they had. A man of God, but a man who, when it suited, manipulated and made use of the beliefs which persisted in the minds of the superstitious and uneducated.

Grief caught in her adult throat, tears from behind her closed eyelids trickled down her cheeks onto the pillow. Witches, men like her father insisted, were the devil's whores, and the only way to cleanse a possessed soul was by the heat of the fire. But an old widow woman, with wrinkled, brown-marked skin, who muttered to herself, who lived on her own with a cat for company and a goat for milk, who had knowledge of healing and herbs, such a one was not a witch, just an old, frail, woman.

True witches kept themselves hidden, for they were the Wise Ones of Light who healed and cared, not killed or maimed. The Craft of the White Witches was passed, in secret, from grandmother to granddaughter, and although her gift was dormant by necessity of carrying her child within her belly, Tiola did not need the Sight to know that she was not watching, in her fretful dream, poor, innocent old Agnes burn at the stake. She was watching herself.

Tiola woke with a start, a scream gurgling, trapped, in her throat, her arms flailing as she struggled to sit up, drenched in sweat. Arms were suddenly around her, a cool palm stroking back her damp hair. For a moment Tiola thought it was Jesamiah – the relief intense, how she needed him!

"*Hush, ssh,* my lady, you be all right, 'twas but a dream. A nasty dream."

Not Jesamiah. More tears, spurred on by disappointment. She needed his level-headed practicality, his soothing tenderness, his solid love. But he was not here, and Tiola had a sudden, urgent, fear that there was something wrong, that he would never be beside her again.

Hetty did her best to offer reassuring comfort and drifted into the Cornish accent that, as a lady's maid, she had been expected to suppress. "Us be 'ere, us bain't goin' nowhere. *Ssh,* drink this'n. Us be 'ere, there be naught t' 'arm thee, Maid." She held the glass of brandy to Tiola's lips, who, gratefully, sipped the liquid and attempted a smile of gratitude.

"Thee be welcome, Miss Tiola, though I as wish I could as do more t' comfort thee." Hetty settled the covers closer around her new mistress's shoulders, tucking her into bed and easing her back into a more content sleep. Repeated, as another flash of lurid pink lightning flared beyond the window and a rumble of thunder drummed across the darkening sky and agitated sea, "I wish I could be more help t' thee."

Squeaks of alarm came from the outer cabin as another crash of thunder roared outside. With a sigh, Hetty left Tiola and went to see what she could do to settle the children into bed. The boat was rocking and pitching, but the crew seemed to know what they were doing, so Hetty had no worry about safety – and she'd still had no warning of a sinking ship, drowning passengers or crew, so was not afeared. She'd had warnings other times that she had not heeded, more fool her!

The children were finally settled, and Miss Tiola was sound asleep. The storm was easing; with luck, it would trundle off to bother someone else somewhere else.

Hetty curled up warm and comfortable into her own bed as the night closed in. Why had she not been warned about those pirates? Although, perhaps, she *had* been warned? There had been an awful feeling of dread as she'd sneaked out of her previous mistress's house by the back door and scuttled away through the kitchen garden. The old lady had been snoring beside the parlour fire. Earlier in the day the wretched woman had used her walking cane to strike a blow across Hetty's shoulder.

"All because I didn't put enough butter on her bloody breakfast toast," Hetty mumbled to herself. Sick of the constant abuse – physical and mental – she'd made up her mind to run away when opportunity presented itself. Where to? No idea. What to do? Equally, no idea. A quick-packed bundle of bread and cheese wrapped in a square of muslin, her stout boots and her best cloak, and she had been off, taking her chance to disappear.

Only, a nagging doubt *had* been slapping in her mind that day. *Don't do it... Don't do it...* She had thought, naturally, that it was her conscience pricking, aided by a hefty stroke of fear for stepping out, alone, into the unknown with a few coins of stolen money and no one and nowhere to go to. To trust to luck and good fortune, to hope that someone would take pity and take her in. It was only later, aboard that pirate ship, that the reality had struck her. Had those nagging doubts been for that reason, rather than for the act of running away? She had ignored the common sense of *Stay where you are. Stay safe.* Being aboard that pirate ship had been frightening, but, Hetty had to admit to herself, warm, comfortable and content here in the dark of the *Lady Of Mercia,* that the experience had, despite the fear and horror, been exciting. And nothing, *nothing,* would ever persuade her to go back to that old bitch who had treated her with less regard than a lump of dirt.

Then more thoughts. Could she trust Miss Tiola about this being fey business? The passing years and slips of the tongue had taught her to be cautious and careful, but Miss Tiola was different. *Fey.* Hetty had never heard the word before, but she liked it. Liked it very much.

The thunder had ceased, although there were still a few distant flickers of lightning. The ship, creaking, groaning and complaining, was plunging over high rollers, lifting and dipping but stable and safe. Soon, they would be across Biscay and nearing Roscoff. That was a place she knew of, at least by name. Her father and several of the men had made regular trips across the narrow Channel to the small Breton fishing village, to meet and trade with friends and 'business' acquaintances.

Business? Trade? She was not that much of a blind-minded dolt! Roscoff was a village becoming renowned for the exchange of contraband. The *Lady Of Mercia* was no smuggler's vessel, although she possibly had some illicit 'trade' stowed in her hold, almost every boat outside of the Navy did, but why, Hetty wondered, did she continue to have this feeling of dread hanging heavy like a lead weight in her mind? Why would Roscoff be a threat?

As sleep took her, words rustled into her mind. *Falmouth. Beware Falmouth*. But she was asleep. Did not hear.

CHAPTER TWENTY-FIVE
SEPTEMBER - CÁDIZ, SPAIN

Someone was patting Jesamiah's face. None too gently.

When I wake up, he thought, *I'll bloody pat their face.*

"Wake up, man. Come on, enough of this, it is time to rouse yourself."

Reluctantly, Jesamiah stirred, opened his eyes and looked directly into the stern, but concerned, face of Captain Edward Vernon.

At least, Jesamiah thought it was Vernon. The man had a bedraggled appearance, disorderly, dirty, hair and a generous amount of unshaved stubble. Captain Vernon, the real Captain Vernon, was a stickler for tidiness and cleanliness. The voice was Vernon's though.

"Fetch him some of that water," Vernon ordered to someone squatting close by. The someone rose, came back with a dented tin mug half-filled with green, scummy water. Vernon took it, held it to Jesamiah's lips.

"Fok, but that tastes as foul as a latrine pit!" Jesamiah grumbled, pushing the mug away.

"You have a familiarity with drinking from latrine pits, then, do you?" Vernon asked, not bothering to conceal his disdain for the man before him. The earlier concern, it seemed, was not directed at Jesamiah's wellbeing but for the fact that he was not awake.

"Aboard your bloody ship I did," Jesamiah retorted. He shifted position, stiff from lying prone on a hard, damp floor. Winced, then yelped as pain in his arm, face, thigh and almost all his body hurtled through him.

"We need you to wake up," Vernon insisted. "They tell me that you speak Spanish?"

Jesamiah blinked at him, not quite understanding. They? Who were 'they'? He peered over Vernon's shoulder, realised their surroundings. A prison cell, packed with crew from the *Bonne Chance*. Thirty or so men?

"What happened?" he croaked, again, wincing, trying to sit up. Hands reached out to help him. Richard Tearle. The 'they' in question?

"Spaniards took us," Tearle explained as he propped Jesamiah against the wall. "We know twenty-eight are dead; another six here will not see many more sunrises. You're one of the wounded. One of the lucky ones to be alive."

Lucky? The pain was increasing. Jesamiah did not believe in luck. It let you down too often. He growled something crude about the consequences of luck.

"How long have we been here?" he asked, wrinkling his nose at the overwhelming stench.

"You've been drifting in and out of consciousness for nine days," Vernon informed him. "Which is why you really do need to pull yourself together and wake up."

The question 'why?' filtered through Jesamiah's mind, but he quickly answered it: *Because this is a Spanish gaol and I can speak Spanish*. Except, he had no wish to wake up or to speak Spanish. Nor did he want any Spaniard to discover who he was. His present name was Oakwood and Oakwood he would stay. End of discussion.

"My arm's broke, my face aches and my thigh feels like it is on fire," he said, looking dismally down at himself. He wore only his torn breeches. Most of the material, on his right leg, was missing, replaced by a bloodied, dirty bandage encircling his thigh. An equally filthy bandage was wound round a crude wooden splint encasing his left forearm. The fingers, poking out from the end, were bruised and slightly swollen. He wriggled them; his arm complained but he could move them. Sort of. He wiggled his toes. They worked too, but when he made to bend his knee, he gulped down a yelp of agony that shot out from the muscles of his thigh. That slice of splinter, then, had done some damage.

His head thumped as if an entire militia were beating to quarters in there. He felt with his right hand. A tender lump the size of a duck's egg – no, bigger, a goose egg. His face throbbed too. He brought his hand lower, felt a stitched gash snaking across his cheek. "Bugger," he mumbled.

Tearle explained. "Surgeon says you have concussion. Been in and out of awareness all this time. Your arm's a clean break, it'll mend, no gangrene. No idea how damaged that leg is; nothing's broken but there might be a lot of torn muscle. It'll take some healing, surgeon says. As for your face, you'll have a scar but he reckons it will fade in time. He says you were lucky there too, could have lost an eye."

"Nine days?" Jesamiah queried. "We've been here nine days?"

"Six. They kept us locked up aboard their Spanish ship at first. The *Santa María del* something or other."

"Santa María del Bartolomé," Jesamiah corrected. Perhaps they were lucky? Most Spaniards, as with pirates, would simply have tossed prisoners overboard. "And where exactly is 'here'?" Not entirely certain that he wanted to hear an answer to his question.

"Cádiz. The Castle Tarif, or some such name," Vernon answered.

Jesamiah again put him right. "Do you mean *Castillo de Tarifa*? Shit."

"Aye, that is probably the only thing we will ever agree on, Acorne," Captain Vernon said, grimly. "Shit."

"Oakwood," Jesamiah reminded him. "If you wouldn't mind. Oakwood. My real name ain't harboured by many friends in these parts."

"I have no care as to what you call yourself," Vernon retorted with a snort. "All I am interested in is getting these fish-faced Spaniards to understand that I and my officers have a right to parole and exchange. So far, the imbeciles are refusing to understand the King's English."

"German," Jesamiah muttered as the overwhelming impulse to

go back to sleep flooded through his thrumming head. "King George of Hanover is German, can't talk a word of English."

"Nonsense," Vernon snapped, "he only makes pretence of not doing so, though I grant his accent is lamentably hard to decipher."

"Met 'im personally 'ave you? Heard 'im mangle the language?" Jesamiah countered.

Tearle interrupted. For the first time, Jesamiah noticed that he had a ragged bloodstained bandage bound around his right bicep and a black eye beginning to turn a lurid shade of purplish yellow. He guessed his own face was a similar colour.

"We need you to negotiate for us, Jes. And Captain Vernon needs to know what they have done with the rest of his men."

"If they discover who I am," Jesamiah repeated his earlier statement, "I'll not be negotiating anything for anyone, I'll be swinging from a gibbet. Where are the children? What happened to them?"

Someone else answered, Lieutenant Coffney, brandishing a grimed bandage around his forehead. "The Spaniards took them. From the little we did understand they thought we were the ones who had kidnapped them in the first place."

Jesamiah frowned. "That's absurd! The Spanish should know it were Barbaries. And that we destroyed them. Doone should have made all that clear back in Gib. As should you, Tearle; I put you ashore with the children for that reason. And to see to their safe return home. You don't seem to have accomplished either."

Richard Tearle snapped an affronted retort. "I made everything quite clear to the official representatives. However, I cannot speak for Doone."

He stopped talking, looked up as there came the sound of a key in the lock and the door swung open. A large, black, iron stew pot that put Jesamiah in mind of a fairy tale witch's cauldron was dumped inside, with the door hastily closed and locked again. The crewmen able to walk rushed forward, clutching battered tin plates. With bickering and squabbling increasing, they pushed forward, anxious to get at the meagre food inside the pot.

Vernon rapped a command to stand still, marched forward with Lieutenant Coffney, shouting at the men to form an orderly line.

"Those at the front yesterday go to the back today!" he insisted, prodding one or two to ensure they complied. One of the two was Buckeridge who, as he passed, scowled at Jesamiah.

Realising that he was hungry, Jesamiah struggled to get to his feet, but Tearle pushed him back down.

"Sit tight, I'll fetch yours. It isn't worth fighting over. I've seen better pig's slop."

Jesamiah had to agree when Tearle handed him a plate of what looked like a brown mess of cow flop.

"No spoon?" he asked.

Tearle shook his head, scooped some of his own mess onto his fingers. "Only way to eat this is close your eyes and imagine you're savouring the best stew your dear ma ever cooked for you."

"We had an African cook," Jesamiah stated. "Big black man called Cecil. He used to let me hide from my brother under the kitchen table and passed me leftovers from his cooking. He made the finest apple pies in Virginia." He cocked his head to one side, wondering what had become of the man. Added, "I don't think my mother even entered the kitchen, let alone cooked anything herself." He tried a mouthful of the slop. The stuff tasted vaguely of fish, confirmed by a chunk of mollusc shell. Crab? Cockles? Snails? It didn't matter, whatever it was, it was vile.

"What's for pudding?" he asked.

"Indigestion and a dose of the squits," Lieutenant Coffney answered with a laugh.

"I'd have been better off staying unconscious," Jesamiah observed.

"We've been feeding you with this stuff whenever you were half lucid," Tearle confirmed, "though we did wonder whether it would finally kill you off."

"Iron stomach," Jesamiah said. "My steward ain't a particularly good cook, unless he puts his mind to it. Who's survived then?" He looked across the crowded cell, at men squatting on their haunches and doing their best not to grimace at the food. Saw Charlie Featherstone – Feathers – one of the gun crew he'd fought alongside. Remembered that Tyburn, Longjohn and Walnut were dead. "Curly, the bald black man, did he make it through?" he asked. Tearle shrugged, said he didn't know.

An hour later the cell, built of stone with a rusted iron-grating for a roof, was like a furnace as the sun moved higher towards noon. There was little shade. The stink of men's unwashed bodies, urine and faeces increased; there was a wooden latrine box in one corner that, if it followed other examples, would have a cesspit with a run-off ditch emptying into the sea, and although it provided a specific place to piss and shit, it did nothing to relieve the stench.

The key scraped in the lock. The same doleful soldier reached in through the open door to retrieve the empty stew pot.

Time to put an end to all this nonsense, Jesamiah thought as he struggled, one-handed, to his knees, grimacing with the pain coursing from his thigh. He shouted, "*¡Hola! Llévame a su comandante. Soy el capitán Jesamiah Acorne y tengo noticias importantes para él.*"

The sullen-faced Spaniard merely glowered at him, retreated and closed the door, but almost an hour later it opened again with two different uniformed Spaniards standing outside in the bright sunlight.

"*¿Acorne?*"

"*Sí.*"

"You come."

Jesamiah nodded, held out an arm for Tearle to help him up. "I'll try my best to sort something out," he said to Vernon, "provided, if this lot don't immediately hang me, you promise you won't be doing so if we ever get out of here."

Vernon nodded. "I can agree to that."

"You'd better. Otherwise, I'll forget about you and just extricate myself."

"What about me!" Tearle called, part indignant, part worried.

"What about you?" Jesamiah answered as he limped, huffing and grunting from the pain, to the door, trying to avoid the worst of the detritus on account of his bare feet, the other men parting like the Red Sea for Moses, to allow him a corridor of space. He was unsteady, his legs and knees, in addition to the protesting thigh, feeling as rubbery as a dead jellyfish. Someone came forward, offered him a crude crutch. "That almost dead chap had this. Take it, you need it; he won't."

Jesamiah nodded his thanks, placed it under his arm, took a tentative step. Still hurt like the blazes, but was an improvement. At the door, he bowed slightly to the Spaniards. *"Caballeros, llévame al encargado, y debe de servir un maldito buen brandy."*

"What did he say?" Vernon asked Tearle as the door slammed shut.

"No idea," Tearle admitted, "though I recognised something about a good brandy."

Everyone was quiet for a while, savouring the thought of a rich, warming brandy trickling slowly down the throat.

"So, what do we do now?" Lieutenant Coffney asked no one in particular.

"We wait," Captain Vernon responded. "We wait and we hope that Acorne manages to achieve something positive. If not, we either attempt escape, or we die."

CHAPTER TWENTY-SIX

Shackles, it had been decided, were not necessary as Jesamiah was not going to be able to run far or fast. Walking was difficult enough, although as a precaution a rope tether had been set around his neck, the other end held firm by one of the soldiers as if he were leading a rabid dog instead of a man in pain. They escorted Jesamiah from the gaol, across a courtyard, up a flight of steps, which were agonising for him to negotiate, across another courtyard and up more torturous steps. Then through a wooden side door that took an age to unlock. He was barefoot, the cobbles of the narrow alleyways they ushered him along burned his feet where the sun struck them, and even the shaded areas bruised and jarred his sore soles.

"¿Where's this?" he asked in Spanish as they entered a side entrance to a grand-looking palatial building, the exterior exquisitely clad in red and white marble. Getting no answer, he repeated the question.

A grunted, *"Casa del Almirante,"* was the only response. It was enough; Jesamiah had heard of it. Were this England, he'd be entering the Admiralty buildings at Greenwich.

At least it was cool inside, although beyond this tucked-away entrance the corridors beyond had no hint of the expense incurred for the front, grander, part of the building. More stairs which took all his breath and energy to climb, and then he was ushered into a room with a large window overlooking what he assumed must be the Plaza San Martín – if memory from what his mother used to tell him about Cádiz was correct. A man in a smart blue uniform, adorned with gold lace at cuff and collar, and an impressive array of medals spread across his left chest, sat at an ornate desk, his back to the window. Bent over something he was writing, his quill scratched on the paper as he wrote.

In Spanish, Jesamiah said, "My mother used to tell me of this building, her father often brought her here when she was a child. ¿It was constructed with the proceeds of the Spanish treasure fleet by the family of one of its admirals, Don Diego de Barrios, was it not? He was an uncle of Mama's. That makes the fellow my great-uncle. ¿Does that make me a part owner of the place, I wonder?" He indicated his crude state of undress and filthy appearance. Added sarcastically, "I'd have dressed more appropriate had I known I was to be honoured with such an invitation to come here."

"And I would have had you flogged, then hanged, had I known you were here in Cádiz," came the answer in reasonable English. "But as it is, your execution has been delayed."

"I'm glad to hear it. May I sit? My wound is killing me."

"No. You may not. Your wounds may have the delight of killing you that I must, temporarily, be denied. I take comfort knowing that your reputed good looks have been scarred by that wound to your cheek."

Ignoring him, Jesamiah sat on the chair on his side of the desk.

The Spaniard made no further comment but pushed the paper he had been writing on, and another identical one, towards Jesamiah. "Two copies. Sign both." Added, "I assume you can read and write?"

Jesamiah picked one of the papers up, studied it, in his mind translating the Spanish to English, being careful not to move his lips, even over some of the more unfamiliar words. Many an observer regarded a man who could read without murmuring aloud to be a man who held some sort of magical skill. Equally, moving the lips indicated a poor ability to read.

"This is my parole," he said, setting the paper down. "There's a hefty sum of gold specified as surety. It states I am to be released into non-specified custody provided I relinquish all weapons and give my oath that I will not abscond." He smiled, indicated his semi-naked appearance, broken arm and bandaged, bleeding thigh. "As you can see, I carry no sword or pistol, and even if I did, I doubt I could use either effectively. Who is this custodian to be?"

"Does it matter?"

"Probably, if he's paid you that much for my release."

"Señor de León. The husband of the eldest sister to the deceased Marquésa Catriona de Molina. I believe, although I find it difficult to do so knowing who, and what, you are, that Catalina, the eldest surviving daughter of the marquésa, says she owes her life to you. It is she who has been pleading for you to be found and released. Again, against my better judgement."

"I expect the money swayed your decision. But, all the same, I have you and her to thank."

"You may thank me by getting yourself and that disgustingly offensive stench you carry, from my clean office."

Jesamiah held out the rope dangling from his neck. "This?"

"Will be removed and you will be taken by carriage to San Vincento. I have no wish, Captain Acorne, to ever see you again."

That was fair enough. Jesamiah selected a quill from a fancy elephant ivory holder, dipped it in the inkpot and signed his name on both sheets of paper.

The Spaniard shook some fine sand over the wet ink, blew away the excess and, rolling one copy of the parole order, handed it to Jesamiah.

"Lose it and you will be hanged," he said.

"I'll guard it with my life. What of my fellow Englishmen imprisoned against their will? Are you to release them also?"

"I am not. Be gone before I change my mind about hanging you."

There was no arguing with that. Jesamiah bowed, turned and headed for the door, indicating with a crooked finger that his escorts were to follow him.

It was only as he was climbing awkwardly into a carriage, a cloak draped around his shoulders that he'd casually stolen from where it had been left on a chair, that he realised he had never asked the official's name. Not that it mattered; these Spanish noblemen's names went on forever because they included countless family references. Why they couldn't be simple 'Juan Smith' was beyond Jesamiah's figuring, despite his knowledge of the language. He unrolled the parole paper, studied the man's signed signature above his own. It was so scrawled he couldn't read it.

CHAPTER TWENTY-SEVEN
ROSCOFF, FRANCE

Roscoff. As a village it was little different from any other small Breton fishing village, the inhabitants, Roscovites, no different from any other fisher-folk who struggled to make a meagre living along any part of a French, Breton, Norman or Cornish coast. There was, however, a difference but not one openly visible, especially where strangers were concerned. Roscoff was flourishing as a smugglers' trading centre. A quiet, protected harbour, within easy reach from Cornwall, Devon, the English south coast, the rest of France, Portugal, Spain – and from across the Atlantic. Contraband passed hand to hand with no one in authority seemingly being aware of it: Spanish brandy, Indian tea, French lace, Dutch genever, Portuguese spices. The use of small villages and deserted coves meant the customs men were unaware of the trade, although suspicion was beginning to be aroused, but what could they do to stop it? One or two poorly armed, inexperienced men against a growing number of wily smugglers? Even so, strangers coming ashore at Roscoff were greeted politely but warily. It was jested among the locals, that the only stranger they had greeted with joy and open arms had been the six-year-old Scots Queen, Mary Stuart, when she had disembarked at Roscoff in 1548 en route to being betrothed to the French Dauphin, François.

The village itself was a scatter of granite buildings nestled along the secluded stretch of coast, with several meagre bothies of wood and reed thatch for the less well-off dotted here and there to north and south. Nearly everyone fished in boats large or small, in good repair or weatherworn and falling apart. Nearly everyone regularly smuggled something in or out, save for the priest, the chandler, the draper and the landlords of four different taverns who eagerly accepted the illicit goods. All readily exchanged goods for contraband, the priest playing his part by allowing the crypt beneath his church to be used for storage. Only the farmers with their inland acres, growing their prestigious crops of highly regarded onions showed no interest in smuggling. Onions carried no import or export tax.

The people of Roscoff knew Captain Ashcroft, welcoming him with smiles and backslaps of joyful greeting – him and the illicit kegs and crates he sent ashore. Mr Doone, too, seemed known for although greeted more formally, he was whisked away to the best tavern as a private guest of the landlord. That was a blessing as far as Hetty was concerned for it meant Doone was out of the way.

The Breton children had been engulfed in joyful hugs, the two boys having been taken from Roscoff itself, the six girls from another village. Grateful parents and families crowded Tiola as she came ashore, word spreading like wildfire on a dust-dry moorland that it had been she who had rescued the children. Not quite true, but near enough not to warrant making a fuss about correcting the assumption. Word spreading, too, that she was a respected midwife.

Almost before she had time to draw breath, Tiola was begged to aid a young mother in difficulty birthing a first child, labouring already for more than six-and-twenty hours.

Without her guidance of Craft Tiola was uncertain whether she had skill enough to be of use to the exhausted woman, but she had felt obliged to do what she could, despite Hetty giving her anxious opinion that perhaps it was not a good idea to interfere?

"I've seen a warning of a woman, heavy with child, surrounded by the darkness of death," she had whispered, but Tiola had waved the misgiving away.

As the afternoon drifted towards evening Tiola fought to deliver a breech-born boy almost too large for his mother to push safe into the world. As a half-moon rose into the darkening sky, the baby slid into Tiola's hands having made a torn mess of his mother and near taken her, and himself, into the Beyond. He was not breathing, his lips were blue, made no cry or sound. Not yet cutting the cord, for he needed every small assistance that his mother could give, Tiola wrapped him in a warmed towel and breathed her own life into his mouth and nose, her fingers pressing and rubbing gently above his tiny heart. Anxious minutes, with grandmother and mother motionless, their own breath held.

"Will he live?" whispered the grandmother. "Has all this effort been in vain?"

Tiola made no answer, continued to breathe into the child's lungs. He stirred – hiccupped and then bawled his indignation, great gulps of life flooding into and through his body.

"Your son, my dear," Tiola said with a smile, handing him to his pale-faced, tired mother before turning her attention to the cord and afterbirth.

Reprovisioned, the *Lady Of Mercia* had sailed for Weymouth with Spokesy remaining aboard, and Doone had sent word that he had arranged accommodation for himself and Tiola at his friend's inn, the Auberge de la Reine Marie. An hour after seeing the child born safely into the world, Tiola, tired, but content, made her way there, escorted by Finch who had waited patiently for her to emerge from the young mother's house.

"Me an' the lads are at the Shovel Blank down along the road," Finch explained as he walked with her up the stairs to her allotted chamber on the inn's first floor.

"I think that would be *Cheval Blanc*, Mr Finch," Tiola said wearily, but kindly.

"That's what I said." He jerked his head upwards. "Doone's on floor above. Bloody man got me and Jasper to 'aul 'is dunnage all the way up there. Gave us no coins for doing so, neither. Tight-arsed basket that 'e is. I checked, there's a solid bolt on y' door. Make sure as 'ow you shoot it 'ome. Young Benson's with me, and them other kiddies is with families 'ere in the village, so all's safe. I'll look fer a liddle boat t'morrer t' take us across the Channel."

Tiola looked around the room as she entered: a fire blazing in the hearth, curtains drawn against the night, the handle of a warming pan poking from beneath the covers of an enormous bed.

Hetty, bending over one of the sea chests, looked up with a smile. "I've unpacked only your essentials, ma'am. Your nightwear and hairbrush, and that nice-scented stuff you like to smooth into your face and hands be on the table by the window over there."

One glance, however, showed Tiola's exhaustion, so Hetty ushered Finch out with a firm thank you. Closed the door, slid the bolt home.

"Has anyone secured you a room, Hetty?" Tiola asked as she sat on the edge of the bed, her hand on her bulge. The child within was becoming active and her back was aching. She'd been aware of the forming life throughout the difficult delivery, nervous for the multitude of things that could, maybe, go wrong for her own child. Nervous that there was a prickling insistence at the back of her consciousness of the Dark Side, the omnipresence of the Malevolents, whispering, urging, her to use Craft to ensure the mother's child – and her own – were delivered safe. Safe? Hah! Had she succumbed to temptation the boy this afternoon would surely have died, and her own babe would be in danger. She had several more months of this: fending off that wicked supernatural interference, and no one, not a soul, to plead help or support from. The Malevolents? They were persistent with their intent. Murmuring also that Jesamiah was in danger, was dying, was dead. Tired beyond belief Tiola had only the merest strength left to bat their mischief aside.

"I'll sleep here in that chair, ma'am," Hetty suggested, nodding over her shoulder at the chair in question as she assisted Tiola to remove boots and stockings. "It looks comfortable enough."

"You will not!" Tiola protested. "This bed is large enough for three fat people, I suspect. I will disappear within it on my own. We will cuddle together and keep each other's cold feet warm."

CHAPTER TWENTY-EIGHT

A night of comfort and sound sleep, although it had been strange not to feel the rocking, dip and lift of the *Lady Of Mercia*, nor the constant creaking of timbers in their ears. Hetty was up and dressed before the sun rose, and wanted Tiola to stay abed while she fetched a tray of food to break her fast. Tiola would have none of it.

"I was tired last night," she said, "but I am rested now. Besides, I need to use the privy and then check that the mother and child are doing well."

"That be for the family t' see to," Hetty insisted, concern for Tiola uppermost in her mind. "You must look to your own health, ma'am."

Tiola's answer was sharp. "To check is a midwife's duty. If you are to remain with me Miss Harriett Blackthorne, then you will learn, and remember, to do things as I say they must be done."

Hetty gazed down at her feet, her face reddening. "I were only..."

Annoyed at her spark of uncalled-for temper, Tiola patted the girl's arm as an apology. "Do not fret, I am out of sorts a little this morning. You meant well for my benefit, and I appreciate it, but there are things I am obliged to do, and caring for a woman who has suffered a difficult labour is one of them. So, let me attend the necessaries, then fetch our cloaks. I will enjoy a hearty breakfast as soon as I have satisfied myself that mother and child are doing well."

"Very well, ma'am," Hetty mumbled, looking down at her boots, then drawing on her courage, blurted out, "but I have misgivings, miss. Something, some warning, be naggin' at me. I cannot hear it clear, but 'tis like a small breeze rustlin' through autumn leaves. A feelin' o' danger, like a mouse feels through 'is whiskers when a night-ghost owl glides silent across a field."

"A feeling of danger for here in Roscoff?"

"I don't know, miss."

"You said yourself that your father used to come here. Perhaps you are worried that you could meet him? That would spark some trouble, would it not?"

Hetty nodded; that it would. But it was not her hateful father causing her concern. Within this whispered warning a woman was involved. And Hetty was afeared that the woman was not herself but Miss Tiola.

Walking back from assuring herself that mother and child were well, Tiola paused and looked over her shoulder as her name was called.

"Miss? Miss Tiola? Is that you, Maid?"

A well-dressed, dapper man, whom she judged to be in his late forties, with a bush of a salt-and-pepper beard and a stout ash staff in his hand, was hurrying to catch her up.

"Do I know you?" Tiola asked as, a little out of breath, he removed his hat and flourished her a courteous bow.

"I know you; you are the image of your dear mother," he replied with a broad smile. "And your brother is Carter Trevithick is he not? I do business with him. I've known Carter for many years. He crewed for me for a while, before he met that wife of his and put his mind to running a Devonshire tavern." He spoke in English, was not a Frenchman. "Most of his stock is the genever I supply him with."

"I'm sure I do not..."

"Nay, nay o'course not. Such talk be not for a lady. But surely you recall me? Rowse Austell? I had the one li'le lugger back along then, the *Truro*, but I've quite a fleet now, *Sennan*, *Redruth* and *Falmouth*."

"All Cornish place names?"

"*Ais*, my little joke on account of my own name being Austell. But I see puzzlement in your eyes?"

"Forgive me sir, but I really do not know you."

His turn, now, to frown. "That is sad indeed, for I well remember you and Miss Pendeen from my visits to Cornwall. Do you not recall, it was I an' m'crew who took you both secretly from a cove near Falmouth? A voyage your brother arranged in haste?"

Fear clamped Tiola's entire being. She did not recall his face or name, but the reason for that voyage... Would she ever forget it? If only she could!

"I... I," she stammered.

Suddenly the man's face reddened and he clapped a hand to his forehead. "Saints save me, Maid, what a dolt I am! You were a child, scared, it was night when we left and you slept almost the entire voyage here to safety in Roscoff."

"I am sorry, sir, but I still do not..."

"An' o'course, given the circumstances of that bad business, mayhap I ought not talk of it. I do apologise miss."

"Mistress. *Mistress* Acorne, I am married now."

"And expecting your own child, I see," Mr Austell said, beaming with pleasure. "Oh, my dear, your ma, she would be that proud t' see what a fine young lady you have become."

"So, you knew my mother?"

"I did indeed. A fine, lovely woman who deserved better than the torment she had been served from that husband of hers."

"I do not think..."

"Nay, nay, I understand, a subject I should also not mention, but I knew your dear mother very well, God rest her soul." He stopped talking. Another man was walking towards them.

Doone. He raised his hat, hallooed Tiola's attention.

Noticing him, Austell lowered his voice. "Forgive me ma'am, I b'lieve I may speak out of turn but I urge you to take care. There has been some uncomfortable gossip whispered about the hanging of your dear mother these recent months, and speculation about what happened to her daughter. 'Tis most odd that the matter has of a sudden been on folks' lips. Someone must have stirred the pot of stinking fish heads, offered enough silver t' set a tongue wagging. I cannot say for certain but, that man approaching may be behind it. Do not trust the Doones. They be a bad lot." Louder, for Doone's benefit, he said, "And I thank you, Mistress Acorne for the aid you gave my niece las' night. A bonny baby boy of whom we will all be most proud. I thank thee again. Good day." He touched his hat, turned and walked away.

"Was that Austell?" Doone asked, coming to her side. "What did he want?"

None of your business, Tiola thought, said, feigning amiability, "A kinsman of the woman I delivered of a healthy boy last night. Did you want me, sir?"

"I did. Be wary of Austell, he does not follow the law where trade is concerned."

"Does he not? And what trade would that be? Your kind of dubious trade or the smugglers' kind?"

Doone blushed annoyance at the intentional reprimand. "Yes, well, it is a damnable nuisance that we are marooned here, but I have been assured that a vessel can take us to Falmouth within two or three days."

Suddenly Tiola realised that she did not want to travel on further with this offensive man. "I am in no hurry to leave. I rather like it here, and I would prefer to keep an eye on the young mother and her child, so I will stay for a while. You need to get back to England, of course; I will be quite secure with Mr Finch to take care of me."

Doone's face clouded with annoyance. "My dear lady, that will not be possible. You are in *my* care, and I will not set aside my promised duty."

"Promised duty? To whom?"

"That knave you so rashly insist on calling husband, for one, and I have already writ to your brother. He will be expecting us."

"Oh?" *Will a letter to Appledore travel faster than us*, she wondered? "I am sure my brother will be content to wait, and Captain Acorne will not mind me remaining here."

"Maybe not, ma'am, but *I* will mind. These small fishing boats are suitable for carrying crucial dispatches, but they cannot take passengers, so I will try to secure a suitable vessel as soon as may be." Doone indicated that the conversation had reached a conclusion by touching his hat, and, excusing himself, disappeared in the direction of the harbour.

Tiola watched him go, swinging his cane and strutting with blatant arrogance. What was he up to? What was he not telling her?

She shrugged, did not need a stranger to warn her to be careful where Ascham Doone was concerned. As for the other, she had fled Cornwall after her father's murder, but she had been a child, wrapped in blankets and kept hidden. She and Jenna had dallied here in Roscoff for but a few hours, leaving to take the long overland route to Nantes, changing horses or coaches frequently, lest anyone unwelcome should be following. From Nantes they had boarded a Dutch merchantman, the *Christina Giselle,* heading for Cape Town. En route, being attacked by a pirate ship – the pirates had lost the engagement, but Tiola had seen Jesamiah, and he her, although at the time he had been unaware of her identity or the future that lay ahead of them.

Despite dear Jenna's caution, it had never occurred to Tiola, since then, that anyone would wish to discover their trail. But Mr Austell made her wonder. Could this be the warning of danger that Hetty had spoken of?

Tiola shook her head. Was it likely that she would be remembered by strangers here in Roscoff? Mr Austell clearly knew her through his connection with her brother, Carter, and her mother, but beyond that...?

Although, as she walked slowly back to the tavern, she did ponder just how well, and in what circumstances, this Mr Austell had known her mother. She'd had a lover. That Tiola knew. Knew also that the Reverend Garrick, the man she had called father, was not the man who had sired her – or Carter, or their brother, Ben.

She stopped walking, looked back over her shoulder, but Mr Austell had gone. There could, of course, be one logical explanation of why he had so willingly assisted her and Jenna to escape that bitter, bloody night. One very logical explanation.

CHAPTER TWENTY-NINE

Despite her previous inclination to remain in Roscoff, Tiola had to concede, after a day of grey skies and continuous, miserable rain, that there was no reason for her to stay. The mother and newborn child were in the capable hands of their family, the remaining English children were becoming bored, and Doone had found a suitable boat – a Cornish brig carrying a cargo of onions. All that was needed to set sail was the rain to scurry away and the wind to turn slightly, which it did come the morning of the fourth day.

With no acceptable or relevant excuses to make, Tiola had found herself boarding the *Mary Charlotte,* bound direct for Falmouth. Designed for carrying cargo, not passengers, she was cramped and stank of onions below deck, but the English children were happy enough to make themselves comfortable for the voyage, which according to the captain would take not much more than half of the day, provided the sea, weather and wind remained favourable.

Finch, Jasper and young Benson had seen to the loading of the luggage, and all three were content to assist the crew where and when needed, rather than sit and do nothing. Thomas had told Tiola that his father had promised him a Cornish lugger for his sixteenth birthday, "So that I may sail her to Lundy, or coves along the Exmoor coast."

"That will be quite exciting for you I should imagine," Tiola had answered.

"Oh yes, unlike this boat she'll be open decked, but I'll have false planking fitted so I may conceal contraband when I wish to. I intend to be a successful smuggler."

Tiola had laughed. "Then you must learn to keep quiet about it. Smugglers who boast of their prowess have very short careers."

Tom had grinned. "Good advice. I'll remember it."

Hetty, overhearing, had commented sharply, "Do something else with your life, young Tom. I see a bad end for you if you take to the Trade."

Cocking her head, Tiola had watched the young lady shepherd the children below. Was that conjecture or a specific warning? Either way, she doubted Thomas would take heed. Like Jesamiah, he had too much of the adventurer within him.

Once under way, Tiola remained above deck, craving the early morning fresh air, and willing the bout of sickness not to affect her. With her advancing pregnancy the nausea had been easing of late, but had not quite gone.

"You look slightly green around the gills?" Doone remarked to her as *Mary Charlotte* headed away from Roscoff harbour. "I always took you to be a good sailor."

"I am usually," she responded with as much of a smile as she could manage. "But the child insists on making its presence known of a morning. I am also not a lover of onions, and it appears their slight sulphurous aroma is not a friend to my stomach." She laughed, "Add to which, I think one or two of those sacks down below contain spoiled goods; there is a distinct rotting compost smell, a sure sign of bad onions."

Doone raised one eyebrow. "I did not know that, although as I leave any food preparation to the cooks, I suppose I have never had need to know it."

"Ah, but you are a merchant who trades with the French; you would not appreciate being sold bad onions."

Doone's turn to smile. "My dear, I rely on others to differentiate between quality or poor merchandise. And I trade in more profitable commodities than French onions."

Such as black slaves, and indentured Irish, she thought.

Mary Charlotte heaved herself up and over a particularly robust roller then plunged down again, leaving Tiola's stomach behind. Unable to keep the sickness down, she vomited over the side.

Doone wrinkled his nose, but produced a leather hipflask and, removing the stopper, handed it to her. "A sip of brandy might help?"

She took a small, tentative swallow, willed herself not to retch again, and wished the man would go away, but it seemed he had no intention of doing so. Instead, he found a pile of empty sacks and made a relatively comfortable seat for her in the lee of the wind. He waved the flask aside as she offered it back.

"Keep it. I have no need of it or the brandy within. But there, colour is returning to your cheeks. Perhaps the upset has passed?"

"*Ais*, thank you, I think my stomach has settled now."

"According to various correspondences the authorities have made since these children were put ashore at Gibraltar, most of their families have been traced, so once we reach Falmouth they will be returned to their kin without delay. Only Harriett seems to have no connections."

"She has no one. I have given her employ as my maid, so there is no need for you to concern yourself about her."

Doone disagreed. "We have no information about her. She might not be suitable; you do not wish to take the common poor into your care, surely?"

"She is educated, can read and write, can sew and embroider, so must have had an advantage at some stage of her life, do you not think? Add to that, I like her. She will be suitable."

Ascham Doone made no immediate response, gazed out to sea for a few minutes before commenting, "I could have found a reliable handmaid for you, had you asked."

"I am quite capable of hiring my own servants, but thank you all the same."

Regretting her sharpness, Tiola thought she had better say something else. She looked at him quizzically. "Why are you so concerned about seeing these youngsters safe home? Forgive me, but you do not seem like a man who has affection for children."

Doone fetched his pipe from his pocket, realised he had no tobacco, replaced the pipe. "I have a particular interest in this case, not for the families but for my own status. There is a House of Commons parliament seat here in Cornwall coming available. I have the opportunity of filling it now the present incumbent has decided to retire. I have every chance of winning the seat, as I can be assured of the votes, but the profile of accomplishing worthy deeds shall not come amiss."

Ah, Tiola thought. *That explains a lot.* Said, "So you will, perhaps, reside in Cornwall soon?"

He snorted disdain. "Certainly not! What an absurd notion! Cornwall is only marginally more contemptible than is Devon. I have comfortable apartments in London within a short walk of the Palace of Westminster. I shall only be in Cornwall by necessity come election time, a month maybe in the summer when the stink of London sewage becomes unbearable, or I have invitations from notable worthies for the winter hunting and shooting."

"But will you not have necessity to visit your grandfather, Sir Ailee, on Exmoor?"

"I will not. The man irritates me with his quaint ideas and notions. He should lay aside his Catholic beliefs along with his misplaced politics."

Tiola assumed he was referring to his grandfather's Jacobite tendencies.

Doone confirmed her thoughts. "It is time these old men understood that the Stuart Pretender in exile is not going to return. His cause is dead, their ideas are broken. Who needs worthless ideas when you can run with practical aspiration?"

When Tiola made no comment Doone changed the subject. "I expect you must be eager to see your brother; it has been a while."

A matter of a few months, Tiola thought, but did not wish to prolong this awkward conversation so continued her silence.

"I have writ to him," Doone said. "I believe he is most eager to be reunited with his only sister."

"*Ais,* I expect he is. There were several boys, I was the only daughter." Tiola got to her feet, feigned a smile. "Forgive me, I think

I must brave the bouquet of onions and check that the children are settled. It will be good to see them reunited with their kin."

She bobbed a curtsey and walked towards the open hatchway, paused at the bottom of the ladder leading below to take another sip of the brandy. Hoped this voyage would not be too long, for keeping her tolerance of Doone on an even keel was becoming a hard task.

CHAPTER THIRTY
FALMOUTH, CORNWALL

Sad at their parting, but relieved, Tiola watched the English children run down the gangplank to the shore, smiled broadly as she saw them being scooped into relieved parents' arms. Apparently, the families had been waiting many days for a boat to arrive from Roscoff, but the waiting was now over and the nightmare, for them, ended.

Ascham Doone was there with the joyful parents, revelling in their praise, soaking up the glory. Fortunate for him that none of the English children had died during their long ordeal; perhaps their hard fisherfolk life had made them tougher than the others?

"Doone's well enjoyin' 'imself," Finch said with a sniff of contempt. "Bathing in the attention of bein' a bleedin' 'ero."

"I think his type excel at play acting in the public eye. To be seen as someone who does his best for others, while doing very little at all," Tiola replied, turning to look at Jesamiah's grumpy old steward. Grumpy, aye, but she didn't know what she would have done without him these past weeks.

Finch sniffed again. "'E's all piss and wind, if'n ye ask me. Any 'ow, that's the last of the dunnage ashore. I'll as find somewhere for us for the night then sort out a coach or summat t' take us up t' Appledore."

"Thank you Mr Finch. The Falcon always used to be a good inn, try there first. You have the money I gave you? Good. Mr Doone said my brother would be here, but I cannot see him, although there is quite a crowd gathered on the quay. I will go ashore, see if he's there. Can I leave Hetty and Tom in your care?"

"Aye. Leave all t' me." He touched his forehead, trotted off ashore.

Tiola wrapped her cloak a little tighter around her for the wind, blowing off the sea, was chill. She walked towards the gangplank which was narrow and sloped at an intimidating angle. She hesitated. She was never settled with crowds and more people were pressing onto the quay, the clamour of laughter and shouted joy hurtling up to meet the screaming gulls performing acrobatics beneath the grey clouds overhead. The air smelled of fish and tar, of damp hemp and those wretched onions.

One of the *Mary Charlotte*'s crew came up behind her.

"You going ashore miss? Can I give you m' hand?"

She accepted the assistance, then stood on the cobbled quay, her body continuing to feel the motion of the sea.

Falmouth. She had not expected to return here ever again.

Her childhood had been spent ten miles distant in a small parish. It was unlikely that anyone here would know her – she had rarely come into town back then. And would that gangly, shy little girl be recognisable now as a woman grown? Even so, she pulled her cloak's hood over her head and kept to the shadows.

Somewhere to the left she could hear a preacher quoting the Bible in forceful rhetoric, words of doom and punishment for accumulated sins. She was reminded of her father. He would proclaim the same sinister predictions of God's wrath 'lest ye repent!'. It was beyond her understanding how men could preach fear and prophesy of eternal retribution in direct contrast to the love, comfort and forgiveness that the Christ himself had preached when He had walked in the Holy Land of his birth. Good outmanoeuvred evil, the light chased away the dark, yet these manic preachers managed to turn everything upside down. Where was their compassion, their mercy, their tenderness? Where was the love? These men were driven by their greed for control and power. Not one of them echoed the humility of Christ. They would find the truth one day, when they passed from this life into Beyond, and it would not be the truth they had been expecting.

She shrugged. The corruption within the Church – any church or religion – was not her concern. Finding Carter, her brother, if indeed he was here, was her priority. If she remembered correctly, The Falcon was on the far side of the market square further along the quay. She would start there. She skirted a group of revellers taking advantage of the joyous occasion by celebrating with strong Cornish cider, laughed as an inebriated man took hold of her arm and wanted to dance with her. Politely, she indicated her increasing bulge and declined, squeezed her way through the crush. Another, firmer, hand took her arm, she half-turned, expecting a similar offer. Simultaneously a voice proclaimed, "Sister! Doone has delivered ye to us as he said he would!"

She spun around. Her brother. Not the one she was expecting. She looked into the triumphant, calculating grey eyes of Jed Garrick, her eldest brother, older by a full fifteen years. From his clothing, hat and the Bible clutched in his hand, he had been the bigoted preacher loudly proclaiming a few moments ago.

"So, you have followed in Father's footsteps and devoted yourself to God," Tiola said, trying to mask the sudden fear which was coursing through her body from reaching her voice. Jed had been as frightening to her in childhood as had her father. Of all that man's children, Jed was the apple that fell closest to the tree. The one most alike the father. Arrogant, cruel and opinionated.

"I have indeed, Sister, and I vowed upon my ordination to seek revenge on for his murder."

"Revenge? That particular due was paid by the murder of our mother. You saw to her arrest. You encouraged her hanging."

"She was a witch, the devil's whore. She should have burned in the cleansing fire of justice, not hanged from the common gallows tree. My earthly father tried many times to tame her, turn her to God..."

"He what? He raped her when it pleased him. He beat her so savagely that he broke her ribs, her arm, even when she was heavy with child. Beat her so wickedly that she lost the child."

Jed Garrick ignored her interruption, tightened the grip on her arm. "I have been searching for you, Sister, making enquiries, tracing where you disappeared to. As have, at my insistence, those of the law, for you have charges to answer. Mr Doone has been most obligingly helpful."

"What charges? What nonsense is this?"

Garrick signalled to two burly men, built like lumbering oxen and stinking about the same. Falmouth constables.

"The charge of murder. We have belief that you were complicit with that bloody act our mother committed. And for your part in murdering a father and a priest, Sister, you shall also hang."

CHAPTER THIRTY-ONE
OCTOBER - SAN VINCENTO, SPAIN

"¡Check!" Catalina announced in triumphant Spanish.

Jesamiah grunted. This was the fifth game this week that she had won. And she was only twelve years old, for goodness' sake!

"You're too good for me," he conceded, also in Spanish. The girl spoke no English, which Jesamiah considered to be gross negligence on the part of her parents who had both spoken it very well.

"Papa taught me," she confessed. "He used to let me win at first, but soon realised I was winning anyway." She was silent as she put the chess pieces away in their wooden box. When she looked up, her eyes were glistening with tears.

"I miss him. I miss Mama, my little brother, my sisters..."

Jesamiah shifted on the large, comfortable couch he was sprawled upon, giving her space to sit beside him. He'd been confined to the bed on the other side of the room until four days since. Prior to that, the torn and bruised muscles in his thigh had been too painful and delicate for him to get up and move about, apart from to use the adjoining privy. The leg still hurt abominably, but with the aid of a crutch was not quite so bad now, as long as he moved sparingly and limped slowly. The Spanish physician who had been caring for him had removed the stitches from his face, had said that the resulting scar would fade and the full healing process for his thigh would take some time. The more the patient rested, the quicker that would be. Unfortunately, Jesamiah was an impatient patient.

A breeze blew in from off the sea, ruffling the lace curtains. It was a pleasant room, one he'd had before when he'd been feverish from wounds received; wounds also inflicted by the Spanish. That time, Francesca had nursed him back to health. This was Calderón's house, a grand place resembling a small palace, cool, light and airy, overlooking San Vincento's modest harbour and the imposing fortress on the other side of the bay. From the bed Jesamiah had observed some of the shipping which came and went. Fishing boats, cargo boats. Three Spanish warships, two of them not well sailed and in poor condition. The third had been at anchor for a few days undergoing careening – cleaning of her hull. The *Santa María del Bartolomé*. Jesamiah would recognise her anywhere.

He held out his right arm, inviting his niece to snuggle closer. "Mind m' wounds," he said in Spanish as she curled against him. "I love you lots, sweetheart, but I'll toss you over that balcony beyond the window if you catch my leg."

Catalina attempted a weak smile. "¡I would like to see you try!"

"¡Don't tempt me, Miss!" He brushed his thumb over her cheek, wiping away the tear trail. "Even though I only knew him a short while, your father was a good man. He did not deserve to die as he did. None of them did."

He had told the girl, after she had asked, some of how her parents had been murdered, but had missed out the horrendous details, saying only that they had died honourably and quickly. He knew she did not believe him about the quickly bit, but that was a truth they each kept to themselves.

"Your family physician said I can start doing more walking tomorrow," he said, changing the subject to something more positive. He waved his broken arm about. "This splint's coming off, too. I'll be back to normal soon."

Catalina wriggled closer, mumbled into his chest, "But that will mean you will be leaving."

"Not yet, I still have business to finish. Though I'd be happier to know my wife and my ship are safe and sound."

"¿Shall I ask my uncle if he has any information?"

Before he could answer, the door opened and a well-dressed man of about fifty came into the room. He carried a tray laden with food and a carafe of wine. Tucked beneath one arm, a sheaf of papers secured within a leather folder. An Englishman, but spoke in perfect Spanish.

"Luncheon, sir. And your aunt is looking for you, Miss Catalina. For the same reason. Tidy yourself and fetch your sisters. I believe they are playing in the garden. Make sure they wash their hands and comb their hair. You too, of course."

Reluctantly, Catalina got to her feet. Out of eight offspring only the three girls had survived the ordeal of kidnap: Catalina and her twin seven-year-old sisters. Outside of Jesamiah himself, only the three girls to continue the paternal family line, to inherit and to keep the memory of two wonderful people alive. It was a burden the young girl knew she had to carry, and Jesamiah's heart ached for her. Most of her cousins who had been stolen away with her had survived, a relief for their parents – brothers and sisters of Catalina's mother – but a cruelty of fact to the orphaned girl herself.

"Off you go," Jesamiah said. "And no squabbling with your sisters during luncheon, you know it vexes your aunt."

"Everything vexes my aunt," Catalina grumbled as she dawdled towards the door. Jesamiah agreed with her, but did not dare say so.

The man set the tray down on the table next to Jesamiah, the folder of papers beside it, then opened the door for the girl, closed it behind her.

In English, Jesamiah said, "I don't know how that lass is going to cope with the life that is now ahead of her." He peered under the linen cloth to see what he had been brought to eat. It looked edible. Although he was none too keen on Spanish food – too much fish; he had enough of that at sea – this was not cooked from anything that once had scales, a shell or too many arms, though. It was meat, good, honest, meat.

The man also answered in English, a clear, educated, Surrey accent. "She is like her father, sir. She will manage."

"Perhaps, Alfred, but I worry about her. Anyway, have any dispatches or letters come from Gibraltar or England for me?"

Jesamiah asked. He asked at least three times a day. Always received the same answer.

"No, sir. Nothing."

"My letters were sent out?" He asked that on a daily basis, too.

"Yes sir. I saw to their dispatch myself."

Alfred – he only used that one name, although he had not divulged or explained why – had been Calderón's personal private secretary for many years, and appeared happy to be continuing his role for Jesamiah. It was that or find himself out of a job, which he would be once Jesamiah left.

"But no replies yet?"

"No, sir."

Jesamiah had dictated several letters to Alfred – each only containing his own requirements; he did not want to be accused of spying or tittle-tattling secrets. A letter to Skylark in Gibraltar, care of the tavern he should be staying at; a letter to the master shipbuilder enquiring about *Sea Witch*. Three letters to Tiola who should, by now, be safe with her brother, Carter, in North Devon. One to Carter himself, telling him to take especial care of Tiola. And one to Squire John Benson praising young Thomas and indicating that he'd be happy to have the lad aboard again. It had been several weeks now since the first ones had been sent. He should have heard *something* back from one of the recipients, surely?

Jesamiah tucked into the dish of food: *Jamón Iberico*, cured black pig ham that over a period of months had been salted and dried. Served as thin, tender slices with chunks of buttered bread it proved to be a delicious mid-day meal. Grinning, Jesamiah reached for the second dish, one he had already expressed as a favourite, remembered from his Virginia childhood: *Natillas de Leche*, a spiced egg custard that his mother had asked their cook to make. An old recipe tracing back through the centuries, and believed to have originated from the kitchens of Spanish nunneries. He ran his finger round the empty dish, licked the residue then poured himself more wine, offered some to Alfred who refused.

"Not while I am working, sir."

"And is there any further news of Captain Vernon and the crew of the *Bonne Chance*?"

"None that I am aware of since the last report about them, sir. The men are still being held within the Castillo de San Marcos, the fortress converted from the remains of a Moorish mosque on the banks of the Guadalete River, about six miles to the north-east of Cádiz. I believe they continue to have certain licence to roam and are treated adequately. The agreement of parole remains intact. The officers have the freedom of El Puerto de Santa María during the hours of daylight, but are not to venture beyond the town, and are to return to the fortress by dusk. If they do not, the lives of the men of the crew, who do not have as much freedom having to remain within the fortress, but are not confined to cells, shall be forfeit. Ransom has been suggested for the officers, I believe, but it seems Captain Vernon has refused compliance unless all of his crew are included."

"And they are held there because the river is now only populated by cargo ships trading the famous Spanish sherry? The strength – or lack of it – of the Spanish Navy cannot be spied upon because the fleet, such as it is, is at Cádiz?"

"Precisely so, sir."

"And the *Bonne Chance*?"

"It has been commandeered by that same Spanish Navy."

Jesamiah laughed. "Have they the skill to sail her?"

"Probably not, sir."

"So. These papers?" Jesamiah pointed at the leather folder.

Alfred removed the tray of empty dishes and opened the folder. "These," he said handing a few to Jesamiah, "are the last of the invoiced statements. Legitimate trade with merchants in Portugal, France, England and the colonies. As we have already established, these past weeks, the señor's business was thriving. It is a worthwhile investment."

"Except, as I have already said, I don't want the business, despite having made agreement to become a partner."

"Full owner now, sir. Señor Calderón had left his half to his son. With no son surviving I think it likely the entire ownership should, legally, become yours."

"Except, de León, the eldest brother of Calderón's deceased wife, believes it should all become his."

Alfred formed one of his rare smiles and slightly inclined his head. "Which is why, Captain Acorne, we have so diligently scoured my deceased master's paperwork to ascertain what is what so that you can bargain about the estate and the business to suit you, when it suits you."

Jesamiah grinned back. "Aye, that's what we've been doing on the face of it, but privately we've looked for things that we are *not* going to divulge to anyone."

Alfred nodded agreement. "Precisely so, sir." He handed over another few papers. "This is the final tally for Señor Calderón's other legitimate business. Profitable but, although it is not my place to remark upon it, somewhat distasteful."

Jesamiah looked at the papers, at the columns of Alfred's neatly written figures. Bought, sold, profit. Slaves. Black African slaves. "I see the last lot of the poor buggers set sail the week the Barbary pirates attacked?"

"Yes, sir."

"No more were bought or sold on?"

"No, sir."

"Your doing?"

Alfred tinged slightly with pink embarrassment. "I'm afraid so sir. I do not hold with slavery."

"Neither do I, so no need to stow the facts away from me." Jesamiah studied the second sheet, wrinkling his nose in disgust at the marked up monetary gain at the expense of human suffering. He slapped the paper down. "Doone. He was selling to Doone?"

"Along with the legal wine and fruit, oranges, lemons and such, sir, yes. I believe Sir Ailee Doone sold the slaves on to various Bristol merchants to maximise his own profit. Buy, sell, but not have the onerous burden of shipping them to the Americas."

"Bastard," Jesamiah muttered. Said louder, "So this is all of it? All the legal stuff is now collated and sorted?"

"It is, sir."

"And the rest?"

Alfred retained his solemn expression as he gave Jesamiah the last, thick, bundle of paperwork. More columns of figures, bought, sold, profit, but they listed different things from the official items. Dutch genever. Brandy, French lace, tea, spices, expensive rare dyes.

All smuggled goods, alongside the dates and names of the sellers and the recipients.

Jesamiah glanced through, smiling occasionally as he recognised a name. Finally, he folded most of the papers in half and handed them back to Alfred. "These for burning I think, along with the other bundle I saw this morning. I can remember what – who – I need to remember."

"Those this morning have already been disposed of, sir. These will follow shortly."

"And that's it then?"

"That is it, sir. Señor Calderón's study is bereft of anything incriminating, of anything that should not be there, and of anything that no one else should read or possess. Those last papers, though, sir, that you still hold in your hand?"

"Are for me to keep and for you to forget about."

"Duly forgotten, sir."

It had taken these several weeks to sift through and read everything of a dubious nature. Clearing the deck of anything that could incriminate the good name of Jesamiah's kindred and friends. Not that it mattered, now, to them, but for the sake of the three surviving girls Jesamiah had wanted to ensure that nothing troublesome remained. And there were some items which would be useful for his own, confidential, knowledge. Alfred, loyal to Calderón for many years, had been wholeheartedly complicit, although Jesamiah did wonder how much of his helpfulness had been for his own protection. It was unlikely that he'd not received generous reward for ongoing silence.

With everything that the business, or Jesamiah had no use of, gone up in smoke, only ashes remained. If Tearle, the Doones, Spymaster Harley or any other nosy sod wanted evidence of wrongdoing they were going to be unlucky.

Only one question remained unasked.

"Alfred?"

"Sir?" Alfred paused while collecting together the debris of luncheon.

"What do you know of Señora Francesca Escudero?"

Alfred smiled. "A fine woman, sir, I was saddened to learn of her death. She was a guest here quite often, a good friend of my master's. But you know this from your previous stay here."

"I mean what do you *know* of her?"

"Nothing beyond what I have already indicated. She was a kind, generous woman."

"And a good spy."

Tucking the bundle of papers beneath his arm, Alfred lifted the luncheon tray. "I couldn't say, sir."

Couldn't or wouldn't? Jesamiah thought. Realised he was not going to get anywhere with this particular line of conversation – perhaps a good thing for it did emphasise Alfred's loyalty and discretion.

Jesamiah said instead, "See to the disposal of those papers, then invite this Señor de León to a meeting. I have one or two business proposals to put to him."

"Very good, sir. I will add, sir, that Señor Calderón held Señora Escudero in very high esteem."

Jesamiah nodded. "So did I, Alfred. So did I."

CHAPTER THIRTY-TWO

Señor Rafael Celestino de León was a man who liked to get his own way. So did Jesamiah. The difference, de León expected to achieve his aim through no one questioning his self-assumed position of authority and his dogmatic bullying; Jesamiah was prepared to bargain for it.

"I believe I have you to thank for arranging my parole. I sincerely thank you, Señor de León," Jesamiah said in Spanish, after Alfred had poured coffee for both men and discreetly retired from Calderón's study, although Jesamiah had no doubt that he was listening from beyond the not quite closed door.

De León, having no English, also spoke in Spanish. "It was my wife's niece who insisted. Catalina persisted in ensuring your release. It was unfortunate that the *Santa María del Bartolomé* was under the impression that you were the kidnappers of our children, not their rescuers."

"Someone gave out irresponsible information. I would like to know who that someone was." Jesamiah said this to be polite. He had a good idea who the someone could have been, Doone, but that was not a relevant subject to discuss with de León. "The thing is, I have certain interests that I need to take care of, interests that I can only take care of by remaining as owner of this merchant wine company."

"You are not the legal owner. My deceased brother-in-law merely, and unwisely, offered you a partnership."

"A partnership I agreed to. A partnership legally contracted. And a partnership which clearly states in legal jargon, that the other half of that agreed partnership reverts to the other half's nearest kin in the event of the other half's death. And you, Señor, are not Calderón's nearest 'other half' kin."

"Nor, Capitán, are you."

Jesamiah sipped his coffee. Why couldn't Finch make it taste this good? "Sí, you are right, I am not, but the nearest kin is a twelve-year-old girl. She should inherit."

De León blustered into his coffee and set the cup down on the table next to him. "¿A girl to inherit? ¡That is ridiculous!"

"Sí, I agree to that also, so therefore, by default, I am the nearest kin as I am his only nephew." *Got you, you bugger,* Jesamiah thought.

"I will never agree to such a thing. You will be hearing from my lawyers." The Spaniard rose from his chair, one of the comfortable pair that sat either side of an ornate marble fireplace. Not that there was a lit fire, not with the sun outside climbing steadily towards its noon zenith. Winter evenings were a different matter.

"Oh, we can both bandy our lawyers about, pay them an excessive fee and end up none the better for it. Sit down, señor and give me the courtesy of listening to what I have to say."

Snorting a huff of contempt, de León sat.

"I want to retain my partnership because the three girls, especially the eldest, Catalina, need an inheritance. They now have no parents to see to their welfare. The least we can do, as their devoted kindred, is ensure they have a secure future and dowry enough for a good marriage."

Reluctantly, de León shrugged agreement.

Jesamiah stretched his injured leg, winced at the protesting muscles. It had taken great effort to descend the stairs to this study, leaning heavily on his crutch, the banisters or Alfred's arm, but an upstairs bedroom, no matter how luxurious and delightful was not an appropriate venue to bargain for the future security of Calderón's three daughters. "I also appreciate," Jesamiah went on, "that your share of income from Calderón's wine trade is of importance to you and your family. You have investment in it, have enjoyed the benefits of a share of the profits for many years."

"I worked alongside my brother-in-law, may God ensure the eternal rest and peace of his soul." The man crossed himself. "I have no intention of losing all for the likes of you."

Going to cross his legs at the knee, and instantly realising that was not a good idea, Jesamiah covered the resulting indrawn breath of pain with a cough. "Now, there you go again with the negative insults señor. You only had a minor role in running the business; your 'work' as you put it, did not involve much effort. However, I would not dream of seeing you, or your dear wife and delightful children made destitute." A lie. Jesamiah could not care less about the prospects of this pompous oaf. As far as he was concerned he could go rot, but that would be of no help to Catalina or her sisters. "As inherited owner, I have the power to make new decisions. I want to grant you direct ownership of one quarter of the company."

De León did not even attempt to disguise his astonishment.

Jesamiah nodded. "*Mm-hmm,* you heard aright. One quarter will become entirely yours, if you agree to my conditional terms."

"¿Which are?"

"Mutually agreed and contracted agreements for Catalina to jointly inherit half of the business upon her coming of age, or her marriage, whichever comes first."

Another blustered snort. "¡I am not prepared to relinquish my ownership…!"

"*My* half. I will pass joint ownership to her in order to ensure that things continue to be run correctly. The fourth quarter is to be jointly owned by the two younger sisters – and again, myself."

"That is three quarters for you."

"It is, but my control is to ensure that any money-grubbing prospective husbands don't grab the assets. Again, all this with conditions, of course."

"¿What conditions?"

Jesamiah ticked them off on his fingers. "One. Catalina and her sisters are to remain within this house, their home, with suitably employed servants and tutors at least until they marry – even then,

Catalina will retain sole ownership. Two. In my absence, Alfred is to be their guardian and carer. He is also, in my absence, to be appointed as managerial secretary with full responsibility for the business."

"I object to that. He is a servant."

"He is a trusted and trustworthy employee of the family, and now also employed by me. His continuation here is non-negotiable." Jesamiah paused, allowed his guest to huff, puff and pout a little. "Three. There is to be no trade, whatsoever, in slavery."

"Slaves make good profit."

"That they might but I do not buy or sell human beings. No slave trading."

De León shrugged, reluctantly agreed.

"Four. When Catalina and her sisters are of age and receive their share of the business I will relinquish my main interest, but remain as an absent partner for fifteen percent of the profits."

"¡Too much!"

"Very well, ten. Final amount."

De León opened his mouth to protest again, but Jesamiah cut him short. "Item five. I want a suitable ship to take me to Gibraltar. The *Bonne Chance* will be suitable."

De León grunted loudly. "I have nothing to do with shipping. I have no idea where this vessel is."

Jesamiah waved a hand dismissively. "You only need to pay the right people to find out. Item six. The captain, officers and crew of said vessel are to be released and returned to her."

"¡That will be impossible!"

"You have one week to arrange it."

"¡I cannot do this. What you ask is absurd!"

"You are a de León. I have been told that the de Leóns hold great influence over certain dignitaries and nobles. Over the governor of Cádiz, the admiralty and even the king. But perhaps I have been misinformed. Seven. I want my letters. I suspect correspondence that has been sent to me has been intercepted, read and withheld. I want it returned. By this evening."

"I know nothing of your letters, nor can I get you this ship the *Bonne Chance*."

"You, personally, may not know of my letters, but I'm sure you know, or suspect, who does."

Grumbling beneath his breath, de León shuffled uncomfortably in his chair, then asked, "¿And besides a measly one quarter share, what else do I get?"

Jesamiah grinned. "Me gone from here. That should be incentive enough. As for the ship, if you cannot locate *Bonne Chance* I'll settle for any vessel as long as it is seaworthy. You have until next Friday. If these conditions are not met by then I shall take the entire household to England and sell the business to someone I know in Lisbon."

"¡You cannot do that!"

"I can, and I will."

Jesamiah could do as he threatened, and de León knew it. He blustered some more, stated that he would think on it and left, aware that if he wanted to maintain the generous income he was used to, he would need to agree and arrange what he could as soon as he could.

CHAPTER THIRTY-THREE

"So, who is the fellow I am to meet this evening?" Jesamiah asked Alfred, more than a week later, as they finished the splendid lamb cutlet dinner the cook had prepared for them.

Alfred sipped his glass of cognac, enjoying the food, the drink and the company. And his new elevated position of what basically came down to being the head of household in addition to business manager. He had assured Jesamiah that he would not let him, the memory of Calderón or the surviving daughters – particularly the daughters – down. Jesamiah had answered that he was glad to hear it, otherwise he would never have promoted him to the job.

Alfred explained as best he could about the arranged meeting. "His name is Monsieur Ber'ell, some sort of wealthy foreign exiled nobleman who keeps himself to himself. He has recently returned from Seville, I believe, otherwise he would have sought to meet you before now. He resides somewhere private here in San Vincento. He has done business with Señor Calderón in the past: slaves, smuggling, other dubious entities. Beyond that, I know little of him."

Ber'ell? Could this be the man Doone thought was called Burell? The man Jesamiah was supposed to kill, but had no intention of doing so unless he had a good, personal, reason. "Calderón trusted him?" he asked.

"Depends on what you mean by trust. Trust him with certain business arrangements, then probably, yes. Trust him to refrain from slitting your throat in a dark alley? No."

"I know plenty of people like that," Jesamiah remarked. Grinned. "Me included."

"I do suggest that you take a couple of attendants with you, sir."

"I can look after myself."

Alfred gestured towards the crutch propped against a chair and at the linen sling folded on the table, then at Jesamiah's arm, now without the cumbersome splint. "You can manage a hobbled walk, and that arm, although mended, should be resting within that sling. Just how do you intend to fight if you need to?"

"I'll manage."

"You'll be dead. Then where will the girls and your wife be?"

"Probably better off!" Jesamiah jested, then conceded that Alfred was right. "You can come too, then."

"Me? Oh, no sir, I have no ability to fight. Even a spider scuttling across the floor causes me to faint."

"The size of some of 'em I ain't surprised," Jesamiah teased. "I'll be fine. We are meeting in a tavern. I am going to this tavern – and coming back again – by means of a carriage, which will have a driver."

"I'll ensure a footman as well."

Jesamiah sighed. "Very well, a discreetly armed footman. How do I recognise this Frenchman?"

"I am not certain that he is French, he just seems to be known as 'Monsieur'. He will find you, I believe."

"Any word from de León? Any replies to my sent letters turned up?"

"Not one. I do agree it is most odd, but Spain has never had reliable mail, especially where anything connected to England is concerned."

"Well, de León's time is up tomorrow. Let's see what transpires."

The ornate clock on the mantelpiece tinged the quarter hour past nine. Jesamiah checked his pocket watch – Calderón's watch. As with the clothes he wore, slightly altered by a skilled tailor to fit, weaponry, and a few other items he fancied Tiola would like, Jesamiah had claimed several items for his own use.

"I'd better get going, then," he said. "I don't want to keep this fellow waiting."

"No, sir. And sir...? Be careful."

CHAPTER THIRTY-FOUR

La Negra Paloma, the Black Dove, was a discreet taverna on the edge of the town. Only a short ride in the carriage, but too far for Jesamiah to walk there and back. He'd considered leaving his crutch in the carriage, decided against on the grounds that he would look more the fool tipping arse over head if his thigh gave way. He did abandon the sling, however, even though his arm was stubbornly stiff and ached like a raging headache. The carriage driver remained with his horses and vehicle, the footman propped up the bar although Jesamiah had warned him, with stern words, that if he got drunk, he would be out of a job come home time.

Jesamiah sat at a table in a discreet, shadowed corner, a jug of wine and two glasses set before him. The taverna was busy, but not overcrowded, the clientele gentlemen who sat talking in groups or playing cards. In addition to the landlord, a lanky, surly fellow, there was a young potboy and a spot-faced youth helping to clear tables. There didn't seem to be any women around. A male domain? Men seeking molly boys, not petticoated tarts? Not the sort of place Jesamiah usually frequented.

A few minutes passed. He sipped at his glass of wine. A tall, elegant, slim, heavily cloaked man, his hat pulled well down over his eyes, entered the tavern, paused just inside the door, removed chamois leather gloves as he looked around. He walked towards Jesamiah, pulled out the chair opposite, and sat. He removed his hat, laid it with his gloves upon the table, helped himself to a glass of wine. Dark haired, pale skinned, deep lavender-coloured eyes.

"*Tu es monsieur Ber'ell*?" Jesamiah queried in not very good French – he hadn't spoken the language in quite a while.

"Just Ber'ell. I am not French. I have been wanting to meet you, Mister Acorne, for some while now." He spoke in English. A slight, unplaceable accent, but good English.

"*Captain* Acorne. And that makes two of us. I was hired to look for you. To kill you."

Ber'ell raised one eyebrow, chuckled low beneath his breath. "I doubt you would succeed."

Jesamiah doubted it too. This man was...? He didn't know what he was, although he had a shrewd idea.

"May I ask, *Captain,* who hired you? I trust he paid you a suitable fee for endangering your own life?"

"He hasn't paid me at all. He dabbles in blackmail. I don't subscribe to his swaggering extortion. His name is Doone. Ascham Doone. Know him?"

The man sat back in his chair, crossed his legs. "I have heard of him. I do not regard him as much of a challenge."

"Nor do I."

Ber'ell raised his glass in the gesture of an agreeable toast. "If I paid you to kill him, would you be interested in taking the contract?"

"Nope. When I kill Ascham Doone it will be for my own satisfaction, no one else's."

"Fair enough. I believe you are looking for reliable trade arrangements? Might I ask the details? Although I must emphasise, my share of any profit is high.

"I'm continuing Calderón's business on behalf of his daughters. But for now, I require someone for a different task. Someone able to travel fast to Devon, England. Someone who can be handy with sword and pistol if need be. Would you know of anyone?"

"I might. Why is this someone needed?"

"To ensure that my wife is safe. And kept safe, while I concentrate on getting my ship back."

Ber'ell refilled his wine glass, leant forward to refill Jesamiah's. "Your wife? Tiola Oldstagh. The Wise Woman, the White Witch."

Jesamiah felt his throat go dry and a dribble of sweat trickle down the small of his back but he managed to keep his face passive. No one alive, save himself, knew what Tiola was. No one except perhaps the sort of creatures who were near to her own kind? But Doone had hinted. How had he found out? Through this fellow who oozed charm and politeness on the surface, but underneath stank of danger and malice? Or from...? A thought came to Jesamiah's mind, and a few puzzles were partly answered.

"Tiola Oldstagh is another I would like to kill," Ber'ell said, not noticing the pause or silence. "She murdered a dear friend of mine."

"My wife does not murder people."

Ber'ell raised an eyebrow again. "You do not know her as well as you think you do, then. She also destroyed the Arab mutant, Yakub Pasha."

"His ship blew up. The gunpowder exploded."

"Ignited by the power your wife possesses. But I do not refer to him; his mind had twisted many years ago, making him a liability. One of us would have killed him eventually; your wife got to him first."

"One of us?" Jesamiah asked. "One of your kind you mean, not mine? Would this friend have the name of Maha'dun by any chance? My wife did not kill him, the Arab did."

"No, I talk of my friend, Cara'mina. Her mind was twisted too, but I could control her. Your wife did not need to slaughter her in the way she did."

Jesamiah stared at him. So, this Ber'ell had not queried the name Maha'dun? And who was this Cara'mina? He'd never heard of her. "If my wife did kill this person," he said slowly, "she would have had good reason."

"I believe she did have a reason – a good one, in her opinion. Not in mine, however. Cara'mina tried to kill your wife by setting fire to, and destroying, a house. In doing so she killed the wrong people. But that was Cara'mina for you. Careless of detail. 'Hot headed', I think your human term is."

Not able to control the intake of shocked breath, Jesamiah

clenched his right fist. That night had been a terrible night. He'd had no idea of the cause of the fire which had burned a house to the ground and killed two people. How did this Ber'ell know of it? "In which case," he rasped by way of an answer, "my wife has my entire blessing." He wasn't sure if that was the truth, but he was too loyal to say any different.

He tried again about Maha'dun. "Do you know where Maha'dun is?"

Ber'ell shrugged. "You said he was dead. He means nothing to me."

"But you do know of him?"

"He is disloyal and a traitor."

Jesamiah pushed his chair back, got to his feet. "I do not think I can do business with you, Ber'ell, but I might consider doing Doone the favour of complying with his request, should I get chance."

"Then you must take that chance soon, Acorne. For you are the dead man, not I."

Jesamiah walked as dignified as he could towards the door, prodding his supposed bodyguard with his crutch as he passed the bar. "We're done here, go tell the driver to fetch the carriage round."

The man shrugged, left, Jesamiah limping in his wake, but the landlord suddenly stood in his way.

In gruff Spanish, accused, "That man said you were paying the bill. Pay up."

Jesamiah didn't bother arguing, felt in his pocket for coins and slapped them down on the counter. At the door he turned to look back at Ber'ell.

He wasn't there, but a rear door was swinging closed.

CHAPTER THIRTY-FIVE

Jesamiah waited outside, fuming, for five minutes. No protective footman. No carriage. He did get propositioned by an overweight man who stank of garlic, but his growl was enough to see him off. The whole evening had been a waste of time. All this Ber'ell had wanted was to size Jesamiah up – and now, because of the crutch, knew he would be as easy to kill as a rat snared in a trap.

"Where's that bloody carriage?" Tired of waiting, Jesamiah hobbled towards a side alley – his senses alert, his left hand clasped, as well as his stiff fingers could, around the butt of a pistol tucked discreetly into his waistband.

He could smell fresh dung, found the horses waiting patiently, harnessed to the carriage. The driver looked to be asleep in his seat.

"Oi! Wake up you wastrel!" Jesamiah shouted, realised he'd spoken in English, repeated his anger in Spanish. He hurried forward, raised his crutch intending to poke the man awake. Tripped over something beside the front wheel, almost fell. In the dim light from a feeble torch in a wall sconce, discovered the body of the footman. His throat cut. Blood was still running from the wound, his body was still twitching.

Movement behind. Jesamiah pivoted as best he could; without thinking about it, swung the crutch as if it were one of the willow bats that Thomas Benson so enjoyed using for the game of cricket when ashore.

A thump, a hiss of pain and anger, and a figure crumpled to the ground in a tangle of cloak and foreign curses. Without hesitation Jesamiah stamped the crutch downward, heard a distinct crunch of bone as it slammed into the attacker's skull.

Breathing heavily, face contorted as his thigh screamed protest, Jesamiah leant against the carriage wheel, his forehead on his crooked arm. He felt sick.

"You are getting slow and fat, old man," said a voice behind him.

"I've a bloody half-healed injury. It's nothing to do with speed or weight."

"If you say so."

A dull *whoosh*, the sound of moving air... A thud, a splintering of flesh, crunch of bone and sinew.

Jesamiah turned slowly to look. A man with dishevelled black hair, tall, slim, wearing a none too clean velvet coat with several buttons missing, a torn lace cravat and even less immaculate white shirt, was crouched, searching through the coat pockets of his dead victim. He took an iron key and a pouch of coins, put them in his own pocket and, straightening up, noticed the spatter of blood on his boots and black breeches. Tutting, he wiped at the stains, making them worse.

"Where did the axe come from?" Jesamiah asked, nodding towards the grotesquely bloodied weapon dropped from the man's hand and now lying on the bloodied cobbles. "And did you need to decapitate him? There's enough mess here as it is."

"I stole it from a workman's shed because I figured I would need it, and yes, the only way to ensure a bastard like Ber'ell stays dead is to ensure he stays dead. Our kind can heal from most wounds, but we can't regenerate organs or limbs, nor regrow or re-attach our heads. I've been waiting a long time to be rid of Ber'ell." He paused, grinned. "It's good to see you, Jesamiah."

Jesamiah held out his hand, changed his mind and enveloped his friend, Maha'dun, in a hug that would put a bear to shame.

CHAPTER THIRTY-SIX

An hour to summon the Spanish equivalent of law enforcement constables, for Jesamiah to explain – complain – about his footman and driver being slain, of repeating several times that no, he was not responsible for beheading the third victim. That protection was abysmal in this town... By blustering censure Jesamiah managed to deflect too many awkward questions, and eventually, when the bodies were removed, hire a temporary replacement driver for the carriage. He'd considered whether he could drive it himself, but climbing onto the high seat and then handling the tangle of the lengths of all those leather reins did not appeal.

The nearest church clock was striking midnight as Jesamiah settled himself wearily into the carriage, his stomach leaping as it unsteadily lurched forward – a replacement driver, yes, but not a very experienced one, it seemed. The door on the other side opened and a figure tumbled in, slammed the door shut and sat opposite Jesamiah, grinning.

"They never look in the shadows, these imbecile law people. Had I been the assassin I could have easily cut the throats of all of you."

"You *were* the assassin. You cut that monster's head off." Jesamiah contradicted.

"Him, yes, but he doesn't count. He killed the other two. Would have killed you had I not been keeping watch on you."

"On me? You were doing no such thing!"

Maha'dun wriggled, ill at ease, acknowledged, "Well, no, actually I was following Ber'ell. Could have knocked me over with a cannon ball when I saw you sitting there with him!"

"You mean 'knocked me over with a feather'. Why didn't you contact me earlier? Why didn't you let me know you are alive? And where the fok have you *been* all this time?"

"Why would I be knocked over with a feather? That's ridiculous."

"It's an expression."

"Well, it's a stupid one."

Jesamiah sighed. A few minutes in a carriage together and already he was remembering why Maha'dun could be so utterly irritating.

However, Maha'dun did not have opportunity to pursue the incongruities of ridiculous expressions as the carriage was already at the gates to Calderón's small but affluent estate. The horses trotted up the gravel drive, were halted with a loud Spanish version of "Whoa!" at the front door. Alfred was there, lantern in hand, worried expression on his face. He stepped forward to open the carriage door, was surprised to see a companion with Jesamiah. Held the lantern higher to see better.

"Is this Monsieur Ber'ell, sir? He does not look very French."

"No, Alfred, this is a good friend of mine, Maha'dun. Ber'ell did not turn out to be as useful as I had hoped."

"I am sorry to hear that, but not entirely surprised."

"Did you know that Yakub Pasha passed trade information from Ber'ell to Ascham Doone and vicey versey?" Maha'dun said as he climbed down from the carriage. Alfred's nose wrinkled disdainfully at his tawdry state of appearance.

"You know this for fact?" Jesamiah queried, sceptically.

"I do," Maha'dun answered, deliberately staring back at Alfred with an intimidating, hostile expression.

"In that case," Jesamiah said as he put a hand on Maha'dun's shoulder to ease himself down from the carriage, "I'm glad you took the bugger's head off." He gazed at Alfred. "I take it you were not, by any chance, dropping me into the shit with this Ber'ell?"

Alfred immediately conveyed a mixture of affrontery and horror. "I most certainly was not!"

"Are you going to believe him?" Maha'dun asked.

"Any reason why I shouldn't?" Jesamiah answered.

Maha'dun studied Alfred a moment, his eyes narrowed, head to one side. Shrugged. "Ber'ell wanted you dead last time you were here, Jes, so I guess not."

"I have been loyal to this family for many years, and intend to remain so." Alfred disdainfully returned Maha'dun's scrutiny, then looked at Jesamiah. "Would you like me to arrange a bath and clean clothes for your guest, sir?"

"That can wait," Jesamiah answered abruptly, knowing that any clothes Alfred could find would not satisfy the fastidious Maha'dun. "A couple of large brandies will suffice for now. We need to talk as a priority." He led the way to the study, thumped into one of the comfortable fireside chairs, winced and rubbed at his aching thigh.

"How did you get that?" Maha'dun asked, seating himself in the opposite chair and accepting the generously filled glass which Alfred offered him. "That scar on your face? It adds a certain distinction."

"Long story. Yours first."

"Will that be all, sir?" Alfred asked, masking a yawn.

"Aye, go seek your bed. We can look after ourselves."

"Very good, sir, but would you like me to prepare a room for your guest, first?"

"No need," Maha'dun said, patting the pocket where he had put the iron key. "I have acquired suitable accommodation."

Once they were alone together, Maha'dun took several large sips of his drink before launching into an explanation. "When I gained consciousness, I found myself in an open coffin in a church. I slipped away before dawn, left Gibraltar behind and wandered for a bit along the Spanish coast. Eventually came to the mouth of the Guadalquivir River. Stayed there for a few weeks, toyed with going upriver to Seville, or eastward to the mountains, but eventually came back to Cádiz instead, and then to Gibraltar again." He took a gulp of the brandy, rolled it around his mouth, savouring the taste, inspected his broken and dirty nails. "I was missing *Sea Witch*. I thought, perhaps, there might be something similar in an English harbour. Something that could take me away to a new life in the New World."

"But you came back to San Vincento?"

Maha'dun continued to inspect his nails, then looked at Jesamiah, anguish in his eyes. "Well, yes, I heard you were here, and I was worried. Once Ber'ell discovered you..." He flapped a hand, not wishing to explain the obvious.

"How did you hear I was here?"

"From Skylark."

Jesamiah sat forward, excitement lighting his face. "Skylark?"

"Yes."

"When was this?"

"A couple of weeks ago. Where is Tiola, by the way? I do not sense her presence here."

"She's in England, Devon. She is expecting our child."

Maha'dun beamed delight. "But that is wonderful!"

"Yes. How did Skylark know that I am here?"

Maha'dun shrugged. "I never asked."

"Did Skylark get my letter, then? Why no answer! And where was *Sea Witch*?"

"In the water, where else would she be?"

"*Where* – in what water?"

"In the water water!" Maha'dun snapped, irritated at what he considered stupid questions that he could not answer. He stood, made a half-apologetic gesture. "Look, I need to bathe and rid myself of this disgusting apparel. I have the key to Ber'ell's home, I will find all I need there."

Jesamiah too, stood. "And you know this because...?"

Again, Maha'dun shrugged. "Because I used to live there. I was his lover, although there was no love involved. He treated me like a slave – worse than a slave. He was cruel. I took great, overdue, delight in killing him."

Jesamiah patted Maha'dun's arm as a gesture of sympathetic understanding. There was not much he could say, for fear that if he spoke the building emotion would catch in his throat and tears of compassion would show in his eyes. This man – although Maha'dun was not a man, he was a non-human creature who looked like a man – was the most irresponsible, irritating, idiot he had ever known.

But he loved him like an irritating, irresponsible, idiot of a younger brother.

CHAPTER THIRTY-SEVEN

Jesamiah had slept badly. Thoughts insisted on tumbling around in his head, thoughts of his ship, his crew, Tiola, Maha'dun – the fact that he could so easily have been killed last night. Added to that his thigh ached and he could not get comfortable. Soon after dawn he gave up, dressed and went downstairs, seeking breakfast.

Alfred appeared, informed him that it was early but he would rouse the servants to provide something to eat from the kitchens, and that the young ladies were still sound asleep.

"Will the gentleman from last night be joining us?" he inquired.

"Probably not until this evening. He is a night creature, has some sort of skin condition that is exacerbated by sunlight. Bread and cheese will do for me. And coffee."

"Lots of coffee," said a voice from beyond the window, as the curtains moved aside and Maha'dun stepped over the low sill. He was dressed in the traditional Moroccan garb of the djellaba covering his entire body, though a glimpse of shirt could be seen at neck and wrists. On his feet, fine leather babouche. He unwound a corner of the keffiyeh covering his face, the scarf-like headdress held in place by an agal, a length of black cord made of goat hair and worn doubled to keep the head covering firmly in place. He brought his gloved palms together, made a respectful bow. "I trust you have no objection, but I have left my luggage in the courtyard outside. Someone will be able to transfer it from the cart for me?"

"Of course. You all right out here in daylight? I don't usually see you until dusk."

"Needs must, Jes, needs must. Besides, I've been using a potion for my skin. A gypsy woman somewhere along the coast gave it me. It seems to work, though I will need more of it soon. I'm hoping Lady Tiola will be able to provide it, what with her knowledge of this sort of thing."

"The gentleman is staying, then?" Alfred looked in Jesamiah's direction, one eyebrow raised in uncertainty. "Does he also desire breakfast?"

Maha'dun shook his head. "I am grateful for the offer, but no thank you. As for staying, are we not to go to England to fetch Lady Tiola?"

Again, Jesamiah was reminded just how tedious his friend could be. "I haven't a ship. Without a ship, getting to England could be a little problematic. Unless you want to walk or swim all the way?"

Maha'dun was puzzled. "Would it not be a long walk? And I am not a very good swimmer, but if you insist I will try my best. What's wrong with the ship in the harbour, though? The one that threw its anchor thingy over the side a short while ago?"

"What ship?" Jesamiah hobbled to the window, brushed the curtains aside. Stood, staring, astonished, at his beautiful, beautiful, *Sea Witch*, riding at anchor in the bay.

"I received your letters," Skylark explained an hour later, as he sat at the dining room table consuming a hearty breakfast along with Jesamiah. Maha'dun had opted for only coffee, which he laced with a generous dose of cognac from a leather hipflask. "I replied that the repairs were almost completed and we hoped to sail on or around the fourteenth day of October. We were delayed by a Spaniard hanging around – no siege yet, by the way – but a couple of the Navy ships went out and saw her off, so here we are. A tad short of crew, enough to sail, but not enough should we get ourselves into a

Chase. I used your ploy to get here, had Calderón's colours flying from everywhere we could."

The relief Jesamiah felt was overwhelming. "We'll get more men," he said with a wide grin. "Alfred, did that de León sea slug sort out the release of Captain Vernon and his crew?"

Alfred topped up Maha'dun's coffee. The fellow seemed to drink gallons of it. "Not as far as I am aware, sir. Shall I enquire?"

"If you please. Is everything else in order for you to take over here as soon as I leave?"

"It is, sir. Everything is legally signed. The young ladies will be sorry to realise that you have gone – and will be most aggrieved to discover your sending them off to another of their aunts for a few days was a ploy to avoid making a final goodbye."

"They'll get over it. And I'll write to them when I can. There seems to be one hell of a noise going on outside? People shouting. What's happening? Are we under siege or something?"

Skylark was nearest to the window. He peered out. "Seems to be a mob of ruffians coming through your gates. Shabby looking lot. About eighty or so men? You somehow upset the town's folk, Captain?"

Jesamiah joined him. Shabby was not the word for it; a ragged crowd of scruffy tramps. A couple in front appeared to be slightly better dressed, but rabble it definitely was, or...?

"Bloody hell!" Jesamiah declared, putting his coffee cup down and heading for the door. "It's Vernon!"

CHAPTER THIRTY-EIGHT
AT SEA

"I am not happy about being aboard a pirate ship." Captain Vernon had expressed the same opinion several times during the last twenty-and-four hours.

Jesamiah had always made the same answer. "You can go back to that Spanish prison if you prefer."

De León had managed part of the agreed conditions by securing the release of Vernon and what remained of his crew. How he had done so, Jesamiah did not bother to ask but had reimbursed him a substantial amount of money, so assumed a bribe was involved. There was nothing unusual about paying the right people to conveniently leave prison doors open.

Jesamiah had initially wanted to set sail at once, but there had been practicalities to consider: more provisions to take aboard for an increased crew, with that increased crew being cleansed, fed, medically attended to and re-clothed with garments that were not threadbare ragged. *Sea Witch* was no Royal Navy ship, but Jesamiah was not keen on taking fleas and lice aboard, nor having men working his ship in torn rags.

"I am going to have a difficult job explaining to the admiralty that I've lost the *Bonne Chance*," Vernon complained from the quarterdeck of *Sea Witch* as Jesamiah spun the wheel. More wind filled her sails and she gathered speed, leaving San Vincento to recede into the rising evening mist which was cloaking the coast.

"She was developing rot in more than one place," Jesamiah remarked, keeping an eye on the shiver to the edge of the mainsail – there, he had it, *Sea Witch* was running to her best. "If we come across her, I'm sure we can get her back, but with luck we might find you a better Prize to take home."

Captain Vernon bristled with disapproval, but it was his second lieutenant, Mr Lande, who answered for him.

"If you are implying...? Captain! Sir! We do *not* hold with piracy!"

Lande had been sorely affronted back in the prison cell in Cádiz, upon discovering who Jesamiah truly was, his indignation exacerbated by a pirate being released from those squalid conditions before Captain Vernon and the officers, and upon learning from Buckeridge that this pirate scoundrel was also possibly responsible for a past murder. His annoyance had increased threefold now they were at sea, and that same murderous pirate had assumed command.

Jesamiah grinned at the lieutenant. "I don't hold with piracy either, mate, not now I'm a married man with a wife to nag me about morals, but there's nothing in your little Royal Navy rule book that says we can't have a look for that bloody Spaniard who attacked us, is there?" He waited for a response, received only a scowl. "If we find her, Lieutenant, we can dish out some of our own medicine, can't we?"

"She could be anywhere!" Lande protested, raising his arms in irritation.

Jesamiah looked at Vernon. "She was the *Santa María del Bartolomé*?"

"Yes, she was," Vernon confirmed gruffly.

"Then she's still around here somewhere. Ain't that right Skylark?"

Skylark, standing a little to the side of the helm, nodded. "As I told you yesterday, Cap'n, she followed us all the way from Gib, although kept her distance. Seeing what we were up to, I reckon."

"Aye," Jesamiah added, "with Calderón's Spanish colours flying she would not have dared attack you. A different matter with *Bonne*

Chance, though. British Navy? Fair game." He glared purposefully at Vernon. "I could have supplied you with those same trick colours. Saved us a lot of bloody bother."

"We are Navy!" Lande blustered. "We would not sail under false identity!"

"Suit yourself," Jesamiah retorted, "but deception's a damned good way of ensuring you don't get blown to pieces." To Vernon, he said, "Take *Santa María* as a Prize and you'll be the darling of your admiralty and doing a lot of us a big favour into the bargain. She's the only decent ship the Spaniards have in these parts."

"I must admit," Vernon acknowledged, massaging his cheeks with his fingers, "the thought is tempting."

"Will our men not be aggrieved to take orders from a..." Lande was about to say 'pirate' but received a stern glower from Vernon. He coughed, changed to, "From someone other than yourself, sir?"

Jesamiah answered for Vernon. "Well, if they don't do as I say aboard *my* ship they have the choice of either jumping overboard or taking the longboat and their own chance of survival." He stared at Lieutenant Lande. "And that includes you."

Vernon cleared his throat. Tact was required. "Out of courtesy, Lieutenant Lande – and I might add, necessity – we will comply with Captain Acorne. As long as he acts legally, and sensibly."

Laughing, Jesamiah took one hand off the helm to pat Vernon's shoulder. "It might not be sensible to act legal, but I'll do m' best to keep as many of us as I can alive."

His thigh was aching, and his left arm was still slightly stiff, but ever since yesterday he'd hardly noticed the discomfort, and now that he was aboard his beloved ship, what did a few aches and pains matter? He looked at Lande, said gruffly, "I would be obliged for you to make sure that all your men join eagerly with my crew, and follow my and Skylark's orders without question."

Lande glowered disapproval.

Jesamiah noticed. "This isn't for my pride, Lieutenant, it's because I and my crew know this ship better than does Captain Vernon, and if – no, when – we get into a fight, lives will depend on that knowing."

To Vernon, he said, "I'm grieved for the men you lost, some of them were good sailors, good men. I'm not sorry to learn that bugger, your bos'n, Almighty, didn't survive prison." Privately, Jesamiah thought it quite likely that the man's fellow prisoners had not done much to help him survive. Probably even ensured that he didn't. It was also a pity that Buckeridge *had* survived. The man was a troublemaker, and Jesamiah was not at all keen to have him aboard.

Lande responded to Jesamiah's statement with an objection. "Mr Almitty was a reliable fellow who did his duty."

"He was a sadistic bastard who soured the goodwill of your men."

Again, Lande was about to object, but Vernon interceded. "Some men become overly enthusiastic with their duty, Mr Lande. You do not make friends with the crew, but neither is it wise to make enemies of them."

"But, sir, if the men do not pull their weight, they need encouragement."

"I agree," Jesamiah answered, "but unnecessarily poking and prodding at an honest worker with a rattan cane is not how to go about earning respect. Without respect you get resentment, and then you'll not get a crew to work with a will."

The fact that Vernon made no responding comment made Jesamiah assume he agreed. "How's Lieutenant Coffney doing?" he asked Vernon. "That injury of his looked bad."

"Our surgeon reckons he might lose the arm. We are giving him one more day – those salves and medications belonging to your wife do seem to be helping. I thank you for their use."

"Thank her yourself if ever you meet her."

"I remember her in Nassau. A very pleasant young lady. She was with a Dutchman then, was she not?"

"She was. A most unsuitable marriage. He drowned. We don't miss him." Jesamiah smiled to himself; did Vernon know that originally he'd stolen *Sea Witch* off that odious Dutch butterball? "And you did not finish telling me about Tearle when I asked yesterday. I assume he didn't make it?"

"He was well when I last saw him. He left us not far out of San Vincento. Said he was going to make his way back to Gibraltar."

"Well, with luck, I won't ever see him again. I'll not miss him, either." That wasn't quite true, but Jesamiah was not prepared to admit that he rather liked Tearle.

"I am going to be in trouble, too," Vernon said with a resigned sigh, "because I was supposed to take note of what ships the Spanish had in Cádiz harbour. Delivering the children was a ruse we wanted to take advantage of. You," he pointed towards Jesamiah, "were supposed to help me with this by listening out for any hints about whether this siege of Gibraltar was hearsay, or a possibility. We've both failed, there, I'm afraid."

"I can tell you that." Maha'dun tossed the remains of a cheroot he had been enjoying over the taffrail, idly watched the stub disappear into the frothing wake which *Sea Witch* was leaving behind her.

Vernon had no idea why this strange foreigner with startling blue eyes and dressed in Arabic clothing was aboard. He did not seem to have a role as such, not one of the crew, not a passenger. Surely, he wasn't a lover? The thought curdled Vernon's innards. He didn't think that Acorne was 'like that'. But then, who knew with pirates – even ex-pirates?

"Tell us what?" Jesamiah said to Maha'dun, aware that this could end up as a useless, convoluted conversation.

"About the ships at Cádiz. I was there for some weeks."

Vernon studied him with a new, interested respect.

"Don't get too excited," Jesamiah laughed, "Maha'dun's not very good at counting."

Maha'dun snorted. "I will have you know, Acorne, that Lady Tiola taught me to read, write *and* count." He held up both hands, folded down one thumb. "There were this many big boats – ones with little doors in the sides for the cannons. This many," he held up three fingers, "were being repaired. This many," he held up two fingers, "were being provisioned with barrels and kegs and ammunition. They sailed off. No idea where to."

He felt in his pocket for his cheroot case, selected a smoke, lit it using an exquisite silver flint box. Both items he had taken from Ber'ell's apartment, along with a chest of gold and silver coins and precious gems, three wooden chests of clothing and several exquisite weapons. "As for Gibraltar, I hung around the sailors when I could."

He grinned, "That was quite, well, let's say 'pleasurable'. I heard a good bit of pillow talk about a possible siege, but none of the men I dallied with seemed to think it would happen, because it would mean tying up too many ships for too long. At least, that's what they said." He sent a perfect ring of smoke into the fading light of the dusk. "No idea how tying their ships up will create a successful siege. What do they do? Rope them all together or something?"

"It's an expression," Jesamiah explained. "It means doing something useless which stops something useful being done instead. A bit like you, Maha'dun, at times." He glanced at Vernon. "Does that help you out?"

"It does if it's accurate."

Maha'dun sniffed, indignantly. "You do not have to believe me. But I saw what I saw, heard what I heard." Grinned. "Fucked who I fucked."

Both Vernon and Lande scowled disapproval.

"If we can manage to take the *Santa María del Bartolomé*, we might be able to get a few answers from her crew," Jesamiah suggested, ignoring the momentary awkwardness.

"Torture any prisoners, you mean?" Lieutenant Lande looked aghast. "Prisoners are not to be mistreated, they are..."

"Oh, do shut up, Lande!" Vernon snapped, exasperated.

The quarterdeck fell silent. A few of the brightest stars were showing now; to the east, a pale silvery-gold glow as the moon was starting to rise.

"Might I ask?" Maha'dun said, flicking his finished cheroot over the rail and taking out another one from its case. "Why are we heading south when England is the other way?"

Vernon had been thinking the same question, but had considered it prudent not to ask. However, now that this strange foreign fellow had mentioned it... "The wind is favourable for a more northerly heading, do you not think, Acorne?"

Jesamiah checked the compass, brought *Sea Witch* up a point. "That it is, but we're more likely to find our quarry somewhere between here and Gibraltar." He turned slightly to grin at Maha'dun, "And I'm impressed. You actually *know* which way south is?"

"I'm not a complete imbecile," Maha'dun grumbled back.

Jesamiah guffawed. "No, only half of one!"

"So, we *are* going after the *Santa María del Bartolomé*?" Vernon queried, unsuccessfully masking a rise of excitement.

"We are." Jesamiah touched his thigh, then the scar on his face and wound one of his blue ribbons, returned to his hair from his cache in his cabin, around a finger. "They have a debt to settle."

Vernon's face broke into a broad grin. He nodded, clasped his hands behind his back as he balanced against *Sea Witch* rolling slightly to larboard.

"Good," was all he said. "Good."

CHAPTER THIRTY-NINE
EARLY NOVEMBER

"On deck down there! There's a sail ahead – this side of the pointy end!"

Captain Vernon had been semi-dozing in one of the comfortable chairs in Jesamiah's Great Cabin. Roused by the shout floating in from above through the open stern windows, he frowned. "Did he say 'pointy end'? And what side is 'this side'?"

"One of these days I'll get around to teaching Maha'dun more of the correct words," Jesamiah said, yawning. Rising from his own chair he shrugged on his buckram coat, buckled on his cutlass and slid a pistol through his belt. He glanced at his pocket watch. Five minutes after midnight. "And he doesn't know left or right, so there's no point in telling him about larb'd and starb'd."

Vernon raised his eyebrows in disbelief, but followed suit with his own coat and weaponry. Said doubtfully, "Let's hope it's her. Can you trust that foreigner to know what he's looking at?"

"There are many things that Maha'dun is useless at, but two where he excels: fighting and seeing in the dark." Jesamiah laughed as he stepped through the cabin door. "No, make that three; he's also very good at being exceedingly irritating."

"So why in the name of God do you tolerate him?"

Jesamiah stopped, turned round. "Because of those qualities and because you will never find anyone, on this Earth or elsewhere, more loyal. He's already given his life to save mine."

"What!"

Jesamiah realised his clumsy error, masked it by chuckling, "Well, figuratively speaking. A while back he took a pistol shot meant for me. A nasty wound, but turned out not to be fatal."

On deck, Maha'dun was carefully descending the ratlines. Coffee, the Hindustani crewman, was settling himself at the masthead in his stead.

Maha'dun went with Jesamiah and Vernon to the bow, stood silent as the two men gazed through their telescopes into the distant night.

"Do you see her, Edward?" Jesamiah asked.

Vernon nodded. "I see *a* ship's topsails silhouetted against the horizon, whether it's her or not, though?"

"Oh, it's the *Santa María del Bartolomé* all right," Jesamiah said with a grin as wide as a slice of ripe melon. "She's dawdling. Only those top sails set – and even from here I can see they're somewhat lubberly. Most of her crew are probably asleep. The captain snug and snoring in his cot, the officer of the watch curled in his boat cloak dead to the world as well, hidden away somewhere discreet with a brandy bottle tucked beneath his arm for company. If her task is to patrol, keep an eye on English, French or Dutch shipping, she ain't making a very alert job of it is she? And if she *were* any of those nations, not Spanish, she'd not be idling along but making full sail to get where she was going as fast as she could. It's a clear night, plenty of stars, a half-moon, good wind. Merchants – or Royal Navy – don't hang about in enemy waters."

Vernon nodded. "I cannot disagree with any of that. So, what do you propose we do?"

"We slow down a bit, trundle along in her wake as if we are another Spaniard minding our own business. We then wait and see how long it takes for her to become aware of us. When she does, I expect she'll want to know who we are. She'll soon find out."

CHAPTER FORTY

Dawn was just breaking, strips of pink and gold stealthily fingering the fading remains of the night sky. The Spaniard, three cable lengths – just under one half of a mile – ahead, came up into the wind, her sails coming aback, her mainsail reducing in size as her men hauled it in.

"She's heaving to," Vernon muttered unnecessarily.

Jesamiah studied her. No need for his brass telescope, he could clearly see the sea slime caked and trailing beneath her transom, the streaks of salt and the residue masking the glass of her stern windows.

A few minutes later *Sea Witch* was within hailing distance, a Spanish officer, a lieutenant by his dress, leaned over *Santa María del Bartolomé*'s taffrail, a speaking trumpet to his mouth.

"What did he say?" Vernon asked Jesamiah, who had yelled something back.

"We're to heave to. I reckon we can oblige. Skylark, we'll luff, so that the Spaniard rides under our lee."

Skylark nodded, signalled to the skeleton crew on deck with hand gestures – Jesamiah had already given orders for no one to speak. "We're supposed to be Spanish," he'd said. "No English voices."

Not that it mattered, for given the signal the resulting boom and crash of canvas flapping and flailing overhead drowned any words as *Sea Witch* turned into the wind and reduced speed to a slow crawl. Then *Sea Witch* was hove to, her foretopsail set to the mast, her maintops'l countering, almost full, balancing the other as she lay a mere few yards from the Spaniard. She rolled a little, then dipped into a shallow trough, her lower, closed, gunports disappearing momentarily.

The coast was not far off, a vague, distant blur of grey along the larboard horizon. There was not much wind this calm quiet morning; what there was carried a hint of the land, of forest covered hills and fog-misted mornings, the *Barbas del Levante* – the Beards of the East Wind.

The Spanish officer called again.

"He wants to know where we're bound," Jesamiah said, then shouted back in Spanish. "Veracruz. We were chased by a bloody English frigate yesterday evening; just waiting for the dawn to get a fix and head off west. I'd appreciate you doing your job to escort us safe out of these bloody English-infested waters." It was an excuse he had used on several occasions. It usually worked.

A response came. Jesamiah grinned. "I'll not translate that. It weren't very polite."

The Spaniard was drifting. Orders came, carried by the wind, for her to get under way, and her men scurried to the braces. Her fores'l billowed and she slowly began to gather way.

"Looks like they want to leave the party," Jesamiah said as he stepped to the helm and took over from Bert Moody. "I don't recall telling them they could go." He grinned. This was what the sea was all about! This was living! "Set the t'gan'sls. Mr Skylark – all hands on deck!" he shouted as *Sea Witch* also gathered way. "Prepare to grapple!"

With sudden panic the scratch crew aboard *Santa María del Bartolomé* realised what was happening, the panic spreading like a gust of storm wind as Jesamiah ordered the Spanish colours of Calderón to be struck and his own run up to replace them. His colours had, a while ago, been a leering skull above two crossed bones, but Tiola had made him change from that threatening pirate presence. Now, he had a red flag with a large English Oak acorn sitting in its cup above crossed oak leaf branches. Unmistakably, Acorne's ship.

"Lively now!" Jesamiah shouted. "Pass word for Mr Featherstone to send a ball off from the larboard bow chaser, give 'em more of a scare."

He smiled as he heard, "Look lively lads!" echoing back along the deck from Lieutenant Lancelot Lande – Three 'Ells. Despite his grumbling, at least the man was pulling his weight.

A moment later, the bow chaser roared its potential carnage, the gun lurching inwards as it fired, a plume of smoke, the whine as the ball crossed the short distance and landed with a spout of water within a yard of the *Santa María del Bartolomé*'s hull.

"Prepare boarding parties!" Jesamiah yelled, as he handed the wheel back to Bert Moody. He nudged Vernon with his elbow as he headed towards the quarterdeck rail. "All lookin' good, eh? Grousy!" he shouted to Mr Partridge. "You have command of the guns. Curly – I'm pleased t'see you survived Spanish hospitality! You! Buckeridge, muster your men there, jump to it! Come on Edward, I'll show you how ex-pirates do this!"

The men of *Sea Witch* needed no further orders as the ship nudged alongside the Spaniard. Anything to hand, belaying pins, pistol butts... anything and everything that could make a noise was being used to hammer against the rail – the Hindustani, Coffee, had an old metal bucket.

Excited, eager, voices rose to a scream. *"Death! Death! Death!"*

The pirate chant that every victim dreaded to hear.

"We pipe down when going into battle!" Vernon shouted. "Otherwise, how can the men hear orders?"

"Don't need many orders!" Jesamiah yelled back. "We know what to do without bein' told how to do it!"

Despite his disciplined naval training, less than a minute later Vernon found himself shouting along with the rest of them and, pistol in hand, joining in with the drummed, steady beat. His own men, aboard his own ship, always fought with a will for the hope of a share of any specie, but this was different, this was more primeval, more rugged, more – he hated to admit it – exhilarating.

"Steady there!" Jesamiah yelled to his men from where he stood in the chains, one arm linked through the shrouds. "Steady!" He looked up, canvas was rapidly disappeared, picked men from both crews were standing ready at the rail, grappling irons in their hands. One of them was Buckeridge, his face a surly mask of disdain.

"I trust all your men will fight well?" Jesamiah called to Vernon.

"They will," came the assertive reply.

They'd better, Jesamiah thought, then shouted his order, "Let loose!" Instantly, the grapples flew across the small distance between the two ships, pulling them even closer together. "Board!" Jesamiah screamed as he leapt the yard or so from one ship to the other, Vernon close to heel, other men doing the same all along the length of *Sea Witch*'s deck.

A jolt of pain up Jesamiah's thigh as he landed slightly awkwardly, but no time to think about it. The Spanish were coming forward to repel the attack, many more scampering up from below in various states of undress. Two officers appeared. As Jesamiah had guessed, most of those aboard, apart from the essentials on watch, had been asleep. A slovenly and lubberly mistake, given the trailing presence of another, unknown, ship for much of the night. Their mistake. And they would pay dearly for it.

He fired his pistol at a man running towards him, a raised axe in his hand. The man fell, instantly dead. Jesamiah reversed the spent weapon and used it as a club on the next man, striking at the head, felling those who came at him as easily as if they were old, rotten-to-the-core trees. He could see Maha'dun further along the deck, his Arabian garb billowing like a maiden's ball gown, blood spattering from victim after victim as he hacked forward with a rapier in one hand, a dagger in the other. No time to watch his crew, though, for Jesamiah had his own battles to fight. More and more Spaniards were rushing up onto the deck, all sleep-drowsiness or surfeit of last night's drink gone as they struggled for their lives.

A musket ball whistled past his left ear; he heard someone behind scream as the ball lodged home. He was not able to turn around, see who lay dead or wounded. A blade slashed in front of him, he swept forward with his cutlass, felt the impact wrench up his arm, ignored the blood that fountained from the throat of the Spaniard before him.

No time to look or think. Push forward, use the pistol to crunch down on heads or wrists, the cutlass to slash and strike. Step by slow step, careful not to slip on the blood running along the wooden deck, careful not to trip over dead or wounded men.

He aimed another pistol butt blow, the recipient swung away, brought his arm up, wielding a belaying pin, struck Jesamiah's shoulder. He yelped, dropped the pistol as pain tore up and down his left arm, the mended broken bone reminding him of its barely healed status. Angry, Jesamiah drove his cutlass home, ripping it through the man's belly, then stepped aside, drew his dagger from his belt.

Two men were grappling together, one trying to drive a dagger into the other's neck. The blade touched, drew blood, the Spaniard wielding it leered at his victim, Buckeridge, and tightening his grip jerked his arm for a final slash – his eyes widening in surprise as Jesamiah's cutlass blade tore into his spine, severing through flesh, sinew, bone and muscle. He crumpled to the deck, not dead yet, but never to walk again.

Buckeridge had the graciousness to nod his thanks.

"Finish the bugger off," Jesamiah said through panting breath, "and if I hear one more lie about murder from you, I'll cut your bloody throat myself. Understand?"

"Aye, sir," came the swift response and a respectful, quick, salute.

A temporary truce or a final settlement? Jesamiah had no time to consider the matter; a Spanish officer was coming at him, sword raised, teeth bared, nostrils flaring. Their blades came together with a clash of steel, sparks flying as the two men exchanged savage blows, then they locked, the one blade sliding along the other until the hilts clashed. The Spaniard's face was close to Jesamiah's, his breath stank as he hissed in broken English "You die, English pig!"

"¡Not today, Spanish bastard!" Jesamiah thrust the dagger held in his left hand up under the man's ribs, his full weight behind the blade, thrusting the dagger further, up into the heart. He stepped back, yanked the blade out, blood gushing as it came free, didn't see, only heard, the man fall to the deck as another leering bastard was before him, brandishing an axe.

The only sounds, the hiss of a blade, the clash of steel on steel, an occasional *crack* from a fired pistol or musket. No shouting, no screaming, only the pitiful cries of the wounded and dying, and the heavy, laboured breathing and desperate grunts of effort as the last few men fought on against the Spaniards who refused to surrender. The smells were rank. Acrid gunpowder, sweat, piss, faeces, vomit. The stink of disembowelled guts, the strong tang of blood.

No sign of Vernon. God, but Jesamiah hoped he wasn't dead, he'd have one bugger of a lot of explaining to do if he was.

He saw Maha'dun again, wrestling with a Spaniard – a moment only, for within seconds the man was flying over the rail, his arms frantically windmilling against the early morning blue sky. A splash. He would drown, quickly, if he was fortunate enough.

Jesamiah turned, his leg slithering a few inches along the blood and gore-wet deck. His thigh protested, he grabbed for a stay, righted himself, made ready to fight the next man, but no one was there. A few, last, *pop, pop* sounds as pistols came from below deck. A curdling scream, and then, save for the creaking of the two ships and the wind grumbling through the shrouds and rigging, silence. Then, suddenly, an uprush of elated cheering; Skylark was bringing down the Spanish colours. A moment later, up flew Jesamiah's own.

And there was Vernon, coming up from below, his face, breeches and shirt bloodstained, his grogram coat torn in two places, the gold lace of a shredded epaulette dangling, ragged, from his shoulder, but a grin as wide as the Atlantic creasing his face.

"The Spanish captain is dead," he puffed, labouring to gain enough breath to speak. "The lazy bugger was barely from his bed, as drunk as Bacchus."

Jesamiah grinned back, gave a half-hearted naval salute – he was suddenly too tired for anything more formal. "The *Santa María del Bartolomé,* and most of what is stored within her is yours, Captain Vernon."

"Most?"

"I'll have a good portion of any cognac we find, and a decent percentage of anything of value to share with my men."

Vernon nodded; that was fair enough, but, "We will have to hand over anything of worth to the Admiralty at Greenwich, who then pay a portion to King George and his government. Only then do we receive our portion of what is left."

"Bugger that," Jesamiah declared. "How are they to know what we find? Keep what is suitable, let them have the rest."

Vernon looked doubtful. "I am an honest man, Acorne, but..."

"But?"

"Well, you make a good point, but there is a small matter of honour and loyalty."

"To whom? I'd say your priority is loyalty to the men who serve with you. The men who give their lives, often for nothing except *your* honour and a handful of silver if they stay alive long enough to get it. However, if virtue will play on your conscience, Captain Vernon, I'll tally everything and give you a generous portion to deal with how you want. That way you – and your Greenwich Admiralty – will never know how much was here originally."

"That will still not be truthful."

"The truth, Edward, can be expandable when you want it to be."

CHAPTER FORTY-ONE
AT SEA - OFF THE COAST OF SPAIN

Captain Edward Vernon renamed his Prize *Morning Glory*, knowing the admiralty would want to change it to suit their own preference, but *Morning Glory* would suffice for now. There were minimal repairs to be done, although quite a lot of general maintenance, for the Spanish rarely cared about keeping a ship in good order.

They buried the dead at sea, the English and Spanish together. Jesamiah had remarked that as the Spanish were mostly Catholic in faith, a Church of England service was perhaps not suitable?

Vernon had dismissed the concern. "The Lord's Prayer is relevant to any faith."

"Hindus, Jews, Muslims and such might not agree with you there," Jesamiah had retorted.

"Do you think there were any Hindus, Jews or Muslims amongst the dead, then?"

Conceding, Jesamiah had dropped the subject. Tiola had always insisted that a deity was a deity whatever one's personal belief, so perhaps it did not matter what prayers were or were not spoken.

The Spanish prisoners had been securely locked in *Morning Glory*'s hold, the English crews, come evening, enjoying a few hours of relaxed pleasure on *Sea Witch*'s deck. Jesamiah, backed by Maha'dun and several of the men – from both crews – had been all for hanging the prisoners. Vernon had vetoed the suggestion, saying they would be put ashore come morning. "We'll be long gone before they reach Cádiz and raise an alarm."

As the day had progressed there had been several close calls for Jesamiah's temper to rise to the surface. By evening he'd already experienced the sharp side of Vernon's authoritative nature more times than he cared to, but didn't have the energy to disagree with him. *Santa María del Bartolomé – Morning Glory* – was Vernon's ship now and he could do what he wanted with it. *Sea Witch*, however, was a different matter.

The moon was riding high, the stars were sprinkled like rice scattered at a wedding across a clear sky. The two captains were sampling a bottle of Spanish brandy in Jesamiah's cabin after an evening feast of roast pork and beef – also provided courtesy of the Spanish. The two ships were anchored in shoals off a secluded bay to the south of Cádiz. That had been another disagreement. Vernon had wanted to make all haste to Gibraltar. Jesamiah had not. He'd won the naval captain round by saying that he'd receive more acclaim were he to tidy the captured ship up, present her in good order rather than one that showed herself as a whore with ragged skirts and a probable dose of the pox.

From on deck Jesamiah heard Maha'dun laugh, then strike up yet another gay tune on a fiddle he'd found. He was a good player, had a good voice. He'd declined the offer to join Jesamiah and Vernon, making the excuse that he preferred to be out in the night air with his cheroots. Truth was, he was even less inclined to keep on an even keel temper-wise where Captain Vernon was concerned. Vernon did not trust him. Maha'dun disliked Vernon. It made sense to avoid each other where possible.

Tentative, sipping at and enjoying the brandy, Jesamiah said, "I don't suppose you'd consider releasing two dozen or so of your men into my care, would you?"

"No. I would not."

Ah, that was pretty succinct. Never one to give up where something he wanted was concerned, Jesamiah tried again. "I'm a little short-handed. You'll find replacement crew at Gibraltar. I'll be happy to pay for their decommission. Twenty men, maybe?"

"I said no. Any man leaving the service will be deemed a deserter."

"But if you signed them off as dead..."

"That would be a lie."

"Yes, but..."

"I said no."

Jesamiah tried an alternative tack. "They all did well today. Yours and mine. Are you going to promote anyone? Give them greater responsibility, more pay?"

"I doubt it."

"Charlie Featherstone and Curly – I don't know his given name – would make good choices. A replacement bos'n maybe?"

Vernon spluttered into his brandy and sat forward. "Curly, as you call him, is Emmanuel Mabuse. And how could I grant him promotion, may I ask? He is a black man, a Ni..."

Jesamiah cut him short. "Don't use that word. It's offensive to the Africans. I won't have it spoken aboard my ship."

"I have no care what words you do or do not use, I cannot give responsibility to black men."

Blind prejudice. "Yet you're happy for black men to sail your ship or to give their lives?"

"That is different."

"No, it ain't."

"They do not have the same feelings as we white men do."

"That's foking rubbish. They are men, no different from us save for the colour of their skin."

Vernon snorted. "I suppose you are also against slavery?"

"I am."

"Well, Mabuse is not a slave. He gets paid like any other sailor."

"Yet he cannot terminate that service unless he's of no more use to you. Then he gets chucked out and left to fend, somehow, for himself."

Again, Vernon snorted. "Is it any different aboard a pirate vessel?"

Jesamiah leant forward, his intention to emphasise his point. "Yes, it is. Anyone wounded gets a fair share of any Prize, plus extra for their trouble. If they're still able, they stay aboard. Many a ship's cook has lost an arm or a leg. Many a pirate has lost an eye. Besides which, a black man has just as much right to wield authority if he has the capability to do so." There was no use in arguing further though. "What about Featherstone, then?"

"He drinks too much."

"Don't we all!" Jesamiah said, leaning back again and raising his glass in mock salute. "I have no objection to giving either of them a good position aboard *Sea Witch*."

"I said no."

Jesamiah sighed, drained his glass, rose from his chair and stretched. His thigh was throbbing like African war drums. "I'll go and end the celebration above, and then turn in. It's been a busy day. You'll be comfortable enough aboard *Morning Glory*, I reckon."

As a dismissal it was about as succinct as Vernon had been.

CHAPTER FORTY-TWO

"I would rather you came to Gibraltar to confirm the run of events," Vernon stated for a third time since dawn had flooded the sky. It was now almost noon. "I am expecting a court martial enquiry over the loss of *Bonne Chance*. I am not concerned for the favourable outcome, but your testament, Acorne, would be useful."

The two ships, *Sea Witch* and *Morning Glory*, were riding together at anchor. *Morning Glory*'s longboat was returning, having taken the last of the prisoners ashore to the deserted sand dunes – minus their clothes, boots and hats. It would be a long, hard walk to Cádiz as naked as the day they were born, barefoot and hatless beneath the sun. The wounded from Vernon's crew were being made comfortable below deck in the good care of his surgeon – Jesamiah was reluctant to lose that particular man; he was good at his job. Thanks to him, the scar on Jesamiah's face was fading nicely, his thigh not aching so much and the broken arm nothing more than the occasional twinge.

Jesamiah answered, also for the third time that morning, "And I would prefer to head north to England."

"I could order you to accompany me."

Jesamiah tossed Vernon a disdainful glance. "You can order as much as you like, I'll not comply. And before you say it, you know perfectly well that *Sea Witch* could outmanoeuvre, outrun and outgun your *Morning Glory* any day."

"Or night," Maha'dun muttered from where he stood a yard behind Jesamiah, his head and body swathed in clean Arab garments, a more than adequate barrier against the bright sunshine.

Vernon smiled, the sort of expression that preceded a possible victorious chess move. *Check*. "But you are aboard my ship, not yours. I could prevent you and your foreign monkey-friend from leaving."

Maha'dun laughed, went to step forward, his hand dropping to the hilt of the fancy rapier he wore at his side.

Jesamiah touched Maha'dun's arm, shook his head. "Captain Vernon is having his little joke. You know, Edward, a short while ago I thought we had a chance to become good acquaintances; I think I was being too optimistic. Never mind." His turn to smile, his turn to swing the game to his favour. *Checkmate*. Reaching into his inside coat pocket, he brought out two sealed letters. "I have here my written account of Spain attacking *Bonne Chance* and everything else that has happened since. I've included details of what Maha'dun saw at Cádiz – not much I admit, but I'm guessing it will all be of help to you."

He held up the second letter. "This one, is for your superiors in Greenwich. It is my official complaint against you for breaking the law by pressing someone – me – from the American Colonies into service. I am prepared to do my own pressing by pressing charges against you."

Vernon's face suffused to an angry colour of something between tomato and beetroot. "That is preposterous!"

"No, it ain't. But I'll destroy the letter, and give you this first letter, when I have the extra crew I need. Twenty men, I believe we agreed?" They had agreed nothing of the sort. "But I'll accept fifteen volunteers in addition to Curly and Mr Featherstone."

Hands were busy about the deck of *Morning Glory*, bringing in the longboat and setting the ship straight. The nearest men had been able to hear every word. Several looked up with expressions of alarm. More had a look of interest in their eyes.

"Mr Lande," Vernon called his lieutenant over from where he

stood on the windward side of the quarterdeck. "Fetch me the ship's log, and then muster the men."

"Aye, sir."

"You can take ten volunteers," Vernon rasped through part-gritted teeth. "And I never want to see you again."

"Plus the two I named. That'll be acceptable."

Vernon spoke briefly to the men, explaining that they would replenish crew at Gibraltar, but *Sea Witch* was short-handed. "Ten volunteers prepared to transfer, step forward."

"Excuse me, sir, Captain," Charlie Featherstone saluted. "Might I ask, what about our owed pay?"

"Captain Acorne will cover any payment due from when we left Gibraltar."

Jesamiah opened his mouth to protest. That would be quite a bit of silver. Vernon tipped his head slightly, glowering a challenge for him to voice the objection.

Jesamiah shrugged. "Fair enough."

"And we won't be cast as deserters?" That was Curly.

"You will not. I will discharge your names from the ship's log." Vernon pointed to the leather-bound book his lieutenant was holding.

"Sir?" Lande said. "Is this wise?"

"Are you, by chance, questioning my authority Mr Lande? If you are, I suggest that maybe you would be better off putting yourself forward as one of the volunteers."

Lande swallowed hard. "No, sir, of course I am not, sir."

"Then I am glad to hear it."

A handful of the men were whispering between themselves. Some shook their heads, others were nodding. Ten took a step forward.

"Permission to collect our dunnage, sir?" Featherstone asked.

"Granted, but look lively. We weigh anchor in five minutes. Mr Lande, take note of their names." To another sailor, said, "Heed the hourglass. Five minutes. No more."

A matter of moments for the men to collect their belongings and swing the heavy sea chests or canvas dunnage bags over the rail from *Morning Glory* to *Sea Witch*. Curly, Featherstone and nine more men that Jesamiah did not know too well. And Buckeridge, the tenth man.

"You can take him as part of the bargain," Vernon announced with curt finality. "He is a troublemaker. You deserve each other. Good day to you Acorne. Mr Lande? Have you noted those names? Good. Then get us under way if you please."

Aboard *Sea Witch*, the men mirrored the activity aboard *Morning Glory*. Weighing anchor, stowing the wet, weed-slimed cable as it was winched inboard, setting canvas, hauling on the yards.

Buckeridge, looking about him, dared to ask Jesamiah a question. "Captain?"

"Aye?"

"I ain't sure about a truce a'tween us, but I thank you for saving my life. An' I'd like to know, if something as I heard a few of your reglar men talkin' about be true?"

"And what's that?"

"They said as how you'll be, one day, goin' after that black-bellied pirate bastard, Charles Vane."

"I might be. If opportunity ever arose."

"Right then, that be good enough for me. Truce it is." He spat on his palm, held it out towards Jesamiah.

Ignoring the outstretched hand, Jesamiah said, "Such familiarity aboard a Royal Navy ship would result in an instant flogging."

"Just as well *Sea Witch* ain't Navy, then."

"I do things my way," Jesamiah emphasised. "Cross me and you'll become shark bait. Tell me, though, why are you so keen set against Vane?"

Buckeridge answered without hesitation. "One of the men he killed in the Azores was my brother. I thought you was t' blame. I were wrong there, but Vane has to pay. I want justice done."

"I've more than one score to settle with him myself," Jesamiah conceded, taking the man's hand and giving a brief, acknowledging squeeze, "but I have other, more pressing things to see to first. And one of them, Mr Buckeridge, is to get this ship under way."

Buckeridge saluted, jogged off to join his new crew mates.

"You trust him?" Maha'dun asked.

"Not in the slightest. But if what he says is true, he might come in useful if ever I do meet up again with Charles Vane."

CHAPTER FORTY-THREE
NOVEMBER 1715 - THE PAST, CORNWALL

A knife slashed across the Reverend Garrick's shoulder blade, slipped sideways, leaving a scratch only, but drawing blood through his otherwise pristine white linen shirt. His outrage, his shout of fury. He hurled his wife aside, the back of his hand smashing across her face, a bruise instantly reddening there. She fell with a cry, caught her side on the wooden bedframe, breaking a rib. She gasped as the pain tore through her, but anger outrode any hurt. Her hatred boiled. Hatred against his cruelty, his indifference, his superiority. Hatred burning into anger. Anger against his sneering contempt, his church-bound hypocrisy. Anger against the torment of repeated, endured, rape. And fury that she had caught him attempting to rape a child. Her child, her daughter.

The blade glinted in the light of the single lantern, struck upward again. Found its mark this time as she plunged it into his flesh, forcing it to scrape against bone, then into the soft pulp of the heart.

Her daughter, Tiola, screamed again, her mother's sobs of disgusted anger in her ears. Her father's bubbling shout of rage turning to gurgled gasps of bloodied breath. Then silence.

Jed Garrick, the eldest son, calling, anxious, from the kitchen two floors below.

"What is it? What is happening up there?"

His heavy boots treading on the wooden stairs, Mother, thinking quickly, bundling Tiola beneath the bed.

"Hide! Stay there, stay quiet. Whatever happens, stay quiet!"

Jed at the bedchamber door. Mother blood-spattered, the knife in her hand. Jenna, her maid, appearing from her room in nightgown and nightcap. Jed, raging fury, hauling his mother away, swearing and cursing at her. Calling her foul, accusatory names, calling her the devil's whore.

"Look after Tiola!" Mother cried as she stumbled down the stairs. "Jenna, see to Tiola's safety!"

And then, the mob. That baying mob. Tiola watched, scared, from the window as Jenna bundled together what they would need. Warm clothes, mother's jewels; from the kitchen, a loaf of bread, a small round of cheese, a cold venison pie. Some wrinkled apples. A kitchen knife that would serve well as a defensive dagger.

"Come away from the window, child. Dress yourself. We must leave! Hurry!"

But still Tiola stared out of the window, transfixed, seeing with her new-awakened full ability of Craft all that was happening down the hill in the village. Seeing through the mist of the downpour of rain the villagers roused by her brother, Jed, from their homes. Saw the torches flaring in the wind and hissing in the rain. Saw the hastily-tied noose and her mother, hands bound, kicking and struggling, unable to plead for mercy as the noose, slung over the bough of the gallows tree, tightened around her neck. Unable to plead, yet again, that she was new with child. Or perhaps Jed did hear her? Tiola saw his leer of contempt. His disgust that such a child was created from a lover's seed, not a husband's.

Even if they had heard, would the mob heed her cries? It was known, in the way that superstitious folk insisted they knew these things, that the daughter born to Elswyth Garrick was not sired by her husband. Tiola was a strange child, the result of the devil's work, planted there by the mother's wicked prostitution on a night of the full moon. The night when the devil had his way with the witches who worshipped him.

No one helped Elswyth Garrick. No one dared show sympathy for the devil-tainted.

Tiola watched as her mother hanged, slowly strangled, slowly suffocating as the mob jeered and taunted, and as Jed Garrick stood, hands on hips, laughing his spiteful vengeance against the woman he despised. Laughing his triumph over her treachery, her betrayal, her witchcraft.

The dreams. The dreams of blood, of screams, of death, of murder... The dreams of the past seeping from those restless moments of sleep into Tiola's mind, resurrecting the memories. Memories that were always there, thrumming behind her eyes until she fell to her knees among the foetid detritus of her prison cell, spewing up what little was in her stomach. The past, haunting her present. The past refusing to let her be, refusing to go away. The past, mocking that now it was her turn to hang.

CHAPTER FORTY-FOUR

LATE NOVEMBER 1719 - LAUNCESTON, CORNWALL

Hetty smiled at the prison gatekeeper as she always did. He smiled back, as he always did, although his smile was hopeful lust, unlike her pretence of interest in him. She had discovered, during those first awful days, that her cheerful smile, fluttering eyelashes and a little more showing of her bosoms than was decent, gained her admittance to the gaol a lot quicker than did indignant demands. Mind, it had been Finch making those demands, and by no stretch of the imagination was he as pretty as Hetty.

Approaching Falmouth that distant autumn afternoon – a grey, overcast day that had threatened rain – everyone had felt relief, even elation, at finally reaching England. A coach would take them on to North Devon, but instead, a nightmare had begun. The coach had left carrying only young Thomas Benson and Jasper: Tom with orders to return to his parents, Jasper to meet with Captain Acorne and the crew of *Sea Witch,* assuming they had arrived, as intended, at Appledore.

That aggressive preacher had accosted Tiola and the town constables had arrested her. Ascham Doone had done nothing, nothing at all, to intervene, and Hetty had felt remorse ever since. The arrest was her fault. She should have, could have, prevented it!

Scrying, Mistress Tiola had called her 'gift', but Hetty called the unwanted visions an intrusive curse. Were they warnings of possible predicted outcomes, or future certainties? It was the latter causing her fear. If what she saw in her mind were things yet to happen, then horror and grief by the barrel load awaited. She had been warned of Falmouth, and had disregarded the warnings. Now Miss Tiola was paying the price. At Falmouth the visions had started happening for real. Tiola, gentle, kind, Miss Tiola, arrested, accused of murder. Sentenced to hang. And there was nothing that either she or Mr Finch could do to stop it. Who would listen to the pleading of a fifteen-year-old girl or a scruffy, middle-aged, seaman who, apart from a perfunctory ability to read and write was an uneducated nobody?

The Falmouth magistrate had held no liking for women, particularly women who were accused of murdering their fathers. He had not listened to reasonable explanation, had not listened to anything beyond the accusation thrust by Tiola's own eldest brother – a preacher at that, so a man, according to the law, to be believed. The magistrate's decision had been clear: transfer to Launceston assizes for trial. A trial that had taken place, a trial that had condemned Tiola to hang as soon as she gave birth. There would be no reprieve, no commuting the sentence, no compassion.

Compassion? A woman who pleaded her belly, who carried the proof of being with child could not hang, for that would be murder of an innocent. That same innocent, however, would, from the day of its birth, be orphaned if there was no father or family to take it in. Condemned to a life of poverty and misery. Examined by a jury of matrons, Tiola had been fortunate in that her pregnancy was advanced and obvious. Other women, in their first months were often not believed. They hanged, the unborn babes dying with them.

Fortunate? Perhaps not, for only the very fortunate survived the deprivations of gaol.

Launceston Castle, what was left of it after Thomas Fairfax and Cromwell's Parliamentarian troops had decimated it during the Civil War, occupied a scarped and terraced rock knoll rising sharply to a height of one hundred feet above the River Kensey. The town itself – they said it as 'Lahnsen' – had encroached beyond what little remained of the castle walls, with the gaol building itself, erected in the late 1600s, occupying the centre of what had once been the bailey. The County Constable, Sir Hugh Pyper, had not maintained it, allowing the squalid place to fall into disrepair, with male and female prisoners incarcerated in the one, dismal cell. In 1692, with his position granted in perpetuity for himself and two succeeding generations, Sir Hugh had agreed to invest £120 into making suitable repairs and changes. The money had not gone far, and the so-called improvements were not plentiful: one narrow corridor with a single window of two feet wide by less than that high; opposite it, three small dungeon cages, two for men, with the one for women even smaller, measuring nine feet by five feet. With earthen floors, no water and no sanitation, all soon became offensive in condition and smell.

An upper room had been converted into a chapel, although it was more frequently used as a store room, with food and water being lowered through holes in the floor to the inmates below, and waste hauled up in a bucket. The gaoler, mean spirited as he was, often thought it amusing to deliberately spill the stinking contents. It saved him carrying the bucket outside to empty it. With the main entrance door rarely opened, save to escort prisoners in or out, there was no hope of escape, no chance to breathe in fresh air or exercise cramped, aching limbs.

The only advantage Tiola had was money. Money talked enough to secure food and blankets, to provide feeble light. Clean straw for the floor, ale to drink, but that was all. Hetty considered it her duty to visit the gaol twice a day, a duty only possible by paying a fee for the privilege. And keeping sweet the young guard, the gaoler's only son, so that he ignored the sign above the archway which read: *No admittance except by an order from the sheriff or magistrate.*

"Good morning Master James," Hetty said, shifting her basket from one arm to the other, and reaching inside to bring out a hot meat pasty. Providing James with something to eat for his apparently always empty belly helped gain access to the gaol without question or delay. Secretly, Hetty did think that Mr Finch's original idea of 'blowing the bloody gate open' and breaking Miss Tiola out was a good one, except Tiola herself had vetoed the plan on the grounds that if she ran, she would either not get far or would be forever running.

"Better than 'anged," Finch had grumbled out of concern for her, but she had been adamant.

"They will not hang me while I am with child," she had said, with more conviction than she felt. The thought *Jesamiah will come for me before then,* something for her to cling to, but it was now late November, and still he had not come.

Hetty felt guilty about leading poor James on; he was a spot-faced youth, gap-toothed from a poor diet and dressed in a guard's uniform that was too big for him. She had considered offering to take the seams in, but had realised this could suggest a more intimate relationship. For all her guilt, she still flashed more ankle and swayed her hips as she walked through the arched gateway beside the gaoler's small, cluttered house, and headed up the hill, tossing a parting smile at James over her shoulder.

One foul man had occupied the other cell, but he had died two weeks back of gaol fever, and another young woman shared the cramped conditions with Tiola – Hetty brought her food, too. A child really, fourteen years of age, heavy in pregnancy and facing the gallows. To be hanged because she had killed the brute who had raped her.

Hetty climbed the stone steps to the upstairs chapel, knelt in the puddles from the leaking roof and peered through the hole to the cell below.

"Miss Tiola? Ma'am? Be you there?"

"I would not be elsewhere, Hetty dear," came Tiola's tired voice as she heaved herself from a corner which she kept as clean and dry as she could, thanks to the straw Finch lugged up the hill twice a week.

"Where's Doryty?" Hetty asked, puzzled.

"She gave birth to a girl yesterday evening. A frail little thing that I doubt will survive long, if not already dead. I did what I could to help, made Doryty comfortable, assisted her to suckle the child for a first and last time."

A sob choked Tiola's voice. "That wretched gaoler ordered the babe to be away at first light, then hanged the mother soon after."

Tiola gazed up at Hetty's face, tears streaking her cheeks. "She was naught but a child herself. What type of world do we live in, Hetty? Where is the justice for innocents?"

Hetty lowered her basket down through the hole, watched as Miss Tiola took out the bread, cheese and flagon of ale – ale was preferable to water, for at least it was not tainted with any foulness. The provisions were all for herself now that Doryty was gone.

Tiola took the small bunch of red-berried holly from the basket.

"Finch picked it for you," Hetty called down, "he thought the bright berries would cheer you."

"It was very kind of him," Tiola replied. "Thank him for his thoughtfulness, but can you take them and put them on Doryty's grave, assuming they have already buried her, and you can find out where they laid her to rest. Ask your young James, not his miserable father."

"I will," Hetty said, thinking that perhaps she would have to show James Cooper more than a flash of ankle to find out. "But his father'll not be bothering anyone for a while. He got kicked by a horse down at the blacksmith's last night. Drunk, him and the smith, so I hear, larking about near the stalls and the mare booted him in his privy bits. Word is that he'll not be pestering any more women, or sheep again. I don't know how his wife put up with him, God rest her soul. Mind, perhaps it's because she died several years ago that he's become the foul old letch that he now is. I'm sad that James might be taking after his father. I hope not, although his lusting eye is proving useful for us."

"Hetty?" Tiola said, interrupting, her hand resting on the bulge of her belly. "Promise me that you will take care of my baby when it is born, until Jesamiah gets here?"

"Of course I will ma'am, you need not ask – but he will be here soon, I know he will."

With a spark of hope, Tiola gazed up at her. "Have you seen him here in your visions?"

"Oh yes, ma'am!"

As a lie, it was probably one of the biggest Hetty had ever told.

CHAPTER FORTY-FIVE
THE ISLES OF SCILLY, ENGLAND

Wind and weather were not favourable. Both had sent constant squalls and gales ever since they had left Spanish waters, causing frustrating delays and shortened tempers. On several days, because it had been so overcast, Jesamiah had found it nigh on impossible to take the necessary observations of the sun or stars to determine *Sea Witch*'s position of latitude. Instead, relying on his natural instinct and knowledge of dead reckoning he had to hope for the best. All right when at sea, but danger lurked when nearing land, especially when visibility was poor. A few minutes' lack of concentration, half a mile in the wrong direction, could mean an abrupt and fatal end to a voyage.

On this day, the twenty-third of November, *Sea Witch* was clawing her way under reefed topsails; the wind had backed from north to southwest, giving more advantageous sailing to the east-northeast, but it was a wind that was strong enough to lay *Sea Witch* over as she thrashed along, heading for the Cornish coast. Jesamiah had wanted, had intended, to sail more westward, direct for Appledore and the North Devon coast, which meant sailing towards the Bristol Channel to the *north* of Cornwall, but it was not to be. They were now too far south of Cornwall. And as the elements were still not being in the slightest bit co-operative, he would have to settle on dropping anchor at Falmouth or Plymouth, then take a coach up into Devon in order to collect Tiola, Jasper, Spokesy and Finch.

The wind screamed through the weather-rigging and battered at sailors' ears and cheeks, the squalling rain stinging flesh like dozens of merciless, pinprick arrows. Enormous grey waves roared towards the ship, the starboard bow beginning the ambled climb as each wave hit here first, *Sea Witch* hauling her bowsprit up and up towards a sky that was as dismally grey as the slate-coloured sea below. Then her roll, falling slowly over, the bow still rising – a moment of limbo followed by the ponderous slide down the other side, white foam creaming all round as she dawdled into an even heel again, leaning slightly into that tormenting wind. Her stern then rose as the last of the wave passed beneath her keel, and the corkscrewed motion was completed, only for the next wave to repeat the movement again, and again.

They were approaching the English Channel and depths of between ninety-three and one hundred fathoms. At noon, the weather had cleared slightly, although the sea was no less grey and restless, the wind no less strong, the rain no less threatening in its intent to release yet another downpour. The cloud had cleared enough, and Jesamiah had achieved good navigational readings – a location about one hundred miles west-southwest of Scilly. He balanced on the deck, standing near the helm, paid no heed to the pitch and roll. Too many years' experience had acclimatised his body to the motion of his ship and the belligerent sea. He was, however, frowning. They would need to reef again soon, and were they too far to the north? Like many a sailor he was only too aware of the Navy disaster of 1707 when, sailing too close to the scatter of islands almost an entire British fleet had been destroyed with many hundreds of lives lost as ship after ship, in the wrong place, had ploughed onto rocks.

There were myths and legends about the islands; in particular, myths about a drowned land of Lyonesse. It was said, or so Jesamiah had read, that on certain nights the screams of the drowning could be heard, and at low tide the ruins of houses and churches could be seen as ghostly shadows beneath the water. Thinking about this lost land as he studied what little he could see of the horizon ahead, Jesamiah made a mental note to ask Tiola about it. She'd know the true story.

He cocked an eyebrow at Maha'dun, standing leaning against the quarterdeck rail, trying to light yet another of those damned cheroots of his. Would he know of Lyonesse? He'd been around a long time, or so he claimed. About to call out to him, Jesamiah changed his mind. Grinned.

"Give it up Nightm'n! You ain't ever goin' t' light the bloody thing in this wind!"

Maha'dun's face, part covered by his keffiyeh, puckered into an angry snarl and he threw the cheroot overboard. The wind caught it, blew it back at him. His indignant outrage was not soothed by Jesamiah's burst of laughter.

"I'd go below to my own quarters," he grumbled at Jesamiah, "but I am not permitted to smoke down there, am I?"

"No, you are not. This is a wooden ship and we carry gunpowder. Your smokes, and the way you tend to leave them around, still lit, could send us all sky high."

"I've tried giving them up," Maha'dun whinged. "Can't do it."

"Then try harder?" Jesamiah suggested.

"But I like them."

"And I don't."

Hearing the conversation, shouted against the wind, Skylark proffered a suggestion. "Maybe Miss Tiola can help you wean yourself off them when she rejoins us?"

Maha'dun's gloom brightened. "That's a good idea!"

Jesamiah made no comment. Tiola would be too busy with their baby to bother about nagging Maha'dun to do something he didn't want to do.

He was missing her. Missing their secret ability to use mind words. Was she all right? How was the child? How big was she now with not long to go? He resented being denied the delight of sharing her pregnancy, but also, he was relieved. Some women, he knew, grew tetchy or hated their ungainly bulk. Ah, Tiola would be doing well in Devon with her doting brother, Carter, and his wife to fuss over her. Not long now and they would be together again.

Provided he could navigate safely along the Channel into a suitable harbour.

By mid-afternoon the wind was continuing to be more favourable, but visibility remained poor and the winter night would soon be closing in. Jesamiah checked the compass, stood on deck, pondering. What was it he had read in that pamphlet published by Edmund Halley? Something about ships endangering their passage by passing to the north of Scilly, rather than safely to the south? He chewed at his lip, uncertain, doubting his memory. Was it the other way round? North, south? South, north? Halley had emphasised the mistake of failing to take into account the magnetic variation of 7° west, and had mentioned several errors that were in the pilot books for the area, which placed the islands too many nautical miles from where they actually were. Jesamiah had no pilot books which perhaps, in this instance, was a blessing. No, he was certain he remembered the correct recommendation: a course of nothing more northerly than 49° 40' in order to steer clear of danger.

He was also aware of a strong north-setting current that was running at about seven nautical miles to the twelve hours, well sufficient to carry a ship into difficulty. As with many a current, Jesamiah sensed its presence by the feel of his ship beneath his feet, by her creaking and groaning, by her discomfort and mithering. And this particular current had every opportunity to build to a greater strength because of the wind direction.

He made a decision.

"We'll take soundings," he said to Skylark. "We need a longitude reading – if only some bright spark would win that bloody Longitude Act and come up with a simple and practical solution for us to get one!"

"I doubt that will ever be likely. If there was a way, we'd know it by now, surely?" Skylark observed, before calling for the lead-line to be swung out.

"What's longtitude?" Maha'dun asked.

For a moment Jesamiah wondered whether it was worth explaining. Maha'dun had trouble grasping simple facts, let alone difficult ones. "Longitude is a way of determining exactly where we are. We know how to obtain the longitude measurements for most places on land, but accurate navigational observations on an ocean swell is much harder, and to reckon longitude you need to know the accurate time. Pocket watches are unreliable, and pendulum clocks don't work at sea."

"They tick-tock wrong?"

Jesamiah laughed. "Aye, they tick-tock wrong. Longitude is measured by lines that run around the earth vertically – up and down – unlike latitude, which is measured horizontally, round and round."

Maha'dun pursed his lips. "I've no recollection of ever seeing any lines going either up and down or round and round."

Jesamiah, realising his friend's puzzlement, wondered how else he could explain, but was saved by a call from the leadsman.

"One hundred and forty fathoms. We're in the Soundings, Captain!"

"That gives us an approximate idea of where we are, then," Jesamiah said. He thought a moment as *Sea Witch* heaved herself over another wave, watched as her bow rose up and up, faltered, then plunged downward again. *If Tiola was here,* he thought, *she would know. Her gift of Craft would sense our position, sense any danger.* "But she's not here," he muttered to himself, "she's safe in Appledore. Even if she were with me, she'd not be of use. Not until the child is safely born."

"What's that?" Skylark asked, not hearing correctly.

"I said we're too far to the north to continue heading as we are," Jesamiah said as he stepped to the wheel and took over from the helmsman.

"When do we see these littertude lines then?" Maha'dun asked, still puzzled.

CHAPTER FORTY-SIX

FALMOUTH, CORNWALL

Harbourmasters, in Jesamiah's opinion, should all have been drowned at birth. This one was no exception. He was faffling about calculating a fee, meticulously entering details in his ledger, humming and hawing about a suitable anchorage.

No, I am not unloading or selling cargo. No, I do not know how long I will be here. No, we will not require... and so Jesamiah's patient answers droned on.

"All I want," Jesamiah finally growled, "is to anchor safely for what might be a week or two. One of my men is securing me a coach to North Devon so I may collect my wife. I intend to get there and back again as fast as possible."

"You'll set correct anchors?"

"Of course." Did this idiot think he was a wet-behind-the-ears imbecile?

"Coach you say? Roads are not good from here. Not after all the rain we've had. 'Osses'll be fetlock-deep in mud."

"I am sure we will manage."

"That there Bodmin Moor is not too healthy a place to cross. You got a good blunderbuss to use against highwaymen?"

Good grief! "I have pistols and muskets. And I'm a good shot."

"Might not get a seat on a coach. Private carriage maybe? We're inundated with folk come to town for the election."

Jesamiah felt obliged to ask: "What election is that then?"

"Member of Parliament. It's been brewing for some while now, our previous chap dithering about retiring or no. God finally made up his blithering, senile old mind for him. Silly old fool can't do much Parliamenting from six foot under, can he?" The harbourmaster's burst of laughter turned into a fit of coughing. Gaining his breath, he continued, "Us who have our right to vote will be electing someone new tomorrow. Mind, it's probably a done do. Enough of us been paid to vote for him. Smart young fellow, but I don't personally like 'im. Got shifty eyes, and only interested in his own advantages. Couldn't care a cat's arse for Kernow folk. I'll vote for him though."

"For whom?"

"Why, Doone o' course. Ascham Doone. Who else?"

"What! You are jesting, aren't you?" Jesamiah's surprise was genuine.

The harbourmaster shrugged. "Why would I jest about something like that? I would rather the fellow spent more time here in Cornwall, not up there in Lunnon, but whoever heard of an honourable parliamentary chap who actually visited his constituency more than once a year – apart from at election time? At least Doone understands business."

By that, you mean he's as corrupt as they come? "Where is he lodged, do you know?" Jesamiah asked, not voicing his thoughts.

"The Falcon. I doubt he'll agree to see thee though, Cap'n. Not unless you intend to cast a vote."

"Oh, he'll see me. I know him."

"Do you? What sort of person is he then? Got any insider knowledge have thee?"

"Oh aye, I have that. My sincerest advice? Do not vote for him."

CHAPTER FORTY-SEVEN

Outside the harbourmaster's office Maha'dun pushed himself off the wall he was leaning against and, tossing away the stub of his cheroot, announced, "Doone's here."

"So I have just discovered."

"He's dining with some Marked Crow in that tavern over there." Maha'dun pointed towards The Falcon. "They serve dreadful brandy. Watered down stuff, more bilge than brandy."

Jesamiah smiled to himself. Maha'dun was starting to add the occasional sailing term into his vocabulary. The smile changed to a frown. "You were supposed to be hiring us some transport, not quenching your thirst."

"Done both at the same time. Hired a Berline carriage and a driver willing to take us at night as he knows the road. No footman with it. I guessed we didn't need no raggedy-arse idiot tagging along as a useless bodyguard. Never found a coaching footman yet who could shoot straight. I assured the driver that we could look after ourselves. Bodmin Moor, so he says, is noted for its highwaymen. Can't say I've ever had any trouble."

"You've been across Bodmin before then?"

"Couple of times, when I've had a job to do. Never had any bother with highwaymen." Maha'dun chuckled. "Left a couple of them dead behind me though! Anyway, the driver will be ready to leave within the hour."

Jesamiah did not dare ask how Maha'dun managed to arrange such things; the ability to conjure transport was one of the things he was good at. Presumably, his apparent infinite wealth had something to do with it. He said, "Let's pay a visit to Doone first, shall we?"

Sensing an interesting squabble, Maha'dun grinned and swept along in Jesamiah's wake towards The Falcon.

"Hello Doone, surprised to see me?" Jesamiah toed a stool out from beneath the table and sat, without receiving an invitation. "I believe I'm owed some money for delivering those children. A job you scurried away from doing because you knew there would be a few difficulties involved. Like the Spanish making a bloody nuisance of themselves."

"Captain Acorne, I admit to being surprised to see you, but that is because I would not have expected you here in Falmouth."

"Of course not. You never expected to see me anywhere at all." Jesamiah tipped his chin towards Doone's companion. "So, you're the Marked Crow? One of Doone's hangers-on, eh?"

Not rising to Jesamiah's baiting, Doone introduced his companion. "This is the Reverend Garrick. He has been most helpful in securing my prospective seat in the House of Commons."

The man, dressed in sombre black, nodded disdainfully at Jesamiah.

"Did you achieve the other task I set you?" Doone queried.

"What? Murder Ber'ell on your behalf? That was his name, by the way. Ber'ell, not Burell. I guess his and your friend, Yakub Pasha, did not care to correct your error. No. I did not kill him."

Maha'dun stood with arms folded, fully clad in his Arabian garb, behind Jesamiah. "I disposed of him. He was a Marked Hawk. Overripe for harvesting."

"And who might your foreign friend be?" Doone asked Jesamiah, raising a questioning, and disapproving, eyebrow.

"This?" Jesamiah jerked his left thumb over his shoulder. "This is..."

Maha'dun interrupted. He removed the keffiyeh from his face and gave a slight bow. "You know me very well, Doone. Your grandfather assisted me with a few essential tasks a short while ago."

Doone snorted. "My grandfather employed you to keep unwanted noses away from our personal concerns on Exmoor. You proved yourself to be most unreliable."

"If you say so. But I am a Seeker, a Night Walker. I eradicate those I need to kill, not those I am ordered to kill by ignorant idiots. Your grandfather happened to be useful to me, so I used him."

"You are a rude, crude, lazy drunkard and we were pleased to be finally rid of you," Doone stated. He took another mouthful of the rabbit pie which was before him. Chewed, swallowed.

"I do not like the proximity of this foreign-garbed heathen, Master Doone," Garrick announced, putting down his knife and fork and pushing his plate aside. "I trust that these people are not friends of yours?"

Jesamiah chortled. "Neither of us considers Ascham Doone a friend, you have no worry on that count."

"You have proof that this Berell is dead?"

"Ber'ell," Jesamiah corrected Doone. "My word and that of Maha'dun is proof enough."

A muscle at the side of Doone's right eye twitched. "I heard that Maharden was dead."

"You heard wrong then," Maha'dun said. "You Doones are all hard of hearing. Or is it that none of you has the brain to listen?"

Jesamiah held out his right hand, palm uppermost. "I want my money, Doone. My money, my wife, and your silence."

"The admiralty will pay you all in good time. But silence? About what?"

Jesamiah folded his arms and rested them on the table. "You threatened the safety of my wife. You do one thing to harm her and I'll ensure everyone in England, aye, and beyond, gets to hear just what a corrupt, lying bastard you are."

Doone wiped his mouth with his napkin, leant back in his chair.

"Making idle threats when I have witnesses is most unwise, Acorne."

"Oh, I assure you, these are not idle, nor threats."

"Whatever they are is of no consequence. What I knew about your wife – although I still doubt the accuracy of that particular term – is now irrelevant. I discovered the facts behind her fleeing Cornwall those few years ago from my companion here, who was most anxious to see her brought to justice for the murder of his father. Once I deduced who she truly was, I managed to assist him achieve his aim. For a mutual assistance, of course."

Jesamiah did not move, stared at Doone, then the Crow, as Maha'dun had called him – for the sombre black clothing, presumably. Garrick? Tiola's name had once been Garrick. Was this man a relation? Then, murder? Father? Tiola had fled England because of the death of her father. Was this the secret Doone had discovered? Relief flooded Jesamiah. Not her Craft? Oh, thank God! She was safe!

The reverend formed an expression which was part contemptuous smile, part delighted sneer – and had not an ounce of religious humility or compassion about it. "I am Tiola's eldest brother, and I swore, on the day that my father was butchered by the whore who was his wife, and the slut who was passed as his daughter, that I would ensure just punishment for his death. Punishment for them both."

"Are you accusing Tiola of murdering her father?" Realisation slammed home. "What... have... you... done... with... my... wife?" Jesamiah said to Doone, very quietly, very slowly and very dangerously.

"I have done nothing at all," replied Doone, pushing his empty plate away from him and folding his napkin to lay over it. "I merely returned her to Cornwall because her brother asked me to. Her fate from thereon was nothing to do with me, but decided by a court of law. She is at Launceston gaol, awaiting her time to hang."

Jesamiah slammed to his feet. "Nothing? You did *nothing*? You fucking bastard, you handed her to this... this... petty minded, bigoted... *crow*? Knowing that she could hang for a crime she did not commit?" Jesamiah's hand went to the hilt of the cutlass at his side. Maha'dun grabbed his arm.

"No, my friend. If you cut their miserable throats here you will hang alongside her. Come away. Come. Come away."

Hissed into Jesamiah's ear, "Be sensible. Leave this to me."

CHAPTER FORTY-EIGHT

Twice, waiting for Maha'dun, Jesamiah made a move to leave the hired carriage. The pair of harnessed horses were equally impatient, stamping and snorting in the cold November dampness. The driver was walking about, stamping his own feet and clapping his gloved hands together to keep warmth circulating.

"He goin' t' be long, then?" he asked Jesamiah through the open carriage door.

"He's here!" came Maha'dun's cheerful voice from the far side of the carriage as he opened the door and climbed in, dragging a small wooden trunk behind him.

"We'll be gone for only a few days," Jesamiah said, nodding towards the luggage. "How many changes of silk drawers do you need?"

Maha'dun closed the door and settled himself on the seat next to his friend. "I go nowhere without clean clothes."

"At least it's only one chest, not your usual half-dozen," Jesamiah muttered.

"We ready then?" the driver asked as he closed the other door with a solid thump. "Direct to Lahnsen?"

"Launceston, aye."

"Tha's what I said. Lahnsen."

The carriage rocked as the driver hauled himself to his seat and made himself comfortable, lurched as he whipped up the horses. With a clattering of shod hooves on the cobbles, the creaking of wood and leather and rumble of iron-bound wheels, they were off, up the hill out of Falmouth heading for Launceston, sixty or so miles, two or three days, away.

The night was cold. Jesamiah took a thick blanket from the seat opposite, tucked it over his feet and knees. Said, "You have blood on the hem of your thobe."

"Have I?" Maha'dun looked down, swore. "Bugger. Oh well, I doubt anyone will be brave enough to notice. I cut his throat as he stepped from the tavern privy."

"Whose throat? Doone or Garrick?"

"Doone is a shit, but he is of no great consequence. The Marked Crow was a different matter."

"I would have preferred to be done with the bugger myself."

"Better I kill him than you. You'd hang. You'd be suspected, Doone would have seen to that. But I assured that you had a witness who'll put you sitting here in this vehicle for a good hour."

"Doone could as easily condemn you."

Maha'dun laughed. "He would not dare."

Jesamiah asked another question. He remembered Tiola using the word once. "Seeker?"

"It is what I am. What I do. I am a Seeker."

"Seeking what? Who? These Marked Crows? I get the crow bit, all dressed in black as Garrick was, but care to explain 'marked'? You go around slitting the throats of preachers, do you?" Added beneath his breath, "Don't blame you for that."

"Not just preachers. Any who need dispatching. The different birds describe the target. Crows are usually religious types. Hawks, buzzards, peregrines, different ranks of the well off. Nightingales are whores – of either sex. Magpies are thieves. Pirates are jackdaws. Sparrows, common folk."

That all made sense. The carriage rumbled over a wooden bridge, the horses' hooves echoing hollow into the cold night. On the far side, the driver urged them into a steady trot.

"Marked? By whom?"

Maha'dun reached into a pocket, withdrew a small leather flask of brandy, offered it to Jesamiah then took his own generous gulp. "No one. They are born marked. The Seekers were created to be rid of them. Some we find easy, the young are often cocky and careless. Others, who keep themselves hidden in the shadows, we might not come across until they're old and senile. There used to be many, many of them, many of us too; aren't so many now, though I guess there will always remain a few, especially if they breed before we can get to them."

"But marked as what?"

"Living Malevolents. The evil-souled. The opposite of Miss Tiola and the goodness of her kind. Yakub Pasha became one through his own greed. That Crow, Garrick, he was born marked. Tainted through his rotten sire. Not sure how we missed the both of them. Hid behind their narrow-minded religious nonsense I suspect."

"And Doone?"

Maha'dun shrugged. "Sadly, he is not one of the marked. Though if he were, I'd have him as a vulture. One who feeds on others. The right time to be rid of him will come, I promise you."

"So, you are a professional killer. Yet my Tiola admires you?"

Maha'dun looked at Jesamiah through his bright, sapphire blue eyes. "You admire me, too."

"No, I don't, you're an irritating idiot."

"I've heard Tiola call you the same on occasion."

That was true. Jesamiah laughed.

"Besides," Maha'dun fiddled for a cheroot, lit it. "Besides, it was the Wise Women, the Old Ones of Craft, Tiola and her kind, who created us, the Seekers."

CHAPTER FORTY-NINE

Tiola could not sleep. The cell was bitter cold, damp and miserable. Frost was in the air, maybe there would even be snow soon. Could she survive much longer? Almost, were it not for the child, she welcomed the thought of approaching death, of passing Beyond and being freed from this ongoing nightmare.

She knew that was defeatist, that others endured. She herself had endured in the past, although all those memories of past-life existences were hidden from her during these months of being with child. What was that old saying? You never missed something until you no longer had it? She would get her Craft back once she had given birth, but she could well be dead by then.

She could sense, rather than hear, the torment of the Malevolents in her mind, sniggering and snickering. Goading and tempting.

~ *Use your Craft. Keep warm, keep alive.* ~

~ *Save yourself. Use your Craft.* ~

~ *Save your baby! Use your Craft*! ~

Hardest of all to ignore: ~ *Use your Craft. Talk to Jesamiah*! ~

Draping a blanket around her shoulders she got up from her nest-like bed – thank goodness for the clean straw and blankets that Finch and Hetty brought her – and walked around. It was a small cell. Four paces, turn. Three paces, turn. Four paces, three... Her ankles were swollen. Her back ached as much as her head. As much as her heart. Sighing, she sat down again, pulled the blankets close and laid her hand on her swollen belly. She was large, not far off her time now if the child was born to term. If. And then that would be it. They would take her, still bloodied and exhausted from giving birth, to the gallows on the castle green to hang. They'd not wait, they'd not allow her the chance to suckle or cuddle her child. She might not even see it, might not even know if it was a boy or a girl.

Best to be done quick, without fuss, they'd say.

Where was Jesamiah?

She got up again, went to the bars and stared out across the narrow corridor to the single, grated window. Gazed at the small portion of night that she could see beyond. There was only blackness and the rough, castle walls. No view of the sky or the stars – if there were stars. Perhaps it was cloudy. Perhaps rain was coming, perhaps snow. Perhaps a frost sparkled on the ground. Perhaps Jesamiah was on his way. Perhaps he would be here tomorrow, or the next day? Perhaps, perhaps, perhaps!

There had been a lot of rain, a blessing for there had been several days of intolerable heat back when it had been summer. Except, the roof leaked and the wet came through the many holes in the floorboards of the chapel above, formed as many puddles below, made everything damper than it already was. But it was colder now. Freezing. The ground outside, and in, would turn to ice. There was no warmth for her, or the baby. Only the straw and the blankets.

She was lonely. Doryty had been company. Even that filthy man who had been incarcerated in the cell next door had been a bulwark against loneliness, despite his lewd habits. Doryty had made Tiola laugh the first time he'd masturbated in front of them.

"Put it away, grandad," she'd said, scathingly. "I'm surprised ye like anyone seein' tha' li'le withered thing. I've seen rats with bigger pricks!"

Again, Tiola laid her hand on her belly. There had been little movement these past few days. No kicking, no fluttering. Tiola leant her head against the cell's bars, closed her eyes and made no attempt to stop the tears from slithering down her cheeks. The baby was dead, she was sure of it.

~ Use your Craft. Find out. ~

"No, I will not. In case I am wrong. I will not endanger my baby for the sake of my own ease." She began walking again.

Where was Jesamiah? She needed him so much, but he could not see her like this. There was nothing he could do to bring her comfort, nothing he could do to ease this pain that was tearing her apart. Nothing he could do to bring a dead baby back to life.

Wherever he was, it was just as well that he was not here. Not here to witness and endure the agony of watching her hang.

CHAPTER FIFTY

They arrived at Launceston three days later, the journey, to Jesamiah's frustration, taking longer than anticipated. They had made good progress that first evening, covering the eleven miles to Truro in ten minutes over the two hours. There, with the need to rest the horses, they had spent the night at an inn, setting out again at first light, swinging up towards Bodmin at a steady pace. But up on the open moor the driver slowed the horses to a walk, and not far from the remote inn, halfway across the moor, snow had come blizzarding in like a wild monster let loose from its cage and bent on vengeance.

"We can't go on in this!" the driver had yelled through the punishing north-easterly wind. "The inn be not far ahead. We'll take shelter there a while."

Taking refuge there, Maha'dun enjoyed the fine brandy the inn served. The driver and horses content to wait for better conditions, but Jesamiah was restless. Any other time, he would have enjoyed the brandy too, but he had Tiola on his mind.

As he served a steaming hot venison stew to his guests, the landlord made no secret of where the drink had come from. Contraband – smuggled goods from France and Spain. With pride he explained that it was carried by sturdy Dartmoor pack ponies along the 'Gentlemen's' secret ways having been landed along the southern Cornish coast, the inn being a suitable exchange point. From there, goods were sent on to wherever they were wanted – as far as Bristol or London. No one bothered this remote inn, not even the military or makers and keepers of the law, for most of them took advantage of their own illicit share of anything cheap to buy... and any potential troublemakers all too easily met with 'accidents' out on the lonely expanse of the moor.

Despite his distraction, Jesamiah was impressed by the smooth organisation of the Trade. He had noticed the two kegs and several wooden boxes which had appeared from hidden places on the carriage, and then rapidly disappeared again into the inn's storeroom. And he noticed their driver did not pay for his or the horses' lodging. No need to ask why, and every need to pretend that he had not seen anything.

"Been a Gentleman's Rest ever since 1547," the landlord had also boasted. "The first owner, a retired seaman, started building the day King Hal passed to God in January of that year. By the time Bess were on the throne various Traders saw the advantage of such a suitable location."

The snow had changed to sleet during the night, and by early morning, to rain. With the snow washed to slush, the track was wetter and muddier, but passable and they arrived in one piece at Launceston as the church bells rang two of the clock in the afternoon. Jesamiah went straight to the gaol.

There, Maha'dun found him, two hours later, sitting huddled in an alcove of the high outer stone wall, sheltering as best he could from the bitter wind and sleeting rain.

"Idiot of a gaoler won't let me in," Jesamiah mumbled through his coat pulled high around his ears and chin, his hands tucked under his armpits. "Visitors have to get permission from the sheriff or the constable."

"So where are they to be found?" Maha'dun asked, squatting down beside Jesamiah and pulling his own woollen robes closer for warmth.

"Other end of Cornwall, and London."

"Oh."

"If I tried to find this sheriff I could be gone for several weeks. Which might be too late."

Maha'dun got to his feet, stared up at the stone walls. "Anywhere climbable?"

"No, I've walked round twice."

A sound, footsteps scrunching on the gravel of the ascending lane alerted Maha'dun. He turned to see who was coming. A young girl, huddled into a woollen shawl, a basket on her arm. Beside her a man, equally huddled, carrying a large sheaf of straw.

"Finch!" Maha'dun called, striding forward, arms open in delighted welcome. "Jesamiah, it's Finch!"

Jesamiah scrabbled to his feet, peered through the drizzle of rainy mist. "What are you doing here? You were meant to meet the rest of the crew at Appledore?"

Finch deposited the bundle of straw on the ground. "Aye, and so were Miss Tiola meant t' be there. Never got that far did we? Me an' the girl 'ere, as stayed all this while t' keep eye on 'er." He peered at Maha'dun. "An' where did you spring from? We thought you was dead."

"I wasn't."

Finch sniffed. "Looked it t' me at the time. Oh well, obviously y' weren't. Still smokin' them demmed cherryoots o' yourn? Got any spare baccy?"

Maha'dun rummaged in his pocket, gave Finch a small tin.

"Ta. Silver's nigh on run out, Cap'n. I'm 'elpin' re-thatch a barn at a farm nearby t' earn some money. The girl 'ere's servin' at one o' the inns. An' if we don't get more silver t' pay fer necesstities soon, I reckon 'er servin'll be more than pourin' ale an' dishin' out stew!" He motioned pulling an imaginary skirt up to his waist, his meaning plain. He scrutinised Jesamiah's face. "I likes the scar. Suits you."

"Now I'm here I can pay for things." Jesamiah recognised the girl now, one of those they'd rescued from the Barbary pirates. Couldn't remember her name.

Seeing his consternation, Hetty bobbed a curtsey. "I'm Hetty, I've been taking care, as much as I can, of Miss Tiola."

"Then I thank you. Is she all right?" Jesamiah hardly dared ask.

"No, sir, she's as thin as a twig, despite her big belly and even though I take her as good quality food as I can get." Hetty proffered the basket, flipping back the cloth cover to reveal a small loaf of bread, a portion of cold pie and two apples. "An' she has a bad cough. Gaol cough. I reckon she caught it from the bugger who were in the cell beside her a few weeks back. He had a hacker of one. They hanged him. Good riddance."

Jesamiah reached for the basket. "Perhaps if I take this, that beardless young bugger at the gate will let me in."

"James? He's conscientious. He sticks to the rules like a fly caught in honey," Hetty said. "His pa is the gaoler, miserable bugger that he is, but he's even more miserable on account of he can't walk at the moment, laid up in bed upstairs at the gaolhouse yonder."

"Why's that then?" Maha'dun asked.

Hetty bobbed him a curtsey too. She remembered him being among Captain Acorne's men.

"An 'orse kicked 'im in the balls," Finch said, guffawing. "Word is that 'is prick's 'angin' 'alf off."

"James is taking full responsibility for the gaol right now," Hetty explained. "I wonder if there's a way we can take advantage of it?

Hetty took the food to Tiola, with young James escorting her and carrying the straw. He delivered the straw and food basket, lowering both down through the hole in the cell's ceiling, mindful of the puddled floor and the soft wood starting to rot.

"The roof is leaking," Tiola complained, looking up at his face peering down at her. "Some slates are dislodged." She'd said the same for the past several weeks.

"I'll make sure that my pa passes word to the constable," James promised. He'd also said the same for the same weeks.

Walking back to the gate, her hand in his, Hetty asked, "Can you not get someone to fix the roof? Someone from the town?"

"Pa could, but who would pay fer it? Pa certainly won't."

"If I found someone, would you let them do the repairs as a charitable gesture?"

James scratched at his fluff of a beard. "Well, I shouldn't really. I'd need to ask Pa first."

Hetty smiled at him, lifted his hand, deliberately brushing it against her breast. "Why does he need to know? He can't see anything from his bedchamber window, can he? It's above the gatehouse, looks out onto the lane, not across at the gaol. At least, that's what you told me the other day."

"*Ais*, but..."

"Maybe it would please him, when the job's done, that he won't have to worry about leakages and rotting wood? You'll be showing that you can get things done, to save him fretting."

She kissed James demurely on the cheek, then sensuously on the mouth. "And it would please me. It would please me a lot."

James kissed her back, then blushed. "I would like t' please thee. Really, I would. I 'spect t'would be all right. D' you think t'would?"

Uncertain, he peered down the steep lane; the ragged man who always escorted Hetty when there was straw to carry was on his way back down the hill – and there was no sign of that other surly man with the black hair and sailor's gait. He kissed Hetty's cheek again and waved as she set off after Finch.

"I 'ope thee find summ'n fer the roof!" he called.

CHAPTER FIFTY-ONE

Jesamiah found lodging for himself and Maha'dun at one of the better inns, Finch and Hetty assuring him that they were suited to the rooms they already had, Finch especially, now that he had enough silver to pay for his board. Hetty's bed and food came free with her work. Jesamiah sat with Maha'dun in a secluded corner, having picked at a generous serving of gammon, potatoes and chutney, not enjoying it, for he knew Tiola only had bread and cheese. He'd wanted to break into the gaol to be with her, but Hetty and Finch had persuaded him against the idea.

"If you get caught you'll end up in trouble, then how will you be able to help?" Hetty had admonished.

Jesamiah had hated taking advice from a mere slip of a girl, but Maha'dun had agreed with her logic.

"You going to eat that?" Finch asked, pointing at the half-eaten plate of food.

Jesamiah shook his head. "No. You have it."

Finch didn't need a second invitation. "Any 'ow, as I were sayin'," he said through a mouthful of food, "we sent young Benson off to his ma and pa that same aft'noon we got t' Falmouth. It's prob'ble Master Carter, Miss Tiola's other brother, don't know what's 'appened."

"And Donréal? Where's he?" Jesamiah asked.

Finch looked at Hetty, who stared back at him.

"Donréal?" Jesamiah repeated. "The Spanish lad?"

"I knows who 'e was," Finch mumbled, not looking at his captain.

A moment of silence.

"Was?" Jesamiah asked quietly.

Finch became suddenly busy with what remained of the gammon.

"I didn't realise that you did not know. He's dead," Hetty blurted out. "There was an accident at Lisbon. We buried him at sea. Miss Tiola was distraught."

"Dead?" Jesamiah repeated. "How?"

Hetty told him, leaving out that the Portuguese soldiers had tried to molest Tiola.

"Doone had nothing to do with it?"

"No, sir. It was just an accident. He fell, hit his head."

Jesamiah closed his eyes a moment, sighed. "Poor lad. At least, perhaps, he is now with his mother and little brother."

"Young 'Edgepig Benson took it 'ard," Finch said, now the worst had been accounted for. "They was good friends, them two lads."

The potboy arrived to take away the empty dishes. Maha'dun ordered more drinks. "I made a few enquiries earlier," he said, "got the driver of our carriage to ask around. He's found himself a bed at the livery yard, by the way. I told him to stable the horses and wait for further orders. He's quite content to get paid and not have to do anything to earn it."

"What sort of enquiries?" Jesamiah asked, half-hearted, unsure whether he was really interested or not, his mind on the news about Donréal and how – what he could do – to help Tiola.

"It seems this constable, Sir Pepper, or whatever his name is..."

"Pyper."

"Whatever. Seems he comes down to his estate with a pack of rich followers and unwanted relatives every winter for your Christmas celebrations, but mainly to enjoy the hunting. He's expected any day now."

Jesamiah sat forward, suddenly excited. "You're sure of this?"

Maha'dun nodded. "I am."

"That means I might be able to buy Tiola's freedom. How well off is he?"

"He needs money," Hetty answered. "James told me that the Pypers spend more than they have."

"And we know where this estate of his is?"

"A few miles north of here," Hetty answered.

"Just as well we have a private carriage to use then, eh?" Jesamiah was grinning, suddenly everything looked more hopeful.

"Finch," he said, "get yourself to Appledore on the next Flyer. See if any of the crew are kicking their heels waiting for us to turn up there. Go with them to Falmouth to meet with Skylark. Have *Sea Witch* ready to sail at a moment's notice. As soon as I get Tiola released we'll be out of here."

"But what about the gaol roof?" Hetty protested. "You said you and Mr Finch would see to it. I told James I would find someone."

"Mend it t'morrer mornin'. Take the Flyer t'morrer aft'noon?" Finch suggested, accepting the pint tankard of ale which the potboy placed before him. "Just 'ope it don't bleedin' rain or snow agin t'night."

CHAPTER FIFTY-TWO

James watched two men approach the gaolhouse gate soon after daylight had become more than the bleak misery of a grey mizzle. One, carrying a bag of tools, was the sailor-type who had been hanging around yesterday, the other was the man who always came with Hetty, this time, carrying a ladder instead of straw. Of Hetty there was no sign.

When the men were a few yards from the gatehouse James straightened from his position of lounging against the wall and attempted to look menacing and professional. It was a poor attempt because beyond a wooden quarterstaff he had no weapons and two of the spots beside his nose had burst that morning, so were weeping pus and looked sore and angry. His father was also shouting from the confinement of his upstairs room, bellowing, none too pleasantly, for ale and breakfast.

"Who are you?" he challenged.

Jesamiah smiled congenially. Introduced himself as Jesamiah Oakwood and explained that he was waiting for Sir Hugh Pyper to return from London.

"He was supposed to be here by now," he grumbled. "I've been commissioned to do some improvements to his house. Cannot start until he gets here. Meanwhile, I hear you have a roof that needs mending? Might as well get that done. Do something useful whilst I'm waiting."

"He bain't expected until first week December. Sevr'l days off yet. An' who be there t' pay thee?" James asked doubtfully. "I bain't sure if Pa – he be gaoler – 'll agree t' this."

"I'll sort it all with Sir Hugh," Jesamiah promised. "I've heard talk that the King's Inspectorate will be coming to Cornwall; we can't have Sir Hugh accused of not doing his duty, can we? If there's work that hasn't been done your pa will be the one blamed for it. Now, where's this hole? I want to get done before this bloody rain starts again."

As he spoke, Hetty appeared, trotting up the hill. She carried a basket, wore a huge smile. "I've brought some nice things for your father, James," she called as she came closer. "Poor soul has been confined to his bed these past days with only you to look after him – and no disrespect, James my lad, I doubt you have yet managed to master cooking a nice pheasant pie as good as your dear dead mother could. God rest her soul." She proffered her laden basket. "I've a jug of ale in here, too, and a honey syllabub. It's a large jug of ale. I thought your pa would like a large jug." With a broad smile, she handed the basket to the young lad. He peeped inside, grinned at the contents.

"That the building?" Jesamiah said, walking through the open gateway and beckoning Finch to follow.

James set the basket down on the gaolhouse doorstep and started to anxiously trot after them. "I'd as best come an' all!" he cried.

Hetty swore beneath her breath. She had to keep James here with her, keep him out of Captain Jesamiah's way. She went towards the open kitchen door of the adjoining gaolhouse and pretended to trip on a loose cobblestone. "Oh! Oh, my ankle!"

James ran back to her.

"Oh, it hurts!" Hetty wailed, sitting on the cobbles and pulling up her skirt to her knees to assess her injury. "I think I've broke my ankle!" She pulled her skirt a little higher.

James crouched down to investigate, trying not to stare at her garters, revelling in touching her stocking, removing her boot to inspect the damage. "I think as 'tis only sprained," he said. "Do y' think thee can walk?"

"No! Oh no!" Hetty sobbed, throwing her arms around his neck. "You will have to carry me indoors, I can't sit out here. Perhaps a bit of a rest and a sip of ale might help. Oh, it hurts!"

"That girl's a natural actress," Jesamiah chuckled as he set the ladder up against the gaol wall and motioned for Finch to climb up to see what damage there was to the slate tiles.

For himself, he went to the only door, found it bolted and locked, as he expected it would be. Around the side, he peered through the metal grill of the single window.

"Tiola? Tiola! It's me! I'm going to get you out of here!"

Startled, relieved, flustered, Tiola hurried to the bars of her cell, peered at the small window, her heart leaping at the sight of him. Oh! He had come! He had come at last! All the same, she answered gruffly. "You most certainly are *not* going to do anything illegal! I will not run from the law for the rest of my life. If you have anything stupid in mind, forget it! I have no intention of running anywhere. Go away."

"No. I intend to buy your freedom, but until then, you are not staying here, I..."

"Who is that on the roof?" she interrupted, stepping back to look up through the hole in the ceiling.

"It's me Miss. Finch," Finch called down. "Slates are all come adrift. Shoddy workmanship. Won't take m' long t' make this 'ole wider, shinny down, pull you up an' out..."

"You will do no such thing!"

"Tiola..." Jesamiah began.

"Do not 'Tiola' me! In my condition I am not able to 'shinny' anywhere. Nor am I able – or inclined – to leave here. I will stay put and face what I must face."

"But..."

"Mr Finch," she called upwards, "I would be obliged, since you are up there, for you to do what you can to mend that hole."

"But..." Jesamiah tried again.

"I will have no buts, Jesamiah, I am *not* going anywhere. If you can legally purchase my freedom, then please do so, although I resent being bargained for like a mare or a cow, but I will *not* be branded as a gaol-breaker. Please, go away. You are making all this so much harder for me."

"I don't bloody want to go away. My place is beside you. Maha'dun is with me. He found me in Spain. He isn't dead."

"I know he is not dead. Have they told you of Donréal? There was nothing I could do to save him. Oh, Jesamiah, my dearest love, I very much appreciate your concern, but you are distraught. I can see it in your face – where did you get that scar? Where have you been? What have you been doing all this while? No, do not answer, I am not interested. Fighting, I assume. I just cannot trust you to act sensibly can I?" Tiola fought back tears, not wishing to allow him to see her weep, not wishing for him to realise how frightened and lonely she was. Losing her temper seemed a better option. "I love you and I so want you to tell me that everything will be all right, but I need to conserve my strength for myself and our baby. I do not have enough in reserve to spend it on your idiocy, so please, *please* Jesamiah, go away!"

She turned her back on him so that he would not see the tears rolling down her cheeks.

"You comin' up t' 'elp me?" Finch called. "Slates are bloody 'eavy things and you want me t' get that coach soon. An' it's goin' t' bloody rain agin."

Using damp logs, for that was all he had, James stoked the fire in the living room of the house. The place was small and none too clean. Hetty sat in the only armchair, her foot swathed in an ice-cold wet towel, tears – genuine tears – trickling down her cheeks. James assumed they were for the pain in her ankle, though he had not queried that it did not look very swollen.

How could she tell him that as he had carried her withindoors a vision had swamped her with such dread that she had almost fainted?

The vision: a dark, storm sky. The sea, rough and angry. A ship – sailing away or toward? Sunset or sunrise? These, she could not tell, but the rest was all too, too clear. Miss Tiola, her belly swollen to term, the wind blowing her hair.

And a gallows noose around her neck.

CHAPTER FIFTY-THREE
DECEMBER 4TH 1719

"Women near their time be tetchy, you can't do more t' 'elp by mopin' an' 'angin' around 'ere. Leave 'er be," Finch had advised those few days ago as he and Jesamiah had mended the roof, both being careful for the supporting beams were rotten. Poor, cheap quality wood, even poorer, cheaper quality workmen used to build the place.

Jesamiah had snorted disagreement, but privately took Finch's point. At least he could make his wife as comfortable as he could. He sent things for her – blankets and a small bed, admitted, it was not much larger than the one they were used to in *Sea Witch*'s cabin, but a bed was a bed. A squirrel fur cloak, boots, generously lined with rabbit fur. Woollen socks and gloves. A clean gown and two linen undershifts. A charcoal brazier. A lantern. Candles. Hot food.

The gaoler, generously paid not to notice the items being delivered, was hobbling around knock-kneed and bent double.

"You can always sell the things later on," Jesamiah had suggested.

The gaoler had liked the idea, so stayed within his own house, leaving the supervisory role of the gaol to his son.

Every day Jesamiah went with Maha'dun in the hired Berline to discover whether Sir Hugh had arrived at his country estate. The place was made ready for him and his party of guests: servants had replenished the kitchens for expected meals, dust sheets were removed from furniture, beds aired, fires laid and lit in the great hearths. Cobwebs dusted, spiders evicted, mice and rats trapped. But still the man had not arrived. Every day Jesamiah returned to Launceston dejected, more afraid and more worried. Every day Tiola became nearer to giving birth.

Hetty reported back to him each evening, although there was nothing new to tell. That she had permitted James a kiss and a discreet fumble to keep him sweet, and distract him from her obviously not sprained ankle, she kept squarely to herself. The lad had asked her to marry him, which was awkward but useful, for she had told him she would need to think on it. "We are both very young," had been a suitable avoidance and delaying excuse.

By the fourth day of December the wind had turned hostile. A bitter wind that found its way through cob or stone walls, through thatch and slate alike. That squinnied under doors, squirmed around window frames and strode through broken panes of glass. That swooped down chimneys, swirling smoke and soot along with it. The cold it carried bit deep through clothes and mantles, to sear to the bone. It viciously toyed with anything not tightly secured down, like a spiteful cat torturing a captive mouse.

Still no one had arrived at Sir Hugh's estate, although with sodden tracks, muddy roads and rivers ready to burst their banks, it was not surprising that prospective guests were reluctant to venture into the West Country, even if the prestige of the host's social status was alluring.

"It's my birthday today," Jesamiah said to Maha'dun as their driver negotiated the carriage up the drive to Sir Hugh's grand house, the horses' hooves splashing through puddles, the carriage wheels sending up fountains of spray.

"Perhaps I'll be awarded a present of this bloody man actually being there this time." Jesamiah did not sound very hopeful.

Maha'dun peered out of the carriage window to gaze up the man's drive stretching ahead of them, wrapping his keffiyeh tighter around his face to block as much light from his skin as he could, although because of the rain, the day was grey, bleak and dismal.

"From what I can see, there doesn't seem to be much activity going on."

"When is your birthday?" Jesamiah asked, for want of something to say as Maha'dun resettled himself.

"No idea. Nightwalkers don't have birthdays."

"What? No celebration? No presents!"

Maha'dun grinned beneath his face covering. "An exhaustive tumble with an amorous lover is all I need to keep me happy. Oh, and a bottle of cognac and a box of best cheroots."

"I'll get you the last two for Christmas. Can't help with the first."

"Ssh!" Maha'dun hissed as the carriage slowed to a halt beside the grand flight of Caen stone steps to the even grander mahogany front door. He thrust his head out of the window again. Ignoring the rain removed his keffiyeh briefly, sniffed, his nostrils flaring. Ducked back into the carriage, said, "Doone is here."

"What? How do you know?"

"I can smell him."

"That awful perfume stuff he wears? It's strong, but not that strong!"

"I smell different things than do you. I can smell souls. He's here, I say."

"Gentlemen, make yourselves comfortable. Mine host is not yet arrived, but I have been given instructions to offer full hospitality, on his behalf, to any guests intrepid enough to brave this inclement weather. Refreshment? Brandy, I think." He nodded to the servant hovering at the door to the library. "Our guests will be staying for dinner." He gestured to the wind disturbing the bare-branched trees beyond the rain-drenched windows. "And the night? How far have you come, Acorne?" He did not wait for an answer, went straight on to give orders to the servant. "See to it that my guests' horses are stabled and their driver is made comfortable."

"Very good, sir."

Jesamiah exchanged a wry look with Maha'dun. They had

enquired after Master Doone at the door but had not expected to be invited in.

"Thank you for the offer of dinner, but no, we will not stay. We'll accept the offer of brandy, though," Jesamiah said, then sat down in one of the upholstered armchairs beside the blazing fire. "How did the election go?"

Doone preened. "You are addressing the new Member of Parliament. I won by a most generous majority, in light of which, Sir Hugh was only too delighted to write and offer me an invitation to join his house party here. He has been a most beneficial patron. May I ask what business you have with him? Ah, here's our brandy. Sir Hugh has an excellent taste. His coffee and chocolate are as flavoursome; he has his own plantations in the Colonies, of course. Now, there could be honest employment for you, Acorne. I happen to know that Sir Hugh seeks a vessel which can make fast passages across the Atlantic. Or, maybe you are interested in more dishonest dealings? Most brandy is smuggled."

"Did you know," Maha'dun said to Jesamiah, savouring his glass of strong liquid, "that our host here, Ascham Doone, the honourable member of the British Parliament, handed Yakub Pasha, the bastard who slaughtered people dear to you in Spain, a list of names, giving instructions to eliminate certain of those same names?"

"Names? A list?" Jesamiah answered.

"I have it here. I could not comprehend the written squiggles earlier in the year, but now that I have mastered the technique of reading I find it most informative." As he spoke, Maha'dun fished beneath his robes, pulled out a crumpled piece of paper from an inside coat pocket, handed it to Jesamiah.

Jesamiah read it aloud.

"Winnard Doone – eliminated. Robert Harley – dying. Francesca Escudero – eliminated. Leandro Escudero – missing: unimportant? Captain Jesamiah Acorne – to be eliminated. Calderón – to be eliminated. Henry Jennings – unimportant." He laughed. "Henry will not like being referred to as 'unimportant'. As for these others..."

"The interesting thing about that note, Jesamiah," Maha'dun interrupted, "is that I saw Yakub Pasha pass it to Ber'ell. Ber'ell was the one Master Doone, here, wanted you to kill."

"You could not possibly have seen any such thing!" Doone protested. "Aside of which, how could you be certain that what you have is the same note?"

Maha'dun reached forward and took the dogeared piece of paper from Jesamiah, held it to his nose and inhaled. "It has the scent of all three of you on it."

Doone snorted.

"I also guess, although I cannot be certain, that because of this list, Ber'ell told Pasha where to find Calderón and his family. Funny that Master Doone so desperately wanted him dead, silenced, isn't it Jes?"

"Most funny," Jesamiah answered, not laughing.

"I know nothing of this nonsense." Doone was contemptuously dismissive.

Maha'dun continued his conversation with Jesamiah. "And I am not very happy that it was this same Member of Parliament who handed Mistress Acorne to that religious fanatic who was her brother."

"A brother who was bent on seeing her hang for a crime she did not commit," Jesamiah finished for him. "You claimed to know her secret, Doone. I thought it was another secret that you threatened me with. But I assumed the wrong danger. The accusation of murder was your threat, wasn't it?"

"I put two and two together, yes. It is my duty, as an M.P., to see justice done."

"No, Doone, you have stirred mud where there was none to stir. My wife is innocent of all this, and I think you had better put right the mischief you have sown, or I might have to inform certain people, like Sir Hugh, that you are a rotten apple in his barrel."

Doone laughed outright. "*All* of Parliament is a rotten apple! We do not do the job for love of King and Country, we do it for what we can get from it as personal gain."

Jesamiah, quick to laugh, formidable when angry, narrowed his gaze. There was no laughter; he was angry. Very angry. "I intend to see you hang, Doone, for the murder of Francesca Escudero, and my kinsman and his family. To hang because you organised the kidnapping of innocent young women and children. And because you have targeted my wife. I expect I can think of a few other reasons as well."

"Superficial accusations, Acorne. None of which are provable, nor would any magistrate listen to you. You are known as a pirate, I am an elected member of His Majesty's Government. Are you truly so set on making a public fool of yourself? I can easily arrange for you to spend a few hours in the stocks, if that is so."

"I have no care about you putting your backside on a seat in the Commons, you can be as corrupt as you choose in that place, but I do care about the distress my pregnant wife is being put through." Jesamiah rose from his chair and went to the desk to one side of the room, rummaged, found what he wanted. "So, you can write a letter exonerating my wife. Issue her a grant of pardon."

Doone snorted indignation. "I cannot do that. I have not the authority."

Maha'dun chuckled. "Is he admitting that he is not as important as he says he is?"

Jesamiah held out a quill. "You have studied law; you know exactly the correct words to put down. Write, or I'll make sure that seat in parliament is a damned uncomfortable one."

Grunting annoyance, Doone seated himself at the desk and wrote. Done, he handed it to Jesamiah. "I think," he said in the most unfriendly manner, "that it is time for you to leave."

Jesamiah went to the window. The rain was coming down as if someone was emptying water by the bucketload, the wild wind swirling it into rivulets and rippling puddles. It would not be a pleasant journey back to Launceston.

"On reflection," he said, looking through narrowed eyes at the hateful man before him, "I think you had better come with us. Add weight to the authenticity of this letter."

"You can think all you want, Acorne! I am not leaving these premises. Now, be gone, or do I summon assistance to have you removed?"

A brass paperweight was on the desk. Jesamiah picked it up, nestled it into the palm of his hand and cracked it against Doone's skull as he turned away towards the door. Doone fell, unconscious, like a dropped brick.

"Master Doone has been taken unwell," Jesamiah explained to the anxious servants as he and Maha'dun dragged Doone to their summoned carriage and bundled him inside.

"The poor chap has been afflicted by these seizures before. We'll take him to the physician in Launceston. Give our regards to Sir Hugh if he ever gets here."

CHAPTER FIFTY-FOUR

Tiola sat hunched before the brazier. It threw out scarce warmth, but with blankets, better clothing and the fur cloak she was at least warmer than she had been. And a little drier, although the roof still dribbled rain onto the ceiling above, forming puddles which dripped into the cells below. The wind was moaning, coming in gusts and battering against the walls and roof. Occasionally there came an ominous creak. The draughts had guttered her lantern out several times; she had given up trying to keep it alight.

There was nothing that could help her ease the dull, persistent backache which had been nagging since noon. Neither standing, sitting, nor walking eased it, and come dusk, she accepted that she was in labour. Too early by a few weeks, although she was not over-alarmed. As a midwife she had helped to birth many an early born child, except usually the mothers' dates were not reliable. The important thing would be to keep the baby warm. She busied herself sorting blankets.

Realised too, that the fourth day of December was Jesamiah's birthday. He was now twenty-and-six years old. It would be good to present him with a healthy son for his special day. Not good to burden him with what must inevitably follow.

Hetty, coming mid-afternoon with a meat-filled pasty and fresh ale, had told her that Jesamiah and Maha'dun had gone again to find Sir Hugh Pyper. "Not that they're having much luck, and the weather is rousing something dreadful, but I suspect it keeps Captain Acorne busy."

Tiola walked. She sat, she walked again. The pains were coming more frequently. Hetty would not be visiting again until morning. Neither would James, nor his father come for they never stirred from their house after dark. Tiola looked towards the window – Jesamiah had fixed oiled parchment over it, stopping the worst of the wind, but a corner had ripped and now it flapped uselessly, like a bird with a broken wing. As she watched, a fresh gust seized hold and the parchment danced off with the wind as it raced across the castle green. For a moment the torn parchment caught on the cross rail of the gallows, flapped there, a stark reminder of what was to come, was then whisked away, tumbling and prancing in dizzying spirals against the wild, dark sky.

Tiola was a midwife, knew what to expect, what to do, but delivering someone else's child was quite different from labouring to bring your own into the world. She breathed steadily through another, stronger, pain. Another burst of wind came roaring inward. She heard its sound lift over the castle walls, dip, then hit the gaol as if a vengeful giant were wielding a sledgehammer. The walls shook. The single wooden, bolted door, rattled. Then the roof gave another groan, the rotten timber joists grating against stone walls, slates shifted, slid to the ground outside, smashing and splintering. With the movement, the change of weight, the rotten supporting beams gave way and the roof at the far, door, end caved in. Tiola hurried to a corner as far away from the devastation as she could get. Crouched there, her arms over her head as the creaking, groaning, crashing and grinding swelled to its height of tortured sound.

And her waters broke.

"Oh, the Goddess help me!" Her cry was part sob, part scream as she huddled, frightened and alone, beneath her cloak to shield herself from the swirl of choking dust.

"Someone come. Please. Someone come!"

CHAPTER FIFTY-FIVE

Hetty was serving ale to four boisterous cowmen, regulars who enjoyed their pints after a hard day working with the beasts on the farm. She enjoyed the tavern, although rough hands groping her buttocks or breasts were not as welcome, but on the whole the clientele were pleasant people – workmen mostly, farmhands and labourers, although the occasional gentleman or gentlewoman made use of the private room to the side. The work was hard, the hours long, but she earned a few shillings and the landlord did not mind her disappearing twice a day to visit the gaol. Captain Acorne had offered to provide more silver so she need not work, but she had refused. Serving customers, collecting empty pots, sweeping the floor... it kept body and mind busy.

She set three pewter tankards of ale down on the table, automatically brushed aside the hand that was squeezing her bottom.

"That's enough of that!" she said, neatly sidestepping the man's gripping fingers. "Groping is five pennies extra."

The tavern door opened, letting in a squall of rain and wind. The fire blazing in the hearth flared and sent out a cloud of smoke. A vision spun into Hetty's mind – darkness, a roof falling in, Miss Tiola crouched in pain in a corner. She slammed the last tankard down, slopping some of the ale over the brim, ignored the growl of protest from its recipient. Running to the kitchen she snatched up her cloak, darted for the rear door.

"Where d' ye think ye be goin' young maid?" called the landlady. "There's stew ready t' be served!"

Hetty did not hear. She ran, head down, through the dark and the rain, knowing the path so well after all this while she needed no light. She had indoor shoes on, soon saturated, the hem of her gown becoming as sodden. Up the hill, pausing only momentarily to gain her breath; on, her fists hammering, urgent, at the door to the gaolkeeper's house.

James answered cautiously. Who would be knocking so frantically at this time of the evening, in this weather? Thieves? Murderers? Gaol breakers? His apprehension dissolved as soon as he saw Hetty's anxious face.

"I think there is something wrong at the gaol!" she gasped.

"It were fine when I las' looked," James responded.

"Please, come and check with me!"

James' father called, irritably, from within. "Who be it? Tell 'em t' clear off, come by t'morrer."

"Please James."

"It's my Hetty, Pa. I'm just goin' out."

His father sniggered. "Ye'd be better off choosin' a more agreeable nigh' fer swivin'!"

James grabbed his greatcoat, shoved his hat on his head and took the bunch of clanking keys from his pocket to unlocked the main gate. Barely had he done so, Hetty was through and running ahead of him across the castle green.

"James! James!" her urgent shout – a scream. "James, the roof has fallen in! Get help! Miss Tiola! Tiola are you all right? Tiola!"

James was there, beside Hetty, elbowing her aside. He drew the two heavy bolts back and the door swung outward with a protesting creak and a cloud of escaping dust. He held his lantern high, the light casting eerie shadows across the piled devastation of fallen timber, broken slate and debris.

Coughing, Hetty tried to climb over the rubble, realised it would be hopeless. "Miss Tiola!" she shrieked again. "This is hopeless

James! We can't get in this way. You'll need to climb up, get in from the top."

James stared at her uncomprehending. "I can't climb," he finally admitted. "I as goes dizzy if'n I climb on a chair."

"You're bloody useless!" Hetty yelled. Then, "Ssh! I hear something!"

Faint, urgent, Tiola calling for help. "Hetty! My baby is coming!"

"Fetch help!" Hetty shouted, shoving James back towards the gate. "We need strong hands and the midwife!"

CHAPTER FIFTY-SIX

Doone was trussed up like a goose ready for the Christmas pot. Maha'dun had thrown a blanket over the man's head because when he had gained consciousness his enraged glower had been annoyingly unnerving.

"If you won't let me kill him, let's at least keep the bugger covered and quiet," Maha'dun had muttered.

The 'quiet' had not been a problem, for Jesamiah had stuffed a bundle of old rags into Doone's mouth and tied a firm gag in place. The blanket provided the rest.

The horses had swung along at a reasonable trot, despite the rain and wind, for the road, although rutted and muddy, had been sheltered by thick woodland on each side and was well drained by the natural slope of the terrain. Then the road descended down to the river. The driver slowly approached the one place he was uncertain of, Poulston Brygge. Built originally in Norman times the stone bridge spanned the River Tamar and had witnessed many a drama through the passing of centuries, from flooding to pitched battle between Cromwell's and Fairfax's drab Roundheads and the Kings' flamboyant Cavaliers. For all their clash of weapons, belief and fury, the Civil War skirmishers had been of little consequence in comparison to the Tamar in full flood. On the outward journey the main arched span had already been partly hidden by the deluge of water rushing down from where the river rose a few miles inland from the north coast of Cornwall. The two additional flood spans were barely managing to divert the excess flow. But more rain had fallen since then. More rain was scudding down the steep, saturated, hillsides to swell the river below.

Carriages had been swept away in past years, horses and passengers drowned. Slowing the horses, the driver approached with care, his team of two had ears flat back, heads high, nostrils snorting, eyes rolling. They too, were uncertain. The driver gathered the reins, brought the animals to a halt, heaved on the brake and climbed down from his seat, holding aloft a storm lantern. Water swirled around his feet, covering the stone bridge. Water which was more than just puddled rain. He walked forward a few steps, the sound of the gushing river in full spate tearing through the confines of the three arches loud in his ears. He could not be sure. Was the bridge intact? He edged forward another few inches. Had the flood come over the top, would the current carry away those who tried to cross the bridge? He could see broken trees and debris swirling in the raging water below, shook his head, went back to the carriage where Jesamiah and Maha'dun were both peering out.

"I ain't riskin' it," the driver declared. "Not safe t' drive over what I can't see."

"I'll walk ahead," Maha'dun offered, opening the carriage door.

"Beg pardon, sir, but no! That's a fair current runnin'. It can sweep this entire carriage away, you'd not have a chance."

"He's right," Jesamiah said, more familiar with the hazards of water. "Where else can we cross?"

The driver scratched his beard-stubbled chin. "There's a ford near Tamarton. Might be too deep t' cross, but it's a few miles 'igher upriver, and the water be not so wide there, with grazin' land each side t' take up the overflow."

"How far?"

The driver scratched his chin again. "A few miles. Five, six, mebbe?"

"Good tracks on the other side?"

"*Ais*, a fair few."

Maha'dun interrupted, sceptical. "You know the way? How do you know the way?"

"I were born in these parts, been familiar with these lanes since I were a tacker astride m' first pony."

That suited Jesamiah enough. "We're in your hands, then. Just try to make as good time as possible. I want my wife released without delay."

The driver touched his whip to his forelock, relieved at the decision. "I'll do my best, sir." He had some skilful manoeuvring to do to turn the carriage round, but once back on the road he urged the horses into a steady trot. He liked the two men he was carrying around, even though the foreigner was a strange one, and the other was probably not as honest as he outwardly seemed. What did it matter? They paid well.

And truth to tell, now that they were jogging along safer tracks, he was rather enjoying the adventure.

CHAPTER FIFTY-SEVEN

Hetty had managed to wriggle over the pile of timber and rubble, scraping her knees and elbows, laddering her woollen stockings beyond repair and tearing her skirt, none of which mattered; Tiola was her only concern.

"Are you injured?" was her first question, was relieved to receive a shake of the head.

"No, but I am in labour."

That small moment of relief fled. "I don't know what to do Miss. James has gone for the midwife, but I don't see her managing to climb over that mess back there."

Tiola took several breaths to ride the next contraction before answering. "Clear the bed can you? And a space. There are candles and a tinderbox in that wooden trunk. We'll need light and blankets. Strip the bed – the linen sheet will be better to wind the baby in. I will need linen strips too. Have you a knife?"

"Yes, ma'am."

"We will need it. Empty the piss bucket, we'll use it for the afterbirth. The bowl I use to wash will be needed too. We will need water, no chance of hot water...?" Tiola paused to breathe, in through the nose, pause, out slowly through the mouth, containing the increase of pain. "Cleanliness is important, Hetty, but we will do what we can. The babe is early born, we must keep it wrapped up warm when it comes."

Again, frightened, Hetty repeated, "I do not know what to do."

"But I do, just do as I tell you. We will get through this." Tiola sounded more positive than she felt. It was one thing assisting others to give birth, entirely another when it was yourself. Especially when instinct – experience – was screaming that there was something wrong.

James and the few men who had volunteered to help, had managed to clear some of the debris from the doorway, enough for the town's second most experienced midwife to scramble over in a little more dignified manner than had Hetty. Old Agnes, the matriarch midwife, had refused to come out, not caring to brave the weather for a convict, so it was left to Chaucer, a woman who attended the brothel whores in their time of need, because no one else would do so. Chaucer, once a whore herself; before that, the youngest daughter of a well-to–do family, disgraced through circumstances not of her own doing. Men raped and were rarely punished for it. Only the shamed women suffered. Chaucer was not her real name, no one knew it, but the whores who took her in twenty or so years back had nicknamed her for the books she loved reading and the stories she related from them. *The Canterbury Tales* had always been her favourite.

She had attended the other poor girl, Doryty, who had birthed a child and then hanged immediately after. The baby had not survived long; the same two outcomes probably awaited this poor lass.

"The child's not helping its own passage," she stated, sitting back on her heels before Tiola. "Leaving all the work to you, but you are fully dilated, and despite your ordeal here, strong. Between us we'll get the little imp delivered. It's probably a boy, reluctant to leave his warm bed for this cold, wet, world."

Tiola nodded as the contractions came closer together. For six hours now she had been labouring. There could be many more ahead.

One of the lanterns Chaucer had brought began to gutter and

Hetty replaced the candle inside. Another hour. The men had cleared what they deemed necessary from the doorway, there was still rubble and timber to be stepped over, but not a pile of debris more suited to a mountain goat.

James's father had issued orders for Tiola to be moved to somewhere more suitably restrictive and to be chained to ensure no escape attempt was made. Chaucer had refused to comply stating, furiously, that a woman in strong labour was unable to run anywhere. Once the child was born this would be a different matter, but with the main gate locked and barred what would Tiola do? Climb the castle walls? Chaucer had sent James off with a flea in his ear, telling him to tell his father what he could do with his chains and fetters!

An hour later, midnight had come and gone; the baby's head had crowned. It would soon be all over. Hetty at her back, Tiola squatted, panted rather than pushed as Chaucer knelt, ready to catch the child as each wave of contraction did its job.

"We have the head," Chaucer said. "Just a little rotation at the next push to ease the shoulders... Look, the moon's come out to bring us a welcoming light. Nothing finer than the Moon Goddess to see a babe into our arms."

She sounded positive, tried her best. "Though those scudding clouds are not helping us. Hetty, bring me that lantern closer. Tiola, do not push, wait for the next contraction, work with our Mother Nature, not against Her – there! We have it!"

The baby slid into the night-dark, moonlit-shadowed world. Tiola lay back, exhausted.

"A boy," Chaucer said, wrapping the child in the linen Hetty handed her.

He had been dead for several days.

CHAPTER FIFTY-EIGHT

The moon was riding against a cloud-chased sky, her light reflecting on darkened windows, puddles and sodden ground as the carriage rumbled into Launceston High Street. The nearest church clock struck a single note. One a.m.

Jesamiah jumped down from the carriage, stiff and tired. It had been a long journey, with, because of flooding and fallen trees, several more detours along uncertain tracks. The horses stood, coats steaming, heads down, as exhausted as their driver who had done them proud to get here in one piece. Maha'dun had promised him a handsome bonus of gold sovereigns.

"What'll I do with 'im?" the driver said, easing his own sore back and numb backside while nodding over his shoulder at the snoring lump beneath the blanket within the carriage.

"I suggest march him up to the gaol, secure him in there," Maha'dun said – he was the only one who didn't appear to have any aching limbs. "If we claim he's a robber we captured on the way here, they'll be obliged to open up for us."

"That they would," Jesamiah retorted, "but then they will not listen to his testimony of Tiola's innocence will they?" He looked up and down the street, saw only a tom cat; no one else seemed to be awake. "I doubt our landlord will open up and let us into our rooms. You happy enough to stable the horses?" he asked the driver.

He nodded, stretched and yawned. "I'll curl up in some hay. Wouldn't be the first time."

"We'll stay in the carriage then, keep an eye on our guest. That suit you, Maha'dun?"

"You mean you'll bundle into blankets and spend the rest of the night snoring along with Doone like some sort of out-of-tune duet orchestra, while I keep watch? And without a single cheroot left to smoke?"

Jesamiah grinned. That was precisely what he meant.

The driver climbed back up to his seat, and walked the weary horses forward along the street towards the livery yard on the corner, Jesamiah and Maha'dun following behind, the horses' shod hooves clip-clopping at a slow plod. At the stables, the driver began unharnessing the animals, aided by Maha'dun. A bleary-eyed whiskered face appeared at a small window above the cobbled yard. The ostler, yawning and stretching. "You back then? Where y' been? Y' fine t' see t' them 'osses y' sel'? I ain't comin' down."

"I can do better without your bumblin'!" the driver called back.

"Suit y' sel'. That you Cap'n Acorne? There were some sort o' t' do up at gaol earlier. Roof fell in or summin', an' then midwife were called. There's t' be the 'anging first thing, they say. Should be a good turn out, 'er bein' pretty an' all."

Jesamiah was off, running for the castle gaol; yelled over his shoulder, "Maha'dun! Keep watch over Doone. Don't let him go anywhere!"

Hammering at the gaol's gate, Jesamiah stood swearing and cursing for more than ten minutes, kicking at it in between blows with his fist. He was just deciding to go back into town and find a keg of gunpowder to blow the bloody thing open, when James appeared, clad in unlaced boots, jacket and nightshirt, and carrying a lantern high.

"Do you know what time it is?" he snapped. "If you wake my Pa, he'll be throwing you in gaol quicker than a goose hisses."

"Good. That's where I want to be. Is my wife harmed? The roof? I hear it collapsed? Why are you here, abed, not clearing..."

"All sorted hours ago. No 'arm done, save for we'll be needing a new roof."

"No harm? What about my wife? Where is she? They said the midwife..."

"No 'arm come t' er neither. Midwife's still there. Not 'eard no babbi squawklin', so it ain't arrived yet."

"Open this bloody gate."

"I will, but don't be askin' to come out again afore sunrise. Y' got me out o' m' bed once already this night."

James unlocked the gate and Jesamiah was through before it was barely opened wide enough – plucking James' lantern from his hand as he did so.

"Tiola?" Jesamiah stepped over the rubble – all that had been done was a suitable space made wide enough to scrabble over, the real work of clearing up, he guessed, would start in daylight. "Tiola?" he called again, holding his lantern high to see into the interior gloom. Dust continued to swirl, the spinning motes catching in the beams of moon and lantern-light.

"We're here!" That was young Hetty's voice, sounding tired and strained.

The faint glimmer of lanterns guided him: two shapes, Hetty rising from where she had been sitting coming to meet him, another woman crouched beside Tiola who was semi-recumbent on the bed, a linen-wrapped bundle clutched in her arms. Jesamiah nodded to the woman, went straight to Tiola who looked up at him, tears pricking from her sunken tired-bruised eyes to glisten on her pale, hollow cheeks.

"I'm sorry," she murmured.

He sat beside her on the edge of the bed. "Sorry? For what? None of this was your doing."

"Sorry that I lost the baby," she whispered. "Your son did not live." A fresh sob choked in her throat. Not many months ago she had assisted this wonderful man's mistress to give birth to a boy, a boy who also had not lived. Two sons, both of whom never took a breath. Life could be so cruel.

Gulping down his own tears Jesamiah put his arm around her shoulders, drew her close. Touching a forefinger to the bundle in her arms, and not knowing what to say, he asked, "Is this him?"

She nodded.

Gently, he took his son from her and cradled him in his own arms, peeled back the linen and gazed at the small, wrinkled, scrunched-up face. His son's eyes were closed, he looked as if he were asleep, save for the blueness shading around his lips and the translucence of his skin. Jesamiah stroked his forefinger down the little lad's cheek. He was cold to the touch. Had black hair, tiny hands, small curled up fingers.

"What did you name him?" Jesamiah whispered, hearing the choke in his voice, which turned into a hastily swallowed sob when she answered.

"Rue. After our dear friend."

"He would've liked that," he said, almost unable to speak.

Tiola groped for Jesamiah's hand, clung to it, her fingers crushing his, stared, wide-eyed, frightened, at him. "I'm scared. My Craft has not returned, it should have come back when the child's cord was cut."

"Perhaps because the child is...?"

But he did not finish his thought. Tiola suddenly went rigid, arching her back, gasping for breath through a pain which tore like thunder through her body.

"Just the afterbirth," Chaucer stated simply, putting her hand gently on Tiola's belly.

But Tiola shook her head, pushed the hand away.

"Take the boy," she said through panting breath to Jesamiah. "Lay him somewhere safe for now – there's another coming!" She laughed, nervously, not daring to hope, to let tentative joy flood in. "I didn't know! I've carried twins! Oh, please, please, let this one be alive!"

Jesamiah made a nest of straw over to one side, placed the dead boy within it, turned away, but as an afterthought turned back and pulled from his hair one of the blue ribbons he always wore. Carefully, he looped it around his son's left wrist, secured it there. "So you know you're my son," he whispered before tucking the linen shroud tightly around the lifeless little man.

Tiola screamed as a contraction swept through her. She flailed for Jesamiah's hand. Quickly, he was at her side, her hand gripping his.

"Head's crowned!" Chaucer said excitedly, "ease back m'dear... wait, yes, here it comes! You, Acorne, come here, catch your baby. Yes, use both hands, support its head. One more push Tiola, just one more..."

A wet, tiny, slippery, sticky, blood-spattered wrinkled thing slid into Jesamiah's open hands. Its eyes were screwed up in a puckered little red, angry face. The eyes blinked open. Then her mouth, and she squalled her outraged indignation.

"A girl," Chaucer announced with cheerful laughter, "and one with a fine pair of lungs!"

Tiola was concerned. "Wrap her well in blankets. Early born babes are troubled by the cold."

Hetty passed blankets to Jesamiah who wrapped his daughter carefully and then handed her to his wife.

"I guess this will mean I'll have to squirrel away a hefty dowry for her. And, in years to come, spend most of my money on the latest fashion in dresses, yards of French lace and be prepared to shoot unsuitable beaus." He grinned. "What do we call her?"

Tiola smiled, tired, sore, relieved that one of the two had fought to survive. "Christina? For the ship where we first met?"

Jesamiah shook his head. "That was a sea battle I lost, her captain was better than those of us aboard *Mermaid*, in hindsight, fortunately so. What about Jenna, or your mother's name?"

"No, this little one deserves her own identity." Tiola gazed at her beautiful, tiny, daughter and the baby opened her eyes. Swirling within their deep, sapphire blue, Tiola saw the wonder of the entire Universe reflected there. The galaxies, the stars, the planets, her eyes reflecting the blueness of the oceans of the Earth itself.

"Merrin," Tiola said. "It is an old, old Cornish name. It means Pearl of the Sea."

Jesamiah fought tears. Tears of grief for the dead boy, tears of joy for the living girl. He had thought he'd wanted a son to follow in his footsteps, a son he could teach to shoot and fight and be a man, but looking at his daughter he realised he did not want to do those things at all.

"Hello Merrin, my little pearl," he said softly, leaning forward to stroke her soft cheek. "I guess I'm going to have to make you pretty poppet dolls to play with, and learn how to dance."

CHAPTER FIFTY-NINE

Dawn strode in with a return of the rain, although the storm had blown itself out, and the wind was swinging around to the north-east, threatening more colder days to come. The midwife, Chaucer, had gone, taking Hetty and the dead baby with her, promising to lay the little mite within a recent-dug grave.

"Cissy Cartwright lost her babe a few days back, another wee boy; I'll see to layin' your lad in with him, they'll be company for each other. It'll not be a Christian burial in the churchyard, o' course, both babes not yet Christened, but there's a little plot in the woods just beyond the churchyard wall that I use for these innocents who don't make it safe into the world. Nice and peaceful it is there. Best not tell anyone. The Reverend's a bit of a stickler for Church rules. How they reckon God will turn away babes from Paradise for lack of earthly formality, is beyond me. Cissy will make a suitable wetnurse, too. You'll be wanting one. She has several other childer, one more for her titties'll make no difference." She didn't labour the point of why a wetnurse would be needed. Nor did she mention that the dead baby of the girl who had hanged was laid to rest in the same grave.

With Tiola cleaned and made comfortable, Jesamiah had stretched out beside her on the narrow, creaking, bed, nestling her and their sleeping daughter in his arms. Exhaustion had taken all three of them into instant sleep, and it was only the murky, grey daylight that had woken him. And, once he was awake, a noise that at first he could not place.

Hammering? Were they making a start on the collapsed roof? Voices too, now that he was listening. Then realisation slammed home. They were ensuring the gallows out on the castle green was ready for use! Panic ripped through him. What to do? Run? Fight? Where was that letter? Where was Maha'dun, Doone? Oh! Why had he fallen asleep? Idiot! Fool! Imbecile!

Tiola awoke, settled the stirring baby to feed at her breast for the essential nourishing colostrum; milk would not come in for a day or so. She felt quite calm and accepting. Now that the time was near, now that she knew Jesamiah was here to take care of their daughter, what was to follow this morning did not seem so frightening. Birth, life, death. That was the natural order of things.

"Calm yourself, Jesamiah," she said. "You must look to Merrin's welfare, not mine. I can take care of myself, she cannot."

"It is my job to take care of you both, and I should be doing it, not sitting here, being useless," he said, brushing straw from his coat and raking fingers through his hair. His chin was stubbled, no chance to shave and make himself presentable. "I have a letter here, your freedom. I must get it to the right person." He kissed them both on their foreheads and headed for the open door, treading carefully over the strewn rubble. Was aware that he could easily scoop mother and babe into his arms and walk away – was as aware that they would not get far.

"Jesamiah. I am all right," Tiola insisted, shifting the child to her other breast and guiding her to suck. "Trust me, but promise you will give precedence to your daughter's care over mine. I must have that promise."

"I cannot!" Jesamiah cried. "I cannot do that!"

"You must!" Tiola again insisted. "Promise me. You *must*!"

Feeling sickness rising into his throat, his body beginning to tremble, Jesamiah reluctantly nodded. "Very well, but I intend to stop this nonsense in any way I can."

"Then do so," Tiola responded pragmatically, "but legally, within the law. I will not condone anything else."

Bugger that, Jesamiah thought.

He had the letter, a bit crumpled, in his coat pocket, made his way outside into the morning drizzle. Onlookers were already beginning to gather, several others were coming through the open gate – he could, indeed, scoop Tiola up and run for it, risk the both of them being shot. He sighed. She would not come with him, he had to resign himself to that.

"Who do I see about presenting a letter of pardon?" he asked a man balancing on a ladder affixing the hemp noose to the gallows crosstree bar.

"The County Constable, I reckon," he answered, not looking round from what he was doing.

"And if he isn't here?"

"Gaoler, perhaps? No idea, mate, it ain't never occurred afore."

Word had spread. More people, eager gawpers from Launceston and the immediate vicinity, were appearing. The gaoler, pulling on his second-best coat and best, plumed hat came shuffling from the gaolhouse, followed by his son, James.

Jesamiah had watched many a hanging, several bringing the demise of men he knew well, friends and crewmates. He regretted their passing – a life of piracy almost inevitably brought death by hanging, unless battle or disease got to you first. But this was different. This was Tiola, his wife, the mother of his child, the woman he loved. He saw Maha'dun striding up the hill, his Arab clothing fluttering in the wind, something concealed in his hand, probably a pistol, prodding at Ascham Doone's back to make him walk in front. Jesamiah waited until they were both near, then marched up to the gaoler.

"I have here a letter of pardon!" he exclaimed, thrusting it into the startled man's hand.

The gaoler inspected it, read the words. "Not signed by the Constable. Ain't legal. Who's this signature then, anyway? This Right Hon Ascham Doone? Never 'eard of 'im."

"That would be me," Doone said, stepping forward and, taking his hat off, sweeping a deep bow. "Honourable newly elected

Member of Parliament. And that letter is as worthless as a clipped penny. I was forced against my will to write it. I demand this fellow, Acorne, and this foreign ruffian be arrested and charged with kidnap and assault."

The growing crowd drew nearer to listen, intrigued. Jesamiah glared at Doone, his hand itching to draw his pistol and shoot the bastard between the eyes.

Someone else stepped forward, removed his hat which he twiddled around and around between his hands. The carriage driver.

"Beg pardon, master gaoler, the authenticity of that letter I cannot attest to, but I can vouch that this man, who calls himself Doone..."

Jesamiah clenched his fists, shifted his glare to the driver. If he was going to speak up for Doone he would soon be a dead man.

"I do not *call* myself, I *am* Ascham Doone!"

"This Doone chap," the driver continued, "did not seem to come here against his will to me."

Jesamiah allowed himself to relax a little.

"I've driven these two gentlemen for several days now. Yesterday we went to collect Mr Doone here. He had plenty opportunity to leave the carriage, never did so. Seemed quite happy to snore the night away beneath a pile of my best blankets."

"Look at him now," Maha'dun piped up. "Are we preventing him from leaving?"

"They are distorting the truth!" Doone thundered, "I demand the three of them are arrested."

The gaoler shook his head. "I got more important things t' be seein' to this mornin' than botherin' with a fallin' out between bloody Parliamentarians and their servants. If you claim you shouldn't be 'ere, then get yerself t' Westminster an' be gone with ye. I'm a king's man. My gran'sire fought for King Charles, not for you Cromwellian Parliament lot."

Doone tried spluttering that as a Member of Parliament he was nothing whatsoever to do with Oliver Cromwell, but his protestations fell on deaf ears. The gaoler tore the letter in half and handed it back to Jesamiah. Barked at his son to usher the crowd to an orderly distance behind a roped-off area, and for proceedings to begin.

With alarm Jesamiah realised that while they had been arguing Tiola had been fetched from the gaol by two women from the town; one of them, the midwife, Chaucer, carried the baby. Tiola's thick, long black hair had been plaited and wound around her head, almost like a crown. She wore a simple, plain, but clean gown. She looked pale and tired, with dark circles beneath her eyes.

Jesamiah ran forward, his arm outstretched, but a military man was suddenly there, an eight-foot pikestaff barring his way.

"Behind the line, sir, if you please. No approaching the gallows."

Jesamiah grasped the wooden pikestaff. "Bugger off, that's my wife."

"I don't care if she's the Queen of Sheba. Spectators stand behind the line. Or I'll arrest you and lock you in the gaol."

~ Jesamiah. No fuss, please. You are making things worse for me. ~

Tiola's plea nudged into Jesamiah's mind.

~ But I... ~"

~ Please. If you love me, you will take our child and do nothing more. Let the law unfold as it must. ~

His throat tight, trembling, Jesamiah took his daughter from Chaucer, stood, as near the gallows as they would let him, and watched helpless as Tiola was stood up upon a barrel and the hempen noose placed around her neck. She had refused a hood, stood there, her gaze fixed steadily on Jesamiah's face.

~ I love you, ~ she said.

"Oh God! No!" Jesamiah screamed, as the hangman kicked the barrel away and Tiola's body swung beneath the gallows bar.

As the noose tightened around her neck, she took a deep breath, held that lungful of air, willing herself not to struggle against her body's natural instinct to fight the stranglehold of rope biting into her windpipe. It could take up to twenty minutes or more for death to come by strangulation. Hanging was never quick or painless.

This was how her mother had died. There had been no one there to offer comfort, no one there to speak for her, to grieve for her. The villagers had howled for vengeance, led by the malicious hatred of

Jed Garrick, who sought revenge for the woman's adultery and for the crime of bloody murder.

Tiola clearly saw her mother's choking, distorted face in the air before her, but saw also the serenity in her eyes. Serenity, for the dying woman knew that her daughter was safe, and the man she loved would never have his identity discovered by those who must never know it.

Tiola smiled at her mother. And the rope snapped.

The crowd gasped, Jesamiah thrust the baby into Hetty's arms and ran forward, but was pushed back by the soldier.

Tiola knelt in the muddied grass, taking great gulps of air, but all too quickly her arms were grasped by the gaoler who trundled her like an unwieldy milk churn to the side while the barrel was replaced.

"Did you not use new rope? You imbecile!" he shouted at the hangman. "Get another noose set!"

The hangman growled some incomprehensible swear word, followed by, "What do you think I'm bloody doing?"

Jesamiah was beside himself – was aware that Maha'dun was gripping his arm to stop him plunging forward, vaguely heard his friend urging him to do nothing or he too would hang.

Tiola was again lifted to stand on the barrel, a fresh noose around her neck. The hangman did not wait; to an accompanying cheer from the crowd, kicked the barrel away.

Again, Tiola willed her legs not to flail for the foothold which was not there, willed her body to go limp, not to fight that overwhelming instinct to claw for air. Willed her heartrate to slow, willed her bladder and bowels not to empty. Willed calmness... and again the strands of the rope parted.

Uproar coursed through the crowd, part disappointment, part excitement.

"Two times!" someone shouted, Jesamiah thought it might have been the midwife woman, "two times the rope has broke! If there be a third she be granted God's Judgement of innocence!"

Jesamiah swallowed vomit. Kept his gaze, steady, on the woman he would willingly give his own life for.

Doone was at his side. "Luck runs with the devil and his whore," he muttered. Jesamiah swung round, intending to hit him, but Maha'dun was there first, throwing a full-bodied punch to the bastard's jaw, knocking him to his knees.

"I enjoyed that," Maha'dun said, massaging his bruised knuckles.

Jesamiah returned his attention to Tiola who was on all fours, taking deep breaths to refill her lungs.

~ *I am all right. Just winded.* ~ Her calm voice in his head.

~ *Once more, you must endure once more*! ~ Jesamiah answered. ~ *I can't bear it*! ~

"Get on with it!" the gaoler roared, frustrated, angry.

The barrel was replaced, a third rope was hastily fashioned into a noose, thrown over the gallows' cross tree. The gaoler himself picked Tiola up from the grass and dumped her on the barrel. He shoved the hangman aside, dragged the noose around her neck, jerking it so that the hemp chafed against her already bruised and aching throat. He stepped back, gave an almighty kick with his boot to the barrel and simultaneously thrust his hands into Tiola's back so that she swung forward and back.

"Run, my dear! Run with Jenna, run far from here, keep yourself safe!" Her mother's desperate words buzzed in Tiola's mind. Those last words as men had come tramping into the house to drag a murdering whore away, Jed directing them, screaming abuse at the woman he hated.

"Run Tiola! Live! Live for me, and for the line you carry, live!"

Swinging by the neck from the gallows, the rope tightening, strangling, Tiola kicked against the searing pain. Her mother had died to distract attention from her daughter, died to give her opportunity to escape. Her mother had not held the Craft, had not been a witch. There had been nothing that she could do to save herself. But Tiola *was* a witch. Her Craft passed from grandmother to granddaughter, and as she'd known it would, it had returned with the birth of her daughter.

Tiola cleared her mind. Concentrated on the rope, the hemp strands, splitting, fraying, severing... Had known that there were only certain ways that a true witch could die. Strangulation by hanging was not among them.

For the third time, the rope broke.

CHAPTER SIXTY

The carriage rumbled along the muddy lanes, the driver singing at the top of his voice in between encouraging his team to 'trot on, there, boys!'

Maha'dun, surprisingly, was doting upon the baby nestled in his arms, although he did, hastily, pass her to Hetty when a sudden obnoxious smell wafted from her swaddling linens.

Jesamiah and Tiola were sitting opposite, their arms linked. Jesamiah was asleep, Tiola was dozing. Her neck was sore, her throat aching and her voice no more than a whisper, although she had assured her beloved husband that all would heal.

He had her written pardon, signed by the gaoler and the hangman, in his pocket. The crowd had cheered, exultant at witnessing the rare oddity of a noose breaking three times – God's Divine Judgement indeed, that no man alive, from king to humble peasant, could contest this sign of innocence.

Even Doone, massaging a sore jaw, had applauded and offered his congratulations. A public display of graciousness for the benefit of the crowd, of course, marred only slightly by Jesamiah's soft spoken words to him.

"If you, or even your shadow, ever, *ever* cross my path again Doone, you'll be a dead man."

"Are you threatening me again, Acorne? I would be careful, there are many witnesses here."

"Threaten? Oh no, Doone, that was no threat, that was a promise." To back his statement, Jesamiah yanked one of his blue ribbons from his hair and stuffed it into Doone's coat pocket. "The next one will be tight around your neck," he hissed, "remember that."

Tiola wriggled more comfortably into Jesamiah's arms, nestled her head deeper into his shoulder. They were heading, with all speed, to Falmouth where *Sea Witch* was waiting at anchor. From there, Jesamiah intended to sail west, as far west as was necessary away from England.

Opening her eyes, Tiola watched Maha'dun take the re-swaddled baby into his arms. He was the most incongruous 'uncle' that any child would ever have, but would be the most protective.

Tiola smiled, closed her eyes. The horses were trotting steadily, their shod hooves rhythmically beating a tattoo of sound on the hollow ground of Bodmin Moor. The carriage wheels rumbled and swished through puddles, lulling her back to sleep, the sound, she fancied, whispering a name in the mud and the rain.

Jes-a-miah. Jes-a-miah. Jes-a-miah...

DROP ANCHOR

AUTHOR'S NOTE

Gallows Wake is purely a work of fiction. Most of the main characters never actually existed – save for one or two who have 'supporting cast' roles – but there are a few historical facts dotted in here and there.

Bodmin Moor. Its Cornish name was *Goen Bren* and pre- 1812 it was known as Fowey Moor, but I have kept its present name to eliminate confusion. The dreadful place that was Bodmin Moor Jail (as featured in Winston Graham's novels, and the TV series *Poldark*) is now only frequented by visitors interested in the organised ghost tours. It replaced Launceston Gaol in 1838.

In 1637, contemporary accounts noted that Launceston Castle was 'so ruinous that every small blast of wind threatened to shatter it down'. In 1690, the complaints were made to the king that the constable, Sir Hugh Pyper, had allowed the gaol to fall into disrepair and the male and female prisoners were sleeping together in the same quarters. Two years later, Pyper was granted the post of Constable in perpetuity for two generations after him; in exchange, he agreed to invest £120 to repair the place. The bailey was used for hanging executions.

It was rare for a hangman's noose to break three times – but it *did* happen, and when it did the convict was deemed innocent as per an

Act of God. Hanging pre-the 1800s, before the 'long drop and a short stop' and a rope knotted so that the neck was instantly broken, was a long, drawn out torture. It could take up to twenty minutes for someone to die, although death could be hastened by friends and family running forward to grasp hold of the struggling body to add weight and a quicker death, from which we get the term 'hangers on'. Captain William Kidd was sentenced to hang on 23 May 1701 at Execution Dock, Wapping, London, accused of piracy, although it is now thought that he was not guilty of the charge. He was hanged twice. On the first attempt, the rope broke and Kidd survived but was hanged again minutes later, and this time died. Had the rope broken a third time... Poor man.

The inn I have used on Bodmin Moor is, of course, Jamaica Inn, although it was not known as that in Jesamiah's time. An inn has stood on the main road (modern A30, before the bypass was built) since 1547. The current building dates from 1750, and it was famous for smuggling – a fact which Daphne Du Maurier made full use of in her novel of the same name.

Poulston Brygge is the old name for Polson Bridge in Cornwall, spanning the River Tamar. And several lives – including a carriage and horses – were lost to flooding. There really was a skirmish there between the 'Roundheads' and the 'Cavaliers' towards the end of the English Civil Wars.

Much of the detail of the scenes aboard the *Bonne Chance*, are, to those who study the history of the British Royal Navy, somewhat inaccurate. This is deliberate on my part because I decided to stay with the familiar. Prior to the middle to latter half of the eighteenth-century, the British Navy was not as it became by the time of Admiral Lord Nelson and Trafalgar in 1805. There was no standard uniform, for instance, in the early 1700s – although many captains, lieutenants and sailing masters wore dark blue coats with gold braid (lace) on the cuffs and a standing collar to signify their wealth and social status. With these coats, red waistcoats and 'gentleman's apparel', which included white breeches and powdered wigs, was worn. In the early 1700s the 'tricorn' was still called a 'three-corner' hat. The shape of officers' hats changed by the end of the century.

Edward Vernon was a real, and highly respected, Naval officer, known as 'Old Grog' because of the Grogram material he used for his coats. This is a coarse fabric made of silk, combined with mohair or wool and stiffened with gum. In 1740 Vernon (then a Vice-Admiral) introduced watering down the run ration which sailors called 'Grog'.

There were no formal exams or training for officers – the ranks were purely down to experience, ability or, more usually, the financial means to buy a position. Prior to the 1740s, the Royal Navy had only three clearly established shipboard ranks: captain, lieutenant, and sailing master – midshipmen did not appear until a few years later, so, my use of this term is author's licence.

I mention the Royal Marines: I believe that I am accurate about the Holland Regiment and John Churchill, the first Duke of Marlborough, and that '*in 1702 six Regiments of Marines and six Sea Service Regiments of Foot had been formed for the War of the Spanish Succession, their most significant achievement being a successful assault on Gibraltar, although it had been sailors of the Royal Navy who had captured the Rock itself.*' I also say that '*After the Treaty of Utrecht in 1713 four of the regiments had been redeployed as line infantry, men aboard the Bonne Chance being from the Gibraltar Foot.*' In fact, only three were formed and the Gibraltar Regiment of Foot and their adventures with Jesamiah are entirely made up. Gibraltar did endure a long siege, however, but not in 1719.

For those interested, Tom Benson existed. He lived at Appledore, North Devon, and he did become a smuggler when he grew up. He held various positions of authority and ran a small fleet of ships. Unfortunately, he got into debt and tried to clear it by deliberately scuppering a ship and falsely claiming the insurance. The captain was hanged and Thomas fled to Portugal, never to be heard of again.

The Doones I have blatantly borrowed from R.D. Blackmore's *Lorna Doone*. They are known as a thoroughly bad lot in the realm of Exmoor-based fiction and I couldn't resist using them.

The saying 'knocked me down with a feather' was first used in print form in the early 1800s, so I might have taken an anachronistic liberty to use it, but in my defence, it was probably in use verbally long before that date.

A note on Spanish, and in particular, Spanish punctuation. I didn't want to use much dialogue in Spanish, with clumsy translations for readers who have no knowledge of the language. (As I haven't – thank you, Nicky Galliers for your assistance here!) I also didn't want to keep saying things like *"He said in Spanish"*, but needed to indicate they were still speaking the language. So, where appropriate I have included Spanish punctuation to indicate a difference, which is a little odd compared to our English usage.

A question written in Spanish has *two* question marks, one at the start and one at the end of the sentence: **¿...?** and the same for exclamations: **¡...!** – so I've included these in the dialogue. Incidentally, when I originally wrote the first Sea Witch Voyage (back in 2006!) I have no idea why I made Jesamiah half Spanish. He just *was*. He can speak Spanish. I can't, so I'll blame any confusion about Spanish and its punctuation firmly on *his* shoulders, not mine.

Finally, women who 'plead their belly' (were pregnant) were not hanged until the baby had been born. A few were reprieved, usually either dying anyway or having their freedom paid for by rich relatives. Most women, however, were hanged soon after giving birth. Probably two of the most famous women in this situation were the pirates Anne Bonney and Mary Read, both of whom were pregnant when captured and tried alongside the pirate Captain 'Calico' Jack Rackham in October 1720. Rackham and his crew were hanged, Read died of fever in April 1721. Anne Bonny's fate is unknown.

But *that* tale will be told in another story, the seventh Jesamiah Acorne Voyage, *Jamaica Gold*.

GLOSSARY

Used in *Gallows Wake* or throughout the Sea Witch Voyages

NON-SAILING TERMS

Agal – also spelled iqal, egal or igal. An Arab male accessory usually of black cord, traditionally made of goat hair and worn doubled to keep a headdress in place.

Babouche – boots.

Berlin or Berline – A type of covered four-wheeled travelling carriage with two interior seats. Initially noted for using two chassis rails and having the body suspended from the rails by leather straps. The term continued in use for enclosed formal carriages with two seats after the suspension system changed from leather straps to steel springs.

Drang – a narrow passageway between buildings.

Drashed – Devonshire word for thrashed, a beating.

Genever – Gin

Keffiyeh – or kufiyah, also known in Arabic as a ghutrah, shemagh, ḥaṭṭah and, in Persian, as a chafiyeh. A traditional headdress fashioned from a square scarf and is usually made of linen or cotton. Commonly found in arid, desert regions to provide protection from sunburn, dust and sand.

Ope – an opening or passageway between buildings.

Thobe – or thawb or tobe, known by various other names in different Arab regions. A flowing ankle-length robe, usually with long sleeves.

NAUTICAL TERMS

Aback – a sail when its forward surface is pressed upon by the wind. Used to 'stop' a ship.

A-cockbill – having the tapered ends turned upward. Said of the anchor when it is hanging ready from the cathead.

Aloft – up in the tops, at the masthead or anywhere about the yards or the rigging.

Articles – Each man when coming aboard a pirate ship 'agreed the Articles'. Some pirate ships were run on very democratic lines. The crew elected their captain, agreed where to sail, divided the 'spoils' fairly etc. Most rules were sensible things like no naked flame below deck, each man to keep his weapons clean and ready for use, and no fighting aboard ship.

Bar – a shoal running across the mouth of a harbour or a river.

Bare poles – having no sail up, the bare mast.

Belay – to make fast or secure. Also: 'Stop that', 'Belay that talk!' would mean 'Shut up!'

Belaying pin – a short wooden rod to which a ship's rigging is secured. A common improvised weapon aboard a sailing ship because they are everywhere, are easily picked up, and are the right size and weight to be used as a club.

Bell (ship's bell) – used as a clock, essential for navigation as the measurement of the angle of the sun had to be made at noon. The bell was struck each time the half-hour glass was turned.

Best bower – the larboard (or port) side anchor. There are usually two identical anchors on the bows of a vessel, the second one is the small-bower.

Bilge – the lowest part of the ship inside the hull along the keel.

They fill with stinking bilge water or 'bilge'. Can also mean nonsense or foolish talk.

Binnacle – the frame or box that houses the compass.

Boatswain/ Bosun/ Bos'n – usually a competent sailor who is in charge of all deck duties.

Bos'n's chair – a platform on ropes made to form a chair-like structure, and hauled aboard.

Bow – the front or 'pointed' end of the ship.

Bowsprit – the heavy slanted spar pointing forward from the ship's bow.

Brace – rope used to control the horizontal movement of a square-rigged yard.

Brig – a two-masted vessel square-rigged on both masts.

Brimstone – formerly the common name for sulphur.

Bring It Close – the telescope.

Broadside – the simultaneous firing of all guns on one side of a ship.

Bulkheads – vertical partitions in a ship.

Bulwark – the raised wooden 'walls' running along the sides of a ship above the level of the deck.

Cable – 1) a long, thick and heavy rope by which a ship is secured to the anchor. 2) A measurement of length = 120 fathoms or 240 yards.

Capstan – a drum-like winch turned by the crew to raise or lower the anchors or other heavy gear.

Careen – the process of beaching a ship, heeling her over to her side and cleaning the underside of weed, barnacles and worm; making essential repairs to the part of a ship which is usually below the waterline. A careened ship will go faster and last longer than one that is not.

Cathead – vertical beam of timber protruding near the bow, used for hoisting the anchor.

Cat o'nine tails, or 'cat' – a whip with many lashes, used for flogging.

Caulk – to seal the gaps between planks of wood with caulking (see Oakum).

Chain shot – two balls of iron joined together by a length of chain, chiefly used to destroy masts, rigging and sails.

Chandler – a merchant selling the various things a ship needs for supplies and repairs. Originally, a chandler was a candlemaker, from which we get the word 'chandelier'.

Chanty/shanty – a sailor's work song. Often lewd and derogatory about the officers.

Chase / Prize – the ship being pursued. (Usually capitalised)

Cleat – wooden or metal fastening to which ropes can be secured. Can also be used as a ladder.

Clew – the lower corners of a sail, therefore 'Clew up' – to haul a square sail up to a yard.

Close-hauled – sailing as close to the direction of the wind as possible.

Cordage – rope is called cordage on board a ship.

Colours – the vessel's identification flag, also called an ensign. For a pirate, the Jolly Roger!

Courses – lowest sails on the mast.

Crosstrees – horizontal cross-timbers partway up a mast to keep the shrouds spread apart.

Deadeyes – a round, flat, wooden block with three holes through which a lanyard, or rope, can be threaded to tighten the shrouds.

Dolphin striker – a short perpendicular gaff spar under the cap of the bowsprit for guying down the jib-boom. Also called a martingale.

Doubloon – a Spanish gold coin.

Fathom – a depth of six feet of water.

Flukes – the broad parts, or palms, of the anchor.

Fore or for'ard – toward the front end of the ship, the bow.

Forecastle – pronounced 'fo'c'sle'; raised deck at the front of a ship.

Fore-and-aft – the length of a ship.

Forestay – the rope leading from the mast to the bow.

Fother – to seal a leak by lowering a sail over the side of the ship and positioning it so that it seals the hole by the weight of the sea.

Futtocks – 'foot hooks'.

Futtock shroud – short pieces of rope which secure lower deadeyes and futtock plates to the top mast rigging.

Galleon – a large three-masted square-rigged ship used chiefly by the Spanish during the 1600s.

Galley – ship's kitchen.

Gaol / gaoler – pronounced 'jail' and 'jailer'.

Gasket – a piece of rope to fasten the sails to the yards.

Grenados – early form of hand grenade.

Grapeshot or grape – small cast iron balls bound together in a canvas bag that scatter like shotgun pellets when fired.

Gunwale – pronounced 'gun'l'; upper planking along the sides of a vessel. 'Up to the gunwales' = full up or overloaded.

Halliard or halyard – pronounced 'haly'd'. The rope used to hoist a sail.

Hard tack – ship's biscuit. Opposite is soft tack – bread.

Hatch – an opening in the deck for entering below.

Hawser – cable.

Heave to – to check the forward motion of a vessel and bring her to a standstill by heading her into the wind and backing some of her sails.

Heel – to lean over due to action of the wind, waves or greater weight on one side. The angle at which the vessel tips when sailing.

Helm – the tiller (a long steering arm) or a wheel which controls the rudder and enables the vessel to be steered.

Hold – the lower space below the decks for cargo.

Hounds – Projections attached to either side of the mast just below the masthead to support the trestletrees.

Hull – the sides of a ship which sit in and above the water.

Hull cleats – the 'ladder' or steps attached to the hull via which entry is gained to the entry port.

Hull down – a vessel when it is so far away from the observer the hull is invisible owing to the shape of the earth's surface. Opposite to hull up.

Jack Ketch – the hangman. To dance with Jack Ketch is to hang.

Jolly boat – a small boat, a dinghy.

Jolly Roger – the pirates' flag, called the *jolie rouge*, although its original meaning is unknown. The hoisted flag was an invitation to surrender, with the implication that those who did so would be treated well and no quarter given to those who did not.

Jury-rigged – makeshift repairs.

Kedge – a small anchor used for mooring to keep the vessel secure and clear of her mooring ropes while she rides in a tidal harbour or river. Also used to warp (haul) a ship from one part of the harbour to another by dropping the kedge anchor, securing a hawser to its wooden or iron stock and hauling the line in.

Keel – the lowest part of the hull below the water.

Keelhaul – an unpleasant punishment: the victim is dragged through the water passing under the keel, either from side to side or bow to stern.

Knot – one nautical mile per hour.

Landlubber – (or lubber) a non-sailor.

Langrage – jagged pieces of sharp metal used as shot. Especially useful for damaging rigging and killing men.

Larboard – pronounced 'larb'd'; the left side of a ship when facing the bow (front). Changed in the nineteenth century to 'port'.

Lead line – (pronounced 'led') a length of rope used to determine the depth of water.

Lee – the side or direction away from the wind i.e downwind.

Lee shore – the shore on to which the wind is blowing, a hazardous shore for a sailing vessel particularly in strong winds.

Leeches – the vertical edges of a square sail.

Letter of Marque – Papers issued by a government during wartime entitling a privately owned ship to raid enemy commerce or attack enemy ships.

Lubberly – in an amateur way, as a landlubber would do.

Luff – the order to the helmsman to put the tiller towards the lee side of the ship in order to make it sail nearer to the direction of the wind.

Marlinspike – a pointed iron tool used to part strands of rope so that they can be spliced.

Maroon – a punishment for breaking a pirate ship's Articles or rules. The victim was left on a deserted coast (or an island) with little in the way of supplies. Therefore, no one could say the unlucky pirate had been killed by his former brethren.

Mast – vertical spar supporting the sails.

Masthead – the highest reach of a mast

Molly boy – a homosexual prostitute.

Nautical mile – similar to a land mile, but wetter! About 1.18 miles (1.9 km)

Oakum – a material used to waterproof seams between planks on deck etc. Made of strong, pliable, tarred fibres obtained from scrap rope or rags which swell when wet.

On the Account – or the 'sweet trade'; a man who went 'on the account' was turning pirate.

Painter – a rope attached to a boat's bow for securing or towing.

Piece of Eight – a Spanish silver coin worth one peso or eight reales. It was sometimes literally cut into eight pieces, each worth one real. In the 1700s a piece of eight was worth a little under a modern five shillings sterling, or 25p – this would be about £15 - £20 today. One side usually had the Spanish coat of arms, the other two lines symbolising the limits of the old world at the Straits of Gibraltar, the exit into the Atlantic Ocean from the Mediterranean. In later designs two hemispheres were added between the lines representing the Old and New Worlds. Pieces of eight were so widely used that eventually this sign was turned into the dollar sign – $.

Port – the left side of a ship. Remember it for the consumption of the after dinner drink: "Oh! There's no port left!"

Privateer – an armed vessel bearing letters of marque, or one of her crew, or her captain. A 'privateer' is theoretically a law-abiding combatant.

Quarterdeck – a deck at the rear of a ship where the officers stood and where the helm is usually situated.

Quartermaster – usually the second in command aboard a pirate ship. In the Royal Navy, the man in charge of the provisions.

Rail – timber plank along the top of the gunwale above the sides of the vessel.

Rake – when a ship strikes another with a broadside of cannon.

Ratlines – pronounced 'ratlins'; horizontal lines tied across the shrouds to form a rope ladder for climbing aloft.

Reef – 1) an underwater obstruction of rock or coral. 2) to reduce the size of the sails by tying them partially up, either to slow the ship or to keep a strong wind from putting too much strain on the masts.

Rigging – the ropes which support the spars (standing rigging) and allow the sails to be controlled (running rigging).

Round shot – iron cannon balls.

Rudder – blade at the stern which is angled to steer the vessel.

Run – to sail directly away from the wind.

Sails – in general each mast had three sails. (See diagram).

Sail ho! – 'I see a ship!' The sail is the first part visible over the horizon.

Scuppers – openings along the edges of a ship's deck to allow water to drain back to the sea rather than collecting in the bilges.

Scuttle – 1) a porthole or small hatch in the deck for lighting and ventilation, covered by the 'scuttle hatch'. Can be used as a narrow entrance to the deck below. 2) To deliberately sink or wreck a ship.

Shank-painter – the stopper (a short rope) that secures the shank and fluke of the anchor to the cathead.

Sheet – a rope made fast to the lower corners of a sail to control its position.

Sheet home – to haul on a sheet until the foot of the sail is as straight and taut as possible.

Ship of the Line – a Royal Navy ship carrying at least fifty guns.

Ship's biscuit – hard bread. Very dry, can be eaten a year after baked. Also called hard tack.

Shrouds – ropes forming part of the standing rigging and supporting the mast or topmast.

Sloop – a small, single-masted vessel, ideal for shallow water.

Spar – a stout wooden pole used as a mast or yard of a sailing vessel.

Spritsail – pronounced 'sprit'sl'; a sail attached to a yard which hangs under the bowsprit.

Square-rigged – the principal sails set at right angles to the length of a ship and extended by horizontal yards slung to the mast.

Starboard – originally 'steerboard', pronounced 'starb'd'. The right side of a vessel when you are facing toward the bow.

Stay – strong, *very* thick ropes supporting the masts.

Stem – timber at the very front of the bow.

Stern – the back end of a ship.

Swab – a disrespectful term for a seaman, or to clean the decks.

Sweeps – long oars used by large vessels, especially galleys.

Tack/tacking – to change the direction of a vessel's course by turning her bows into the wind until the wind blows on her other side. When a ship is sailing into an oncoming wind she will have to tack, make a zigzag line, in order to make progress forward against the oncoming wind.

Tackle – pronounced 'taykle'. An arrangement of one or more ropes and pulley blocks used to increase the power for raising or lowering heavy objects.

Taffrail – upper rail along the ship's stern.

Tompions – muzzle-plugs to protect the bore of cannons from salt corrosion etc.

Transom – planking forming the stern.

Trestletrees or trestles – framing that holds the weight of the topmast.

Trim – a term used for adjusting the sails as the wind changes.

Waist – the middle part of the ship.

Wake – the line of passage directly behind as marked by a track of white foam.

Warp – to move a ship by hauling or pulling her along on warps (ropes); also the name of the ropes which secure a ship when moored (tied up) to a jetty or dock.

Weigh anchor – to haul the anchor up; more generally, to leave port.

Widowmaker – term for the bowsprit.

Windward – the side towards the wind as opposed to leeward.

Yard – a long spar suspended from the mast of a vessel to extend the sails.

Yardarm – either end of the yard.

ALSO BY HELEN HOLLICK

https://viewauthor.at/HelenHollick

THE JAN CHRISTOPHER MURDER MYSTERY SERIES

A Mirror Murder

A Mystery of Murder

To follow:

A Mistake of Murder

There will be more!

THE PENDRAGON'S BANNER TRILOGY

The Kingmaking: Book One

Pendragon's Banner: Book Two

Shadow of the King: Book Three

THE SAXON 1066 SERIES

A Hollow Crown (UK edition title)

The Forever Queen (US edition title. USA Today bestseller)

Harold the King (UK edition title)

I Am The Chosen King (US edition title)

Alternative short stories by various authors

1066 TURNED UPSIDE DOWN

Betrayal: Short stories by various authors

Free on Amazon

NON-FICTION

Pirates: Truth and Tales

Life Of A Smuggler: In Fact And Fiction

Discovering The Diamond (with Jo Field)

RICHARD TEARLE - WITH HELEN HOLLICK: THE NORTH FINCHLEY WRITERS' GROUP

HOW TO SAY 'THANK YOU' TO YOUR FAVOURITE AUTHORS

Leave a review on Amazon

http://viewauthor.at/HelenHollick

'Like' and 'follow' where you can

Subscribe to a newsletter

Buy a copy of your favourite book as a present

Spread the word!

A VARIETY OF AMAZON READERS' COMMENTS

"Helen Hollick takes the reader into a completely different world, where each real person has his or her own vivid story. Beautifully written. Highly recommended."

"Ms. Hollick is a truly magnificent author! She brings to life all of the characters of that turbulent time in a way that's absolutely spellbinding."

"What a wonderful read! I so totally enjoyed this book. It is obviously thoroughly researched."

"You can tell when you're in the hands of an accomplished writer."

"A good, easy to read mystery story, goes very well with a nice glass of red!"

"From the very first page I was hooked."

"What a story! Can't believe that I've come so late to Helen Hollick's wonderful writing."

FIND HELEN HOLLICK ON AMAZON

https://viewauthor.at/HelenHollick

or order from any bookstore

Please do leave Helen a review for any of her books.

Thank you

Helen

Made in the USA
Middletown, DE
03 October 2022